The carriage jerked and jolted to a halt. The door opened, and a black-clad figure stepped inside. Rachel struggled to keep her expression neutral.

"'Ere, now," he said. "Where's the guv'nor?"

"This is Lord Westhampton's carriage," Rachel replied, "if that is what you mean. Westhampton is back at his estate."

The man was silent for a moment. Finally he asked, "Are you the missus, then?"

"I am Lady Westhampton," Rachel admitted.

"Right. Well, I'm thinkin' you can deliver the message, then."

"The message?" Rachel felt as if she had stepped bizarrely into a scene from a play, one in which everyone knew the lines except her.

"Aye. Tell 'im he needs to watch 'is back. 'E's gettin' too close. There's some'un wishes 'im ill." He nodded, then sprang from the carriage.

Behind him, Rachel gazed in stunned silence.

* * *

"This is a suspense tale with a witty twist."
—*Romantic Times* on *The Hidden Heart*

CANDACE CAMP

Secrets of the Heart

HQN™

ISBN 0-373-77162-2

SECRETS OF THE HEART

This edition published by arrangement with Harlequin Books S.A.

® and ™ are trademarks of the publisher. Trademarks indicated with
® are registered in the United States Patent and Trademark Office, the
Canadian Trade Marks Office and in other countries.

www.HQNBooks.com

Printed in U.S.A.

Secrets
of the
Heart

1

Rachel leaned back against the soft velvet squabs of the carriage seat and stifled a sigh. She glanced across at Gabriela, who was curled up in a corner of her seat, asleep. She envied the girl the easy sleep of youth.

Rachel had not been able to fall asleep, despite the monotonous rumbling of the coach. She could not dismiss the odd feeling of ennui, even sorrow, that had plagued her ever since they'd left Westhampton yesterday morning. When Michael had handed her into the carriage, she had felt a distinct urge to turn back and say that she had decided to delay her trip for a few more days. But, of course, that had been impossible. She had already put it off three days longer than she had planned. She had to get Gabriela back to her guardians; they were waiting for her at Darkwater.

A shout outside the carriage startled Rachel from her reverie, and she lifted a corner of the curtain to look out. She could see nothing but the dusk of evening, the branches of the nearby trees a darker shape against the grayness. Then there was a shout from the coachman, and the carriage lurched forward. In the next moment, Rachel heard the sharp report of a gun. She dropped the curtain with a gasp.

The coachman's voice rang out, calling to his horses, and the carriage jerked and jolted to a halt. Rachel grabbed the leather loop beside her seat and held on. Across from her, Gabriela let out a squeak of surprise as she tumbled unceremoniously to the floor. The girl scrambled back up onto the seat and turned to look at Rachel, wide eyed.

"What is it?" Gabriela whispered. "What happened?"

"I don't know." Rachel tried not to let her fear show. She could think of no good reason for the sound of gunfire or the coachman yanking his animals to a stop. What came to her mind was highwaymen, although it seemed bizarre to find them this far from London.

She heard voices and turned toward the door, her fingers curling into the palms of her hands. She would be brave, she thought, reminding herself that she had Gabriela now to look out for, and she tried to envision what her redoubtable sister-in-law Miranda would do—or her friend Jessica, with her soldier's daughter's courage. But she could not help a brief, desperate wish that Michael had decided to accompany them to Darkwater.

The door opened, and a black-clad figure stepped

inside. Rachel struggled to keep her expression neutral. He was a smallish man, she told herself, and it was only the black attire and the scarf across the bottom of his face that made him seem sinister. She would give him her money and he would leave, and the incident would be over with no harm to anyone.

The man's eyes above his mask looked startled, and he glanced around the carriage, then returned his gaze to Rachel. He looked, she thought with some astonishment, puzzled.

"'Ere, now," he said somewhat plaintively and jerked down the scarf to reveal his entire face. "Where's the guv'nor?"

Rachel's fear subsided dramatically as she looked at his face, almost comical in its dismay. "I beg your pardon?" she asked, pleased at how calm her voice came out.

"The lord," the man went on. "This is 'is carriage, ain't it? I saw the sign on the door."

"This is Lord Westhampton's carriage," Rachel replied, rather puzzled herself now. "His coat of arms is on the door, if that is what you mean."

"Aye, that's the one. Westhampton. It's 'im I'm wanting."

"I am afraid that you are in the wrong place, then. Westhampton is back at his estate."

Their visitor was silent for a moment, digesting this news. Finally he asked, "Are you the missus, then?"

"I am Lady Westhampton," Rachel admitted.

"Right. Well, I'm thinkin' you can deliver the message to the guv'nor, then."

"The message?" Rachel felt as if she had stepped bizarrely into a scene from a play, one where everyone knew the lines except her.

"Aye. Tell 'im Red Geordie sent it. Tell 'im he needs to watch 'is back. There's some 'un wishes 'im ill."

Rachel stared at the man. "Excuse me?"

"'E's gettin' too close, I'm thinkin' and there's them as don't like it. Word's out that there's those as wants 'im taken care of." He stopped, then gave a short nod, seemingly satisfied with his words.

Rachel blinked, unable to think of an adequate reply.

The man grinned then and said, "Sorry. I'll be needin' to take somemat—you know, for the boys." He nodded toward Rachel. "Them earbobs'd do nicely."

Rachel gasped, her hands flying up to cover the emerald studs in her earlobes. "No! Not these. Michael gave them to me. It was a wedding present."

He paused, considering this information. "Oh. Well, I wouldn't want to cross the guv'nor, that's a fact."

"How about money?" Rachel offered, digging into her reticule and pulling out a small purse of coins, which she offered him.

The small man grinned and took the purse, opening it to peer inside. "Aye, that'll do it, my lady."

He gave a respectful tug of his cap toward her, still

grinning. "I can see you're a cool 'un, just like his lordship. Pleasure doin' business with ye." He nodded toward Gabriela. "Miss. Good evenin' to ye both."

He pulled up his scarf to cover his face again and turned, opening the door and springing lightly down from the carriage.

Behind him, Gabriela and Rachel gazed at each other in stunned silence. There was the muffled sound of voices outside the carriage, then the whinny of a horse, followed by the noise of hoofbeats.

"What in the world—" Gabriela began, her eyes round as saucers in her face.

"I have no idea," Rachel replied frankly.

The door was jerked open again, but this time it revealed the worried face of her coachman, who peered up into the carriage. "Are you all right, my lady?"

"Yes, we are fine, Daniels. No harm done."

"There were four of them, ma'am, with pistols. Jenks and I thought it best not to challenge them, what with you and the young miss in the carriage. His Lordship'd have my hide if anything happened to you."

"You were quite right," Rachel reassured him, though she knew that his statement was more hyperbole than fact. Michael was the most reasonable of men, not one to blame his servants for something out of their control. "Westhampton would not want you to risk your lives or ours that way. You did well. Let us drive on to Darkwater, if you please."

"Aye, my lady." The coachman gave her a respectful nod and shut the door.

They could hear him climb back onto his high perch, and a moment later the carriage started forward again. Rachel looked over at her charge.

"Are you all right, Gabriela?"

"Oh, yes!" The girl nodded emphatically. "But it was terribly exciting, wasn't it?"

"Rather too exciting, I'd say," Rachel replied dryly.

"Yes, I suppose," Gabriela said, sounding unconvinced. "But I've never seen an actual highwayman before."

"Nor I."

"Did you not know him? He seemed to know Uncle Michael. Isn't that strange?"

"Very," Rachel agreed. "I cannot imagine how he could know Michael...."

Michael was not the sort of man who had a passing acquaintance with highwaymen. Now, if it had been her brother Dev the fellow had claimed to know, Rachel would have had little trouble believing it. Until he had married Miranda and settled down, Devin had known his share of unsavory characters. But Michael? The idea was absurd.

Michael was a quiet, scholarly man, kind, responsible, reliable and generous—the very epitome of a gentleman. His title was one of the oldest and most respected in the land, and, unlike his father, Michael had never done anything to tarnish it. He was happiest on his estate in the country, overseeing the various renovations of the house and outbuildings, and experimenting with the newest innovations in agriculture and land management. He corresponded with men of like nature and interests, ranging from gentleman farmers on vast plantations in the United States to men of science and letters at universities here and on the Continent. He was hardly the sort of man to have met a highwayman, let alone have one deliver vague warnings about danger to him.

What was it the man had said? That Michael was "getting too close." That some vague personage "wished him ill." Too close to what? And who was this enemy?

Rachel could not imagine Michael having an enemy. Whatever disagreements he might have with anyone, they were courteous and usually concerned some scholarly subject that few people had even heard of. The worst that she had ever heard anyone say about him was that he was too respectable, bordering on dull. Hardly the stuff of threats to do him bodily harm.

"It's ridiculous," Rachel told her companion firmly. "Michael doesn't have an enemy in the world. The man must have made some sort of mistake."

She looked at Gabriela, who was still looking a little troubled. The poor child had experienced too much death for such an early age. Gabriela's parents had died when she was only eight years old, and she had been raised by her great uncle until he, too, had died last year, leaving her in the care of a guardian who had been friends with her father many years before. It was through this guardian, the Duke of Cleybourne, that Rachel had come to meet the fourteen-year-old girl. The duke had been married to Rachel's older sister, Caroline, who had died, along with their daughter, in a tragic carriage accident. Rachel had remained close friends with Cleybourne and often worried about his descent into a black pit of grief in the years after their deaths.

Then Gabriela had come to Castle Cleybourne last Christmas, and with her, her governess, Jessica Maitland, a flame-haired beauty with a tragic scandal in her own past. Jessica and Cleybourne had fallen deeply in love, but even that happy time and the security it brought Gabriela had been marred by the ugliness of violent death. A killer had struck at the castle, doing away with one of the other guests and even almost murdering Jessica herself.

It was little wonder that Gabriela's fears would be roused by the stranger's threats, however vague and absurd they were. Gabriela had spent the past two months with Michael and Rachel, for they had taken her home with them after the wedding in order to give the duke and his new duchess a honeymoon, and she had grown quite fond of them both.

Rachel reached across the carriage to take one of Gabriela's hands in hers and squeeze it gently. "Don't worry, Gaby. I am sure that it is all some silly mix-up. He can't have meant Westhampton. No one would wish Michael ill. It's clearly a mistake, this talk about his getting 'too close' to something.

To what? A political theory? A scientific discovery? Some new method of crop rotation? Those are scarcely the sort of things one kills over.''

Gabriela had to smile, and the worry receded from her eyes. ''You are right. Who could have anything against Uncle Michael?'' She squeezed Rachel's hand in return. ''You must be very glad to be married to him.''

There were many, Rachel knew, who would say the same thing to her. Her husband was titled and wealthy, the descendent of one of the best families in England. That in itself was enough for her marriage to be considered a success. But Michael was also thoughtful and kind. He provided her with a generous clothing and household allowance. Though he preferred life in the country, he did not try to impose it upon her. She was free to live as she chose, to spend her time in their elegant house in London, giving the parties she was justly known for, paying calls and in general living the life of a Society hostess. She had a large circle of friends and admirers, and was adjudged one of the reigning beauties of the *Ton*. In short, her life was perfect…as long as one did not mind the fact that her marriage was a sham.

There was no love in their marriage. They lived apart, had never shared a bedroom, never even spoken words of love or passion. And it did not help matters a bit to know that it was all entirely her own fault.

Rachel gave her young companion a smile, hoping the girl would not notice the brittleness of it. ''Yes,''

she agreed, settling back into her seat. "I am very
lucky to be Lady Westhampton."

Torches burned in front of Darkwater. It was a
beautiful house, named for a nearby tarn that was
black as night, not for the house's limestone walls,
which were pale, almost golden in the Derbyshire
sunlight. At night one could not see its graceful lines
or centuries-old mullioned windows, only grasp the
vague outline of its considerable hulk. But Rachel
had grown up here, and she knew it without having
to see it. She flung open the carriage door as soon as
the vehicle rolled to a stop and leaned out to look at
the house.

Jenks scrambled down from the top of the carriage
to pull down the steps and help Rachel and Gabriela
out. Even as they emerged, the front door of the
house opened, and two footmen came out carrying
candles to light the ladies' way into the house.

"Lady Westhampton!" A middle-aged man,
dressed in the formal attire of a butler, hastened out
the front door, smiling broadly. "I am happy to welcome you to Darkwater again! We have been expecting your arrival any time this past day."

"Hello, Cummings." Rachel smiled warmly at the
man who had been the butler here since she was a
child. "Allow me to introduce Miss Gabriela Carstairs. Miss Carstairs is the ward of the Duke of Cleybourne."

The man bowed gravely to Gabriela. "May I welcome you to Darkwater, Miss Carstairs? The Duke

and Duchess have been waiting eagerly for your arrival. Ah, here they are now.''

Foregoing formality, the members of the household were hurrying out the opened front doors despite the chill of the night air. In front were a tall, stunning red-haired woman and a man of dark mien, both smiling broadly. Slightly behind them came another couple, a pretty pregnant woman and a devastatingly handsome man, followed by a young girl of about Gabriela's age.

''Gaby!'' The redhead, who was the new Duchess of Cleybourne, threw her arms open wide to her charge. She had been the girl's governess for six years before marrying Gabriela's guardian, and she looked upon her almost as her own child.

''Miss Jessie!'' Gabriela flew into her arms and hugged her tightly. When she was at last released, she turned to the man beside the duchess, smiling up at him a little shyly. ''Your Grace.''

He smiled, lighting up his dark face. ''Have you forgotten, Gabriela?'' he asked lightly. ''I thought we agreed we were not to be so formal.''

''Uncle Richard,'' she corrected with a smile, and when he, too, held out his arms to her, she went into them quickly for a heartfelt, if somewhat less energetic, hug.

The duke and duchess turned to Rachel, who had been caught up in hugs by the other couple, her brother Devin, the Earl of Ravenscar, and his wife, Miranda, who was several months along with child.

There were more greetings all around, with Richard introducing his new ward to the earl and countess.

"And," Richard went on, with a smile to Gabriela, "there is someone else who has been eagerly awaiting your arrival. Lady Ravenscar's sister, Miss Veronica Upshaw, is here visiting, and she is just about your age, fifteen last month. Veronica..."

The girl stepped forward, smiling at Gabriela. She was a pretty thing, with light-brown hair and blue eyes, though there was little about her that resembled her sister Miranda. She was, Rachel knew, Miranda's stepsister, rather than any blood relative, the daughter of the woman whom Miranda's father had married when Miranda was in her teens. Mr. and Mrs. Upshaw lived much of the time in London, Miranda had told Rachel, but all had agreed that Devin's country estate was the best place for the young girl. There would be time enough for London in a few years, when she had her coming out.

Rachel smiled a little, thinking that these two girls would probably have their coming out in the same year. The *Ton,* she thought with unabashed delight, would doubtlessly reel under the joint assault upon it by the formidable team of the duchess and the countess. Rachel intended not to miss a party that Season.

Laughing and talking, the group went inside. The girls retreated to Veronica's room upstairs, both of them thrilled at finally having someone their own age to talk to, while the adults returned to the music room, where the two couples had been wiling away the evening before Rachel's arrival.

Their conversation turned first to polite inquiries as to Rachel's trip. With studied calm, Rachel replied, "It was all right, really, except for being stopped by a highwayman."

The four other people in the room stared at her speechlessly for a long moment. Then Devin sprang to his feet, his ready temper rising. "What? Are you joking?"

"No. Not at all. It was the most peculiar thing."

"Peculiar!" Dev exclaimed. "That is hardly how I would describe it."

"Oh, yes, you would, if you had been there."

"Rachel! Why didn't you tell us immediately?" Miranda cried, getting up a little awkwardly and coming over to her sister-in-law. "Are you all right? You weren't hurt, were you?"

"No. I just lost a few coins, that is all. He did not threaten me at all."

"What the devil was he doing all the way up here?" Cleybourne asked. "Have you heard anything about this chap before, Dev?"

"No, not a bit. I can scarcely think it would be profitable patroling the byways of Derbyshire."

"I'm not at all sure that profit was his primary motive. He indicated that he was taking the money mostly for show—so his men would not suspect."

"What? Suspect what?" Dev looked at Rachel suspiciously. "Are you sure you aren't having us on?"

"No, I promise you. I told you it was most peculiar. He seemed—well, he apparently thought Michael was in the carriage. He said he saw the coat of arms on the door. I'm not sure if he meant he was lying in wait for his carriage—I cannot imagine how he would know that it would be coming by any time soon—or if he was traveling to Westhampton and just stumbled upon us.''

"A highwayman was meeting Michael?" Miranda asked. "Whatever for?"

"He said he wanted to warn Michael. So he told me to give Michael this message—that someone wishes him ill, that Michael is 'too close,' and there are people who mean to stop him."

Her words were met with another stunned silence.

"Are you sure you heard him right?" Dev asked finally.

"Yes. Ask Gabriela. She witnessed it all. That is what he said. Then he said he was sorry, but he would have to take something to make it look right, or something like that. And he wanted my emerald studs, but I protested and said they were a bride's gift from Michael, and he took a purse full of coins instead. Then he left."

"I'm sorry," Jessica said tentatively. "I don't know Lord Westhampton as well as the rest of you. What did he mean?"

"I don't have any idea," Rachel replied frankly. "I was hoping Richard or Dev would have some idea—that perhaps there was some sort of male activity involved which you conspired to keep secret from us females. Or from me, at least—so I wouldn't worry or be afraid or something."

"I haven't a clue," her brother responded, looking perplexed. "And if I were in on some male secret, you can be sure that Miranda would have wormed it out of my by now." He cast a fond glance at his wife, who gave him a dimpled smile in return.

"Maybe it is some sort of code," Miranda mused. "I know Westhampton told me once that he had always been fond of puzzles and things like that."

"Yes, he is.

"The fellow must have been mad, that is all I can think," Richard added. "Best thing, I suppose, is to send a message to Westhampton, let him know what happened. Perhaps he, at least, will understand it."

"Yes, I guess you are right," Rachel agreed. "I will write him a letter tonight."

"I shall send one of the grooms up to Westhampton with it first thing tomorrow," Dev assured her. "I'm sure there's nothing to it, but best be safe, you know."

So later that night Rachel sat down at the small secretary in her room and dashed off a letter to Michael, telling him everything that the stranger had said to her and adding a few questions of her own. Dev entrusted the missive to his head groom, who would leave at dawn the next morning on one of Dev's excellent horses, so that Michael would know as soon as humanly possible about the strange occurrence.

But knowing that she had done all she could to warn Michael—if, indeed, there was any truth to the highwayman's words—did not bring Rachel peace of mind. As she dressed for bed and took down her hair, her thoughts kept returning to the events of the evening, much as a tongue sought out a sore tooth. Suddenly everything connected to Michael seemed unsure and awkward.

She and Michael were not close in the way that Dev and Miranda, were. There was not that intimacy between them that seemingly only love and passion could bring. But she had thought that she knew Michael well. She knew the subjects that interested him, the foods he liked and disliked. She could have named the tailor and boot maker he frequented, and the clubs to which he belonged, the names of most of his friends and even those of some of the people with whom he corresponded.

However, the encounter with the Cassandra-like highwayman had left her wondering how much she really knew Michael. The man "Red Geordie" had spoken of seemed to be someone altogether different from the Westhampton she knew—a person involved in something that threatened someone else, someone who needed to be warned. Someone who would be acquainted with a highwayman. She kept thinking that the odd man must have been mistaken, that he was talking of another man besides her husband. Yet he said that he had recognized the crest on the side of the carriage. He had called him Westhampton—or had it been she who had offered the name and the man had simply agreed?

Perhaps, as one of the others had suggested, the intruder had been quite mad. Or it was all some bizarre hoax. After all, neither Dev nor Richard had known what the man was talking about; they had been as much in the dark as she. And Richard had been friends with Michael since before Rachel herself had met him. Surely he would know if Michael was somehow involved with a highwayman. But Rachel could not escape the thought that a wife should not have to depend on someone else's knowledge of her husband to be sure of him. Surely she, as his wife, should know him the best of all! Rachel felt sure that if Miranda had been in her situation, she would have known exactly what Dev was involved in.

Rachel sighed as she sat down in front of the vanity and began to brush out her hair. She studied her reflection in the mirror as she did so. She was still an attractive woman, she told herself. Her hair was thick and black, and moonstruck admirers still wrote odes to her green eyes. She had retained the slim figure of her youth, and no wrinkles marred her skin. She was twenty-seven, still young.

She paused in her brushing for a moment, looking intently into the mirror. Had she changed since the day Michael had met her? But she knew the answer to that question—the change had all been inside her.

Her hand tightened involuntarily on her brush. She had married as she was supposed to, as Society expected and her father had demanded. But in doing her duty, she had given up her hopes and dreams. She had denied the longings of her heart.

Rachel could still remember the awful pain of her decision. There had been nothing else she could do, she knew. Her father had been right; had she not married Michael, it would have been scandal and ruin for her family and herself—as well as for Michael, who had been entirely innocent in the whole matter. She had done what she had to do, but in doing so she had condemned her heart to despair. She had married Michael and had said goodbye to the man she loved.

2

Rachel remembered with clarity the evening that she first met Michael. It had been at a rout of Lady Wetherford's, a boring crush of an affair, attended, it seemed, by half of London Society. She could not remember exactly who had been there; indeed, she only vaguely recalled Lady Wetherford introducing her and her mother to Lord Westhampton. Her first impression of him had been merely that of a tall blond man, several years older than she and good-looking in a rather nondescript way. Knowing Michael as she did now, Rachel felt sure that he had been impeccably but plainly dressed, his clothes dark and formal and nothing that would attract attention. He would have been the perfect picture of an English gentleman, for, indeed, that was what Michael was.

But Rachel had paid little attention to him, smiling—for that evening she had been able to do little else but smile, so radiant was the feeling inside her—and returning the usual polite chitchat about the

weather and the crush of the party and the opera,
which she had attended the evening before. All the
time they had talked, her senses had been tuned to
the rest of the room, seeking out the same person
whom she sought at every social occasion, the man
who had engendered her radiant joy that night. For
she remembered the evening, not because of Michael,
but because that was the night when Anthony Birkshaw had told her that he loved her.

Even now, a faint smile touched Rachel's face at
the memory.

Rachel was nineteen, and in the midst of her first
Season. It was a year late in coming, a result of her
family's usual state of impecunity. Cleybourne, her
older sister's husband, had given her mother the
money for Rachel's debut the next year, and Rachel
was well aware that it was up to her to do her best
to recoup the family's fortunes. Few expected her to
attain her sister's success, for Caroline had married
a duke, the highest rung on the ladder of nobility.
But Rachel had the Aincourt good looks and a pleas-
ing personality, and her family was one of the best
in England—albeit one seemingly incapable of holding on to money. It was generally expected that she,
too, would make a good marriage.

Rachel did not question her role in such plans. It
was, after all, the way people of her class married.
There were no longer the arranged marriages of old,
of course, where a wedding was primarily an alliance
of two families for purposes of wealth, power and

political advancement, and the couple might not even have met each other before their wedding day. But, still, the aristocracy did not marry for love, as her mother had drummed into her head from childhood; they married for the good of their family, both present and future.

In the case of the Aincourt family, this dictum nearly always translated into marrying wealth. For generations the earls of Ravenscar had gained and lost money, but more gold, it seemed, left their hands than entered them. The reason for this, Rachel's narrowly and dogmatically religious father believed, was a Papist curse laid on the head of the first Earl of Ravenscar, who was given Branton Abbey during the Dissolution by his friend King Henry VIII as a reward for his loyalty and friendship. Edward Aincourt, Lord Ravenscar, had torn down the abbey and used its stones to build his family's home. The Abbot of Branton, legend said, had had to be dragged out bodily from the abbey, and as Ravenscar's men had done so, the abbot had laid a curse upon the earl and all his descendants, declaring that "none who live within these stones shall ever know happiness."

Whether it was the result of the curse or simply the nature of a family too given to pride and profligacy, it was true that the Aincourts had rarely been happy in affairs of either the heart or the purse. It was good, everyone agreed, that the Aincourts were also a family tall and graceful in stature and of handsome mien, for they were always able to replenish their fortunes through marriage—though there were those who pointed out that it was perhaps this tendency that doomed them to live out the curse's prophecy of unhappiness.

In this particular generation of Aincourts, the lack of money had grown acute. The earl, a religious man of stern views, had not extended his religious beliefs to living an ascetic life. He loved to live well and buy beautiful things, as had his father before him, and as a result, the family fortunes had declined at an ever greater rate. It was generally considered up to the daughters of the family to provide for the family, as the earl had parted with his only son, Devin, the heir to the family title and what remained of the family fortune. Devin had, in his teen years, given himself over to a life of what his father deemed pagan excess, for years loving a married woman and refusing to marry as his father wished.

So Rachel dutifully expected to marry as her father determined, but she could not help but dream secretly that her marriage would turn out to be one of love as well as duty, as her sister Caroline's had been. Everyone knew that the Duke of Cleybourne loved his wife to distraction, and she had seemed to love him in return, though later the truth of her feelings had been proven to be more shallow. At the very least, Rachel intended to enjoy her time on the marriage market, wearing the new dresses and ball gowns bought for her debut, going to parties and balls and fetes, enjoying the plays and operas and other amusements that London had to offer a girl who had spent most of her life on a crumbling estate in Derbyshire.

Rachel was an immediate, dazzling success. Her life was a whirl of social activities that would have left anyone but a vibrant young girl exhausted. She received her invitation to Almack's. Every dance saw her card filled within minutes after her arrival. She had a choice of corsages sent by hopeful suitors for every ball, and there was never a shortage of young men calling at her house.

But Rachel had eyes for only one man. She met Anthony Birkshaw two weeks into the Season, and as soon as she saw him, she knew that this was the man of her dreams. He was a well set up young gentleman a few years older than she, with a frank and open manner that charmed her instantly. His hair was dark brown, thick and falling carelessly over his forehead, and his eyes, she thought, were those of a poet—large and brown, rimmed with thick, sooty black lashes.

And he was, miraculously, as taken with her as she was with him. He did not, of course, make a cake of himself as Jasper Hopkins was wont to do by dancing the two dances with her that were all that was proper from a young man not a girl's fiancé, then pointedly standing apart and watching her the rest of the evening, not dancing with any other girl. Anthony was all that was proper and courteous, dancing and chatting with other young women, not devoting himself so exclusively to Rachel that he caused gossip.

That night, after their waltz together, as they had taken a long promenade around the ballroom, Anthony had told Rachel that he loved her. Her feet had scarcely touched the floor the rest of the evening.

She spent the rest of the summer in a giddy state of love. Given the assiduous way young unmarried girls were chaperoned, she was almost never alone with Anthony. Their love subsisted on looks, daydreams and waltzes. She "ran into" him now and then as she walked with her maid to or from the lending library, fueling a renewed love of reading. When he sent her a posy, she slept with it by her bed, and when it began to wither, she carefully pressed the flowers between heavy books and saved them. Every now and then, at some huge rout or ball, they were able to sneak away together for a few moments, get lost in the crowd after a dance or during a midnight supper, and find a spot in the gardens or some dim alcove in the house. There, briefly, they could whisper of their feelings, pour out the excitement that thrummed in them whenever they were together, even exchange a chaste kiss or two. Rachel lived for those moments.

Lost in her haze of love, Rachel was scarcely aware of how often Lord Westhampton came to call or led her onto the dance floor. She was too wrapped up in Anthony to take much notice of any of her other suitors, but she had not even put Michael among that group. He was almost ten years older than she, as well as a friend of Caroline's husband, and she merely assumed that he was part of the circle of friends around the duke and duchess. As she and her family were living for the Season at the enormous Cleybourne House, their own house in London having been sold some years before, it did not seem untoward to her that one of the duke's friends often came to call or was frequently included on their various outings. He did not form part of the circle of young men around her at parties, maneuvering to be the one to bring her a glass of punch, pick up a dropped glove or lead her down to supper. Had she been older or less naive, she would have realized that his absence had in fact signaled to her parents a more serious intent. He was too mature and important, too serious in his regard, to have joined the group who pursued her. He was not a man who wanted to flirt and admire; he was a man who intended to marry.

She did not think much about him, but if she had, she would have said that she liked Lord Westhampton. He was quiet, a good listener, and if she made a social gaffe or a naive remark, he would only smile a little and smooth it over. Because she did not count him as one of her circle of admirers, she did not feel any pressure to sparkle or enchant him as she did with many other young men. Though she was not interested in any of them except Anthony, it was accepted that the number of suitors in one's circle was the mark of a young woman's success in the *Ton,* so it would not do for people to see that the knot of admirers around one was shrinking away. So she had to flirt without seeming bold, had to be witty and lively and respond to their attempts at wit without ever seeming to favor one over the others.

With Westhampton, she found, she could talk more easily. She did not worry about trying to appeal to him or needing to maintain a certain image. She sim-

ply treated him as she always had any of her older
brother's or sister's friends. It did not take her long
to realize that if she had a problem concerning social
etiquette or needed to find out who someone was and
where they fit into the pattern of the *ton,* Lord Westhampton was the person to ask.

Then, one day late in July, her father called her
mother and her into the library. Her heart speeded up
a little, and her cheeks flushed attractively. Such a
summons from Ravenscar meant something important was up, and her thoughts jumped instinctively to
Anthony Birkshaw. He had asked Ravenscar for her
hand in marriage! In her young, love-drunk mind, it
was the only possible outcome to the summer.

Her father stood behind one of the library tables,
looking large and imposing, as he always did. Rachel
had grown up fearing the man. Stern and religious,
with no sense of humor, the Earl of Ravenscar had
little liking or understanding of children. He rarely
saw his own progeny except on Sundays, when the
family went to the church in the village and afterward
endured a long reading from the Bible by the earl,
followed by a careful catechism from him concerning
their religious training at the vicarage and what particular sins they had committed that week. He lived
by the precept that children were placed on earth to
honor and obey their father, and any form of rebellion
was immediately and thoroughly quashed.

The youngest of the three children, Rachel had
grown up seeing the battles that raged between the
earl and his son, finally ending in a cataclysmic rup-

ture in which Ravenscar had thrown Devin out of the house and told him that he would no longer be received there. Since that time, Rachel had not seen her beloved older brother until this summer. The aching hurt and loss of that split, the terror of her father's purple-faced rage, were indelibly imprinted on her psyche. Rachel had managed to avoid such painful and frightening confrontations by staying out of her father's sight as much as possible and never crossing him openly. Her thoughts were her own, but she was careful never to reveal them to Ravenscar.

On that particular day almost seven years ago, however, her father was smiling and pleased. "Well, Rachel," he said cheerfully, "I imagine you have some idea why I've called you in here today."

"I—I think so," Rachel answered a little hesitantly. She would not have thought her father would have been this pleased about Anthony's proposal. She knew nothing about his finances, of course, but he was a younger son of a younger son, his lineage perfectly respectable, of course, but without a title or any prospects for one, and not, she would have assumed, a man of such wealth as to make her father beam with pleasure.

"I'll warrant you do," Ravenscar went on in a hearty avuncular way. "Lord Westhampton is quite a catch. Not a duke, of course, like your sister…" He gave this little quip the chuckle he thought it deserved, and went on. "But still an excellent prospect. Title. Lands. Family dating back to one of William the Conqueror's barons. Yes, I am quite pleased that

Westhampton has taken such a fancy to you. Offering a very generous settlement, of course—haven't worked out the details yet. Of course, he wants to ask you the question himself. But I think we all know what your answer will be, eh?''

"Lord—Lord Westhampton?" Rachel got out through suddenly bloodless lips. There was a strange roaring in her ears, and she thought for a dreadful moment that she might actually faint. "Lord West-hampton has asked for my hand?"

"Why, yes." Her father cast her a look of surprise that quickly turned dark and suspicious. "Why? Were you thinking it was someone else? Have you given your affections to another?" His voice rose with each question until it was close to a shout.

"Nonsense," Rachel heard her mother say smoothly, moving up to wrap a hand around her daughter's arm. "Of course she has not given her affections anywhere. I am sure she was just surprised that a man of such consequence as Lord Westhampton had been so taken by her. Any young woman of proper modesty would be. He is quite a catch, as you said, especially for a mere slip of a girl."

"Yes, no doubt you are right." Ravenscar accepted her explanation easily, for he could not imagine his youngest daughter, the one with the least spirit of any of them, opposing him.

Rachel's mother, fingers digging into Rachel's arm, then told her husband that she and Rachel must decide exactly how to dress and act for Westhampton's upcoming proposal, and she deftly steered her daughter out the door, leaving Lord Ravenscar to congratulate himself on landing yet another excellent son-in-law, an accomplishment that he was sure was in large part a reflection of his own consequence.

"Whatever are you thinking?" Lady Ravenscar snapped as she led her daughter down the hall and into the ladies' sitting room, where she closed the door firmly after them. "You gave me quite a turn. I thought Ravenscar was going to explode. Is it really such a surprise to you? Westhampton has been haunting Cleybourne House all summer."

"But—but he is a friend of the duke's. I thought—"

Her mother let out an exasperated sigh. "And to think I imagined that you were handling him skillfully! Ah, well, it's no harm done. No doubt he assumed you were merely becomingly modest and innocent. Men in love, fortunately, are great fools. Now…we need to plan. Doubtless he will be coming over this afternoon to speak to you, since Ravenscar has given his permission. We must decide what you shall wear. Perhaps Caroline will lend you her Lucy to put up your hair. You must look just so—beautiful, yet not as if you were anticipating his question."

"But, Mama!" In her panic, Rachel reverted to her childhood name for this woman who was in general far too cool and reserved for a more affectionate name than Mother. "I cannot accept Lord Westhampton! I…"

Her mother stared at her in astonishment, and Rachel's words faltered to a halt.

''Are you mad?'' Lady Ravenscar's voice was like the crack of a whip. ''What do you mean, you cannot accept—'' She drew in her breath sharply. ''No! Was your father right? Have you given your affections elsewhere? My God, girl, what have you done!'' Fear and fury mingled in her face. ''Do not tell me you have let a man have his way with you!''

''No!'' Rachel gasped, shocked. ''How could you think that? I have never—he would never—''

''Good.'' Lady Ravenscar relaxed a little. ''Then it is nothing that cannot be put right. Who is this man? I cannot believe that I have not seen this happening.''

''It is Mr. Birkshaw. Anthony Birkshaw. And he has done nothing untoward. He has been all that is proper and correct. He would never have incurred gossip by dangling obviously after me.''

''Birkshaw!'' Her mother's first look of puzzlement changed quickly to one of horror. ''Anthony Birkshaw! That penniless pup? He dared to try to engage your affections! Oh, Rachel, how could you have been so foolish? What have you said to him? Have you promised him— But, no—no one would regard a silly girl's promise as binding when he had not had the courtesy or courage to speak to your father first.''

''He has not asked me to marry him,'' Rachel assured her. ''I tell you, Anthony—I mean, Mr. Birkshaw—has been all that is proper. We have made no promises, done nothing that anyone could construe as wrong. I swear it. But I—I love him, and I know that he returns my feelings. I thought today, when Father called us into the library, that it was he who had asked for my hand.''

Her mother looked at her with a touch of pity. ''My dear girl, you cannot think that Ravenscar would have approved such a match, can you? Mr. Birkshaw could not hope to get his permission. He has no money. No prospects. His father is the third son of Lord Moreston. The family runs to males. A plague would have to hit for him to come into the title. And it is only a barony, anyway. I cannot imagine how the man could think he could aspire to the daughter of an earl.''

''I don't think he thought much about my father's title,'' Rachel replied with rather more asperity than she was accustomed to using with her mother. ''It was me he fell in love with.''

''Then all I can say is that he is a proper ninny and so are you.'' Lady Ravenscar shook her head. ''Well, you had better put such foolish thoughts out of your head—and with no time wasted, either. You have to accept Westhampton this afternoon—and with no unhappy looks, either, to give him second thoughts.''

Rachel's heart turned in her chest. ''But, Mother, how can I accept him? I don't love him! I scarcely even know him! I—I love another man!''

''There is no reason for him to know that,'' Lady Ravenscar retorted. ''And it would be best if you got that thought out of your head instantly, as well. Your father would never let you waste yourself on Anthony Birkshaw. I can scarcely believe that you have been so foolish as to have given your heart to a—a pauper!''

''He is not a pauper!''

''Bah! You know nothing about the matter!'' Her mother faced Rachel, her lovely face set in cold, adamant lines. ''Do you think any of us married for love? That any of us knew our husbands before we became engaged? I can assure you that I did not, and neither did your sister.''

''But Caroline and Richard love each other.''

''Your sister was wise enough not to give her heart until she had given her hand,'' Lady Ravenscar snapped. ''I cannot believe that you are acting like this. You were always the most biddable of my children, the one I could count on to be reasonable. Obedient.'' She paused and gathered her composure, then started again. ''What did you think we were coming here for? For you to have a summer of parties and fun? Your father had to swallow his pride and accept a loan from Cleybourne to enable you to have this Season. You knew the reason for it. You knew what you were expected to do.''

''Yes, but—'' Tears glittered in Rachel's eyes. The dreamworld she had been living in this summer was crashing down around her ears. She could see now how foolish she had been, believing that the man she had fallen in love with would be an acceptable spouse in her parents' eyes. She had let herself believe that her love and the brilliant match she must make would somehow turn out to be embodied in the same person. "I cannot!" she cried out in a low voice. "I cannot marry Lord Westhampton when I love someone else!"

"You can, and you will." Lady Ravenscar's voice was implacable. "I am sorry that you were so silly as to let your feelings be engaged. Obviously I was not careful enough. I did not see this foolish romance developing and nip it in the bud. For that, I apologize. But I will take care to correct that mistake now. I will tell Caroline to inform the butler that you are no longer home if Mr. Birkshaw calls."

"No!" Pain stabbed through Rachel's chest like a knife. "Mother, you cannot—"

Lady Ravenscar gave her a long, level look. "If I have to, I will tell Ravenscar, and he will send the young man on his way."

"No!" The thought of her father railing at Anthony and barring him from their house filled her with even more fear. Her father was terrible in a temper; there was no telling what he might say to Anthony—or do to him. It would not surprise her if he took a cane to the young man.

"You will get over this infatuation," her mother went on, her cool voice like a knife lacerating Rachel's heart. "I know it must seem to you that your world is ending, but this feeling will pass, and soon. Young girls' fancies always do. In a few weeks, after you have gotten involved in planning the wedding and choosing dresses for your trousseau, why, you will look back on this calf love and realize how absurd it was."

"No," Rachel said in a choked voice. "I will not."

"You must try. Because I can assure you that you will not marry Mr. Birkshaw. You can turn down the best offer you could hope to receive if you insist, but you still will not marry Mr. Birkshaw. If you think about it, I am sure you will see why Birkshaw has not offered for you. He knows that he cannot: I imagine he barely has the money to support himself, let alone a wife. It is my best guess that he must marry money himself. Perhaps he was foolish enough to think that you had some."

"It was not about money!" Rachel cried. "We love each other."

"Well, it is a love without hope," her mother said remorselessly. "Your father and I will never allow you to marry him. And if you are so foolish as to turn down Lord Westhampton because of this piece of lunacy, I can guarantee that you will regret it the rest of your life."

Rachel could no longer hold back her tears. She began to sob, sinking into the nearest chair and covering her face with her hands. Her mother watched her with exasperation for a moment, then pulled a dainty handkerchief from her pocket and handed it to her daughter.

"Cry it out, then," she said. "And when you are done, lie down with a cool rag over your eyes to keep the swelling down. You cannot meet Lord Westhampton this afternoon with puffy eyes."

"I cannot marry him," Rachel repeated through her tears. "It would kill me."

"No. I assure you that it will not. You are not the first young girl to fancy herself desperately in love, and you certainly will not be the last. It never kills them. Of course, if you choose to turn down the prospect of being Lady Westhampton, of having a husband who adores you and will answer your every whim, of owning two of the most admired homes in the country and a limitless number of dresses and jewels—" Lady Ravenscar broke off with a sigh. "Well, we cannot make you accept him, though what your father will say about it, I dread to think. It will be a wonder if I can convince him not to pack us all up and go storming back to Darkwater in a rage, and, lord knows, that will be the end of all your hopes. But one may hope he will see reason. You are admired by other men—though none, of course, as fine a match as Lord Westhampton. There might be another chance for you to get a decent offer before the end of the Season, when we shall all have to return to the country to finish our lives in penury."

Rachel thought with horror of continuing to stay here this Season, going to parties and trying to attract a husband, when all the while her heart would be breaking. "Mother, I cannot...."

"Then you plan to live the rest of your life a spinster? For you will have no more opportunities to meet marriageable men. We cannot afford a second Season for you, and I can assure you that your father will have no desire to do anything for you if you cross him in this.''

Rachel shuddered, thinking of her father's ire. She had never been on the receiving end of one of his truly terrible rages. ''Mother, please…''

''Child, I cannot help you. You have only two choices—do your duty to the family, accept Lord Westhampton and have a nice, satisfactory life, or refuse and remain with us until we die, and then I suppose you will have to live as a companion to your sister Caroline.

''I want you to lie down now. I'll send the maid up with cucumber slices and a cool cloth for your eyes. And I want you think about what you are going to do. I want you to consider what will happen to us all if you do not marry Lord Westhampton. I want you to remember this Season and all we have done for you so that you could get a good offer and have a good life. Then decide whether you want to shame your family this way. Whether you are really willing to refuse to do what you are expected to do. What you *have* to do. I am sure you will come to the right decision about how to answer Lord Westhampton.''

Even now, Rachel thought, closing her eyes, she could feel the pain she had felt all those years ago, the numbed, emotionally battered state in which she had stumbled to her room and lain down on her bed. Exhausted with grief and plunged into despair, she had cried until she could cry no more, while the maid fussed and dried her tears and did her best to repair the damage her outburst had done to her face.

She had lain there and thought, as her mother had told her to do. She knew, bitterly, how foolish she had been, how much she had lived in a dreamworld. And she faced the void of her future, living immured in Darkwater, the object of her father's displeasure, constantly reminded of what an undutiful daughter she was and how she had failed the family. She could not marry Anthony without her father's permission, at least until she was twenty-one, and she knew that her mother was right—her father would not give her permission to marry Anthony, the man who had ruined her father's plans for gaining a wealthy son-in-law. And she knew, too, with sinking despair, that her mother was right about the state of his finances. Lady Ravenscar always knew such things. Besides, it explained why, despite his love for her, he had not asked for her hand. He had known that he would not be acceptable to her father; probably he, too, must make a good match.

Her dream of love died that afternoon. She faced the world as it was, the world in which a daughter married as she ought, as her parents desired. She saw reality, in which love did not hold sway, but only cold, hard reason. Her whole being ached at the thought of joining that world. But in the end, she had risen and let her maid dress her in the afternoon dress her mother had chosen, had let Caroline's Lucy do her hair up and hide the telltale redness around her eyes with just the barest touch of rice powder. Then she had gone downstairs and accepted Lord West-hampton's proposal of marriage.

3

Michael jerked awake. He lay still for a moment, drifting back to reality—sweating, heart pounding, hot blood racing. He had dreamed of Rachel. He could not remember the details of the dream, but the feeling was clear—the same mingling of excitement and pleasure, underlaid with sorrow, that was always there when he dreamed of his wife.

Being with Rachel was a different thing entirely. The same feelings were inside him, but amplified many times more and shot through with the thrum of nerves and uncertainty. In his dreams, at least he was able to talk to her without turning into a stiff priggish fool, as he did in real life. In dreams he was able to kiss and caress her to the point of thunderous, pulsating lust. The sorrow came as his mind swam back to the surface of consciousness and reality seeped in.

It was always worse after she had been here for a visit. Then the dreams would come frequently and with intensity. They tended to fade with her absence.

It was easier to live without her, as he had discovered after they had been married for a year or so. Great as the joy was in being with her, the pain grew to an excruciating point, until he could no longer bear living with her, being with her every day, aching with love and passion for her, yet never fulfilled. Never truly being her husband. It was an almost unbearable thing, to love her as he did—and to know that she did not love him in return, that she never had and never would. To know, in fact, that since she had married him, she had lived her life in muted sorrow, aching, as he himself did, for someone she would never have. He knew how she felt; he wished with all his heart that he could take that sorrow from her. He also knew, worst of all, that it was he who had condemned her to that life.

With a sigh, Michael pushed aside the covers and got out of bed. The caress of the cool air on his overheated skin was pleasant, and he did not put on his dressing gown as he walked to his dresser and poured himself a glass of water from the carafe that stood there. He drank it thirstily, then strolled over to the window and pushed aside one edge of the heavy velvet drape to look out into the night.

His bedroom looked out upon the sweep of driveway and trees that led up to the front of the elegant house. Beyond lay the view of hills that typified the beautiful Lake District of his home. It was not daylight yet, but the dark was lightening, so that one could make out the dim shapes of trees and shrubs in the gray light. It would soon be dawn, he knew,

when the light would turn golden, then burn away
the mists. There was no point now in trying to go
back to bed and sleep. He supposed that he should
put on his dressing gown and slippers, and light a
candle. Start his day.

But it seemed a pointless effort to him. There was
nothing in the day before him but loneliness and the
ache of loss. It would be so for many days more, he
knew. Experience had taught him that. The house
was still too full of memories of Rachel, too alive
with her presence. Hope still rose in him crazily that
he would turn a corner and see her there, or that he
would hear her laughter ringing down a corridor. She
had been here longer than normal this time, almost
three months, and Gabriela had been with them, too,
so that there had been the sound of a child's laughter
in the house, as well, a sound missing from here for
many, many years.

Rachel had been happier, he thought, than he had
ever seen her—at least since their marriage, that is.
She had been pleased for Dev and Richard, glad that
they had finally found love in their lives. She loved
both her brother and brother-in-law deeply, and their
unhappiness had further dampened her spirits. Con-
versely, their joy had brightened her own emotions.
And Gabriela's presence had also brought her happiness. The girl was lively and bright, and somehow
her being there had made everything smoother with
Rachel and Michael. It was hard to maintain formality with Gabriela around, laughing and chattering,

throwing herself with enthusiasm into everything around her.

It had brought home to Michael how much Rachel would have enjoyed children—another thing of which she had been robbed by marriage to him. He had wanted to give her children, had thought that he would. That had been back in the early days, when he had believed that she would grow to love him someday, that the depth and intensity of his love would eventually warm her heart to him. He had thought they would have a normal marriage in time, with intimacy and its natural result: children. He had lived in a fool's paradise, not knowing that the woman he loved had already given her heart to another man.

He had been naive not to see that she was in love, he supposed. He had known too much about books back then and not enough about the heart of a woman.

He had been almost thirty when he met Rachel, far too old to still know so little about love and courtship. He had grown up quiet and bookish, in chosen opposition to his father. His father had tainted the Westhampton name with scandal. An outdoors man with huge appetites, the former Lord Westhampton had lived exactly as he pleased. He had eaten and drunk to excess, never counting it a good evening unless he went stumbling and belching to bed. He had been wild in his youth, gambling, drinking and wenching, and his ways did not change much when at last Michael's grandfather forced his son into marriage.

Michael had been more like his mother, a quiet, intelligent woman who loved books and knowledge far more than the usual feminine pursuits of clothes and parties. Michael had seen the pain in his mother's eyes, and he had known that his father was the cause of it. He had hated his father for his excesses and his bullying, and he had vowed never to be the sort of man his father was.

Michael had learned to ride and shoot and hunt; he had been taught the manly art of boxing, as well as the more gentlemanly art of fencing. His father had insisted on his learning these things, which to him constituted the education of a British gentleman, and Michael had learned them as he did everything, with quiet determination. But while he did not have it in him to do any less than the best he could in such sports, he did not love them as he loved the education of his mind. His happiness lay in books and in the quiet hours he spent reading and puzzling out the mysteries of the universe. He had a thirst for knowledge that equaled his father's thirst for liquor.

He despised his father for his loose, hedonistic ways, for the shame he had brought upon his family's name and the pain he had brought to his gentle wife, and he had vowed early on never to be like his father. Where his father was prodigal, he was wise with money, recouping the family fortune that his father had tried his best to throw away. Where his father was greedy, he was abstemious. And where his father blustered and roared, he kept his temper in check. Michael was controlled, intelligent and circumspect. He enjoyed his time at Oxford and made friends among the men of letters and science whom he met there. After his father died—from a broken neck in a fall off a horse one night as he rode home inebriated—Michael spent most of his time in solitude at the family estate in the Lake District, reading, restoring the estate and corresponding with those of like mind.

The only time he had veered from his quiet life had been during the war, when Sir Robert Blount—a friend of his who worked in the government—had begged for Michael's help in catching a ring of Napoleon's spies operating within England. His friend had asked Michael to try his hand at deciphering the coded messages that the spies were using, knowing that such puzzles were precisely the sort of thing that Michael enjoyed. He had soon broken the code, and had found himself being drawn more and more into the game of intrigue. He told himself that he did it only for patriotism and for the intellectual challenge, but he knew, with some degree of shame, that he enjoyed the excitement and danger of it, as well. There was something elementally satisfying in using his wits and physical skills to defeat his opponents, a certain giddy pleasure in escaping danger. He discovered that he had a heretofore untapped talent for disguises and accents, that he was able to mingle with people of widely varying classes and places without being detected. His unobtrusive demeanor and his attractive but unremarkable looks made it easy to disappear into any crowd.

After the war ended, his life settled into its former quiet routine. It bothered him a little that he missed the excitement of the intrigue; the love of danger reminded him too much of his father, and he hated to see in himself anything of the former Lord Westhampton.

He was not actively looking for a wife. When he chanced to think about the matter, he assumed that he would someday marry someone of appropriate birth and like interests, a woman with whom he could raise a family and share a life. He was not expecting the thunderbolt of passion that struck him the first time he saw Rachel Aincourt.

He was in London for part of the Season, as was his custom, and he had attended a large party with his friend Peregrin Overhill. Perry had been waxing enthusiastic over a new beauty in town, but as Perry was the sort who often raved over some girl or other, though without ever actually pursuing them, Michael had, frankly, paid little attention to what he had said about Lord Ravenscar's youngest daughter. He had little doubt that she was lovely to look at. Michael was friends with the Duke of Cleybourne, and his duchess, Caroline, Ravenscar's oldest daughter, was, indeed, a beauty.

But when he entered the crowded ballroom and caught sight of Rachel, slim and tall in her elegant white dress, the word *beauty* scarcely seemed adequate to describe her. Her face glowed, the fair skin touched with pink at the cheeks and as soft as velvet. Her green eyes, fringed with lashes as black as the curls on her head, were brilliant and huge. And when she smiled—well, there were not words to convey how his heart had turned within his chest, and his life, formerly so routine, organized and calm, suddenly became a chaotic and glorious tumult of feeling.

All his previous thoughts of a pleasant marriage flew out the window. He knew as soon as he crossed the room and spoke to her that this was the woman he wanted as his wife. This soft-spoken girl with the dazzling smile awoke in him such passion, such emotion, that he knew he could never feel this way about anyone else.

He set about courting her in a gentlemanly way— never, of course, doing anything untoward or extreme, but consistently calling on her, taking her for an occasional ride in his high-wheeled tilbury, dancing the politely curtailed two dances at balls. He was aided in his efforts by the fact that he was already friends with the Duke of Cleybourne and therefore had frequent access to his house. Both the duchess and Lady Ravenscar, alert to every nuance of interest from a marriageable male, were sure to include him in any party they made up, whether for a picnic or a night at the opera or taking in the newest play at Drury Lane.

Michael did not delude himself that he was a figure of high romance to a young girl, but he was aware that he was considered a marital prize, being not only titled and wealthy, but also quite presentable in looks and manner. He knew that Rachel did not love him, but he was hopeful that in time he could win her heart. She did not turn down his offers of a ride along Rotten Row, and she always seemed happy enough to talk to him whenever he made up one of their party. He would have moved more slowly, allowing her time to develop some affection for him, but he knew from Cleybourne that Ravenscar, perennially strapped for cash, was likely to give his daughter's hand to the first eligible man to make her an offer. Given that one of the most likely men to offer for her had been Sir Wilfred Hamerston-Smythe, a widower old enough to be Rachel's father and from whom many had suggested his wife had died to get away, Michael knew it was not a matter of conceit to think that Rachel would be happier married to him.

He had not really considered the possibility that Rachel would turn down his offer. Daughters generally married as their parents wished, and she, too, would have known that his offer was among the best of her options. So, even though Rachel's demeanor when accepting his proposal had been subdued and even, he thought, a little red eyed, he had put it down to the remnants of a girl's romantic hopes that her future husband would be a knight from a fairy tale, come riding to rescue her. He would make her happy, he told himself. He knew that he was probably a rather dull, bookish figure to a young woman, but he thought that his gentle wooing, his respect and love and consideration of her would engender in her some

affection that he could build into, if not the fire of
passion, at least a warm glow of love.

He had not realized then that not only did she not
love him, she loved someone else.

Just thinking about it now was enough to pierce
his chest with pain. Michael sighed and dropped the
curtain, walking away from the window. He wrapped
his dressing gown around himself and slumped down
in a chair, his gaze turning inward to the time over
seven years ago when he discovered, only two days
before the wedding, that his fiancée had eloped with
another man.

Their wedding was to be celebrated here at Westhampton in the picturesque stone Norman church in
the village, where all the earls of Westhampton had
been married for longer than anyone could remember. The house was packed with friends and family
who had come to celebrate the wedding, and still
more were staying in the inn in the village and with
Sir Edward Moreton, a neighbor whose kind lady had
taken on the burden of lodging several of the wedding guests.

It was a joyous occasion. Michael could not remember a time when he had been so happy. He
thought that Rachel had been warming to him during
the past few months. Once they were engaged, they
had been allowed to spend more time together in
comparative solitude. While Rachel's mother or sister
was always with them when he came to call on her,
they now often sat discreetly apart from the engaged

couple, allowing them to talk more freely. And at balls he was now allowed to dance with her more than twice in an evening without calling down gossip upon their heads.

The fact that she seemed to like him more the more she was around him made him hopeful that he would be able to win her love completely once the massive production of the wedding was over and they were finally alone together.

It was two days before the wedding, and as Michael strolled with Rachel from the music room after a convivial evening of song and merriment among their friends, he was thinking with anticipation of the time when they would at last be alone together. He did not intend to consummate their marriage that first night; it would be, he thought, too frightening for a young woman still virtually a stranger to him. No matter how much he wanted Rachel, he intended to take his time and build her trust in him, to awaken her gradually to passion. He had long ago vowed that no woman would suffer at his hands, and he certainly would not inflict any pain or fear upon Rachel, whom he loved.

But it would be wonderful just to be alone with her, without the constant presence of a chaperon—to be able to talk with her, to laugh and do as they pleased, to get to know one another, to kiss and hold her, to take her hand, without anyone there to watch or gossip. There had been times in the last few months when he had wondered if that moment would ever arrive.

Rachel, he thought, had been quieter than usual all evening, and as he looked down at her, it seemed to him that she was a trifle pale. She was, he supposed, nervous about the wedding approaching so rapidly.

As they passed the conservatory, empty and dark, he took her arm and whisked her inside the door. Rachel looked up at him, startled, her eyes wide.

"What is it?" she whispered.

He smiled down at her. "No need to be frightened," he told her.

"What?" Rachel stared at him and let out an odd little laugh. "What do you mean? Frightened of what?"

"I don't know. The wedding. We'll get through it well enough. Everyone always manages."

"Oh. Yes, I suppose they do." Rachel gave him a small smile. "I am a little nervous, I guess."

"Don't worry. I shall be there with you. Just dig your fingers into my arm if you feel that you are about to faint. I'll prop you up."

"All right."

He thought that there was the glimmer of a tear in her eye, but she glanced away just then, and when she looked back up at him a moment later, he saw that her eyes were dry. Michael put his hand under her chin and gazed down into her face.

"You trust me, don't you?" he asked softly. "Please believe that you always can. I will not hurt you, I promise."

"Oh, Michael…" Her voice broke with emotion,

and her hand came up to curl around his. "I am not...worthy of you."

He smiled. "What nonsense. You are worthy of any man."

Overcome by the love that swelled his heart as he looked at her, he bent to kiss her. Her lips were warm and soft beneath his, hinting of such pleasure that he almost could not bear it. He wanted her in that moment more than he ever had before. His blood pounded in his ears and thrummed through his veins. He thought of Rachel's body pliant in his arms, of her mouth opening to him in passion.

His arms went around her, and he pulled her close against him, his kiss deepening. Heat surged through his body, and he pressed her body into his, delighting in her softness. His lips moved against hers, tasting the sweetness he had dreamed about for months. He thought of the days and weeks ahead, of introducing Rachel to the delights of the flesh, of exploring her body with his hands and mouth, of teaching her the pleasure they could bring each other, and a tremor of lust shook him.

The last thing he wanted to do was to end the kiss, to release her and step back, but he made himself do it. He must not frighten her with the extent of the passion pounding through him.

Rachel stared up at him, eyes wide with surprise. Her lips were soft and moist, dark from the pressure of his mouth, and the sight of them was enough to stir his lust all over again. Michael carefully took another step back, clearing his throat.

"I beg your pardon. I should not..." His mind was too clouded with desire to think of anything rational to say. "Perhaps we should, um, say good-night."

"Yes, my lord." Rachel's words were barely a whisper, and she whirled and hurried from the room.

Michael took a step after her, suddenly worried that it had been fear he had read in her eyes, not merely surprise. Then he stopped, thinking that if she was a little frightened, his chasing after her would only increase her fear. No doubt his sudden kiss had startled her. It had not been, he thought rather disgustedly, a suave or subtle move on his part. It was not like him; in general, he was a man who was in control. But Rachel's beauty tested his control, and over the months of their engagement he had had to exercise an iron control over his desires. With the end almost in sight, he had let his guard down. He would have to be more careful, he thought, to keep his distance from his fiancée until after the ceremony.

Right now, he told himself, the best thing to do would be to leave her alone. If his passion had upset her, her mother or sister would be much better at allaying her fears than he.

Michael retired to his study and poured himself a brandy.

He was still there over an hour later, his blood cooler, reading a book and sipping at the last of a second brandy, when there was a polite tap on the door. It was the butler, looking faintly embarassed.

"My lord..." he began somewhat tentatively. "The, ah, head groom wishes to speak to you. I told him you were in your study, but he was most insistent. He would not say what it was." The butler looked displeased at that notion, but continued. "However, he seemed to feel the matter was urgent. I am sorry to disturb you, but, as it was Tanner..."

"Yes, quite right." Michael rose from his chair, faintly curious. He supposed there must be some problem with one of the horses—or perhaps one of the guests' animals. Tanner was a normally phlegmatic sort, not the kind to urgently seek his employer's counsel.

Tanner was waiting for him just outside the door leading into the back garden, holding his hat in his hands and twisting the soft cloth nervously. Michael had known the man since he had come there as a groom when Michael was just a boy, and there was something in his leathery face that made Michael suddenly apprehensive.

"What is it?" he asked without preamble, striding over to the man. "Is it Saladin?" He named his favorite mount, a black stallion of unusual grace and speed.

Tanner looked faintly surprised. "What? Oh, no, my lord. Nothing like that. Saladin's as fine and fit as ever. 'Tis something else entirely." He paused, looking at Michael uncomfortably. "I'm hoping you won't take this the wrong way, sir. I wouldn't have even come to ye, 'cept that the lad generally has a good head on his shoulders. He's not the sort to go startin' at shadows."

"I'm sorry, Tanner. I'm not sure—who are you talking about?"

"One of my lads, sir. Dougie. He's a good boy, one of the best I've had here, and I would say trustworthy. He came to me just now with a story...."

"Yes?" Michael encouraged him when the other man's voice trailed off. "A story you thought I should hear?"

"Exactly." Tanner sighed, then said in a rush, "The thing is, the lad thought he saw Miss Aincourt."

"Miss Aincourt?" Whatever he had expected the head groom to say, it had certainly not been this. "My fiancée?"

"Yes. That's right. Down below the gardens, along the path that leads to the meadow."

"The meadow! When? You mean tonight?"

"Aye, sir." The other man looked away, not meeting his gaze. "Maybe thirty minutes ago or so. Dougie was taking a walk before bed, and he comes back inside, lookin' all distraught, and he pulls me aside and he says he seen Miss Aincourt down there."

"He must be mistaken," Michael said automatically. "At this time of night? I just saw Miss Aincourt a little over an hour ago, and she was going up to bed."

"I asked him, sir, and he swore up and down that it was the lady herself. He was taken aback to see her, he said, so he moved a little closer. He..." The groom hesitated, then went on in a rush. "He saw that she was talkin' to a man."

Michael went suddenly cold. His fingers curled into his palms. "Go on," he said, amazed at how even his voice sounded.

"Dougie thought it was you at first, so he was goin' to turn and leave, only a horse whinnied. He looked an' seen there was a bay tied to one of the trees, kind of back in the shadow. Now Dougie knows horses, and this wasn't one of ours, so he— he didn't know what to do, sir. He was thinkin' he shouldn't leave Miss Aincourt out there alone, an' he reckoned the man was a stranger, 'cause of the horse. So he stayed, watching, tryin' to decide. And then, well, the man led his horse out, an' Dougie saw his face. It was no one he'd ever seen afore, he said. An' he—he helped Miss Aincourt onto the horse and mounted it after her, an' they—they rode off."

The groom studiously examined the flagstone walkway beneath his feet. Michael felt as if someone had just knocked the wind out of him. He remembered suddenly the look on Rachel's face after he kissed her—surprise, he'd thought, then wondered if it had been fear. Had the force of his passion scared her into running from him? Then he remembered that she had seemed a little odd all evening.

He took a breath and tried to clear the confusion from his head. "He is certain?"

"He swears it is what he saw. I wouldn't have bothered you if it had been some of the other lads. But Dougie...well, I've never known him to lie or even exaggerate. I asked him over and over, an' he insisted he hadn't been mistaken. There was no smell of gin on his breath. I didn't know what to do, sir, but finally I decided I had to tell you and let you decide, you know...." His voice trailed off miserably.

"I will look into it straightaway," Michael assured him grimly. "I needn't tell you—"

"No one else heard it, and they won't. I already swore Dougie to silence. He knows he'll be turned off without a reference if he breathes a word of it to anyone else, including the other lads."

"Thank you, Tanner."

He went back into the house, feeling strangely numb, and knocked on Lord Ravenscar's door. Ravenscar came to the door, glowering, with his nightcap on his balding head and a dressing gown flung hastily around his shoulders.

In a low voice, Michael explained what he had learned. Ravenscar stared back at him blankly for a long moment, then his cheeks flushed red. "What? What are you saying?" he barked. "Do you dare to imply that—"

"I am not implying anything," Michael responded coolly. "I am just asking if Lady Ravenscar might step into Miss Aincourt's room and see if she is in her bed."

Ravenscar looked as if he would have liked to shut the door in Michael's face, but after a moment he turned away, and Michael heard him talking to his wife. Michael stepped a few feet away and waited.

A few moments later Lady Ravenscar rushed out of the room, a dressing gown wrapped around her, the ribbons of her nightcap fluttering as she rushed down the hall. Michael caught only a glimpse of her face, but he saw that it was white and taut with fear. He was suddenly sure that she knew something her husband did not.

Lord Ravenscar went down the hall after her at a more stately pace. Before he reached the door, his wife stepped back out into the hall. If possible, her face was even paler than before. She looked at her husband, then at Michael, fumbling for words. Impatiently, Ravenscar shoved past her into the room. Michael strode down the hall to Rachel's mother and took her arm to steady her. She looked as if she were about to faint.

"She's gone, then?" he asked in a low voice.

Lady Ravenscar nodded dumbly, tears pooling in her eyes. She raised her hands to her cheeks. "I don't know what he will say." She cast an anxious glance behind her toward the room into which her husband had gone.

Michael steered her into Rachel's room and closed the door behind him, guiding Lady Ravenscar to a chair. Ravenscar stood in the middle of the room, shock turning to rage on his face.

"Are any of her things gone?" Michael asked quickly, forestalling the imminent explosion from Ravenscar.

Lady Ravenscar shook her head. "I don't know. I don't think so. Her vanity set is still there." She gestured toward the dresser, where a silver-backed set of brush, mirror and comb lay.

Michael glanced around the room. The bed had been turned down, the fire banked. A woman's white nightdress and dressing gown were tossed onto the bed. She had dressed for bed, he surmised—no doubt because of the presence of her maid—then had discarded the nightclothes and redressed, slipping out into the night. There was no sign of a letter on the bed or anywhere else. He wondered if she had gone out wothout intending to leave the estate, or if she had left her things behind to conceal what she had done for a while longer.

"Do you have any idea who he is?" Michael asked Lady Ravenscar.

"Of course not!" Ravenscar snapped.

Michael noticed that Lady Ravenscar cast a furtive glance at her husband but said nothing. He turned to Lord Ravenscar. "They have not been gone long, and Dougie said they were riding double. It is quite likely that we can catch up with them if we leave quickly. I will send down to the groom to saddle two horses if you want to accompany me."

Ravenscar, still looking as if he might fly into a rage at any moment, nodded his head shortly. "I'll get dressed."

He strode out of the room. Lady Ravenscar started to follow, but Michael laid a hand on her arm. "Do you know his name, my lady?"

Rachel's mother cast him an agonized glance. "I—I'm not sure. There was a man—the silly girl thought she had developed a *tendre* for someone. But I made sure he was not admitted to our house any longer and that she was never alone. She hasn't seen him in four months, I would swear it. I thought she had forgotten him.''

"What is his name?'' He had to know, though it cost him some pride to ask.

"Anthony Birkshaw.''

"Birkshaw.'' Michael cast around in his mind for a face to go with the name. He faintly remembered a darkly handsome young man among the flock who had hung around Rachel before her engagement. "She loved him when she accepted my proposal?''

"Love? The chit doesn't know what love is!'' Lady Ravenscar retorted contemptuously. "She was flattered, and he was a presentable young man. I explained to her that it was impossible. She knew where her duty lay. I cannot imagine what can have possessed her to throw away her future like this.''

Her duty. The words lay like lead in his chest. He was the duty her family had laid upon her. He had known she did not love him, but there had been hope. But the knowledge that she loved another, that she had fled from Michael at the last moment, unable to bear the thought of wedding him, cut through him like a knife.

There was a part of him that wanted in that moment to simply go back to his room and shut the door, to let her go to her love, to simply wrap himself around with his misery and let Ravenscar answer the storm of questions from the guests.

But he knew that he could not. He had seen the light of fury in Ravenscar's eyes. He could not allow him to catch up to Rachel alone. Besides, her reputation would be damaged beyond repair if word of what she had done this night got out. The scandal would stain his name, as well, of course, but he was the injured party, after all, and, after this, once again a highly eligible bachelor. He cared little for London Society, anyway, and he could ride out the storm alone up here at Westhampton, far away from the pitying glances and malicious whispers about what had driven the Aincourt girl to take such drastic measures.

It would be Rachel who would be excoriated by the gossip. Leaving a bridegroom almost literally at the altar…eloping to Gretna Green, with the several nights spent alone with a man, unmarried, that that would entail…her reputation would be in shreds after this. Whispers would follow her all her life. There would be many hostesses who would not invite her to parties or receive her if she called on them. Of course, given what Lady Ravenscar had said about Birkshaw's finances, doubtless Rachel would not be able to afford to move in her family's social circle any longer, anyway. She would be living in some rented room, not sure where her next meal was coming from, mending her dresses because she could not afford new ones, no doubt burdened even further by children whom she would have to worry about feeding, too.

Michael supposed that such a gloomy picture of

Rachel's future should have assuaged his spirits somewhat, but he found he could not bear to think of her in such dire circumstances. She had been un- utterably foolish. Why had she accepted his pro- posal? Why had she not told him that she loved someone else? But the ruin of her life was too cruel a punishment for her adolescent mistake. He had to find her and stop her from throwing away her future.

So, turning away from Lady Ravenscar, he went out to ride after Rachel.

4

Michael sighed and stood up, running his hands over his face tiredly. It had been a long time since he had thought about the night when Rachel ran away from him. For the first two years of his marriage, that night had haunted him constantly, but over time the memory of it had blessedly receded. But when it did come to mind, as now, it was vivid and painful. He could feel once again the leaden sorrow in his heart, the dread of what he would find when they caught up to the escaping couple, the anguish of knowing that Rachel was so revolted at the thought of marrying him that she was willing to forfeit her reputation—not to mention a life of ease—in order to avoid becoming his wife.

He had come to know in that evening the depths of pain which love brought...as well as the extent to which love for Rachel had wrapped around his heart and all through his body, to the point that he could not despise her no matter how much he wanted to, could not wish for her the misery his wounded heart cried out to inflict on someone. Pride and bitter hurt had called out for revenge, yet he had known, even as he rode grimly after her, that in the end, given the chance, he would not exact that revenge.

The upstairs maid crept quietly into his room and was clearly startled to find him up. She scurried about her business, scraping the ashes from the fire and lighting a new one, then slipped out. Michael rang for his breakfast tray. After that, his valet would bring heated water for shaving and lay out his clothes, and his day would begin. But for now, Michael stood before the fire, holding his hands out to the warmth, welcome in the chill of a spring dawn, and watched the flames dance—and remembered the night he brought Rachel back.

He and Ravenscar rode grimly through the darkness. It had not been difficult to follow the escaping couple. From the bottom of the gardens, the tracks of the doubly loaded horse led along the edge of the meadow and onto the road, where they had clearly headed east, toward the village. There, he and Ravenscar stopped to enquire at the inn whether a couple had stopped, and the innkeeper cheerfully responded that indeed, a young man had come by seeking to hire a carriage only an hour or so earlier, and there had been, the innkeeper thought, a young woman waiting out in the yard for him, but as she had been wearing a hooded cloak, he had not gotten a proper look at her.

"Friends of yours, my lord?" the innkeeper asked, curiosity mingling with the friendly respect in his face.

Michael smiled with a look of ease that he did not feel, glad that his experiences dealing with spies during the war had engendered in him an ability to dissemble, and replied, "Yes, a foolish young man who took offense, I'm afraid, and rode off into the night. I must see if I can bring him back before he puts his poor wife through much more trouble."

"Ah, I see. Yes, I thought he was awful unprepared-like, seekin' a vehicle at that time of night. 'Course, I had nothin' to give him, and I told him so. No place nearer than Coxley would have an inn big enough to be hirin' out post chaises. That's where I told him to go."

"Very good. Perhaps I will catch up to him there. Thank you for your trouble." Michael tipped the innkeeper a goldboy just to ensure his continued allegiance and strode out to rejoin Lord Ravenscar.

"The fool tried to hire a post chaise here at this time of night," Michael said. Anger surged through him—how could the man have enticed Rachel to run away with him, knowing that he had not even made arrangements for their escape? He was clearly an idiot or a scoundrel or both.

They pushed onward and ran the couple to ground in Coxley not long after midnight. There was no bustle of a carriage being prepared in the courtyard of the inn, but the lights were on inside the place, and an irritated innkeeper opened the door to their knock.

On hearing they were seeking a young couple, he jerked his thumb over his shoulder toward a closed door across the hall from the public room.

"They're in the private sitting room there, sir, and if ye can talk some sense into that young man's head, it'll be a great favor to me, I'll tell ye. Fool wants me roust out me grooms and set him and his wife up in a post chaise. At this time of night. I told him he'd have to wait 'til the morning, like any decent body would, but he's been carrying on like a scalded cat about spending the night in a 'grubby country inn.' I ask ye—"

"He'll win no awards for tact," Michael agreed calmly. "Don't worry. We shall handle him for you. Go back to bed and don't worry about it. They will be leaving with us."

"Thank you, sir." The innkeeper nodded his head gratefully. "I can always tell real quality, sir, and yer it, not like some young pups I could mention." He nodded his head significantly toward the closed door, then turned, picked up his candle and waddled off down the back hall to his quarters.

Ravenscar had been waiting impatiently all through the innkeeper's conversation, and as soon as he left, Rachel's father strode across and unceremoniously opened the door and walked in. Michael followed quickly, closing the door behind them.

Rachel sat in a chair across the room, her elbow propped on the arm of the chair and her head on her hand, looking wilted. A young man with a thick head of black hair and handsome features was striding impatiently back and forth across the floor. He swung around at their entrance, but it was clear from the stunned expression on his face that he was not expecting to see Michael and Ravenscar.

"Good God!" he exclaimed involuntarily.

Rachel looked up at the force of his exclamation, and she froze when she saw their visitors. She jumped to her feet, her hands clutching her skirts, and the fear on her face pierced Michael's heart anew. "F-father! Lord Westhampton!"

"Did you think you would get away?" Lord Ravenscar roared, his face flooding red with fury. "Did you think you could just dash off and nothing would happen? Have you gone mad? Are you dead to all sense of propriety?"

"Lord Ravenscar..." Michael began, coming up beside him.

Ravenscar cast him a single cold glance, saying, "No. Unfortunately she is not your wife yet, Westhampton. She is still my concern." He turned back to his daughter, saying, "Your mother is prostrate with grief. You have ruined us all."

Rachel's face turned even paler, and tears welled in her eyes. "I'm sorry. So sorry. I did not want to hurt anyone."

"My lord, it was all my fault." The young man came to stand between Rachel and her father. "I begged Rachel to run away and marry me."

"Of course it's your fault!" Ravenscar roared. "Do you think I don't know that? This one hasn't the wit to come up with an idea like that. But you couldn't keep from seducing her, could you?''

"My lord!" Birkshaw gasped. "I did not touch her, I swear! I love your daughter!"

Ravenscar's face went from red to purple as Birkshaw's words rendered him speechless for the moment.

"You have an odd way of demonstrating your affection," Michael said crisply, stepping into the gap. "Convincing Miss Aincourt to elope with you practically on the eve of her wedding, with scores of guests here to witness the scandal. You have exposed her to unimaginable gossip and encouraged her to break her trust, all the while knowing that you have not the means to support a wife. And you hadn't even the foresight to hire a carriage to make your escape," he finished in disgust.

The other man flushed, whether from anger or shame, Michael was not sure. "I know you have good reason to hate me, my lord, and I beg your pardon. I had no intention of doing wrong to you. It is just that my love for Miss Aincourt is overwhelming."

Birkshaw turned to look at Rachel, and she smiled at him through her tears, love glowing on her face. Michael felt as if a knife had just sliced through his vital organs. He turned and walked away, struggling to compose himself. Rachel had never looked at him with even a third of that emotion, and he saw clearly now that he had no hope of becoming the man she loved. He walked over to the sideboard, staring blindly down at the rough wood surface, seeing only the bleakness that lay over the rest of his life. A life without Rachel. Without love.

"Overwhelming!" Ravenscar barked. "You are a fool. Between the two of you, you have ruined her life. Eloping—spending the night on the road with a man who is not her husband—good God, man, the entire world will know she is a wanton. Her good name is destroyed. Are you such a mooncalf you don't see that? No man would marry her now."

"*I* will marry her!" Birkshaw declaimed dramatically.

"Over my dead body," Ravenscar snarled. "You have ruined us with your silly posing! Do you understand me? Ruined us! Do you honestly think that after what you have done I would allow you to marry my daughter? And how do you propose to take care of her? Did you think of that before you swayed her to run away with you? Eh? What will you do, take her back to your bachelor's rooms? Live on some paltry allowance you get from your father?"

"I will find employment, my lord," the younger man replied stiffly.

"Oh, yes, of course! Secretary to some lord, no doubt. Hah! You couldn't live on the pittance they pay, and even if you could, what man would hire you? Secretaries are responsible men, not the sort who run off with another man's fiancée in the middle of the night. The same is true for any government job. If you had the sense God gave a kitten, you would know it. No one in the *Ton* would have anything to do with either one of you after this. You will be lucky if you're able to find a job clerking. I know your situation. You have to marry money. I'll wager you're living on borrowed funds now. Did you think she had money? Did you think, if you blackened her name, I would have no choice but to allow you to marry her, and you would batten onto me for the rest of your life?''

"It was not like that, my lord." Birkshaw's jaw clenched. "I realize that my prospects are not very good...."

"Not good? They are miserable!" Ravenscar roared. "And you intend to drag my daughter into that? You propose to house her in some tenement in the East End? How will you feed her? How will you provide for the luckless children you will have?''

"I—I don't know," Birkshaw faltered.

"You don't know," Ravenscar repeated with heavy sarcasm. "And for that you have ruined my family.''

A little sob escaped Rachel at her father's words. He turned his harsh gaze on her. "Well, miss, I never expected this of you," he said bitterly. "I always thought that Dev would be the one who destroyed our good name. It was his licentious ways I feared. What a fool I was not to see that you were cut from the same cloth. You are a wanton! A trollop!''

"Father, no, please!" Tears streamed from Rachel's eyes, and her entire body shook with sobs. "I have done nothing wrong!''

"Ravenscar!" Michael swung back around. "That's hardly necessary."

"It is the truth!" Ravenscar thundered, his eyes flashing with the fire of a biblical prophet. He pointed an accusing finger at his daughter. "For the sake of your fleshly desires, you have trampled the good name of your family. It is not only that you will never be received in decent company again. Neither will your mother. I will be too ashamed to set foot in White's again. You are a stain upon the name of Aincourt."

"I am sorry. I am sorry!" Rachel cried, looking at her father pleadingly. "I did not think! I was—it was just—" She covered her face with her hands, unable to go on.

"It's obvious that you did not think," her father retorted disgustedly. "Dragging both our names through the dirt just so you could have your pleasure with this boy! There is no way we can keep this quiet. The house is full of wedding guests. The entire *Ton* will know that you left Westhampton standing at the altar."

Rachel's hand dropped from her face, and she stared at her father with rising horror. It was obvious that until this moment she had not considered the consequences her actions would have for Michael. "No, I did not mean—"

"You have made him look a proper fool," Ravenscar thundered on, disregarding her comment. "You have dishonored an excellent man, broken your trust—"

"Enough!" Michael exclaimed, striding forward. "That is enough, my lord. She will not be ruined, and I will not be dishonored. Because no one will know of this."

"What?" Everyone else in the room turned to look at Michael in astonishment. Ravenscar frowned. "What are you talking about? We cannot keep this hidden."

"Yes, we can. No one will know that Miss Aincourt jilted me if we are married two days hence, as planned."

Ravenscar stared at him. "You would still be willing to marry her? After this?"

Michael carefully refrained from looking at Rachel. "If Miss Aincourt agrees to it. It is the only way to keep it a secret. I am sure Mr. Birkshaw, if he loves Miss Aincourt as he says he does, will ride away and never speak of this." Michael cast a long, intent look at the other man.

Birkshaw's gaze dropped, and he nodded.

"My servants will never breathe a word," Michael went on. "They are loyal to me. I think we can count on you and Lady Ravenscar not to reveal it."

"I should think not!" Ravenscar exclaimed.

"Then the only way it would be revealed is if I repudiate our marriage contract. If we return to the house quietly, and Miss Aincourt and I are married day after tomorrow, no one will be the wiser."

There was a long moment of silence. Michael turned to Rachel. She was wiping tears from her cheeks, her face averted. "Well, Miss Aincourt? Are you willing to wed me Friday?"

"Of course she is," Lord Ravenscar inserted quickly. "She should count herself a fortunate woman that you would even consider allying yourself with her after this."

"No. Let the lady speak for herself," Michael said firmly, his eyes still fastened on Rachel. "Obviously she accepted me unwillingly before. I do not want that to happen again. It is entirely your decision, Miss Aincourt."

Rachel raised her eyes, still damp with tears, to his. "Yes," she said in a low voice. "I will marry you Friday. I am so sorry. My behavior has been inexcusable. I—thank you for your generosity."

Michael nodded once, gravely. He had spoken up because he could not bear to hear Rachel's father harangue her any longer; the thought of her having to return to live with the man, forever the object of his anger and scorn, filled him with disgust. This was the only way, he knew, for Rachel to survive this episode with her reputation intact. But he was also aware, with a touch of self-disdain, that his motives had been largely selfish. He had made his offer because he could not bear to let her go. He had to bind her to him, even knowing that she loved another.

Birkshaw let out an inarticulate sound of frustration and pain and, turning on his heel, left the room. Rachel cast an anguished glance after him but did not move to stop him. Shortly after, the three of them left the inn and rode silently back to Westhampton,

Rachel riding on her father's horse behind him. On Friday, as scheduled, she became Lady Westhampton.

They had been married for seven years now, and she had never been truly his wife.

Michael had still hoped—foolishly, he soon found—that somehow, someday, Rachel would grow to love him, or at least to like him well enough that her innate desire for a normal life, with intimacy and children, would lead her to ease into a true marriage with him. He had reassured her, of course, the afternoon before their wedding, that he would not press her or expect a physical relationship with her, knowing her feelings. But inside, he had still believed that in time, with care and consideration on his part, she would change in her regard for him.

But over the years, their relationship had scarcely changed. They had begun their marriage in a careful, polite way, and they had continued that way. Hurt and still somewhat stunned, not wanting to rush her and cause her any pain, Michael had been scrupulously courteous and restrained with Rachel. They had spent their honeymoon in Paris, once again open to the English now that the war with Napoleon was over. Their rooms had been separate, joined by a door in the common wall that was never opened. They went to operas and plays, and to a ball at the British ambassador's.

They returned home to London, to a life that was much the same. Rachel made her cautious entry into

the life of a Society matron, starting with small card
parties and dinners, and growing to a spectacular ball
by the end of her first Season. Michael helped her
through the sometimes treacherous shoals of a Society life, and she responded with gratitude and, he
thought, a certain degree of liking. But there was always between them a certain awkwardness, a formality. Though they learned sundry small facts about
one another, they remained, on an important level,
strangers. It seemed as though the more awkward he
felt, the more polite and restrained he grew, and Rachel responded in kind, until at last he realized in
despair that there would never be any love between
them. He did not know if Rachel still loved Anthony
Birkshaw. He would not have dreamed of violating
her privacy by asking her; he knew only that she had
not seen the man again after they had wed, for that
was the only stipulation he had made regarding their
marriage. But whether she loved Birkshaw or not, it
was clear to Michael that she did not love *him*.

After a year of marriage, he decided that it was
worse to live with Rachel, loving her, wanting her,
and receiving no love or desire in return, than it was
to live without her. Their parting, as in all things,
was polite, even amicable. He reminded her of his
liking for the country and quiet calm, but assured her
that he had no intention of making her suffer a country existence. She could remain in London, living the
life she enjoyed, while he would retire to the estate
in the Lake District. There had been in him, he
thought, some small, lingering hope that she would

protest that she did not want to live alone in London, that she would go with him, or that they must split their time between the two homes. But she did not. She merely agreed, polite and passionless.

That had been a lonely, bitter trip north for him, and an even harder winter in the snowy landscape of Cumbria. There was all the beauty he had always loved; there were his books, his studies, repairs to the house and gardens, experiments to try in the fields, letters to write and read—in short, all the things that had made up his life before Rachel. But none of them satisfied.

But so it had been for over five years now. He and Rachel lived separate lives. He visited London sometimes during the Season, just to make an appearance; she returned to Westhampton for Christmas. They were married. And they weren't. He had grown accustomed to it, if not reconciled.

There was a discreet tap at the door; then his valet opened it and carried in the tray containing his breakfast. He set the tray on the small table in front of the pair of chairs in the sitting area of the bedroom, then proceeded to pour Michael's tea and remove the covers of the dishes.

"Good morning, my lord," the valet said politely. Garson was a person of rigid ideas concerning etiquette, and he was careful never to cross the line into friendliness with his employer, despite the fact that he had been Michael's valet for almost fifteen years.

He bustled about the room, opening the drapes and letting in the morning glow, then paused beside Michael's chair, waiting until Michael had taken several sips of tea. Michael looked up at him inquiringly.

"You had something to say to me?"

Garson folded his hands prissily at his waist. "There is a person who arrived here this morning. A groom, I believe, from Lord Ravenscar's estate. He left there yesterday morning, as I understand, and rode straight through."

"Lord Ravenscar!" Michael set the cup of tea down with a clank and jumped to his feet. "Why? Is something wrong? Did something happen to Lady Westhampton?"

"He said that all was fine, my lord, or I would have delivered the note he carried to you immediately." With this, he produced a small note from his pocket.

Michael snatched the missive from his valet's hands. "Good God, man, why didn't you?"

Garson looked pained. "I thought to give you a moment to take your tea first, my lord."

Michael grimaced. He broke the seal, unfolded the letter and began to read Rachel's familiar hand. A moment later an oath burst from him, then he sat back down in his seat and read through the note again. "Bloody hell!"

Garson had remained in the room, ostensibly laying out Michael's clothes for the day, but in reality waiting, Michael knew, to find out why Lady Westhampton had sent a letter winging swiftly back to the house she had just left. He paused now beside Michael's chair. When Michael said nothing, he prompted, ''Everything is all right, I trust, with her ladyship?''

Michael tapped an irritated tattoo on the arm of his chair. ''No,'' he snapped. ''Everything is most definitely not all right.'' He paused, then added, ''Pack my bags, Garson. We will be joining Lady Westhampton at Darkwater.''

5

Rachel glanced across the sitting room to where Jessica stood looking down at the bit of knitting in Miranda's hands. Jessica pressed her lips together, then pursed them.

Miranda looked up at her and sighed. "Oh, go ahead and laugh. I know it looks absurd."

"No, it—" Jessica glanced at Miranda, and a laugh escaped her lips. "Actually, you're right. It does look absurd. Whatever did you do?"

"I haven't the faintest idea," Miranda confessed, chuckling, too. "Obviously my education was sadly neglected. I cannot do any of these things that you and Rachel do so easily."

"Ah, but I cannot shoot a gun," Rachel pointed out with a smile at her sister-in-law.

Miranda, the daughter of an American who had grown wealthy in the fur trade, had been raised in a manner almost inconceivable to Rachel. She had accompanied her father on fur-buying trips to the wilds, where she had met Indians and trappers, and learned not only how to shoot but also how to use a knife to advantage. As her father's business had grown, she had moved naturally into it, keeping track of his accounts and investing his money in real estate in the raw, burgeoning city of New York, so that his fortune—and her own—doubled and even tripled. Although Rachel had quickly come to love her sister-in-law dearly—not the least because she had brought Dev back from the edge of ruining his life—there were times when Miranda's bustling energy left her feeling rather breathless and inadequate.

"That's true," Miranda agreed, but added, "However, that is hardly a useful skill when one is trying to prepare for the arrival of a baby. Right now, a blanket would be more practical." She looked over a trifle wistfully at the soft pale-yellow blanket that lay on Jessica's chair. "How did you learn to knit so well?"

"Actually, my father's batman taught me," Jessica, the daughter of a soldier, replied with a small laugh. "He was quite good at darning, mending, and knitting socks. "But fine sewing was not his forte. That is why, while I will knit you oodles of little caps and booties and blankets, you will have to depend on Rachel for the christening gown and the fine embroidery."

Rachel smiled at the other two women. "And I will be delighted to do it. I have been stitching away, Miranda, ever since you told me about your good news."

It was odd, she thought, that only a year ago, she had not even met these two women, yet now she counted them among her best friends.

Miranda smiled, and Rachel was a little surprised to hear Miranda echoing her own thoughts. "Who would have thought that when I married Devin I would also acquire such wonderful friends?" She went on thoughtfully. "You know, I never really had many friends—certainly not ones I can confide in as I can the two of you."

Rachel was not surprised. She suspected that most women Miranda's age would have found her rather too intimidating to make friends with. It was easy to see why Miranda and Jessica had become fast friends in just a few days; they had similarly strong personalities and an open, even blunt, manner. She was rather less certain why either one of them had been drawn to her. She did not have their strength; neither of them would have made the mistakes she had made.

She returned to the sewing in her lap, a long christening robe for Miranda's future child. It was made of elegant white satin, put together with careful dainty stitches. She had finished sewing the plainer underdress and the robe, and now she was adding the rows and rows of delicate white Belgian lace that would decorate the hem and sleeves and edge the yoke of the elegant robe. Inside the yoke she planned to embroider flowers in white thread, giving it a subtly rich look. The finishing touch would be matching satin booties and a cap, both also edged in lace and tied with the same narrow satin ribbons as the front of the robe.

Rachel had been working on the outfit this winter at Westhampton, as well as some other everyday gowns and cotton receiving blankets for the baby's layette. Miranda had told Rachel of her lack of expertise at sewing, and Rachel had been happy to apply her skills to the task.

Rachel carefully stitched along the pinned lace, then removed the pins. Jessica, coming over to her side, gazed down at the gown.

"It's beautiful," she breathed. "You do such lovely work."

"Thank you." Rachel smiled, smoothing out the line of lace. She was aware of a small ache of loss in the area of her heart. It happened now and then as she worked on the baby things—the stab of knowledge that she had never had a child for whom to make such things and probably never would. It was part of the price she paid—the worst part, she supposed—for having behaved so foolishly before her wedding.

But she was practiced enough at dealing with it that her smile did not waver as she thanked Jessica for her compliment, and she looked composed as she began to ply her needle again.

Then the sound of men's voices in the house broke the quiet of the room, and all three women looked up expectantly.

"They're back!" Jessica said happily. Devin and

Richard had gone out riding that afternoon, and the house had seemed rather empty without them.

"Good. I was afraid that I was going to have to tell Cook to delay supper," Miranda said, but the glow that lit up her face belied the asperity of her tone.

Dev was the first to enter the room, his handsome face wreathed in smiles. "Guess whom we happened upon as we were riding home!"

Immediately on his heels followed Richard and another man, tall and blond.

"Michael!" Rachel jumped to her feet, a grin breaking across her face. Her heart was suddenly pounding, and she felt almost giddy. She took a step forward, then stopped, feeling slightly embarrassed. "Wh-what are you doing here?"

"I found I grew quite bored after you left," Michael said lightly, coming forward to take Rachel's hand and raise it formally to his lips. "Westhampton is far too quiet without the sound of Gabriela's laughter."

"Well, you will have more than enough noise here, with Gabriela and Veronica together," Jessica told him with a laugh.

Michael greeted the other two women warmly, congratulating Miranda on her upcoming "happy event." Rachel noticed, with a pang of hurt, that her husband's manner toward his in-laws was easier and warmer than toward his wife.

"I am so glad you could come," Miranda said,

smiling. "We were quite sorry that you had not driven down with Rachel."

"Had I known that highwaymen were going to be popping in on Lady Westhampton's carriage, I would have done so," Michael replied. "I decided that if things like that were going to happen, I had best escort Rachel the rest of the way to London."

"Good idea," Dev agreed. "I had been thinking that I ought to do that myself."

"Don't be silly," Rachel told her brother. "I am sure that nothing else will happen." She turned toward Michael. "I am afraid that you have put yourself out for nothing."

"Not for nothing," Michael answered politely. "I will have the pleasure of your company on the ride to London."

It was the sort of courteous, meaningless thing men said to women they did not know well, Rachel thought. Not that it mattered, of course. Her life was quite pleasant; it was only the sight of Miranda and Jessica with their husbands that made her a little dissatisfied with her own marriage. Many women would be grateful to have a husband such as she did, who placed so few demands on her, yet was unfailingly thoughtful and polite.

"Who was the man, Michael?" Miranda asked in her blunt American way. "Did you indeed know him?"

Michael grinned at her. "Do you honestly think that I am the sort of chap to be friends with a highwayman? No, I am afraid he sounds like some kind

of lunatic, frankly. The only thing I can think is that
it was part of some bizarre jest—that one of my
friends hired this man to play a joke on me, and then,
when I was not in the carriage, he didn't know what
to do except go ahead and relate the tale they had
made up to Rachel.''

"An odd sort of jest," Jessica offered.

"Yes, well, some of the men with whom I corre-
spond are rather eccentric. Dr. Waller, for instance…''

"The scientist?" Rachel's eyebrows shot up.

"Yes, I realize that he is a veritable genius, but he
has been known to have a distinctly odd sense of
humor.''

"I should say so," Dev grumbled, "if his idea of
a joke is to go about frightening ladies.''

Michael had not looked at Rachel as he spoke, and
she had the sudden, intense suspicion that he was
lying. She would have liked to press him on the matter, but she could scarcely accuse her husband of lying in front of her family.

"I wrote him immediately, of course, to enquire,"
Michael went on, turning toward Rachel. "But in
case it was not he or a mistake of some sort, I thought
it wisest to accompany you to London.''

It occurred to Rachel that her suspicion of a moment before was ridiculous. Of course Michael had
not known that man; he did not socialize with thieves
and highwaymen. It was absurd to think so, even for
a moment.

"Thank you," she said. "It will make the ride much more enjoyable."

She realized as she said it that her statement was true. On the drive to Darkwater from Westhampton, she had found herself missing Michael's company. In fact, now that she thought of it, she had felt sad to leave him. He had a quiet, subtle wit and a calm manner that made any situation more agreeable. Intelligent and well-educated, he could talk on almost any subject, and he was too courteous to let his boredom with one's conversation show. It would be nice, she thought, if he would even stay with her in London for a while.

To her surprise, she heard Jessica echo her thoughts. "Perhaps you might stay in London for the Season."

Rachel glanced at Jessica, then back at Michael. She found his gaze upon her before he turned toward Jessica. "Tempting as the thought is, I am afraid that I must go back to Westhampton. It is the busiest time on the estate, as well. I have a number of experiments going concerning the farms."

Rachel knew that Michael's estate manager was privy to all of Michael's plans and it would cause little problem if he happened to stay away at least part of the spring and summer. The reason he would not stay the Season was because he preferred to be alone on his estate. He had lived with her the first year of their marriage—for appearance' sake, she presumed—then after that he had retired to Westhampton, visiting her in London only rarely. He had told her that it would be "easier." Easier, she supposed, for him not to be reminded of her treachery each day by the mere fact of seeing her. Easier not to have to keep up the pretense of civility towards her. It surprised her sometimes that the thought still had the power to hurt her.

Miranda tugged at the bellpull. "I shall tell the servants to make up your roo—" She stopped abruptly, frowning. "I'm sorry. Your customary bedchamber is one of the ones that we are currently renovating...."

Since Miranda and Dev had married, they had been restoring Darkwater piece by piece, beginning with the most desperate areas—the roofs and chimneys and worm-eaten wooden banisters and railings. The more cosmetic changes of painting and papering walls, replacing drapes and threadbare rugs, had followed as soon as the structures of the rooms were made sound. As a result, there had not been a time in the past seven months when there was not hammering or sawing or painting going on in some room or other. Miranda had put on a push to be finished with the family area of sleeping and sitting rooms before the arrival of her baby, knowing full well the value of peace reigning where the baby was, while the noisy construction was relegated to the other wings of the house.

As a result, all the guest rooms besides the ones currently occupied by Rachel and the duke and duchess were unusable, including the one in which Mi-

chael usually stayed when he happened to visit Darkwater.

Miranda cast an anxious look first toward Rachel,
then back to Michael. She was aware, as they all
were, that Rachel and Michael did not have the same
sort of warm, intimate marriage that she and Devin
did—or Jessica and Richard had, for that matter. Rachel had told her long ago that hers was not a love
match, that she and Lord Westhampton "lived
apart." She also knew that when Michael and Rachel
both stayed here, Michael slept in a separate room.
However, that was a fairly common arrangement
among the aristocracy, and it did not necessarily sig-
nify that the couple were not intimate.

Typically, if rooms were short, one would expect
to put a husband and wife in a room together. But
Rachel's was not a typical marriage. Though they had
not, of course, ever actually discussed the matter,
Miranda suspected that Rachel and Michael had
never actually shared a bed. It made for an awkward
situation, and it would be embarassing to even discuss the matter. To make some special arrangement
for Michael would highlight the oddity of their marriage, which Michael and Rachel tried to keep normal
in appearance. Yet it would create an uncomfortable
situation for the couple if she simply stuck him in
Rachel's room.

For a long moment, silence hung in the air, then
Michael said easily, "Well, of course I would not
trouble you for the luxury of a separate chamber in

such a situation. Just tell the footman to put my bags in Rachel's room.''

''Of course.''

''You would no doubt like to wash up after your journey,'' Rachel said quickly, hating the red tint that she knew had washed up her neck into her face. ''I will take you up to our room.''

She slipped out of the room, avoiding looking at anyone, and Michael followed her. She did not look at him, either, as they crossed the entryway and began to climb the stairs. There was no need, of course, for her to show him where her room lay; he knew it well enough after all these years. But Rachel had had to get away from the eyes of the other couples. Her family knew, of course, the state of her marriage, at least in general terms, but it was embarassing to have everyone be reminded of it.

''Don't worry,'' Michael said in a low voice beside her. ''It will be easy enough to have one of the servants set up a camp bed in your dressing room for me. It is ample in size, as I remember.''

''Yes, of course,'' Rachel replied. Suddenly she felt foolish for having offered to show him the room. Of course he knew the way—did he think she had done it because she wanted to protest his sleeping in the same room with her?

They continued up the stairs to the hall above. Rachel tried to think of something to say to break the silence. She wanted to tell him she was glad that he had come to Darkwater, but she could not think of the proper way to phrase it. ''I—um, it was very kind of you to go to the trouble of journeying here. There was no need, I'm sure."

"Perhaps not," he agreed with a formality to equal her own. "However, one can scarcely take the chance. A pretty coward I would look to let my wife travel on to London alone after such an event."

Of course. Appearances. That was all that mattered in their marriage.

She nodded her head and walked down the hall to her room. "Well..." she said, opening the door and taking a step inside. "Here it is."

She glanced around the room, her gaze falling on the wide, high-testered bed on which she had slept all her life. She felt the treacherous blush returning to her cheeks. She thought about having to get ready for bed tonight in the same room with him. He had never seen her in anything less than her dressing gown; they had never shared a room, even sleeping in different beds. She wondered exactly how they would handle this.

"Well," she said again, glancing at Michael and away. "I, um, I guess you would like a chance to freshen up a bit."

Even this situation was awkward, she realized. He would doubtless like to wash off the dust of the road, and of course he would have to change for supper.

"I shall leave you alone," she went on quickly, flashing a brittle smile. "I, um, I'll go tell Gabriela you are here. She will be quite pleased to hear it."

She backed out of the door and quickly closed it behind her.

For a moment she stood in the hall. How had her marriage become what it had? But even as she asked herself the question, she knew the answer: she had done it. The cold, loveless state of their marriage was entirely her fault.

She had not loved Michael when they became engaged, but he had loved her, and he was a kind and patient man. Looking back on it, she thought that perhaps with time they might have found their way to at least a satisfactory relationship.

But before it even began, she had ruined everything....

Three days before Rachel's wedding, her mother took her aside and explained in vague terms what to expect on her wedding night. Rachel was shocked and even frightened. It was somewhat difficult to understand exactly what would transpire, because her mother's speech was so roundabout and couched in euphemisms, but Rachel came away with the impression that it was distinctly immodest and unpleasant, and Lady Ravenscar's frequent, faint assurances that "the pain does not last long" filled her with dread.

She spent much of the next day worrying about her mother's warnings. To make matters even worse, when she walked into the drawing room that afternoon, she found Anthony Birkshaw sitting there talking to two of Michael's cousins. She had not seen him for four months, and the sight of him now jarred her. She had almost forgotten how handsome he was and how his thick dark hair curled upon his forehead. The smile that broke across his face when she entered the room was like a blow to her heart. In a rush, all the feelings she had had for him came back to her, and she wanted to giggle, to cry, to throw her arms around him and to run from the room, all at once. It took all her strength to greet him with some semblance of normalcy.

They said almost nothing to each other after that, but when Anthony rose to politely take his leave, he murmured as he bent over her hand, "Meet me tonight at the bottom of the garden. Ten o'clock."

Rachel did not reply. Indeed, she did not intend to meet him. However much the sight of him had shaken her, however forcefully she had been reminded of the love she held for him, she knew that it would be foolish even to speak to him, let alone meet him in the dark of the garden. However much she loved him, she was honor bound now to Michael.

But then, that evening, Michael unexpectedly kissed her, and his kiss was deep and hungry, completely unlike the gentle, patient Michael she was used to. She had felt the twist of something dark and unknown deep within her abdomen, something almost more frightening than the sudden strong grip of Michael's arms around her, pinning her to him. She was thrown into a panic—a panic that sent her slipping down through the garden to meet Anthony a few minutes later.

Anthony was there waiting for her, and as she hurried toward him, her heart swelled with love. Even after this time, despite all the discouragement her family had given him, he had not given up on her! He had come at the very end, like a knight in a story, to rescue her.

He turned and saw her, and he came to her, pulling her into his arms. He cradled her against him, his head against hers, murmuring, "Rachel, my love...my love. I was so scared you would not come—that they had turned you against me."

"Never!" she cried in a low, choked voice, stepping back and looking up at him. In that moment she was sure that what she said was true: she would love him forever; nothing could ever make her stop loving Anthony. She would be married, tied for life to a man she did not love, her heart all the while aching with the sorrow she felt right now. "I will always love you."

"Then marry me."

"What? I cannot!" She looked up at him, horrified. "I am promised to Lord Westhampton."

"You do not love him!" His voice throbbed with emotion. "You love me. You cannot marry him."

"But Father would never—"

"He doesn't need to know," Anthony argued. "Come with me now. We will ride to Gretna Green and be married. Then you will be my wife, and your father will have no power over you. I will deal with him if he comes after us. And you and I will be together for the rest of our lives."

"But the money—"

"I don't give a damn about the money! Not as

long as we are together. What is money compared to our happiness? Would you rather live in this huge cold mansion without love, or with me in a cozy little cottage?''

"With you! You know I want to be with you!''

"Then what does wealth matter? I will work. Lord Muggeridge told me only last week that he needed an aide. I know he would hire me. There is no shame in honest work.''

"Of course not.''

"And knowing that I would be coming home at night to you would make it all worthwhile.'' His dark eyes shone down at her with love.

Rachel gazed back at him, her heart filled with emotion. She ignored the small cold voice of practicality, listening only to the pounding of her heart, seeing only the sweet love that shone in Anthony's eyes. It was nothing like the fierce fire that had leaped to life in Michael's gaze that evening. Anthony was sure and safe, and the warm, pure glow she felt when she looked into his face was nothing like that breathless twist of sensation that had curled through her when Michael kissed her. Love was what was important, she reminded herself. She was not the mercenary sort who would marry for money.

She thought of making that long walk down the church aisle, everyone watching her, giving her entire life over to a man whom she did not love, a man who was little more than a stranger to her. "But everyone is expecting me to—''

"Damn what they expect of you!'' Anthony rejoined. "What is important is what *you* expect of you. You are too fine a lady, too gentle and good, to marry for money! Please...I cannot stand by and let you give yourself to a man who—"

"No, you are right. I cannot do it!" Rachel cried, panicky at the thought.

"Then come with me. We shall be happier than you could ever be immured in some castle married to a man you barely know, no matter what his title. Give yourself over to love."

For a moment Rachel hesitated. Then she flung herself into his arms. "Yes!" she cried, feeling as if a great weight had been lifted from her. "Yes! I will go with you."

He put her up on his horse behind him, and together they rode through the night. She was blissfully happy at first, clinging to Anthony's strong back and thinking only of the joy that awaited her. It wasn't until she stood in the courtyard of the inn in the village, waiting while Anthony tried to arrange for a post chaise for them, that reality began to sink in. She felt like a criminal, lurking out there in the dark because it would be too scandalous to let anyone see her, and the feeling tainted her joy.

They had to continue on his horse, for the inn had had no carriage to lease, and it was slow going with the double load. As they rode, she thought about what she had done and what would happen the next morning when Michael and her family discovered that she was gone. It occurred to her that she had not even left them a note. Would they think that something had happened to her? Be frightened and set out on search parties?

Her guilt and unease grew, until by the time they stopped at the inn in the next village, she was beginning to realize the enormity of what she had done. She sat huddled in the private dining room, chilled through and through from the night air and numbly tired, while Anthony tried to convince the innkeeper to have a post chaise prepared for them. She could see in the innkeeper's eyes his doubts about Anthony's story, as well as her propriety, and she realized how she must look to him—how she would look to everyone. She wanted to cry; she wanted to turn and flee back to Westhampton.

Then everything grew even worse, for her father and Michael walked through the door. She jumped to her feet, fear flooding her at the sight of her furious father. He began to berate her, driving home what she already had begun to know in her heart: the scandal of eloping would haunt her for the rest of her life. And the stain of it would spread to the rest of her family, too—her parents, even Caroline and Richard, though they had done nothing wrong. She had failed to do her duty to her family. Darkwater would crumble into ruins; her parents would have to live entirely on Richard's generosity.

But worse than her father's words was the look on Michael's white, set face. For the first time she understood what a disservice she had done him. He cared for her. She did not know how much—obviously her proud lineage and the fact that she was one of the reigning and most sought after beauties of London made her an appropriate match for him, but there must have been some affection or desire on his part, as well, to have made him willing to overlook the obvious disadvantage of her family's financial situation. Rachel saw now, in the pain that lay in his quiet gray eyes, that his feelings had been deeper than she knew. Her elopement was a slap in the face to him, a blatant announcement that he meant nothing to her, and though she had not intended it, she could see that what she had done cut Michael deeply.

Moreover, it would involve him in a tremendous scandal. Through no fault of his own, he would be exposed to the ridicule of Society, an object of amusement and scorn for having been left at the altar. Michael had been nothing but kind to her, Rachel knew, and she realized how selfish and wicked she had been to treat him this way. The fact that she had not wanted or intended to hurt and shame him didn't really matter; the fact was that she had, and out of sheer selfishness.

Guilt swamped her, and, oddly enough, she felt even worse when Michael offered to make everything all right by marrying her anyway. The very kindness of his offer seemed to emphasize the enormity of her own selfish wrongdoing.

Tearful and ashamed, she rode back to Westhampton with Michael and Ravenscar, slipping into the house quietly to escape detection. The whole way, Michael never looked at her or spoke to her.

The next morning, she sat quiet and subdued under

another one of her father's lectures. Then he turned her over to her mother, saying he washed his hands of her.

"It is the only way Lord Westhampton can save his own name from scandal," Lady Ravenscar told her. "That is the only reason he swallowed his pride, I'm sure. Still...there is many a man who would not have done so." She sighed. "I cannot imagine what possessed you to act so stupidly. No doubt you will have to spend the rest of your life trying to get him to forgive you." Again she sighed, looking at Rachel with a mingling of puzzlement and, Rachel thought, a touch of pity. "Well, it is probably exactly what you deserve for behaving so foolishly. I cannot think where you acquired such a lack of judgment."

"Nor can I," Rachel responded wryly. No one else in her family would have behaved so, she knew. Even Caroline, who was the closest to her in all the world, had been aghast when she learned what Rachel had done. Dev, of course, would never have agreed to marry to please his parents in the first place.

Lady Ravenscar glanced at her sharply, unsure whether her daughter was being inappropriately flippant. Rachel was saved from having to make a response by a tap upon the door, followed by the entrance of one of the parlor maids.

The girl gave them a polite curtsey and delivered her message. "Lord Westhampton requests Miss Aincourt's presence in the conservatory, if you please."

Lady Ravenscar looked alarmed, and as soon as

the maid exited the room, she turned her worried gaze on Rachel. "You don't suppose he is going to take back his offer to continue with the wedding, do you?"

A frisson of fear ran down Rachel's back. "No," she said stoutly, as much to reassure herself as her mother. "Lord Westhampton would not go back on his word."

"You had better hope so." Her mother looked her over critically, shaking Rachel's skirt out on one side and picking a small piece of lint from the shoulder of her dress. "In any case, I trust you will be appropriately apologetic."

"I will." The weight of her guilt was still like a physical burden upon her shoulders.

Rachel went down the stairs and along the spacious hallway to Westhampton's study. The door stood open, and Lord Westhampton was inside, his back to her. Rachel paused for a moment, steeling herself, then stepped inside.

He turned at the sound of her approach, and their eyes met, then dropped quickly away. "Miss Aincourt. Thank you for joining me."

He gestured toward one of the chairs, and as Rachel walked toward it, he closed the door and came back to where she sat and took a seat across from her.

"I, ah, I wish you had told me, Miss Aincourt."

"I'm sorry." Rachel's eyes flew to his, and her hands curled into themselves in her lap. "I did not mean for that to happen. When I accepted you, I intended to marry you. I was not—'' She paused, the breath suddenly running out of her so that she had to make an inelegant little gulp. ''I was not even going to see him again.''

''Still, it would have been…easier if I had known.''

''I know,'' Rachel agreed miserably. ''I am sorry.''

''It—well, it hasn't turned out well. Not as I had hoped. Or you, I'm sure.''

''No.'' Her voice was barely a whisper.

''Miss Aincourt…I want you to know…'' Michael paused, then abruptly rose to his feet and began to pace. ''I am making a hash of this. What I want to know is, is your father compelling you to say yes to me? I have no desire to force you to marry me. Or for you to feel obliged to do so. We can make an announcement—you may cry off, if you wish.''

Rachel looked up at him, tears swimming in her eyes. He was offering her a way out, not a perfect one, but a far better one than her elopement. If she cried off, everyone would assume that he had done something to cause her to; he was offering to bear the blame for her.

''No,'' she responded in a choked voice. ''I do not want to break it off. Father was right. Even An— Mr. Birkshaw admitted it. He needs to marry well. I know there is no— Anyway, I am a more responsible person, I hope, than I have appeared to be so far. I know that I have given you little reason to trust me, but I promise you that I will never do anything like that again.'' She paused, then added uncertainly, ''Unless, that is, you have changed your mind and would prefer to break it off?''

''I have not changed my mind.'' Michael glanced at her, then away. It occurred to Rachel that he could not bear to look at her for longer than a few seconds, and the knowledge made her heart swell even more with guilt and sorrow.

''Marrying would be the best thing for us to do,'' Westhampton went on, his voice distant and calm. ''I know that it is hard for you. It—is not easy for me, either. But it will prevent any gossip, and you have said that you cannot marry, um, as you wish.''

Rachel nodded, clasping her hands in her lap and gazing steadfastly down at them. ''Yes. It would be best.''

''Knowing how you feel…that is, given the situation…naturally I would not expect, a, um… It would not be a true marriage, of course. I would not press you. We would not share a bedroom.''

Startled, Rachel glanced up at him. *Was he saying that those things her mother had talked about would not happen?* Surprise shot through her, followed by relief. Then she realized, with another pang of guilt and even hurt, that Westhampton was saying this because he no longer wanted her. She had killed his love by her disgraceful actions. She wondered if he despised her now, if he was disgusted by her.

She told herself that of course he must be. She had hurt and humiliated him, yet he felt obliged to marry her in order to save his family's good name from a scandal that she had created. How could he feel anything but dislike for her? It was simply that he was too much a gentleman to tell her so.

"I see," she responded inadequately.

"I hope that you will not find the burden of marriage too onerous," Michael went on in the same stiff voice. "However, I have one...stipulation, I suppose I should say. My family's reputation is important to me, and I will not—I *cannot*—allow it to be besmirched."

Red stained Rachel's cheeks, and she said in a low voice, "Please, my lord, I am so sorry. I promise you, I would not do anything to hurt your name or reputation. I realize that I have acted in such a way as to make you think that I am...irresponsible, even dissolute. But, please, believe me, it was an aberration."

"I do believe so. I know that you are a woman of honor. But, painful as it is for both of us, I must have your assurance that you will not see Mr. Birkshaw again."

Rachel's head flew up, her face horrified. "No! I would not. Lord Westhampton, I will do nothing to harm your good name. I would not break our wedding vows. I swear it to you."

His face was unreadable, his jaw clenched tightly. "I believe you. But not even the faintest appearance of impropriety can—"

"Of course not." She rose, her fists clenched in determination. "I promise you—on whatever you like—that I will not see Mr. Birkshaw again. I will not talk to him or write to him. I know how kind you have been to me, how easily you could have left me to the contumely of the world. I would never repay you that way. I will never dishonor you. Or myself.''

''Thank you.'' The smile Michael gave her was more a twisting of his lips than any genuine smile. He took a step backward. ''Well, then. Until tomorrow.''

That had been the tone of their marriage ever since—formal, slightly awkward and distant. It had been a relief, of course, not to be expected to take her place in Michael's bed. Her heart was broken, and she could not imagine how horrible it would have been to have had to pretend to be in love with her new husband, to let him have his way with her when the thought of even kissing someone besides Anthony turned her to ice inside. She had been grateful to Michael and remained so, but she could not help but feel sometimes as though she had missed out on the most important aspect of life. She had no children. She was not, in any real sense, a wife. Their marriage was such a sham that even the thought of spending the night in the same room with Michael was embarassing to them both.

Rachel glanced back at the room she had just left and wished, not for the first time, that she had not been so foolish that night seven years ago.

6

For at least the tenth time that evening, Rachel glanced over at the graceful ormolu clock that adorned the mantel of the music room. It seemed as though its hands had sped up for the last few minutes, racing toward the time when everyone would decide to leave the room and retire. Her stomach had been a knot of nerves all through the evening, dreading the moment, and she had barely been able to enjoy the conversation with her family or the songs that Veronica and Gabriela had played for them. Indeed, she had felt only half there, the rest of her mind occupied with what she would do when she and Michael climbed the stairs to their room.

She thought about the maid helping her to undress with Michael right there in the room with them, and she blushed at the idea. It would be completely humiliating, of course, and yet...something odd stirred low in her abdomen at the thought. She could not help but wonder how Michael would react to the sight. Would he watch? Would he turn away, polite and disinterested? Indeed, did he ever think about the strangeness of their private life?

Rachel was no longer quite the naive girl she had once been. She had never had any actual experience of the marital act, of course, but over the years she had heard a good bit from other married women who had assumed that she shared in their knowledge of men and the marriage bed. Like her mother's speech, their conversation was usually couched in euphemisms that hindered learning, but she thought she had come to have, more or less, a basic understanding of what went on.

Apparently men were more interested in the act than their wives, she had decided from the comments of her friends and acquaintances, so much so that they often broke their marriage vows by having affairs and mistresses—sometimes, amazingly, to the relief of their spouses. However, she had also gleaned that there were a fair number of other women who enjoyed the attentions of their husbands. And in the past few months, she had been witness to the fact that Miranda and Jessica seemed to take as great a delight in passion as did Dev and Richard. She found her mind turning to the matter more and more often lately, wondering what her reaction would be to lovemaking, whether she would revel in the pleasure—as Miranda obviously did, given the way her mouth curled up and her eyes took on a certain gleam when she alluded to the act that had gotten her with child—

or would, like her mother, view it with cool disdain and resignation.

There was a vast difference between Jessica's and Miranda's situations and hers, of course. They both loved their husbands deeply and were loved by them in return, whereas she and Michael— Well, she was not sure quite what lay between her and Michael, but clearly it was not love. A kind of friendship, she supposed, despite the awkwardness that often hindered them. Certainly she knew that she could depend on him, and there had been times when she had gone to him with a knotty problem. Rachel admired and respected him more than any man she knew. But none of those things involved the sort of heart-stopping emotion she had felt for Anthony Birkshaw those many years ago.

Still, he was the only man in her life. She had not seen Anthony since their ill-fated elopement, just as she had promised Michael, and there would never be any other man. She would never do anything to betray Michael or sully his name.

Therefore, she knew, if ever she was to experience what normally occurred between a man and woman, it would have to be with Michael. So when she thought now and then—with strangely increasing frequency, it seemed—about how it might feel to kiss a man or to feel his hands upon her, it was Michael whom she imagined herself with. It seemed an odd and unlikely thing, however, and at the times when her thoughts strayed in that direction, she was quick to pull them back.

It was silly, really, to think about what she was missing. She knew many a married woman who would have told her that she was lucky, that she had all the advantages of a married lady and none of the difficulties. It was probably true, she knew. It was just that sometimes, like tonight, she could not help but wonder what it would be like to…to have Michael watch her as the maid removed her dress until she was standing in next to nothing…or to have him take the brush from her hand and begin to brush her long, thick hair himself, as she had heard Miranda once say Devin did…or to lie with him beside her in the bed, to hear the steady rhythm of his breathing and feel the warmth of his large, masculine body.

She felt a faint flush creep into her cheeks at her thoughts, and she glanced across the room at Michael. Now that Veronica and Gabriela had quit entertaining them at the piano, he was listening to Miranda describe the renovations she had set in motion around the house. Rachel watched as he nodded, smiling, at something Miranda said, and leaned forward to speak earnestly to her. Around the others of her family, Rachel had noted, Michael was rarely as reticent as he was with her. His gray eyes were alight with interest, and his firm, well-cut lips curved up into a smile.

He was a handsome man, she thought—not devastatingly so, as her brother was, for Dev's green-eyed, black-haired good looks were the sort that made women swoon—but Michael was agreeable to look at, nevertheless. His hair was dark blond, streaked through, particularly in the summer, with lighter strands, and his gray eyes were wide and intelligent. And his mouth was really quite attractive, she thought, with that small scar near the corner that gave his well-bred face a hint of devilishness when he smiled.

Rachel wondered how he would react if he knew what she was thinking. Did he ever regret the decision he had made not to share her bed? Or wonder what it would be like if their marriage was different? She wondered if he had thought about tonight, when they would go up to the same room, and if he had, whether he'd felt the same strange flutter of nerves in his stomach that she did.

So deep in her thoughts was Rachel that she did not notice that Jessica was speaking to her until the second time she said, "Rachel? Did you hear me?"

Rachel started and glanced over at her friend. "What? I'm sorry—were you speaking to me?"

Jessica laughed good-naturedly. "Yes, I was, actually. But I'm afraid I must have been putting you to sleep."

Rachel blushed. "No, of course not. I apologize for my rudeness."

"No need. You are doubtless sleepy, as I am."

Dev, listening to them, added, "We have all turned into country folk, I fear. Here I find I get up about the time I used to be going to bed in London. The light is too good in the morning to waste."

Rachel smiled at her brother. "I am so glad you

have returned to your painting. The work you have done the past few months is beautiful.''

He smiled. "Thank you. But it is all due to Miranda, you know.'' He turned toward where his wife sat, gesturing enthusiastically as she talked to Michael, and the look on his face told Rachel everything she needed to know about his happiness. "Look at her. Have you ever seen such a woman? I think she is talking about crop rotation now.'' Dev chuckled. He looked at Rachel and added more soberly, "It was a good turn you did me when you steered me in her direction.''

"I am so glad," Rachel answered honestly.

"Now if only—'' he began impulsively, then stopped.

"If only what?''

Dev shook his head. "Nothing. I find sometimes that Miranda rubs off on me and I want to step in where I have no business.''

A little self-consciously, he turned away and raised his voice to speak to his wife across the room, "Miranda, my love, I know that you never tire, but you might have some sympathy for poor Michael. He has ridden a long way today, and I suspect he would like to seek his bed.''

Miranda looked instantly contrite. "Oh! I am so sorry, Michael! I did not think. It was so wonderful to have someone to talk to who was interested in such things that I quite forgot you must be tired.''

"I was far too intrigued by what you were saying,'' Michael assured her, smiling. "However, I imagine that you probably need your sleep.''

"I am never tired,'' Miranda protested, then cast a smile at her husband and added, "However, Dev worries—far more than is necessary, but I try to indulge him.''

She rose as she spoke, and as abruptly as that, the evening was over. The others began to rise, smiling and saying their good-nights to one another. Rachel's pulse skittered wildly, though she managed, she hoped, to keep her face perfectly calm.

Michael came over to where she stood and extended his arm to her. Rachel curled her hand around his arm, hoping that he could not feel the trembling of her fingers, and walked with him out of the room. Behind them came Dev and Miranda, talking happily to each other and now and then chuckling. Rachel searched her mind for something to say to break the silence between her and Michael, but she could think of nothing that did not pertain to the fact that they were climbing the stairs to the bedroom that they would share. The more she tried to think of something else, the more it occupied her mind. The silence between them grew until it seemed solid and huge. Rachel was certain that the others must notice, and that thought made her feel even more uncomfortable.

Michael stepped aside politely at their door for her to enter first, then came inside and closed the door behind him. Rachel turned to face him; her hands felt like ice.

Michael walked over to the door of the dressing

room and glanced inside. "Good," he said, his voice far calmer and more matter-of-fact than Rachel felt. "They have set up the camp bed for me." He turned back to face her. "You can ring for your maid if you wish. I will go down to the library and find a book to read, so you can have your privacy."

"Oh. Of course. Thank you." Rachel wondered why she had not thought of the solution herself. It was quite simple, really, and removed much of the awkwardness from their situation.

Michael nodded and walked to the door. He paused, not looking at her, his hand on the knob, and said, "Good night."

"Good night." Rachel watched him as he opened the door and left the room.

It was a great relief, she thought, to have the situation solved so easily. She could always count on Michael. And the odd feeling inside her was not regret, of course, but simply leftover agitation from the long evening of worrying over the matter.

With a sigh, Rachel pulled the bellpull for the maid.

Michael walked quietly down the stairs toward the library. It had been one of the hardest things he had ever done to walk so calmly out of Rachel's room. All evening he had been thinking about the night that lay before him—the long hours of lying only a few yards from where Rachel slept alone in her bed. He knew it would be a miracle if he got any sleep tonight; he would be thinking of nothing but Rachel's soft warmth so close to him and how simple it would be to walk over to her bed and slide beneath the sheets.

He had every right; he was her husband. No one would think the worse of him; no one would even know. Except Rachel, of course... But then, she was all that mattered.

He would never do it, he knew. He had promised Rachel long ago that he would not, and the passage of time did not make his promise any less valid. He had hoped, of course, that she would change, that she would warm to him and welcome his touch, but that had never happened. He felt sure that she would be appalled if he came to her bed tonight.

He could not take advantage of the situation, which meant that he would spend a long, tiring and deeply unsatisfying night plagued by thoughts of her nearness. He was already thrumming with lust, knowing that as he walked to the library and looked for a book, she was upstairs getting undressed and brushing out her hair. This whole evening, he had been thinking of just how much he would like to send her maid packing and do the job himself. He had imagined unhooking the back of her gown and pushing the sides apart, touching the skin of her back, softer than even the satin of her dress. He had thought what it would be like to press his lips to that back, to slide his hands around to her front and up....

He had, quite frankly, heard almost none of the music the girls played and even less of what Miranda had said. His mind had been incapable of concentrating on anything except what he was firmly resolved not to do.

Inside the library, he turned the wick of his lamp higher and carried it with him to the far wall of the library, where books rose in shelves far above the top of his head. Michael meandered along, scanning the spines for something that would interest him enough to keep his mind off Rachel. He was finding it difficult to find such a book.

"Well, Michael…" A man's voice spoke behind him, and Michael whirled around, startled.

The Duke of Cleybourne stood in the doorway of the library, arms crossed and a sardonic smile on his face.

"Cleybourne," Michael said a trifle warily. "You startled me. I am surprised to see you here."

"So am I," Richard agreed, strolling farther into the room and closing the door behind him. "Frankly, I prefer to be with my wife at bedtime."

"Then why are you here?"

The Duke grimaced. "Because I want to know what in the devil is going on. What have you gotten yourself into? Who was that fellow that stopped Rachel's carriage?" As Michael opened his mouth to speak, Richard added, "And don't try that 'jest' business with me. Obviously Dev and Rachel are in the dark, but I know about your secret life."

Michael looked at him for a long moment. "All right," he said finally. "The truth is, I'm not sure, but Rachel said he called himself Red Geordie, and he is a highwayman who has sold me information in the past. But I cannot imagine what he's talking about. I presume he was hoping that I would give him some payment for that bit of useless knowledge.'' He scowled, adding, ''Something that I can assure you won't happen again after I've tracked him down and let him know what I think of his stopping Rachel's carriage and frightening her.''

''So Rachel knows nothing about your helping Bow Street?''

''No. Of course not,'' Michael retorted. ''She doesn't even know about what I did in the war, let alone about Rob asking me to help on the Bow Street cases. Almost no one knows about it—only you and Rob and one or two friends from during the war. The fewer people who know the better—and, frankly, right at this moment I am regretting telling you.''

''Yes, but, good God, man, we're talking about your wife! How can you hide something like that from her?''

Michael shrugged. ''It isn't that hard. Most of the time we are not together. She is in London and I am at Westhampton.''

''Or off haring about in one of your disguises.''

Michael shrugged. ''At any rate, we are not together. It isn't as if she sees me leaving the house and not coming back for a week or two.''

Richard eyed him doubtfully. ''Yes, but hiding something like that from her— Well, I can't think she would like it.''

''Yes, well, that's why I don't intend to tell her. Look, it isn't as if I sat down and decided not to tell

Rachel. But by the time she and I married, the war was long over. There was no reason to tell her about my helping Rob catch a few spies.''

''A few!'' Richard snorted and shook his head. ''You know, most men would have found impressing their new bride with their derring-do during the war reason enough to tell her.''

''Really, Richard...'' Michael looked embarrassed. ''It was hardly derring-do. More brainwork, actually. I would have felt a fool puffing it up.''

''Yes,'' Richard agreed with a rueful smile. ''I am sure you would have.''

Cleybourne knew Michael well enough to know what lay beneath his friend's gentlemanly reluctance to reveal his heroism. Michael hated the idea that he was anything like his father, who had always been one to rush into the face of danger. The former Lord Westhampton had loved excitement—the thrill of the hunt, the rush of adrenaline at soaring over a fence on horseback, the challenge of facing an opponent at swords or fisticuffs. Michael had told Richard once in an unguarded moment that he feared it was his father coming out in him that made him choose to go into espionage during the war.

''All right, so you were embarrassed to let on that you were a hero during the war, saving us all from Bonaparte's spies,'' Richard conceded with a degree of sarcasm. ''But why didn't you tell her when Rob came to you and asked you to help him with the Bow Street case?''

Michael grimaced. ''Well, I would have had to explain about how Rob and I had worked together during the war, and then no doubt Rachel would have wanted to know why I hadn't told her. And everything I could think of to explain it made me sound like a fool. Besides, I thought it was going to be only the one case. It was merely a favor for a friend of Rob's who was a Bow Street magistrate. I didn't know that the Bow Street Runner himself would come back the next year wanting my help. Anyway, Rachel was in London and I was at Westhampton, and I couldn't very well write it in a letter. It was over by the time she came home for Christmas, and then it just seemed like...I don't know, braggadocio."

Richard shook his head exasperatedly. "Of course."

"Besides, it is scarcely a fit subject for a lady," Michael pointed out. When Richard looked doubtful, Michael added, "Would you have told Caroline that you were investigating murders and such?"

"Well, no," Richard admitted. "But I have learned a great deal since then. Jessica would have my head on a platter if I kept something like that from her. And given the way she and Miranda reacted to the dangers they have faced the last year..."

"It is an entirely different matter," Michael argued. "Rachel is not a soldier's daughter like your wife. Nor did some American trapper teach her how to shoot a gun when she was eight years old, like Miranda. Rachel is a gently reared Englishwoman, and she is quite unused to tales of murder and robbery. Good God, Richard, she has no idea what the underbelly of London is like—the poverty and crime, the appalling dirt and disease. She would be horrified to hear about my forays into that world. It would only worry and upset her.''

There had been times when Michael had wanted quite badly to tell Rachel about his cases. It would have been pleasant to have been able to confide in her, to discuss his thoughts on the mysteries that confronted him and to hear what insight Rachel might provide in the matter. But he had always stopped himself. It would have been grossly unfair to relieve himself of his burdens at Rachel's expense.

''Perhaps…'' Richard said, looking less than convinced. ''But I have learned the past few months that women are far stronger than we think. You might be surprised to find that Rachel would take it all in her stride.''

Richard did not add his other thought, that one could scarcely have a full relationship with one's wife if she knew so little about one's life. He knew that Michael's marriage bore little resemblance to his own intense, close and sometimes tempestuous relationship with Jessica. Michael had never told him about Rachel's last-minute elopement with another man, but his first wife, Rachel's sister Caroline, had not been so reticent. It was easy to see, watching the two of them together, that the deep rift had never been healed.

Richard was deeply fond of both of them. Michael had been one of his best friends for almost fifteen

years, for they had met when they were first young
gentlemen on the town in London. And Rachel had
been a rock of support for him during the long, dark
years after her sister's death. He would have given
almost anything to help the two of them overcome
their past and have a happy marriage, but he was also
certain that Michael would not have welcomed his
interference.

"I see no reason to worry her with it," Michael
replied.

Richard shrugged. "Then you had best do a bang-
up job of hiding it from her, for if she finds out, you
will rue the day you didn't tell her. Women hate secrets—if they aren't their own." He paused, watching Michael, then added, "Who wants you dead?"

Michael rolled his eyes. "No one that I know of.
I can't imagine why anyone would. I've made absolutely no progress on the last case Cooper brought
me. I'm no danger to anyone; I have no idea whatever who stole the manuscript."

Richard frowned. "Manuscript?"

"Yes. It was an illuminated manuscript from the
eleventh century. Quite rare and valuable. Belonged
to the Earl of Setworth."

"The stuttering chap?"

Michael nodded. "The same. He came to me because Sir William Godfrey told him about how I
helped Cooper solve the theft of his wife's necklace.
He already had a Runner on it, not Cooper, but they
had had no luck. The manuscript was Setworth's
prize possession, and he kept it in a secret room in

his study. Well, obviously, my first thought—and Bow Street's, too—was that it could not have been a thief off the street. It had to be someone with inside knowledge.''

"One of the servants?''

Michael shrugged. "Setworth swore that none of them knew the mechanism that opened the door to the room. He doesn't even believe that any of them knew that there was a secret room in his study at all. The Runner he hired had investigated them—none of them had left Setworth's employ in the months after the theft, and none of them had shown signs of sudden wealth. And there had been no one let go for over year prior to that, and that time it was only a scullery maid who would have never gone into the study. I had one of the chaps I use sometimes pose as a servant and get hired there. He never heard a whisper of anyone knowing anything about the theft. Setworth swore that no one but his two sons knew how to operate the mechanism, and, of course, he was adamant that neither of them would have stolen the manuscript.''

"Did you believe him?''

"I rarely trust anyone as much as the victims seem to, but I could not find any reason to believe either one of them had stolen it. They seemed to live within their allowances, no large debts or questionable friends. When I questioned the earl closely, he did admit that at a house party a few weeks before the theft, he had shown the manuscript to some of his guests. However, he did not believe that any of them had been able to see what trick he used to open the door. I thought they were the most likely suspects, but when I looked into their finances, none of them had come into any windfall lately. Well, actually one of them had, a chap whose uncle had died and he had inherited, but that had occurred several months prior to the party. They were not all wealthy, of course, but again, there were no large debts or shady acquaintances.''

''Then do you think it was a random thief—an outsider?''

''It wasn't random. Whoever went in had to know about the manuscript and where it was kept—it was the only thing taken. There were no signs of a break-in—Setworth didn't even know it was gone until one morning when he went in to spend a few minutes admiring it and discovered it was gone. It could have been taken any time during the two weeks before that. That was the last time he saw it.''

''Word could easily have gotten around about Setworth's manuscript. Obviously he showed it to people, and people talk. Perhaps some thief heard about it, even heard that it was in a secret room, and he went in and found the room and the mechanism. Perhaps it wasn't as difficult as Lord Setworth thought.''

''Perhaps. But if so, he is a smarter man than I. I visited Setworth House and went to the study and spent the better part of a day trying to find the secret room and figure out how it worked. I finally worked out where it had to be because of the thickness of the walls joining the library with the study. However, I still was completely unable to open it. Setworth had to come in and open it for me. The only thing I learned was that he was not as stealthy in opening it as he thought. I managed to see enough of what he did that later I could have opened it. But, still, that narrows it down to maybe fifty or a hundred guests whom Setworth probably showed it to over the course of the years—and there's no telling how many of them might have told someone else about the clever mechanism.''

"Well, supposing it was the most recent guests, the ones to whom you know he showed it…''

Michael grimaced. "Difficult to establish whether any of them could have done it. There was a two-week period during which it could have happened. It's hard to have an alibi for two weeks running—although one fellow was apparently in bed sick for nearly all that time, plus another week convalescing. And another was sworn to have been in London by his wife and four children, as well as all the servants.''

"Are you saying you have given up, then?''

"I was ready to,'' Michael admitted. "Until this happened. Now I'm wondering if I am close to the answer and just don't realize it. Even if I'm not, I have to go back and try again. I can't let it go if Rachel is going to get dragged into it. If someone really wishes me harm, it would be easiest to do it through her. She will be in London, unprotected.…''

"Do you plan to stay with her all Season, then?''

Michael shook his head. It was a tempting, tormenting idea, one he had been considering all day on the ride to Darkwater. "No. I have sent a note to Cooper to hire someone to keep watch on Rachel and the house. But the best thing I can do to protect her is to solve this riddle and get the miscreant behind bars. Besides, she would know something was wrong if I remained the whole Season in London. I will assume one of my disguises."

"You'll go to Lilith's, then?"

Michael nodded. "Yes. And see if I can get any help from Rob, though he is out of the business now."

Cleybourne looked at his friend consideringly. "It's a risky thing you're playing at. I hope you know what you're doing."

Michael knew Richard was talking about more than the physical danger about which Red Geordie had warned Michael. Richard was worried about the health of Westhampton's marriage. Michael did not tell him what he thought—that there was little point worrying about a marriage that was long since moribund.

Richard did not linger long after that, obviously eager to return to his bride. Michael stayed for a few more minutes before he gave up his hopes of finding a book to keep him occupied. He had given Rachel ample time by now to dress and get into bed. With any luck, she would probably already be asleep. He might as well get it over with, he told himself, and stop pretending that a book would do him any good.

He knew that he would spend the rest of the night thinking about Rachel; anything else would be impossible when he would be spending it so close to her.

He climbed the stairs to her room and slipped inside. Rachel was in bed, eyes closed, her hair spilling like a waterfall across her pillow. Michael simply stood for a moment looking at her. She had left a lamp burning on the dresser for him, its wick turned low so that it cast only a soft glow immediately around it. In the dim light he could see little of his wife; it was his mind that provided the tantalizing images of her nestled between the soft sheets.

He tore his gaze away from her and picked up the lamp, then walked softly across the room into the dressing room beyond. The cot was made up for him, a thin, narrow mattress spread across its utilitarian frame. He had slept on worse in the course of investigations, when he took on one of his disguises; it was Rachel's nearness that would make it difficult to sleep, not the camp bed. He set the lamp down on a chest and undressed quickly. After blowing out the light, he settled himself on the bed and closed his eyes. Sleep did not come, of course. His head was filled with thoughts of Rachel, each one more enticing than the one before.

With a sigh, he turned over onto one side. It was going to be a long night.

7

Miranda reached up to give her taller sister-in-law a hug. "I do wish you would not go so soon, Rachel. You have scarcely been here any time. Why, Westhampton did not even arrive until yesterday." She cast an accusing glance over at Michael, who stood waiting by the carriage.

Michael looked a trifle embarassed. "I am sorry, Miranda...." He fumbled for something else to say.

"Yes, I know, he is a harsh taskmaster," Rachel said lightly, coming to his rescue. She strongly suspected that Michael had insisted on leaving this morning primarily because he did not wish to have to spend another night in the same room with her. That fact caused her a little pang of hurt—was it really so terrible to be around her?—but she, too, preferred not to have to deal with the awkward situation another night.

Rachel went on more seriously. "Spring is an important time of year on the estate farm, you see, and

I know that Michael is taking off more time than he would like to escort me to London. I hate to put him out any more.''

''Well, all right, I won't scold him any further,'' Miranda conceded. ''However, you must promise me that you will return in time for my lying in.'' Miranda's forehead wrinkled in an unaccustomed frown of anxiety. ''I really want you to be with me when the time comes. I—my stepmother will be here, of course, and Lady Ravenscar offered to. But…I would much prefer to have you. Just for support, you know. I am a trifle frightened.''

Rachel's eyes widened at this astonishing admission from Miranda, but she took her friend's hand and squeezed it reassuringly, saying, ''I promise I will be here. I plan to leave London by the end of July, and that will give me over a month before the happy event is supposed to occur. And if you are worried or wish me here earlier, just write, and I will come sooner than that. There will be dozens of other Seasons, but only one first child for you.''

Miranda smiled back at her. ''Thank you. I daren't tell Dev I feel nervous about it. He fusses over me far too much as it is.''

''Naturally. You need another woman.''

''I need you.''

Tears sprang into Rachel's eyes at the unexpected, heartfelt compliment. Several years younger than her brother and sister, she had rarely been the one that others depended upon. In general she regarded herself as somewhat ''less than,'' not as talented as Dev nor as beautiful as Caroline—and fond as she had become of Miranda, she was also rather overwhelmed by the other woman's confidence and ability.

Rachel hugged Miranda again before she turned to say goodbye to the others. Then Michael helped her up into the carriage and climbed in behind her. As the carriage rolled away from the house, Rachel pushed aside the window curtain for a final look at her family.

"I am sorry to take you away from them early," Michael told her.

Rachel turned back to him. "Don't worry. It is perfectly all right. I shall return in a few months, anyway."

She did not add that it would be something of a relief to get away from the other two couples. She loved her family and was very glad that both Dev and Richard had found rare and wonderful loves. But there were times when the sight of the others so deeply and obviously in love aroused a piercing envy in her heart.

It seemed as though everywhere she turned the past two days, she had been witness to some indication of the love that lay between her friends and their husbands—a glance between Jessica and Richard or a quick smile from Dev to Miranda, a brief touch of Dev's hand to Miranda's cheek or Richard, yesterday evening when he had thought no one was looking, lifting his wife's hand to his lips for an affectionate kiss. They were small things, true, but filled with such depth of feeling that no one could have missed the love that underpinned their marriages.

Rachel wondered what it would be like to feel that way, to have a man look at her the way Richard looked at Jessica—a way that never failed to make Jessica's eyes sparkle and her cheeks flush with color. It was clear that it was not only the men who delighted in the physical aspects of these two marriages. There were times when Rachel thought that she would give almost anything to feel for even a moment what Jessica and Miranda obviously felt for their husbands—the excitement, the passion, the overwhelming love. It did not make it any easier to bear to know that she herself had recklessly thrown away any chance she had of such a marriage.

She knew she was a terrible person for feeling these things. Even worse, she could not deny that she envied Miranda for her pregnancy, as well. Over the years that she had been married to Michael, she had come to long for a child. The life she lived, the social round of parties and calls, was not enough to fulfill her. She needed more; she wanted children. And with each year that passed, the longing grew worse.

Rachel looked across the carriage at her husband. She wondered if he ever regretted their childless state. Women were more eager for children, she supposed, but if nothing else, Michael must be aware of the need of an heir. Surely he must want a son of his own to succeed him to the title, to receive his fortune.

He would be a wonderful father, she thought. She could see him walking through the garden with the children—two sons and a daughter, as she saw them in her mind's eye—telling them all about the plants around them, answering their questions and lifting them up so that they could better see the bud on a tree or a hovering butterfly.

"Rachel? Are you all right?"

"What?" She focused on Michael, his words bringing her back from where her mind had wandered. He was watching her with concern, and Rachel realized that there were tears in her eyes.

"Shall I tell the coachman to turn around?" asked gently. "I should not have insisted on leaving. We can stay a few more days without problem."

"No. No. Really." Rachel gave him a smile. "I will be fine now." She cast about for something to say to change the subject. "Do you suppose we will have a visit from your protector?"

"Who— Oh!" Michael's face darkened. "I'd bloody well like to meet the scoundrel—frightening you like that."

Rachel's eyes widened with surprise. For an instant there had been something in Michael's eyes that she had never seen there. She wasn't quite sure what it was.

"I am sure we will not, though," he went on in something more like his usual calm tone. "He got some money from you, and I imagine that satisfied him. No doubt nothing will happen, but—you know me—I like to be prepared."

"Yes, I know." Rachel was well aware that Michael did not like uncertainty or slipshod preparations. Everything he did was done with a meticulous neatness and careful foresight. In many ways he was the opposite of her brother Dev, who tended to act impulsively and emotionally. Or, really, she supposed, it was more that he was the opposite of his father, who had been, by all accounts, a man given over almost completely to his physical appetites.

Even when Michael acted in a way that seemed impulsive, such as coming to Darkwater to escort her the rest of the way to London, or last Christmas, when he had made his way across the snowbound countryside to Castle Cleybourne when she had not made it home, it was not emotion that drove him. Even at those times, he was calm and possessed, thinking clearly and logically. He was simply responding to correct a plan that had somehow gone awry—usually, she admitted wryly, because someone less competent, such as herself, was the person carrying out the plan. He would swoop in and take charge because he considered it his duty.

The journey from Darkwater to London was the longer leg of her trip, and it took them two days to accomplish it. Rachel had made the journey many times, but it went more easily and quickly when Michael was with her. A learned man, he could talk with ease on many topics, and he usually had a ready answer for any question she might ask. He had a lovely voice, she thought, rich and deep, and she enjoyed listening to him.

She wondered what it would have been like if she had not made the mistake of eloping with Anthony.

Would they have made this journey together many times? Would he have wanted to be with her, to talk and laugh with her, or to sit in companionable silence rather than to be with her out of sense of duty?

If it had all happened differently, she thought, she would have known him in the intimate way that most wives knew their husbands. Even when they did not like the man or spend much time with him, wives knew their husbands at an elemental level at which Rachel knew she would never know Michael. There would be an ease and comfort between them, a familiarity, rather than the faintly stiff way they sat together now. They might even have been able to communicate with one another by just a glance or a word, as Dev and Miranda did.

She could not quite imagine what it would be like to know a man in that way, to have a man know her. From listening to other married women talk, she had a fair idea of what the basics of the marital act involved; the idea of it no longer shocked her as it had when her mother had first broached the subject before she married Michael. Indeed, there were times when she found herself trying to imagine how it would feel, wondering—well, yes, she might as well admit it to herself, *wanting* to find out—if she would enjoy it, as many women she knew seemed to.

She recalled one day when she had rounded a corner and accidentally come upon Richard and Jessica locked in a passionate embrace. They had been lost to the world, their lips pressed against each other, their arms wrapped around each other so tightly that it seemed as if they would scarcely be able to breathe. Rachel had stopped, gaping at them, wide eyed, for an astonished moment. Then, the heat of embarrassment sweeping up into her face, she had managed to unstick her feet and turned to move swiftly and silently away. The image had been difficult for her to forget, however.

Rachel wondered now, looking across the carriage at Michael, how it would feel to be crushed in his arms that way, to have his mouth devouring hers. She had been in such turmoil when he had kissed her that once, before their marriage, that she could remember little of the details of the kiss, or the panic that had seized her. If he were to kiss her that way now, how would it feel? She blushed a little, just thinking about it, and quickly turned to look out the window of the carriage. Still, it was a subject that kept returning to her mind again and again during the course of their trip. She thought about it as they rocked along in the carriage, and she thought about it when Michael sometimes rode on his horse outside the carriage and she looked out at him. There was something, she realized, that stirred in her as she watched him astride his mount. He was an excellent horseman, and there was something so physical and commanding about him as he rode that she felt... Well, she was not sure what it was she felt, but it was at once odd and intriguing. It was not the wild leap of love she had felt in her chest whenever she had seen Anthony when she was young and madly in love with him. It was something warmer and lower in her body, not at all giddy, but almost an ache.

And at night, when she lay in her bed in the inn where they had stopped to spend the night, she would think about Michael lying in his bed in the room next to hers. And she would wonder what it would be like to lie beside him in the bed, to sleep with the heat of his body cuddled behind hers. She thought about going to his door and rapping softly. Would he open it to her? Would he take her in his arms?

Rachel told herself it was foolish to even think this way. Michael did not love her or want her. The marriage they had was what he had chosen. If he had wanted anything else, he could easily have said so over the years...or even hinted at it, or made the slightest gesture toward taking her to his bed. But he had not.

She was not sure why she was thinking such things. She normally was not what she would have called a licentious person. She did not even comment on certain men's attributes, as some women of her acquaintance were apt to—in a veiled and hushed way, of course. Frankly, she usually did not even notice the men or the topics under discussion until someone else pointed them out.

She supposed it was because she had been thinking so much lately about having a child. She wanted a baby to hold and cuddle, to lavish her love and affection on, to feed and rock to sleep, even to comfort when it cried and ease its pain. She yearned to hold its warm little body close to her heart. It seemed the worst of ironies that she, who had so much love to give, should have no one to whom she could give it. Because she had the desire for a child so much on her mind, she must have slipped into thinking about the act that would bring a child into existence.

That thought made her feel a little better, less prurient. It was the desire for a baby that drove her, not just some base animal instinct. She wondered what Michael would say, how he would react if she went to him and explained how much she longed for a child. Would he tell her that he, too, wanted one and take her to his bed? Surely, she thought, he would not be so cruel as to spurn her, to turn her away, saying that he did not need an heir that badly.

She thought more than once of doing so, both during the ride or after they reached London. But she could never quite bring herself to face even the embarrassment of asking him to make love to her, let alone the even more humiliating prospect that he might turn her down.

Rachel had thought that Michael would stay a week or two in London with her; it would be fun, she thought, to have her husband as an escort instead of going with her friend Lady Sylvia Montgomery or with Michael's friend Peregrine Overhill, who often acted as her escort. But to her dismay, Michael told her the day they arrived that he would be heading back to Westhampton the following day.

"Tomorrow!" Rachel protested. "So soon? But you haven't had a chance to rest. Surely you could stay in London a day or two. Go to your club, see some of your friends, like Perry, or—or what about that man at the museum who you get along with so well? And we should call on Araminta.''

Michael made a face and said in a teasing voice. ''You just want to have company to call on my sister.''

''Well, it does make it easier when there are two to share her disapproval,'' Rachel admitted.

Michael's older sister, Araminta, was a woman of stern habits and equally stern demeanor, and she had never approved of Rachel as a wife for Michael. She had warned her brother not to marry into the Aincourt family, considering them too profligate in their spending and for generations too wild and flighty in their characters, despite Rachel's father's bent toward religion. When Michael had returned to the family estate in the north after a year of marriage, Araminta had considered it a vindication of her warning. She had actually once told Rachel that it was clear Michael had regretted his choice of her as a wife.

''I am sorry, my dear,'' Michael said. ''But I really cannot afford to spend any more time away from the farm. I am starting a new experiment with legumes this year, and Jenks cannot be counted on to keep the standards scientific. They will be planting before long, and I must be there to oversee it.''

Michael felt a pang of regret at the disappointment on Rachel's face. He would very much have liked to stay with her, to squire her to parties and dance with her until the small hours of the morning. It was, as always, a combination of heaven and hell to be around Rachel all the time—to enjoy the pleasure of looking at her, listening to her, simply being close to her, yet at the same time to suffer through the longing that being with her always invoked in him, to ache for her, knowing that he could not have her, that any move on his part to kiss her or touch her would break the friendly companionship between them. He usually stayed with her until the pain of it grew too great, until the desire in him reached the point where he thought that he must have her or die, and then he would tear himself away from her.

This time, however, he could not afford that luxury. Escorting Rachel safely had not been his only reason for coming to London. He must see his Bow Street ally, Cooper, to make sure he had hired a man to take up a watch on Rachel to keep her safe, and to pick Cooper's brain on the matter of this enemy who thought he knew more than he did. In order to make sure that Rachel was not in danger, he needed to solve this difficult case quickly. It would entail not only talking to Cooper and his friend Sir Robert, but also making use of his disguises to work his way into the underbelly of London and find out what he could among the thieves, prostitutes and other criminals who made their home there. He could scarcely adopt those disguises here, around Rachel, nor could he be chasing down clues if he was spending his time taking her to parties and plays and such.

So the next morning he bade Rachel farewell, raising her hand to his lips for a formal kiss, then turned and quickly walked away. Outside, a groom waited with his horse. He mounted, not turning back to look at the house and therefore not seeing Rachel standing at the window in the front drawing room, watching him. Giving a nod to the groom, he rode off down the street. Two blocks down, out of sight of the house, he turned and headed for a different section of London and the house of another woman.

Rachel wandered back upstairs to her sitting room after Michael left, feeling at loose ends and faintly sad. She knew that she ought to visit Michael's sister Araminta. Etiquette required it, since she had just returned to Town after a long absence and Araminta was Michael's closest kin. By the same token, she ought to visit her own mother, who was happily enjoying life in London, free from the isolation of Darkwater as well as the constraints of a lack of money. Neither one of the women, she suspected, really cared whether they saw Rachel, but they would doubtless be affronted at the slight if she did not come by.

But she frankly did not feel like going to see them. Instead she sank down on a reclining sofa and gave herself over to the same thoughts that had been plaguing her for the past few days. It seemed peculiar to her that Michael had had to leave for home so quickly. Was he that anxious to get away from her? There had been something about his face yesterday when he was explaining why he had to go so quickly, something— Well, perhaps not exactly uneasy, but not precisely comfortable, either. It reminded her a little of the way he had looked when she had questioned him about the man who had stopped her carriage. She told herself that it was absurd to think that Michael was not telling her the truth. Michael was the epitome of honesty.

She stood up, disliking herself for sitting there thinking such thoughts. She would go to visit her friend Sylvia, she thought, and her spirits immediately brightened. Lady Sylvia Montgomery was one of the glittering lights of London Society. Short and plumply voluptuous, she was possessed of a silvery, infectious laugh and an entertaining, neverending supply of gossip. She was adored by her husband, Sir Ian, twenty years older than she and constantly amazed at his good fortune in landing such a wife. And she was exactly the sort of friend who could pull anyone out of despondency.

Rachel rang for her maid. An hour later, dressed in a fetching sea-green dress and matching pelisse, she set off for Lady Montgomery's house.

It was still early in the afternoon, and Sylvia had as yet no visitors. When Rachel was announced to her, she jumped up from her chair with a cry of delight and hurried forward.

"Rachel, my love!" She enveloped her in a hug. "It has been ages since I've seen you. You must have spent all winter in the wilds."

"Yes, I did. We were snowbound at Castle Cleybourne at Christmas and—" she smiled at her friend "—I have a veritable treasure trove of information for you."

"About the duke?" Sylvia's eyes lit up. "I heard

from Lady Aspwich that he had married, but I could scarcely believe it. Is it true? And is it true that the new duchess left London years ago under a cloud?''

''I shall tell you all about it,'' Rachel promised, and they sat down to a cozy conversation regarding the events of the past winter at Castle Cleybourne and the startling past of the duke's new bride.

When she finished, there were a few moments of silence as Sylvia turned over in her head the complicated story Rachel had just told her. Then, somewhat hesitantly, Rachel began, ''Sylvia…''

Her friend looked at her, her attention caught by Rachel's tone. ''Yes?''

''I was wondering…'' Rachel began slowly. ''That is, well, have you ever heard anything about Michael?''

''Westhampton?'' Lady Sylvia asked, her blue eyes growing rounder. ''What do you mean? Heard what?''

''I'm not sure.'' Now that she had started, Rachel realized how vague her concerns sounded. ''About, say, his being involved in something?''

''Something?'' Her friend's finely arched brows rose. ''What kind of something?''

''Something dangerous.''

For a long moment Sylvia stared back at her blankly. Then she began to laugh. ''Oh, I see—you are making some kind of joke!''

''No! No, I'm not. Sylvia…do stop laughing.''

The silvery tinkles of her friend's laughter died away. ''But, Rachel, dearest—that's nonsensical.

Why would Michael be involved in something dangerous? What could it be?"

"I don't know. And I know it sounds as if I have run mad. But, well—" Rachel drew a breath and launched into the story of the highwayman who had stopped her carriage.

Lady Sylvia's eyes grew wider and wider as Rachel talked, and by the time she came to a halt, Sylvia was staring at her, openmouthed.

"Well?" Rachel asked. "Do you see now why I asked?"

"Yes. But what does it mean? What was the man talking about? Who was he?"

"You know as much as I do. Nothing."

"Did you tell Westhampton? What did he say?"

"He said it was nothing, that the man was probably a lunatic."

"Yes, well, he rather sounds like one."

"But you didn't see him. He did not seem at all mad. He seemed perfectly serious, as if he really knew Michael and thought that he was in trouble. Michael suggested that perhaps it was one of his friends playing an elaborate jest on him."

"I must say, he has rather bizarre sorts of friends, then."

"Yes, well, I must admit that some of the men with whom he corresponds are a trifle odd. But it's more that they talk about things that no one else would ever even consider, let alone talk about, and they forget to wear a hat in the rain or something like that but can remember what some philosopher hundreds of years ago said.''

"Oh. Like Lady Wendhaven's uncle, you mean?''

"Well, no, not the kind who run about town in their nightgowns. More like Naomi Armistead, say.''

"The one with pencils stuck in her hair, but then she's always looking everywhere for one?''

"And pulls them out to jot down bits of poetry. Exactly.''

"Yes, well, the Armisteads are all a bit odd. All of them have peculiar names.''

"Biblical.''

"Well, I suppose one can hardly blame them for that, but it does seem to me that their parents could have had a bit more consideration. I mean, Matthew is all right, and Ruth, but it seems to me that to name a boy Job is asking for trouble, don't you think?''

"Yes, I guess so, but that isn't the point. What I'm trying to say is that Michael's friends and correspondents are eccentric in that way, but I wouldn't expect them to hire someone to pretend to be a highwayman and warn Michael of some danger or other. Even if they are pranksters, what would be the jest of it?'' Rachel leaned forward earnestly, all the doubts that had been simmering in the back of her mind spilling out.

"I don't know,'' Sylvia replied doubtfully. "It doesn't seem particularly funny, does it?''

"And if the man is a lunatic, why did he choose Michael to trouble with his lunacy? It was not random. He spoke of him by name. He recognized the crest on the side of the carriage. He acted as if he knew him. But wouldn't you think if Michael had met someone as mad as that, he would have recognized him by my description? By what the man said? He even told me that his name was Red Geordie. Don't you think you would remember someone named Red Geordie?"

"He sounds rather unforgettable," Sylvia agreed. "Do you think that Michael really knew who he was and that he lied to you about it?"

Her friend's words brought Rachel up short. "No," she admitted, frowning. "I would not think that Michael would lie to anyone, much less his wife." She hesitated, then added, "But when he said he didn't know who the man was, he—he looked away from me. And suddenly I just felt that something was wrong. That he was...maybe not lying, but that he was not telling me the entire truth." She looked at her friend, troubled. "Do you think he is hiding something from me?"

Sylvia shrugged. "Sir Ian hides things from me all the time."

"Really?" Rachel stared. "Doesn't it bother you?"

"No, not especially. Sometimes it is because he fears I will scold him. The doctor told him to stop drinking port—the gout, you know—and sometimes, when he comes home from his club, I know he has been drinking it, but he pretends he hasn't. And sometimes he thinks I wouldn't understand something. Men think we are silly creatures, with nothing but clothes in our heads.''

"Michael is not like that," Rachel said positively. "He has talked to me about philosophy and science—and sometimes, frankly, it was too complicated for me, but Michael didn't treat me as if I were stupid."

"Then I would warrant that he is doing it to protect you," Sylvia answered promptly.

"Protect me? From what?"

"I don't know. Perhaps the fact that he is in danger, that the man was telling the truth, no matter how unlikely it seems. Maybe he doesn't want you to worry."

"Well, I would worry, but it would hardly be fair of him to hide it from me. And, besides, that means he's been doing something that would get him into danger, and that would have to be something else I know nothing about."

"Probably something from his past," Sylvia said with a wise look. "Before he met you. Men always get involved in some sort of pecadillo or other when they are young, even someone like Michael. He would be embarrassed to admit his youthful folly to you."

"You really think so?"

Her friend nodded her head emphatically, sending her golden ringlets bouncing. "Oh, yes. And if you want to find out what it is, I know just the thing to do. Come with me to Lady Tarleton's soiree tonight."

Rachel raised her brows skeptically. "And how will that help me?"

"Lady Belmartin is sure to be there. She is great friends with Harriet Tarleton. And Lady Belmartin knows all the gossip there is to know about everyone. If anyone knows whether Michael was involved in something shady in the past, it will be she."

"I can't go about asking people if they know anything bad about my husband!" Rachel protested. "Honestly, Sylvia, how would that look? Nothing would be surer to set everyone gossiping."

"We won't ask her outright, silly! One doesn't have to prod Lady Belmartin to gossip. Indeed, it's hard to get her to stop. We'll just start talking to her, let her get warmed up a little, and I shall say something, oh, something like there being nothing bad that one could say about Westhampton."

"Won't she think it's odd?"

"Heavens, no! She will just take it as a challenge. If there is anything bad to be said about Michael, she will do it."

"With me standing right there in front of her?"

"You obviously don't know Lady Belmartin well. She would be eager to see how you would react. It would be more grist for her gossip mill."

"How horrid!"

"She is, rather. She is bosom friends with Ian's mother—there is another one with a tongue like a serpent—so I have had a lot of experience at dealing with her. I ply her with flattery and let her think I am the silliest thing ever, and I feed her bits of gossip. Just look awestruck at her knowledge of every *on-dit* for the last twenty years and she will be pleased with you.''

Rachel had not really planned on going out that evening; she had felt tired and listless all day. But she thought of spending the long night alone in the Westhampton mansion, and the prospect was immensely unappealing.

Smiling at her friend, she said, "Very well. I am sure that she will have no gossip to spread about Michael: I am simply being foolish. But it will be nice to confirm that. And perhaps a night out is precisely what I need."

"Of course. It is always what one needs."

8

Lady Sylvia arrived in her carriage to take Rachel to Lady Tarleton's soiree at a little before eleven o'clock, only an hour later than she had said she would arrive. Rachel, who knew her friend well, had timed her own toilette so as to be ready thirty minutes late and therefore did not have to wait too long. Sylvia was sparkling in a silver tissue gown and the diamonds that Sir Ian had given her upon the arrival of their first son and heir. Rachel had opted for a more subdued gown of blue velvet that went admirably with her pale skin and dark hair. A matching blue ribbon wound through the curls of her hair, and discreet sapphires glowed at her ears and throat.

Tarleton House was lit up both outside and in, and the line of carriages leading to its front door stretched well over a block back. Once they reached the door, there was another long wait in the receiving line, which snaked through the entryway and up the stairs to the grand ballroom. Lady Sylvia kept them both entertained by commenting behind her fan on the dresses worn by the other female guests.

Rachel gave up any hope of even finding Lady Belmartin in the crush, let alone talking to her, and she decided it was just as well. But Sylvia assured her that she knew exactly where to find her, and once they were through the receiving line, she linked arms with Rachel and guided her through the crowd to a row of chairs lining the wall at the opposite end of the large room from where the group of musicians played.

"Lady Belmartin and Mother Montgomery always sit, and they hate to be near the music, as it makes gossiping more difficult," Sylvia explained as they approached the spot where, as she had predicted, her mother-in-law sat with her friend.

Lady Belmartin was as small and spare as Lady Montgomery was tall and rounded, so they formed an interesting contrast. Both widows, they dressed in black, though it had been many years since their husbands' demises. Lady Belmartin reminded Rachel forcibly of a crow, with her widow's weeds and bright dark eyes, an image furthered by the hair decoration of glossy green-black feathers that rose out of the carefully coiffed twist of hair at the back of her head.

"Sylvia, child," Lady Montgomery said, regally holding out her hand to her daughter-in-law. "And Lady Westhampton. When did you return to London?"

"Only yesterday, Lady Montgomery," Rachel an-

swered, dutifully curtseying to the older woman. Sir
Ian's mother had the ability to make her feel like an
awkward child at her first party, so she generally tried
to avoid the woman if she could.

"Not that many people back in Town yet," Lady
Montgomery went on, adding with a disdainful sniff,
"Though one could not tell it from the crush here
tonight. Harriet never has been able to separate the
wheat from the chaff. I see she even invited that
dreadful Blackheath woman."

She proceeded to rip the poor woman to shreds,
starting with her accent, which hinted of an upbring-
ing in Northern Britain, and continuing through her
hair, dress and manners. She was aided ably in this
endeavor by her companion, who added that the
woman's father was country gentry, at least, but her
mother was merely the granddaughter of a Yorkshire
sheep farmer.

"Of course, they never speak of it. Well, one
wouldn't, would one? But I have it from Lady Feath-
erstone, who grew up not twenty miles from there."

"And there is Lady Vesey!" Lady Montgomery
went on disgruntedly. "I cannot imagine what she is
doing here. Surely even Harriet would not be foolish
enough to invite her."

Rachel swung around to search the room with her
eyes. *Leona Vesey!* She would have to be careful not
to run into her tonight! There were not many people
whom Rachel could truthfully say she hated, but
Lady Vesey was one of them. Leona had seduced
Dev when he was a young man first in London, even

though she was both older and married. She had introduced him to bad companions and widened the split between Dev and their father and—the worst thing in Rachel's opinion—had separated him from his art. Until Miranda appeared and changed Dev's life, Rachel had begun to fear that Leona had destroyed her brother's future. It had given Rachel a great deal of pleasure when Miranda had vanquished Leona, but still, she could hardly stand to see the woman.

"The Veseys are a step away from debtor's prison—everyone knows that," Lady Belmartin added. "Of course, I have heard that Leona has a new admirer—a wealthy one, I would judge by that bauble she's wearing tonight."

"My, Lady Belmartin," Sylvia said admiringly, with a sidelong glance at Rachel, "you know everyone."

"Oh, yes," the older woman agreed with pride. "I have been privy to some of the best-kept secrets of the *Ton.*"

"But I must imagine that there are some people who haven't any secrets, aren't there?" Rachel offered mildly.

Her words earned a hard stare from Lady Belmartin. "Nonsense. Everyone has secrets. It is simply that some of them haven't been found out yet."

"Well, but you must admit that some people lead exemplary lives," Sylvia persisted. "Sir Ian, I'm sure has—"

Lady Belmartin let out a hoot. "Sir Ian is no better

than he should be, as I am sure Lady Montgomery will tell you. But, of course, I do not gossip about my friends.''

''Well, perhaps Ian was not a good choice. Then let's say Rachel's husband. I'll warrant you have nothing bad to say about Lord Westhampton.''

Rachel looked at Lady Belmartin, aware that her hands were suddenly damp inside her evening gloves and her heart was beating faster than a mere conversation would warrant.

Lady Belmartin sent her a piercing look. ''You are married to Michael Trent, are you? Well, I can tell you that his father was an utter roue. A libertine.'' She nodded sharply. ''Gave his poor wife nothing but grief, that one. She died years ago, poor thing, and I am sure his escapades did quite a bit to shorten her days. I have heard that he fathered several children on the wrong side of the blanket. Well, men do, of course, but he never honored his responsibilities. If a man is going to behave in that fashion, the least he can do is support the poor benighted babes.'' She paused, then added judiciously, ''Never knew a better horseman, though. Always threw his heart over a fence.''

''But that is nothing about Michael,'' Rachel said stiffly.

Lady Belmartin shrugged. ''Well, the fruit doesn't fall far from the tree, my dear.''

Color flamed in Rachel's cheeks. ''What? What sort of unfounded calumny is that? Are you saying that Michael—''

"Dear girl!" The old lady chuckled. "Don't take my head off. I merely meant— Well, he is a man, after all."

"He is an honorable man—and nothing like his father."

"No, of course not." Lady Belmartin's eyes twinkled in a sly way that Rachel did not like at all.

Sylvia quickly linked her arm through Rachel's, firmly pulling her with her as she backed away from the older women. "I fear we must go now. I must introduce Rachel to, um, another friend of mine."

"Of course, dear." Lady Belmartin and Lady Montgomery turned back to each other and started in on another hapless vicitim.

"The idea was not to argue with Lady Belmartin but to get information from her," Sylvia whispered to Rachel. "Thank heavens she did not take it poorly."

"It's obvious she knew nothing about Michael," Rachel replied, still feeling rather heated. "She was much too vague—making little hints like that. If she had actually known something, she would have said it outright."

"Mmm. Probably," Sylvia agreed, obviously losing interest. "Well, there you are, then—there is nothing secret in Michael's past. Oh, look, here comes Perry Overhill."

Rachel smiled and looked across the floor, where a fashionably dressed gentleman was hurrying toward them. Peregrine Overhill, better known to his friends as Perry, was an amiable soul, not quite portly, but certainly not slender, either, whose beaming round face could be found at almost every social occasion. Although a friend of Michael's, he had none of Michael's love of the country, preferring to spend his entire life within the environs of London. He was given to a love of clothes, and though he was not the sort who would follow the extremes of fashion—he never put a bouttoniere the size of a nosegay in his lapel or indulged in pink or puce waistcoats—he would generally be dressed in the forefront of style. His first thought, by his own genial admission, was always for his own comfort, but he was also a firm and loyal friend.

Rachel had met him her first Season, a few weeks before Michael came into her life, and ever since that time Perry had been one of the men who made up the circle of Rachel's admirers. Any acknowledged Beauty, single or married, worthy of the name had such a retinue. The names and numbers varied. Some were young men truly enamored for the first time; others were older, confirmed bachelors who simply enjoyed the opportunity for light, meaningless flirtation; still others were, in Rachel's opinion, men who had not the slightest interest in her as a woman but who approved of her style and beauty in a purely esthetic way.

The rules of flirtation were delicate and differed a great deal from the married Beauties to those just making their first debut. A man's interest in an unmarried young woman was considered serious; with a married woman, the purpose was exactly the opposite. For the woman, her admirers were handy escorts when her husband could not or would not do so. They could be counted upon to make pretty compliments or bring one refreshments or stand up with one for a dance. For the men, much of the appeal lay in being able to do all those things without being measured as husband material by calculating mamas. There was, of course, the possibility of an affair between a married woman and one of her admirers, but such a thing would be conducted in secret, separate from the formalized interaction of a Beauty and her *cisibeos.*

Perry was a friend of Michael's and quite fond of Rachel. As he was the only one of her admirers who had remained one of her retinue since her coming out, Rachel was sure that his continued attendance on her sprang more out of Perry's laziness than from any actual love. Rachel found him comfortable to be with, which was one of the factors that made him her favorite escort. The other was that he had been a good friend of Michael's for years, which meant that Michael would not have the slightest reason to doubt her intentions. She had been determined all the life of her marriage not to let the slightest hint of scandal attach to any of her actions.

Perry was grinning broadly now as he approached her through the crowd. Despite his love of fashion, there was almost invariably something a trifle off about whatever he wore—buttons done up wrong or a handkerchief tucked haphazardly into a pocket or a hat a trifle askew. Tonight was no exception; his cravat, knotted in an elegant style and pinned with a large pearl, had gotten turned a half inch off center, giving him a lopsided look.

Rachel returned his smile. Perry's somewhat bumbling ways were part of his charm, as was the boyish aspect of his face, a fact which caused him great despair. His face was round, with apple cheeks, and was usually adorned with a smile.

"Lady Westhampton!" he cried from several feet away and swept her a grand bow. "I had thought the sun was brighter today, and now I know why. It shone because you had returned to the city."

Rachel chuckled and extended her hand to him. "Perry, you goose, stop posing and come here."

He came forward and took her hand, raising it to his lips to bestow a light kiss upon it. "Rusticating must agree with you—you look stunning. But London has been dreadfully dull without you."

"I am sure you found something to amuse you."

"Poor substitutes for you," he retorted.

"Can you not even spare a greeting for me, Perry?" Sylvia scolded.

"Lady Montgomery." He turned slightly toward her to execute another bow. "You are a veritable vision tonight—a, um, star come down from the heavens."

Sylvia tilted her head to the side. "All right; you have saved yourself with that compliment. I shall forgive the lack of greeting."

"I need not ask how you have been," Rachel told

him. "You look exceedingly well, despite your supposed boredom."

He smiled and looked somewhat abashed by the compliment.

"How is Gypsy?" Rachel asked, referring to the ill-tempered, snuffle-nosed pug that was Overhill's much loved pet.

"He has missed you terribly. I shall have to bring him by to see you."

Since Rachel had never known the dog to do anything but snap peevishly at her when she approached it, she had serious doubts about Perry's oft-held claim that Gypsy adored her. But she did not express her reservations, merely smiled and nodded.

"How is Michael?" Perry went on, glancing around. "Did he come with you?"

"Actually, he did escort me to London, but I am afraid that he has left already to return to Westhampton. You know how he is about planting season."

Perry grimaced. "Yes. Well, I will have to take him to task for leaving without even paying me a visit."

"Perry…" Rachel began impulsively. "Do you know anything about Michael's secrets?"

The man goggled at her for a moment in silence. "Secrets?" he asked after a long moment. "Rachel, my dear, what are you talking about?"

"I just wondered, you know, if you knew anything about something he might have done or—"

Overhill was staring at her now in alarm. "Michael

has no secrets. Who has been telling you any differently?'' He glanced at Sylvia.

She held up her hands in an expression of innocence, saying, ''It was not I. Don't look so fiercely at me.''

''But, well, it's absurd to speak of Michael having secrets, especially from you, my dear. Everyone knows of his high regard for you. Who told you this?''

''No one,'' Rachel admitted. She had been watching Perry's face closely as he answered her, and it seemed to her that there was a slight relaxation of his face when she said that no one had told her anything. And had there been something just a trifle nervous in his eyes as he denied Michael's secrets?

Quietly, she told him about the visit she had received from the highwayman, and he listened with rapt attention.

''Danger?'' he said when she had finished. ''Really, my dear, it's nonsense. How could Michael be in danger? I am sure the fellow just wanted money.''

''But how did he know who Michael was?'' Rachel pressed him.

Overhill blinked. ''Well, ah...''

''You see?''

''I see that you have some unanswered questions,'' Perry began carefully. ''But I don't think that they necessarily lead to the conclusion that Michael has kept secrets from you.''

''Secrets?'' a woman's voice drawled behind

them. "The saintly Lord Westhampton? I am appalled."

Perry grimaced at the sound of the voice. "Lady Vesey."

Rachel turned around to look at the woman who stood behind her. She was a small woman with a voluptuous figure, which was tonight rather scantily clad in a gown of green voile. Her ample bosom swelled above the low neckline of the gown, and it was clear from the way the garment clung that Lady Vesey was wearing few, if any, petticoats beneath the evening dress. It was a style of dress adopted by the faster set of the *Ton;* some women even went so far as to dampen their gowns to make them cling even more provocatively, a practice Rachel viewed as unhealthy, as well as immodest. Few women, however, were able to fill their gowns out as well as Lady Leona Vesey did.

Lady Vesey's wild ways had earned her the censure of most of the leading ladies of London Society. She was not received at many houses, and Rachel felt sure that Lady Tarleton would receive a blistering scolding from several of the more prominent women for inviting her to the party tonight. But, despite the disapprobation of the *Ton,* there were few who would deny that she was one of the great Beauties of the last two decades. Though she was nearing forty, age and dissipation had not yet scored their lines into her face—at least not in here in the glow of the candlelight. Her strawberries-and-cream complexion was soft, her lips full and pouting, her golden eyes large and dark lashed, and though Rachel suspected that her face owed much to the skillful application of cosmetics, the result was admittedly stunning.

Rachel thoroughly disliked the woman for her years of wicked influence over Dev, and it was clear that Leona Vesey returned the feeling in full measure. Rachel had been present last summer during a scene at Darkwater where Miranda successfully demonstrated to Lady Vesey that she had lost control over Dev, and since then, Leona had seemed to regard Rachel with even more venom than she had before.

"Rachel…" she purred now in a falsely sympathetic voice. "You should know better than to ask someone like Perry for your husband's secrets. You should have come to me. I would have been happy to have told you all about his indiscretions."

Rachel gave Leona a level look. "Had I thought you had any knowledge or any capacity for telling the truth, perhaps I would have."

She turned back to Perry and Sylvia, regretting the fact that she had said anything to the woman. Her mother would have given Leona the cut direct, sending an icy glance right through her, then turning away as if Leona were not there. Rachel, however, had never been able to deliver such a cutting gesture, even to Lady Vesey.

But Leona was not to be denied. She plowed ahead, saying, "Oh, I know your husband's secrets, Lady Westhampton. A great deal of London does. Perhaps you should ask Lord Westhampton about his visits to Mrs. Neeley. I am sure you would find his answers quite informative.''

Rachel was startled by Leona's words. She had assumed that Leona was simply being annoying; she had not really considered that Leona actually had a tale about Michael to tell her. Even so, she would not have been alarmed had it not been for the fact that Perry stiffened, his eyes suddenly looking as if they were about to pop out of his head.

A chill rippled through Rachel. Obviously the name Leona had just used meant something to Perry. She turned back to Leona.

A smile curved Leona's mouth, and there was a smug set to her face that irritated Rachel beyond measure. "Ah, I see I have your attention now."

"I don't know who you are talking about, but I am sure it is all nonsense. Vicious nonsense."

"Really?" Leona gave a throaty little laugh. "If you were so certain as all that, I suspect you would not be standing there, waiting for me to tell you more. *Mrs.* Neeley—I give her the title, you see, but I am sure it is one purely of courtesy—is the owner of a rather popular gaming establishment. She has been for some years now—about the same amount of time that she has been granting Lord Westhampton her favors.''

Rachel sucked in her breath sharply, as if Lady Vesey had landed her a blow to the stomach.

Beside her, Sylvia said hotly, "How dare you say something like that!"

"I dare because it is the truth. Lilith Neeley has

been Lord Westhampton's mistress for years. He has been seen any number of times going in and out of her house—at all hours of the day and night. His comings and goings bespeak a great deal of famliarity with the woman.''

Perry moved between Lady Vesey and Rachel, saying, ''Lady Vesey, I think it is time that you were going.''

''Oh, yes,'' Leona's voice dripped scorn. ''We must not say anything to sully Lady Westhampton's ears. What does it matter if all London knows about her husband's dalliance with Lilith Neeley as long as Rachel can retain her naive ignorance?'' She stepped neatly around Perry's bulk to look directly at Rachel and say, ''Perhaps if you were not so ignorant, my dear, your husband would not have strayed.''

Leona turned and sauntered off, smugness in every line of her voluptuous body. Rachel watched her go, feeling numb. There was a roaring in her ears, and she could not move, could scarcely think. She was afraid that she might faint.

''Perry...'' She murmured, reaching out a hand, and Perry quickly took it and tucked it into his arm, shooting a significant look at Lady Montgomery.

Sylvia immediately moved closer to Rachel to grab her other arm if need be, and Perry led them through the throng of people to a bench. Rachel sank down upon it, with Perry and Sylvia flanking her. Sylvia took her hand and squeezed it.

''Don't worry about what she said,'' Sylvia said

stoutly. "Leona Vesey has always been a liar. You know she would say anything to hurt you."

"But she said everyone knew!" Rachel looked at her friend.

"I didn't," Sylvia replied. "And that means Sir Ian's mother didn't, either, which is most unlikely."

Rachel turned to Perry. "Perry?"

"Rachel! 'Pon my honor," Perry said. "How can you even ask me? Of course it's not true."

"But I saw you when she said that name," Rachel pressed.

Perry blinked. "Oh, well..." His face reddened. "Of course I had heard the name. But I promise you she is not Michael's, well, his, you know, light-of-love."

"Michael would not be unfaithful to you. How can you think that?" Sylvia added. "Come, now, you cannot let Leona Vesey make you doubt your husband. That would give her exactly what she wants. It doesn't matter to her whether she's telling the truth—or even whether you find out later that it isn't true. She will have disturbed you, made you worry and question Michael. That will be enough for her."

"You are right, of course," Rachel replied, summoning up a small smile for the other two. "I cannot let her see that she has upset me. It would please her no end." She drew a breath. "I think we should promenade around the room and enjoy ourselves." *And let everyone see us do so,* she added mentally.

Rachel was determined not to give Leona the satisfaction of seeing that she had hurt her, and she managed to keep up a good front through the rest of the party. But what she felt inside was a different matter entirely. Sylvia might be certain that Michael would not be unfaithful to Rachel, but Rachel was less so. Sylvia did not know the true state of Rachel and Michael's marriage. Michael's honor was deep and important to him, so much so that Rachel had never even considered the possibility that he might break his marriage vows. But now that Leona had inserted the worm of doubt into her mind, she could not help but think how very likely it might be. Yes, Michael was honorable, but he was a man, after all, with a man's needs. He had been married for seven years to a woman who did not share a bed with him—a woman who had so offended him with her own lack of honor that he would not even touch her.

Many men kept mistresses, even those who said they loved their wives. How much more likely would it be for a man who did not love his wife, whose affection for her had been trampled into nothingness by her betrayal? It should not surprise her, she told herself. If she were not naive, as Leona said, she would not have been surprised. She would have expected it.

But she had not expected it, and it hurt. She was not sure why—wounded pride, perhaps—but it did indeed hurt, as if someone had stabbed her through the heart. She wanted to run home and crawl into bed and cry.

Rachel told herself that there was the possibility that Leona had been lying. As Sylvia had said, Leona was given to lying, and she would seize any opportunity to hurt her. But how had she come up so quickly with a story to tell? It was absurd to think that she had planned it out beforehand; she had not known that she would overhear Rachel asking about Michael's secrets. Indeed, she would have had no reason to think that Rachel would even be at the party; she had only got back into town the day before.

She believed that Sylvia had not heard the story, which lent some weight to its unbelievability, but on the other hand, men did not usually talk to the women of their family about the other world in which they moved, the world of gambling and drinking and mistresses. It was not considered a suitable topic for a lady to hear. A woman like Leona might easily learn of it; she dabbled in that environment herself. But Sir Ian would never have spoken to his mother or Sylvia about a woman who ran a gambling den or the fact that she was the mistress of Sylvia's best friend's husband.

However, she was certain that Perry knew a great deal more about Mrs. Neeley than he would tell her. No matter how much he insisted that Michael and Lilith Neeley were not having an affair, Rachel had seen his face when Leona first threw out the name at Rachel. He had looked as if he had just swallowed his tongue. His claim that he had simply recognized the name as belonging to the owner of a well-known gambling den was, in Rachel's opinion, completely without merit. Had the name had no more meaning to him than that, he might have looked surprised, even a little shocked, at Leona's bad taste in bringing it up in front of two ladies of the *Ton*. But the look in his eyes had not been merely surprise or social shock; it had been something closer to horror. And, even more significant, he had not looked outraged that she would couple Michael's name with such a woman. Indeed, he had not immediately denied the claim; he had just moved to protect Rachel from Leona. He had not denied it until some time later, when Rachel asked him directly.

She tried to remember exactly what he had said. Had he actually denied it, or had he merely skirted the issue? She could not remember now the exact words either of them had used. It didn't really matter, she supposed; she could not rely on his being truthful. Perry was fond of her, but he had been Michael's friend for far longer, and there was, besides, that male bond that excluded women from all sorts of knowledge. She could not really rely on what he told her.

Rachel was not sure why it bothered her so. It was not as if she and Michael loved each other; theirs had always been an arranged marriage, a matter of practicality. Though Michael had once loved her, in the end they had married only to avoid scandal. She supposed that a woman could not expect a husband to remain faithful when he and his wife shared no intimacy. Michael had, after all, been very discreet. She had never heard a breath of rumor about the affair until tonight.

If, of course, there really was an affair. She could not quite shut down the voice of hope inside her.

The thing was, she decided, that she was beginning to feel as though she did not know Michael at all. First there had been the highwayman's strange warning that Michael was somehow skirting close to danger. Then tonight she had heard that he had a mistress—had had one for a number of years. And she had known nothing about either thing! She felt strangely lost. At sea.

Even though they had never had a real marriage, as other people viewed marriage, still Michael was the rock upon which her life was built. She was his wife. Her title, her support, her position in society, even the very clothes on her back, came from him. If she had a problem, she turned to him about it, and even if it was only through letters, he helped her with it. They lived together part of the year; they had shared every Christmas for the last six years—even this past one, when she had been trapped by a snowstorm at Castle Cleybourne, for Michael, worried that she had not arrived at Westhampton, had managed to make his way through the snow to the Castle. That was the sort of man he was—loyal, steadfast, honorable. And she was proud to have him as her husband.

She had never really thought about the matter before, but now, faintly surprised, she realized that it was true—she was proud to be Lady Westhampton. Not because of the wealth or the title, but because of the man that Michael was. The highwayman's assertion and Leona's words had challenged that belief.

She felt as if she had been cut loose from her moorings.

As soon as it was possible to leave the party without feeling that she was running away, Rachel did so. She kept up a pleasant, unconcerned conversation with Sylvia until she was able to bid her good-night at her front door. With an inward sigh of relief, she went up the steps and into her house. The smile she gave the footman who took her evening cape was a trifle wobbly, but that did not matter. She was home now, and safe. She only wished that Michael was there for her to talk to. But, of course, that was foolish. He was the very problem she would have liked to talk about.

She dismissed her maid as soon as she had helped her out of the evening gown, with its long line of buttons down the back, and taken down the intricate curls of her upswept hairdo. Rachel put on her nightgown, then sat down to brush out her curls. She was a little surprised to notice midway through the brushing that silent tears were rolling down her face.

She brushed the tears away, angry with herself. It was not the end of the world, she told herself. Her life would go on as always. Why, she did not even know if Leona had told the truth! She wished there was someone she could ask. She could write to Dev or Richard, of course, but it would not be the same as asking them face-to-face; it would be far too easy for them to lie. Besides, they were friends of Michael's, and, moreover, they would probably consider it their duty to protect her even if it meant lying to her. It was the same way with Perry. She could try to pry the truth out of him, but no matter how much he denied it, she would not be able to trust that he was being honest.

She tried to think of someone else who might know the truth about Michael. The only name that came to mind was his sister, Araminta. Rachel grimaced. She did not want to visit Araminta, much less ask her such a personal question. However, social courtesy demanded that she visit her upon her return to town. And Araminta was someone who could be counted on not to sugarcoat the truth for fear of hurting Rachel, as her friends and family could not.

Of course, as his sister, she might not have been told about the rumors any more than Rachel had been. On the other hand, it was a rumor that reflected badly on Rachel, so it was entirely possible that one of Araminta's friends might have told her, knowing how little she liked Rachel.

It would be humiliating, of course, to go to Michael's sister and ask her such a question. On the other hand, it might be well worth the embarrassment to learn the truth. Anything, she thought, would be better than this wondering and worrying.

Rachel made up her mind and changed it countless times as she tossed and turned in her bed that night, unable to sleep. By the next morning, when she got up, she was certain, however, that she must call on Michael's sister if there was any chance that it might put her mind at ease.

That afternoon she dressed in a dark-green silk day

dress, its only trim an embroidered flounce around the hem, and went to call on Araminta. She took her carriage, even though Araminta's house was not far, because Araminta had more than once criticized what she felt was Rachel's deplorable tendency not to employ the proper trappings of her station in life.

Araminta's home was a cream-colored abode built in the Queen Anne style, and though it was a graceful and attractive place, Rachel had heard her remark more than once with a faint sigh that it could not compare to Westhampton Place. Rachel was not sure what her purpose was, other than a general dissatisfaction with life, but it always made her feel faintly guilty for living there, another of the many reasons that she usually avoided her sister-in-law.

The butler showed Rachel into the drawing room, and a moment later Araminta entered. Unlike Michael, she was not tall, and her figure had an unfortunate tendency toward stoutness, but her coloring was much like Michael's, blond haired and gray eyed. She was seven years older than Michael and still given to dispensing her advice to him freely. Michael's quiet, courteous nature had in her frozen into a rigid propriety.

She greeted Rachel now with a thin smile, saying, "Rachel. I had heard you had returned to London."

"Yes. I have been settling in the past few days." Rachel knew that Araminta's remark was meant to point out that Rachel had been in London for too long without paying her a call.

A small silence fell upon them. Rachel struggled for some way to broach the topic of Lilith Neeley.

"I, um, I stayed at Westhampton longer than I usually do," she said finally, deciding to try to ease into the matter. "The Duke of Cleybourne married shortly after Christmas, and Michael and I took his ward with us to Westhampton."

As she had hoped, Araminta warmed up a little at the mention of a duke. She would love to be able to drop details about the new duchess into her next chat with friends. So Rachel described Jessica in detail, as well as some of the startling events that had taken place at the Castle during the snowstorm before Christmas. Here she had to walk a fine line, giving Araminta the pleasantly important sense that she was privy to the life of a duke without getting into the details of the crime that had been committed at the Castle, which Araminta would disapprove of as being "vulgar and scandalous."

When she was through, Araminta then regaled her with some of the activities in which she had been engaged this winter, during which Rachel had to fight to keep her eyes open and her face set in lines of interest. Rachel tried to work the conversation around to Michael and the family estate at Westhampton, hoping to find some opening to the topic that had brought her here.

However, she could not, and finally, during a lull in their rather stilted conversation, Rachel blurted out, "Have you heard—do you know anything about Lilith Neeley?"

The heat of embarassment flooded her cheeks, and she dropped her eyes from Araminta's face, so she did not see the expression that crossed her sister-in-law's face, but she heard the sharply indrawn gasp that Araminta made. Her gaze snapped back up to Araminta at the sound, and she saw, with a sinking heart, that Araminta was staring at her in horrified surprise.

"Rachel! How can you— I cannot believe that you would bring up such a...a delicate and, frankly, embarassing matter." Araminta set her mouth primly. "I refuse to discuss a woman like that. And I must say, you are doing yourself a disservice if you go about talking about her. In situations like these, it is much better to keep silent."

Rachel felt as if her heart had wound up in her toes. So it was true, then. Michael was having an affair.

9

The "prunes and prisms" expression on Araminta's face had told Rachel what she needed to know; her careful words had confirmed it. Araminta had obviously heard the tales about Mrs. Neeley and Michael, and believed them to be true.

"Our father was what he was," Araminta went on bitterly. "But I never dreamed that Michael would—"

She broke off, rising to her feet, her face closed. "I think it is time that you were going, Rachel."

Irritation flared in Rachel. One would think from the way Araminta acted that Araminta was the one who had been hurt by Michael's keeping a mistress. She stood up, too, saying with some sarcasm, "I am sorry to upset you, Araminta."

"Yes, well, I am sure that you cannot help it. Propriety is learned at an early age, I find."

Rachel had to clamp her teeth together to keep from retorting something rude. Giving Araminta a nod, she managed to get out a clipped goodbye and left the house.

Annoyance at Araminta's set-down distracted her at first, but by the time her carriage let her down in front of her house, Rachel's mind was occupied by nothing but the painful realization that everything Leona Vesey had told her the night before must be true. Michael kept a mistress, had had one for years. And she had not even suspected. What she had feared was true: she did not know her husband at all.

Over the course of that day and the next, she could think of nothing else. Her emotions ran the gamut from hurt to embarassment to anger. She had followed their agreement to the letter—she had not seen or spoken to Anthony since that fateful day, and she had taken the utmost care not to do anything that would bring scandal on Michael and his family. She had been very circumspect in all her dealings with men. Yet he had had no such loyalty to her!

She knew that she had been the one who had first broken trust with him, that she had been foolish and it had killed his love for her. But, she wondered, had she not made up for that long ago? She had been young and in love, and, in fact, she had not actually done anything immoral. She had not given herself to Anthony; she was still as virginal and innocent when she married Michael as she had been the day they were engaged. It seemd to Rachel that Michael could have forgiven her somewhere along the way. Perhaps he might not feel the same way about her that he once had—but why did he dislike her so much that he had sought out another woman?

She was aware that men were apparently driven by stronger desires than women, but she could not understand why he had had to turn to a mistress. Why had he never come to her? In their whole marriage, Michael had never made any advances toward her. Was she so horrible? So undesirable? So unlovable? Had what she had done been so terrible?

Or was it that this other woman was simply so desirable that he could not resist? Perhaps it was because of Lilith Neeley's beauty that he had broken his wedding vows. Rachel wondered what she looked like. Was she a flame-haired beauty like Jessica? A blonde? What manner of face did she have? Was she tall, short, graceful, witty?

Rachel became possessed by a desire to see the woman. She wanted to look at her, talk to her. It would be highly improper, of course, but Rachel did not care. She wanted to meet her, had to meet her.

The problem was that she did not have the slightest idea how to accomplish that. She had no idea where the woman lived, and she felt sure that none of the women she knew would, either. And, frankly, even if they did know, Rachel did not think she could bring herself to talk to any of her friends about it, even Sylvia. And a man, of course, would be horrified by the very notion of her asking about the woman; he would guard the address from her as if it were the most precious secret in the world. Besides, it seemed even more embarrassing to ask a man about the matter.

However, when Perry Overhill came to call on Rachel the following afternoon, it occurred to her that of all the men she knew, he was the one from whom she would most likely be able to wheedle at least an address for Mrs. Neeley. And since he had been with her the other night when Leona broke the news to her, it did not seem quite as embarassing.

"Perry!" Rachel rose and crossed the room, holding out both her hands to him. "You are just the man I wanted to see."

Overhill looked somewhat taken aback. "I am glad. I think. I—you seem in good spirits."

"Only because of seeing you, I assure you. I have been thinking of what Leona told me."

"I was afraid of that. That is exactly why I came by." Perry's good-natured face drew together in a frown. "You must not fret over anything that vicious Lady Vesey said. She would always like to do you a bad turn if she can."

"Yes, I know. But I cannot put it aside that easily. I went to see Araminta yesterday."

"Michael's sister?" Perry looked astonished. "Good Gad, why?"

"Because she was the only one I could think of who might tell me the truth about Lilith Neeley."

Perry continued to stare at her. "And did she?"

Rachel nodded and looked away, feeling suddenly that she might cry if she continued to look into his eyes. "More or less." She paused, then said, "Perry, would you take me to see Mrs. Neeley?"

Her friend could not have looked more horrified if she had suggested that he rip off his clothes and run naked down the street. "Rachel! I can't—you—Michael would have my heart for breakfast if I did something like that. 'Twould be most improper, I assure you."

"I don't care about proper. I want to meet Lilith Neeley."

"You don't know what you're saying. She is, well, I mean—she runs a gaming establishment. That is where she lives—right next door to it. If Michael did not kill me, your brother would do it. Or Cleybourne. You wouldn't want to be the cause of my demise, would you?"

"No," Rachel agreed. "But none of them will know. I won't tell them, so long as you keep your lips sealed."

"I would, I assure you," Perry said with heartfelt enthusiasm. "But it would get out. If I took you there…" He shuddered at the thought.

"Mmm. Yes, I can see that that would be a problem," Rachel said reasonably. He had come around to what she preferred. "Why don't you just tell me her address, and then I shall go see her by myself? You won't be involved. Michael will never know."

"Rachel!" Perry began to splutter, even more agitated than before. "That would never do! A lady going to such a place by herself? Oh, no, no, you cannot do that. I could never—no, absolutely not."

He looked at her in a woebegone way. "Rachel, you are a goddess. The most beautiful woman in London, and you know that I will always be your most faithful admirer. But you cannot ask me to do that."

Rachel sighed, relenting. "All right. I will not ask you anymore."

"Thank you." He nodded, his face relaxing. Then, as he thought about her words, his brow knitted once again, and he leaned forward. "You will not ask someone else to help you, will you?"

"I cannot promise that."

Perry groaned. "Rachel...you will be the death of me. When did you become so—so—"

"Stubborn?" Rachel suggested, chuckling. "I think perhaps since I met Miranda."

"The American? I might have known."

"I think I have depended too much on others all my life. Always the dutiful daughter. The dutiful wife. Perhaps it is time I started taking control of my own destiny."

"This sounds very dangerous. Michael would be—"

Rachel raised an admonitory finger. "Ah, but Michael will not know. Will he, Perry? Because you are not going to tell him, are you?"

"Rachel..."

"Perry..."

"Oh, all right. I won't tell him. But, please, please, promise me you will not do anything that will get you into any trouble."

"I will be most circumspect."

After Perry left, Rachel settled into her chair with a sigh. She knew that her words had held more bravado than truth. She could not think of any gentleman who would be willing to take her to a gaming establishment, let alone give her the address and let her go there by herself. She wished that Miranda or Jessica were there to give her counsel. Miranda would simply have someone in her employ find out. Rachel wondered if one could hire a Bow Street Runner to discover such things; she thought that one probably needed a crime to hire a Runner.

It occurred to her that if she picked one of the younger men, new on the town and probably eager to appear more sophisticated and knowledgeable than he really was, he might be willing to take her there if she pretended that she wanted only to go to see the gambling den. She could wear a domino and mask, so no one would recognize her, and then she would be able to see this Mrs. Neeley, to observe the woman without her knowing. And then, if she still had the courage, she would go up to Mrs. Neeley and ask to talk to her alone. She would reveal who she was and…

Rachel wasn't sure what she would do. She just knew that she had to see her. Had to talk to her. She could not rest easy until she did.

Rachel was still pondering the problem the next afternoon, trying to think of the perfect young man to approach, when the butler stepped into the upstairs sitting room, where she was, and announced that she had a visitor.

"It is a Mr. Birkshaw, madam," Stinson said.

Rachel stared at the butler. His words were so unexpected that it took her a moment to understand what he had said. "Anthony Birkshaw?"

"Yes, my lady. I told him I would see if you were receiving, as I did not recognize the gentleman. He bade me tell you that it was an urgent matter."

What could Anthony be doing, calling on her after all these years? She had not seen him since the night of their elopement, something that had been made easier by the fact that he married an heiress less than a year after Rachel and Michael were married and moved to her home in York. They had lived there ever since, rarely coming to London. Rachel could not imagine why Anthony would be seeking her out now.

"Well, um, tell him I will be down in a moment."

"Very well, my lady." Stinson bowed out the door.

Rachel stood for a moment, her hands clasped to her stomach, wondering if she had done the right thing. She had promised Michael never to speak to Anthony, but it seemed so odd that he would come here after all this time, and she was curious about the reason. She was even more curious to see what he looked like after so many years and what she would feel when she saw him.

She would go down and explain to him that he must not call on her again. That seemed only polite and, while it might be breaking the letter of the vow she had made Michael, it would not violate the spirit of it. *And, of course, Michael had apparently not had any compunctions over breaking* his *marital vows!* It seemed decidedly unfair of him to expect her never to even see or speak to Anthony again, while he conducted a years-long affair with another woman.

Rachel glanced at her image in the mirror, smoothing back her hair and pinching a little color into her cheeks. She hated to think that Anthony would look at her and think how old she had grown. It was vanity, she knew, but she could not help it. She started down the stairs, her heart picking up its beat. She found when she tried to summon up a picture of his face that she could not remember him clearly.

She remembered how at first her heart had felt as if it would break and she had cried herself to sleep every night. She could not remember exactly when the pain had begun to ease or when it had finally slipped away, leaving behind only the bitter memory of her impetuous mistake and the ruination of her marriage.

Anthony was waiting in the formal drawing room, standing before the mantel, his back turned to her. She paused for a moment in the doorway, looking at him. He was dressed in stark black, his coat well cut and of an expensive material. He was shorter and stockier than she remembered; she supposed that she had grown used to Michael's long, lanky frame. His hair was dark and thick, though, as she remembered, curling over his collar.

"Mr. Birkshaw?" Rachel stepped into the room, leaving the door open. She wanted to make sure that there could be no hint of impropriety in their meeting.

He turned at her words. "Hello, Rachel—Lady Westhampton, I should say."

Rachel simply nodded, carefully not offering him the use of her given name. She gestured toward the sofa. "Won't you sit down?"

She crossed to a chair that stood facing the sofa, a few feet away from it, and sat down. For a long moment they looked at each other. He looked much the same, she thought. Perhaps he had filled out a little, but the soulful dark eyes and dimpled chin, the dark hair casually falling across his forehead—all these were the same. Rachel noticed with some surprise that none of these things affected her at all anymore. He was a handsome man; she could see that. But her heart made no leap within her chest, nor did it ache with remembered love. What she felt when she looked at him, she realized, was almost nothing at all except a sense of awkwardness. How odd, she thought, that she could have loved him so and yet now feel nothing but a faint embarrassment.

He looked away from her, scowling down at the floor for a moment, then said, "I am sure you are wondering why I am here."

"I was a trifle surprised," Rachel admitted. He looked troubled, she thought.

"I am somewhat surprised, too. It is just— Well, I could think of nowhere else to turn."

"I am afraid I don't understand."

"I—well, I assume you know that I married several years ago."

"Yes."

"I have not been in Society much since then. Doreen preferred York. London was too large and noisy for her, and she was not well accepted by the ladies of the *Ton*. Her family was of the merchant class, you see. I have grown rather out of touch." He paused, looking down at the floor, then drew a deep breath and continued, "Doreen passed away a few months ago."

"Oh! I am so sorry," Rachel said sincerely, her sympathetic heart touched by the notion of his sorrow. She understood now the reason for the troubled look on his face.

"Thank you."

"I know it must seem terribly hard now," she went on, remembering Richard's grief after Caroline's death. "But it will get better someday. It will no longer hurt so much."

He looked up at her, a faint surprise in his face. "Oh. No. That is not why I am here. Ours was a marriage of convenience. We both entered into it with our eyes open. We had grown fond enough of one another over the years, and I was sorry that she died, but I was not grief-stricken."

"Oh. I see." Rachel was rather taken aback at his cool words. Hers was a marriage of convenience, too, she supposed, but somehow she did not think that she would be so calm and dispassionate about it if

Michael died. Even the thought of his death made her feel a trifle lost. And why was Anthony here? Did he think to take up with her again now that his wife had died? Indignation rose in her at the idea.

"The reason I am here—I am troubled because...well, this will no doubt sound very dramatic, but...I have come to believe that Doreen was murdered."

"What!"

He nodded. "She had a digestive complaint, you see, for several weeks. No one thought anything about it. I wasn't even there. I had gone to visit my aunt. When I came back, she was still ill. The doctor was obviously growing worried. He wasn't sure what was the matter with her. She got worse, and then, after a few weeks, she died. None of us thought it was anything other than illness. But now—" Anthony clasped and unclasped his hands in an agitated fashion. "Now I think that she may have been murdered."

"But that's awful!" Rachel exclaimed, horrified.

"I know. I'm at my wit's end." He stood up as if he could no longer sit still and began to pace across the room.

Rachel watched him for a moment, then said tentatively, "I don't quite understand. Why—well, why did you come to me with this? I am very sorry, truly, but wouldn't it be best to take this matter to the Bow Street Runners?"

"It's the scandal, you see. She would have hated

it, and, well, I do not wish it, either. If it could just be kept quiet…''

Rachel frowned, still at sea.

''I wanted to ask you to ask Lord Westhampton to help me.''

''Michael!'' Rachel stared. ''But wh—''

''I know I have no right to ask him,'' Anthony went on hastily. ''It would be exactly what I deserve if he told me to sink or swim on my own. But I thought, if you asked him, he might agree. It's been several years now. Lord Arbuthnot—it was he who told me about Michael's investigations—holds him in the highest regard. And I dare swear a man of less even temperament would have dealt with my grievous—''

''Hush a moment!'' Rachel snapped, moving away from Anthony. ''Let me think.''

Michael's investigations! She had no idea what Anthony was talking about, but she had the sudden, sure feeling that it tied in with what the highwayman had been getting at. She could find out more from Anthony, but she would have to approach it carefully. If he realized she knew nothing, he would probably fall silent, moving automatically into that male conspiracy of keeping women ignorant.

''I am surprised at Lord Arbuthnot,'' Rachel said, turning to face him. ''What Michael does is not supposed to be common knowledge. What did he tell you?''

''Oh. I—I did not realize it was secret. Well, yes, of course, I can see how it would be helpful if few people knew. Let me think…it was about a year ago. I was in London and happened to run into Arbuthnot. I was friends with his son Henry in school. We talked a bit and, I don't remember exactly how, but we got to talking about Lady Godfrey's jewels being stolen. Anyway, he said that he had heard that Lord Westhampton had helped the Bow Street Runner, that he had apparently done it for years. I—it was unusual, so I remembered it. I am sure Arbuthnot meant no harm."

"No. Of course not." Rachel felt dazed. The idea made sense—in an absurd sort of way. If Michael was somehow involved in a Bow Street Runner's investigations, then the highwayman's warning was not so strange. Michael had probably met him in an investigation. Hadn't the man said something about his helping Michael from time to time? Whatever Michael was working on, that must be what would put him in danger. On the other hand, it seemed quite mad to think that Michael would be involved with the Bow Street Runners at all. Why would he have started helping them, and what did he do? Most of all, why had he never told her anything about all this?

But she knew the answer to that. It was because she did not really know Michael at all. They were man and wife, but Anthony clearly knew more about Michael's life than she did. She had thought that even though they did not live as most married couples did, Michael at least liked her, trusted her. She had thought she knew what he did at Westhampton;

clearly she did not. Just as clearly, Michael did not trust her enough to share this knowledge with her.

"Then will you ask him to help me?" Anthony said after a few moments of silence. "I know it is a great deal to ask of him, but I don't know where else to turn."

"Yes. I will tell him what you have told me and see if he will help you. But he is at Westhampton now. I will have to write to him, and it will be some time before I know." She paused, then added with some bitterness, "And I do not know that my asking will have any effect on him. We are not very close, I'm afraid."

"I am sorry. I am to blame for that."

"No. I am. I was foolish." Rachel came closer to him, her eyes intent on his. "But I have one thing I would ask from you in return for my doing you this favor."

"Yes, of course. Anything."

"I want the address of Mrs. Lilith Neeley."

"Who?" His face went rapidly from puzzlement to understanding to shock. "The woman who runs the gaming establishment?"

"Yes. I want the address of her gambling den. Someone told me that she lives there."

Anthony continued to stare at her. "But why? What could you possibly want with her?"

"It is for a friend," Rachel lied quickly. "Her brother is a notorious gamester, and he is in danger of losing their fortune. She thinks that if she talks to her, she could get her to refuse him admittance."

Anthony shrugged. "Perhaps. But she cannot go there. No lady could go to a place like that."

"She is determined, and I promised that I would help her."

"You are not suggesting that you go there with her!"

"No, of course not. She will take a footman with her, I imagine. And she will go disguised. Please, Anthony, you said you would help me in return."

"Yes, of course I will. It is just—" he sighed "—it is not the best part of town, but I suppose if she goes there during the day, it would be all right." He gave her the address, still looking doubtful.

"Thank you. I will write to Michael this afternoon." She began to walk toward the door, eager now to get rid of him.

As soon as he was gone, she hurried back upstairs to her bedroom. There she dressed quickly and hurried downstairs, not giving herself time to think about what she was about to do. She had to do this, and she refused to admit fear or hesitation into her mind. Whatever consequences came, she would deal with them later. Right now she was determined to act.

She wore a plain dark dress and no jewelry. She did not want to give the impression that she was flaunting her position in Mrs. Neeley's face. It would be difficult enough to get her to talk to her as it was. Over her dress, she put on a long cloak with a hood. It was a trifle warm for the day, but she knew that both Anthony and Perry were right in warning of the scandal if she were seen entering or leaving a gambling den—especially one run by the mistress of her husband.

The footman offered to ring for her carriage to be called up, but she declined, saying with what she hoped was a look of calm that she preferred to walk to the lending library. He would find it odd, perhaps, that she took no maid with her, but Rachel was counting on his not daring to question her.

She slipped out the front door and started along the sidewalk in the direction of the lending library in case the footman or anyone else might be watching. Their street was a wide thoroughfare, with ample traffic, and Rachel felt sure that she would be able to hail a hansom cab once she got out of sight of the house.

In the next block she hailed a hansom and gave the driver Mrs. Neeley's address. He looked down doubtfully at her, and she repeated it firmly, then climbed in and closed the door, leaving him with little option but to go there.

She sat tensely inside the carriage, her fists clenched in her lap, going over and over in her head what she should say and how she should say it. When the cab rolled to a stop, she pulled the hood of her cloak up around her face and alighted cautiously. Rachel glanced up and down the street, having to turn her whole head because of the covering of the hood. It was a narrower street than where she lived, with smaller houses and buildings, and there was, she noted, a tavern at the end of the block. Still, no one walking along the street looked actively dangerous.

After paying the hansom driver, she turned to the house where he had stopped and climbed the stairs. It was a narrow stone house, with freshly painted shutters, clean windows and a gleaming brass door knocker. Not an elegant house, but one on which care was expended.

She knocked on the door, and it was opened by a male servant so tall and with such broad shoulders that he almost filled the doorway. His face was marred by a broken nose and small scars near his mouth and one eye, and one ear looked, strangely, as if a small piece of it was missing. Rachel suspected that he had been chosen more for his abilities in a fight than for any serving skills he might possess.

He leaned down, peering into her face beneath her hood. "Can I help ye, miss?" he asked, looking doubtful.

"I would like to speak to Mrs. Neeley, thank you. Mrs. Lilith Neeley."

He continued to look doubtful but backed up a step, allowing her to enter. He gestured toward a bench in the hall, saying, "Sit here. I'll ask her."

Rachel complied as he closed the front door and marched up the stairs. She glanced into the rooms on either side of the hall. It did not, she thought with some disappointment, look like a den of iniquity. She had imagined something altogether more ornate and colorful, dimly lit, perhaps.

After a few minutes the man came back down the stairs, followed by a slender, attractive blond woman. "I am Mrs. Neeley," she said in a quiet voice, with only a hint of an accent—Northumberland, perhaps, or some other northern county, Rachel thought. "May I help you?"

"I hope so." Rachel reached up and pushed back her hood. "I am Rachel Trent." She purposely did not use her title, hoping again not to appear snobbish, thinking that if the woman did not recognize the name, she could add "Lady Westhampton."

But Mrs. Neeley obviously recognized the name, for her eyes widened. "Oh. My lady—I—"

"I came to talk to you about my husband," Rachel went on.

"Excuse me?" Mrs. Neeley cast a nervous look around her, perhaps seeking support, but the large man had walked on down the hall into some back region of the house. "I am afraid I cannot help you."

"I think you can," Rachel countered, clasping her hands together to hide their trembling. Now that she was standing here, looking at this woman, who had none of the crassness or vulgarity that she had expected from a mistress and owner of a gambling den, Rachel was at something of a loss for words. "Please do not lie to me. I was told about you by several people. It seems as though everyone knows about you but me. Westhampton hid it very well from me. It seems I know nothing at all about my husband." Rachel could not keep the bitterness from her voice. "But I am aware now that you have been Michael's mistress for some years."

The other woman gaped at her, her astonishment

seeming so real that Rachel almost wondered if she had somehow gotten it all wrong.

"Lady Westhampton! No! Oh, my—this is awful!" Mrs. Neely reached out toward Rachel as if to take her hands, then pulled her own back hastily. "I'm sorry. Yes, I do know your husband. Or, at least, I know who he is. But I am not his mistress. I have never been. It distresses me terribly that you should think so. Oh, dear... There is someone else— I mean, I have a... Please, you must believe me. I am not Lord Westhampton's mistress. He does not come here at all. It is something else altogether."

Strangely enough, Rachel found herself believing the woman. Mrs. Neeley looked so genuinely upset and concerned, stumbling over her words, that Rachel felt herself relaxing a little. Had everyone gotten it all wrong somehow? Perhaps there was some rational explanation after all.

"Oh," Rachel said. "Did I—I'm sorry, but—people told me that he had been seen coming in and out of here. And Araminta—his sister—knew about it."

"She did not say that, surely! She couldn't have said that he and I—that we—"

At that moment there was the sound of footsteps on the stairs. Mrs. Neeley let out a small, choked cry and swung around, looking up the stairs. Rachel's eyes followed hers.

Michael was walking down the stairs, buttoning the cuff of one sleeve. He wore no jacket, and his waistcoat hung open down the front. "Lilith, do you know where—"

He stopped, seeing for the first time the two women standing to the side of the stairs, and whatever he had been about to say died in his throat.

"Michael."

10

Rachel's voice sounded small and tinny to her own ears. She felt suddenly as if she could not breathe. *So it was all true, then.... Michael had not even gone home to Westhampton as he had told her he was. Instead he had stayed right here in London with his mistress.* She wondered how many times before that had happened, how often, when she thought he was at home indulging in his solitary, scholarly pursuits, he had actually been in London...but not with her. "How easily you have fooled me. And how often." Tears choked her voice, and she stopped speaking, swallowing to force the sobs back down her throat. She cast a fulminating glance at Mrs. Neeley. "You are an excellent actress, madam."

"No!" Lilith Neeley cried. "No! I didn't deceive you. I—that is—that is not Lord Westhampton."

"What?" Rachel's gaze swung back to the man on the stairs. The man did look a little different from Michael. His hair was darker, more brown than blond, and he needed a shave. His clothes were the rough full-sleeved shirt and loose trousers of a working man, and his boots were scuffed and cheap, not polished to a mirrorlike gleam.

Rachel wavered. Garson would never have let Michael out of the house looking like this. "But I— no." Her face and voice hardened. "Do you take me for a fool, that I do not even know my own husband? Of course it is Michael."

"He looks like him, 'tis true," Lilith said, her voice slipping in her distress into a thicker accent. "But that is because he is Lord Westhampton's brother."

Rachel raised a single eyebrow. "Michael has no brother."

"Not a legitimate one." Mrs. Neeley gazed at her unflinchingly for a long moment.

"What? Oh!" Rachel looked back up at the man on the stairs. There were differences between Michael and this man—the hair color, this man's rather disheveled look and rough clothes. And it would be just like Michael's father to have had an illegitimate child; the man had been a well-known lecher. "I— but you look so much like him!"

"I'm not the only one," the man replied gruffly.

His voice, too, was slightly different, Rachel thought, a little lower and more gravelly, with an accent similar to Mrs. Neeley's.

Relief swept over Rachel so swiftly and powerfully that she went a trifle weak in the knees. This man who was so obviously at home in Mrs. Neeley's house was not Michael at all, but an illegitimate brother who looked enough like him to be his twin.

"He is my brother," Mrs. Neeley explained.

"Oh! Oh, I see." Rachel could not keep from smiling. "Then—are you saying that you—"

"Lord Westhampton is my brother," Lilith Neeley confirmed, nodding. "They are both my brothers."

There was a similarity of coloring to Michael in Mrs. Neeley, for her blond hair was much the same color as Michael's, and her eyes, also gray, had the same shape as Michael's, though she obviously darkened her light eyelashes.

Everything was falling into place now—no wonder people had thought that Michael had a relationship with this woman. This man who looked so much like Michael had been seen coming and going from this house, and people had assumed it was Michael. Or perhaps Michael had even come here to see his siblings.

"But why has he never told me about you?" Rachel asked. "Why has he kept it hidden?"

The man snorted. "Hardly somethin' you'd be tellin' the missus, is it? Particularly a tony lady like yourself."

Rachel frowned at his sneering tone. She was not quite sure whether he disliked Michael, her, or the world in general.

Lilith Neeley quickly put in, "His lordship doesn't know about us, that is why."

There was a noise from the man on the stairs,

something like a grunt, and Rachel glanced up at him before turning back to Mrs. Neeley.

"I see. I—please accept my apology for barging in on you this way and peppering you with questions. I can see now that I had no right."

Mrs. Neeley looked at her, surprised. "It is quite all right, my lady. Pray don't worry about it.

"I will tell my husband about you," Rachel went on. "You don't know him. Lord Westhampton is a very fair and good man. I am sure that he would wish to meet you."

"Is he now?" Mrs. Neeley cast a look back at the man on the stairs, then turned back to Rachel. "Still, my lady, I do not think that there are many husbands who would wish to hear that their wives had come to visit a gaming establishment or spoken to his relatives that were born on the wrong side of the blanket."

"That's right," her brother said, coming down a few steps. "I wouldn't advise telling him that you was here, talking to the likes of us."

"That is because you don't know Michael." In truth, she suspected that Michael would not be pleased to hear about her going unattended in a hansom to the home of a woman whom she thought to be his mistress. Well, she decided, she would think about how to tell him later. Right now she felt too good to worry about such things. And she also was not about to let this sullen stranger denigrate Michael.

"Thank you for seeing me, Mrs. Neeley," she said, holding her hand out to the other woman. "You have been very kind. I should take my leave of you now." She turned toward the man, still several steps above her and gave him a short nod. "And you, Mr.—"

"Hobson," he said. "James Hobson."

"Good day, Mr. Hobson. I hope that you will meet Lord Westhampton someday so that you can see how wrong you are about him."

His only answer was a shrug and a surly look. Rachel turned and walked to the front door.

"Wait." Hobson came quickly down the last few steps. "You can't just walk out there. You won't be finding many hansoms rolling down this street lookin' for fares, at least not until later, when the gentlemen are all leaving, drunk."

"I am sure I will find one soon enough."

"Oh, no, my lady!" Mrs. Neeley exclaimed. "He is right. It would never do. You shouldn't be walking here unescorted."

"I'll see her home," Hobson said gruffly, snatching a jacket and cloth cap from the hat tree by the door. "Come on, then."

"It is quite all right," Rachel assured him, trying for a tone of hauteur. "You need not put yourself to the bother, Mr. Hobson."

"I do if I'm to keep Lilith from burning my ears," he growled, taking her arm firmly in his grasp and steering her through the front door.

"Really, Mr. Hobson, there is no need to push me," Rachel snapped, jerking her arm from his.

"Excuse me," he said, doffing his cap to her. "'Fraid I wasn't brought up right."

"I suspect that any talk of manners would have fallen on deaf ears with you," Rachel shot back tartly, turning and starting up the street.

It was late afternoon by now, and the setting sun was blocked by buildings, so that the street was already growing dusky. Though she would not have admitted it to this man, Rachel was frankly rather glad to have someone accompanying her. She had no idea where her home lay from here or what street she should take to find an available hansom cab. Nor did she know what way she might turn that would lead her into another, more unsavory area.

"Ooh, you're a feisty one, aren't you?" Hobson said in a conversational manner as he slouched along beside her, his hands thrust into his pockets.

"Because I answered you in kind? You are a very unfriendly man, you know." Rachel looked over at him.

He was bulkier and a trifle shorter than Michael, she thought, though with the way he carried himself, it was difficult to tell his true height. It was amazing how much he resembled Michael, though, even with the differences she could pick out. He was more rough and ready, of course, the kind of man who could doubtless take care of himself in a fight. It occurred to her that he might be the reason for the strange things that Anthony had said about Michael.

"Do you pretend to be Westhampton sometimes?" she asked.

He looked at her a little warily. "I have been mistaken for him now and again. Why do you ask?"

Rachel did not answer but instead asked another question. "Do you work with the Bow Street Runners?" she asked.

Hobson whipped his head around to stare at her. "What? How did you— What are you talking about?"

"How did I know about that?" she asked a little smugly, completing his half-asked question. "You would be surprised at what I know."

"I'm beginning to realize that." He scowled at her.

They had reached a cross street, a more major thoroughfare, and he raised his hand for a cab, and when it stopped, opened the door for her and helped her in. He climbed in after her.

"You need not see me home, Mr. Hobson," Rachel said coolly. "I will be quite all right now that you have found me a vehicle."

"That may be, but I have a few questions for you."

Rachel looked at him. It was dim inside the cab, but she could see the hard glitter of his eyes, silver more than Michael's calm gray. She could very well see this man working with Bow Street; she could just as easily see him working on the opposite side.

"I'm not sure I feel like answering your questions right now," Rachel retorted.

"Oh, you'll answer them." His mouth was set

grimly. "You are dealing with me now, not your lap dog of a husband."

"How dare you speak of Michael that way?" Rachel fired back. "My husband is worth ten of you!"

That statement seemed to afford him great amusement. "Ah, yes, it is clear that you think him worth a great deal. No doubt that is why you shun his company."

"I do not shun his company! Michael enjoys the country and—and rural pursuits."

"While you pursue what in the city?" He raised one eyebrow in a lazy question.

Rachel glared at him. "I am not sure what you are implying, but I find you most impertinent."

"No doubt you will find me more so. I want to know why you asked me if I sometimes work with the Bow Street Runners. Did someone tell you Westhampton did?"

Rachel stared back at him defiantly for a long moment, but then she shrugged and nodded. "Yes. A— a friend of mine. He said that Lord Arbuthnot had told him that Michael had helped Bow Street with their investigations."

"Arbuthnot! How the devil would he know about it?"

"I don't know. Anthony just said that Arbuthnot told him something about someone's jewels being recovered. Godfrey, did he say?"

Beside her, Hobson went very still. "Who said this about Arbuthnot?"

"My friend. The man who came to ask me for help."

"What is his name?" His voice was clipped and hard as stone, his eyes glittering coldly. "Anthony who?"

Rachel raised her brows at his tone. "Birkshaw, but I hardly see that that is any of your business."

"I don't know," he said roughly. "Maybe he'd like to hire me sometime, him or his friends. I'm always interested in more business from the toffs."

"Perhaps." Rachel had no intention of revealing anything about this man to Anthony; she was not about to reveal Michael's family secrets to anyone. She quickly steered the conversation away, saying, "I didn't see how it could be Michael he was talking about. But he seemed so certain of it...." Rachel remembered the anxiety that had gripped her when she realized that she knew even less about her husband than she had thought. It was an enormous relief, she realized now, to have learned that none of those things were true, after all.

"No. It could hardly have been Westhampton. He is much too stodgy and dull to do anything like that."

"He is not stodgy and dull!" Rachel protested. "He is a very intelligent and interesting man."

"Oh, yes, I can tell that you are simply fascinated by him," Hobson prodded in a gravelly voice, his lips curving up on one side into an irritating smirk. "So fascinated that you cannot bear to live in the same house with him."

"That is not true! I told you, he prefers the country, and I—"

"You prefer the city," he finished for her. "Doubtless because your 'friend' is here."

Rachel scowled at him. She did not like the way he looked at her; it was far too bold, not as a gentleman would look at her at all. And the mocking way he spoke to her was highly annoying, as if he knew some wicked secret about her.

"Why do you say it that way? What do you mean? It is rude. You are rude."

"Aye, so I've been told. What should I have said instead of 'friend'? Would you like it better if I called him your lover?"

Rachel gasped, shocked by his words. "What! How dare you say something like that?"

"I'm a man for plain-speakin' myself. It's hardly a surprise—of course you would take a lover, as your husband clearly doesn't suit you. Poor sniveling bastard, he's the perfect cuckold—"

He broke off in surprise as Rachel's hand lashed out and slapped him hard against the cheek. The slap surprised her almost as much as it did him, and for a long moment they stared at each other. His eyes were bright and glittering, even in the dim light, his mouth drawn into a tight line.

Slowly, not taking his eyes from her, he stretched out his hand and wrapped it around her wrist. Rachel's eyes widened, and just as she opened her mouth to protest his further impertinence, he jerked her across the seat so that she slammed into his side.

She let out a shocked breath as his arms went tight around her. He bent and seized her mouth in a long, bruising kiss.

Rachel's hands went instinctively up to his chest, but she did not push him away. She could not. She felt as if all her bones had suddenly turned into jelly. Heat shimmered through her, and a yearning like nothing she had ever felt before opened like a flower inside her. She shivered, her hands curling into themselves, lying limply against his chest. For a long moment she was able to do nothing, say nothing, merely drink in his kiss like nectar.

His lips dug into hers, and a small moan escaped him. Then, as if the sound had snapped him back into awareness, he stopped as abruptly as he had begun. He raised his head and stared down into her face, his eyes wide and intense, dark with hunger. Moving a little jerkily, his arms slid away from her, and he moved back until he came up against the side of the carriage. Their eyes were still locked on each other. Rachel could not look away. She was lucky to be able to breathe, she thought, given how scattered and strange she felt.

She raised a shaky hand to her mouth, the realization of what she had done sinking in on her. She had kissed this man! This rude, uncouth, bizarre twin of her husband. And she had felt a kind of glorious, intense pleasure she had never before experienced.

Rachel let out a choked cry and whirled away. Sticking her head out the window, she cried to the driver to stop. Behind her, she heard James say, ''No! Wait—''

He reached for her, but she jerked away, flinging open the door of the hansom. The driver was pulling to a halt as she had directed him, and she stepped out before he was even quite stopped, evading Hobson's hand again.

She heard him curse and lurch toward the door, but she did not glance back at him, just clung to the bar on the carriage beside the door as she scrambled down the step and onto the ground. She stumbled slightly, but caught herself. She hurried across the street to the sidewalk, glancing around her. She saw that she was only a few blocks from her house, back once more on familiar ground, and she started up the street, not turning to look back at the hansom.

Behind her, the man watched Rachel hustle across the street and up the sidewalk, his hand grasping the side of the door, though whether to keep himself inside or propel his body out of the vehicle after her, he wasn't quite sure. Taut and teeming with hot emotions, he watched her walk away.

Leaning out the door, he growled at the driver, ''Follow her 'til she gets inside, then take me back.''

He pulled back inside, closing the door, and watched Rachel's retreating figure as the cab crept slowly down the street after her. When she reached her house and marched inside, he slumped back against the seat and stared moodily into the darkness all the way back to his sister's house.

When he reached Lilith's, there were already a few

gamblers hanging out in front of the gaming house next door, even though it would be another fifteen minutes before it opened for business. He quickly turned and slipped down the narrow walkway between the two buildings and let himself in through the rear door. Running up the stairs, he went straight to Lilith's room and knocked.

He opened it at the first sound of her voice and strode inside. Lilith was sitting in front of her vanity, dressed now in the evening gown she would wear tonight at her card games, and her maid was putting the finishing touches on her upswept hairdo.

"Bloody hell, Lilith!" he growled without preamble, marching over to where she sat. "What the devil did you say all that for? Now I'm in a fine mess."

"She thought I was your mistress!" Lilith shot back. "I swore to her that it was a lie someone had told her, and I almost had her convinced that you never came here when all of a sudden you come trotting down the stairs, looking as if you lived here. What was I supposed to do?"

"Well, you didn't have to tell her I was someone else," Michael retorted grumpily. "Why not tell her the truth? Why not just say that you are my half sister instead of that idiotic story that I am my own illegitimate brother!"

"I don't know. Why haven't you ever told her that?" Lilith stood up and faced him, planting her fists on her hips pugnaciously. "Obviously, it was something you wanted concealed. And you looked so different—it was the first thing that popped into my head. I had just been denying vigorously that you ever came here. It seemed absurd to say then, 'Oh, yes, well, here he is now, how odd.'"

She drew a breath and went on. "Besides, it seems to me that your wife might not take it too well that you have known about me for years yet never told her that you had a sister born on the wrong side of the blanket. Women are peculiar that way. Especially when you visit this sister often and even stay with her instead of at your own home when you are in London, a fact, I might add, which has clearly been noticed if people are gossiping that I am your mistress! And how was I to explain why you were here and why you look as you do? It would have all come out about your investigations, and I cannot imagine any wife not being furious that you have kept an entire life secret from her!"

Michael grimaced. "Well, when you say it like that…"

"How else is there to say it?" Lilith pressed him. "It is what you have done." She sighed and went over to him and took his arm. "I understand why you might not want to tell her about me. Many ladies would be horrified to know that you actually visit your illegitimate sister. Or that you went to her and helped her as soon as you found out she existed." She smiled, taking away much of the sting from her earlier words. "You are the kindest and most generous of men, and I love you dearly for what you have done for me. But not all wives would appreciate your admitting a connection to a woman who owns a gaming establishment and is the mistress of a married gentleman."

"I did not hide your existence from her because I was ashamed of you!" Michael exclaimed, looking horrified. "I hope you do not think—"

"I think nothing bad of you, and you know it. But I am your sister, not your wife. No wife wants her husband to be the subject of gossip. A fine lady does not wish to be connected to a woman such as me."

"Rachel is a good woman. She would not chide me for seeing you."

"Then why did you not tell her about me?" Lilith asked softly, her clear gaze fixed on his face. "Why did you never tell her about your investigations? You have kept many things secret from her."

"God, don't you think I wish now that I had told her!" Michael burst out, pulling away from her and beginning to pace agitatedly. "You have no idea how much I regret not saying anything to her. It becomes a worse tangle daily. I never set out to deceive Rachel. Truly I didn't. But that is not something you reveal to someone you barely know. I was ashamed—not of you, never of you. It was my father I was ashamed of, his wantonness, his careless, selfish behavior—never acknowledging you, letting you live in poverty. He was a blackguard, and how can you admit that to the woman you want to marry? And afterward…well, we have not been close. It never seemed appropriate to bring it up. And then, when I started helping Bow Street, it was so handy to be able to come here when I was adopting a disguise. I didn't want the servants seeing me slipping in and out of the house in all manner of clothes. And I wanted to protect her..." He sighed. "I wanted to tell Rachel about what I do. About you. But after I had not done so for so long, I was afraid of what she would think. I have been a fool. I can see that now."

"You are not a fool," Lilith reassured him. "You are a wonderful man, and she must know that."

"As you said, my wife would see me differently," Michael said with a wry smile. "I don't think she would characterize me as 'wonderful.'"

"Then she is blind," Lilth retorted stoutly. Turning, she went back to her vanity table and sat down to finish her toilette.

Michael followed Lilith and sat down in a chair near her vanity table. "And now she thinks I am two different men. Good Gad, what a coil! I thought for sure she would recognize me when we were sitting in the hansom. She wasn't two feet from me."

Lilith shrugged. "People see what they are told they see. If I dressed up as a man, you would believe I was a man—a small man, grant you, but still a man—because you assume that what you see is true, not a trick. I told her you were someone else, a person who could resemble you greatly, and she accepted it. She saw that you looked different from the person she is used to seeing—she isn't going to think, well, Michael could have put walnut oil in his hair to darken it and donned rough clothes and adopted an accent, or any of the other things you do to disguise yourself for an investigation. She will just think that you are someone else who looks very much like you.''

''I suppose.''

''Besides, you won't ever see her again as James Hobson. There won't be any need for you to keep up the disguise. The next time you see her, you will be dressed as you, speaking as you, your hair lightened again, and she will see all those differences between you and him. She will probably wonder why she ever thought you looked so much like him.''

Michael gave her a faint smile. ''She already told me that Michael is twice the man I am.''

Lilith chuckled. ''You see?''

He nodded. ''Yes, but what about when she tells me, the real me, about you and this James Hobson chap and wants us all to meet?''

''I will say that James Hobson has left the country. It isn't as if you and she will be spending time with us.''

''I guess you are right.''

''Of course I am. It will work out. I promise.''

Michael sighed. What Lilith did not know, of course, and what he would not tell her, was that ''James Hobson'' had just kissed Michael's wife—kissed her thoroughly and pleasurably, the kind of kiss it warmed a man's blood just to think about. It was the way he had dreamed for years of kissing Rachel, the way he had kissed her that night before they were married—and frightened her into running away from him. Just thinking about the kiss made his blood run hot and fast in his veins again, just as it had when it happened. He wanted to taste her again, ached to feel her warm and pliant in his arms.

And Rachel had responded. Unlike that time years ago, she had melted against him, her mouth opening to him, her body trembling with a passion that was unmistakable.

The problem was that she had not been kissing *him.* She had been kissing James Hobson, another chap entirely. The scruffy, surly, illegitimate brother of her husband. The passion he had felt in her had not been for him at all. And no matter how much he had enjoyed the kiss, it made him burn just as much with jealousy.

But as awful and ironic as that was, it was not the worst that had happened this evening. He had found out that Rachel had been seeing Anthony Birkshaw. She had promised him when they married that she would never see the man again, never speak to him, and Michael had believed her. He had trusted in her honor, her integrity; he had believed that she was a woman who would keep her word.

When had she started seeing the man again? What did it mean? Had she played him for a fool all these years? Had she been secretly meeting with Birkshaw since the very beginning?

Jealousy tore through him, almost blinding him to all else. It had been that fierce, furious jealousy that had made him taunt her, had made him jerk her to him and kiss her. Reason might tell him that he did not know all the facts, that the very casual way in which she spoke of the man would indicate that she had nothing to hide. But then, he reminded himself, she had not realized she was telling secrets to her husband. She had thought him only a bastard brother whom Michael did not even know; there would have been little chance, in her estimation, of anything she told James Hobson finding its way back to Lord Westhampton.

He felt his sister's gaze on him, and he knew that she was doubtless wondering why he had sunk into such a brown study. He glanced up and gave her what he hoped was a reassuring smile, but he could see from the worried crease between her eyes that she was not convinced.

At that moment he was saved by a tap on the door, followed immediately by its opening. A man entered. He was well dressed in a black evening suit and snow-white shirt and carefully arranged cravat. He was a year or two older than Michael, dark of hair and eyes, with a short, well-muscled build and a face that was more craggy than handsome. He was not given to smiling a great deal, but when he did, his smile lit up his face, charming anyone around him.

"Hallo, Michael," he said cheerfully, advancing toward them.

"Robert." Michael stood up to shake the other man's hand.

His name was Sir Robert Blount, and he had been Michael's friend for many years. It was he who had first introduced Michael to the intrigue and adventure of countering Bonaparte's espionage during the war, and he who later offered him his first case helping the Bow Street Runners. He was also the man who had first revealed to Michael that he had a half sister, born on the wrong side of the blanket.

He crossed over to Lilith after he shook Michael's hand and bent to kiss her on the cheek. His kiss was perfectly chaste and correct, but there was in his eyes a glow that said he was far more to Lilith Neeley than the friend of her brother.

He was, in fact, the married gentleman to whom Lilith had referred earlier, the man who was her lover and had been for over ten years now. As her brother, Michael could not help but have some reservations over Lilith's love affair with a man who could not marry her. However, since Sir Robert had been her lover before Michael even knew of Lilith's existence, and since she was a grown woman who had been making her way in the world on her own for some years now, he had realized that he had little to say in the matter. As long as he expected to remain on friendly terms with either of them, he knew that he could not lecture them on the subject. Besides, he was well aware that he had little basis on which to be giving anyone advice in the area of love.

He was aware, too, of Sir Robert's marital circumstances, and of the deep and obvious love he held for Lilith. This was no casual affair, but a long-standing commitment which was known by many of the male members of the *Ton*. Sir Robert, though from a good family, had not been a wealthy man. He had through family connections found a good position in the gov-

ernment and had served it with skill and dedication
for several years. The death of an aunt several years
earlier had resulted in a moderate inheritance, which
he had multiplied many times over with skillful in-
vestments. He had been able to leave the government
and live on his fortune three years earlier, and he had
also lent Lilith the funds to buy her gaming establishment. He was prone, also, to lend his presence to
the place on a regular basis, thus solidifying its reputation as a reliable place to gamble.

He was, in many ways, the man closest to Michael.
Yet Michael also knew that there were depths to the
man that he would never know. Despite his quiet
demeanor, Sir Robert Blount was not a man whom
anyone would be advised to cross.

"Going out on one of your jaunts tonight, Michael?" he asked now, pulling up a straight-backed
chair and sitting down beside him. He cast a significant look at his friend's attire.

"I was planning to," Michael admitted. "Now I
am not so sure. Robert...what do you know about a
chap named Birkshaw? Anthony Birkshaw. Have you
ever heard of him?"

Robert frowned, thinking. "In what context? My
work? Gambling?"

"In any context. He is a member of the *Ton*. Married an heiress a few years ago. Daughter of a merchant in York."

Robert shrugged, shaking his head. "Can't say that
the name rings any bells with me. Lil?"

Lilith shook her head. "No. I don't know him. Is it he whom you are chasing?"

"No. It is another matter entirely. Well, at least I know that he is not likely an inveterate gambler if you are not familiar with his name."

Michael chatted with the other two for a few more minutes, until Lilith had to go downstairs to see to her business. Michael then went to his room and shaved and changed into more aristocratic attire. If he wanted to find out social news, he had decided, he had to go to someone who knew such things. So when he was dressed, he took a hansom to the home of his friend, Perry Overhill.

Overhill was in his study, enjoying a glass of wine before venturing out for the evening. He stood up as Michael entered, surprise spreading over his face. "Michael. I didn't expect to see you here. I thought you had gone directly back to Westhampton." He strode forward with a smile to greet his friend. "Must have misunderstood what Rachel said."

"Hallo, Perry." Michael shook his friend's hand warmly. "No, you didn't misunderstand. Rachel thinks I am back at Westhampton. I stayed because I'm looking into something. I'm at Lilith's. Disguise, you know." He gestured toward his darker hair.

Perry frowned. "I thought there was something different about you. I say, old man, you've gotten yourself into a dicey situation."

"I know." Michael sat down with a sigh.

"No, I don't think you do," Perry said earnestly. "Rachel's got the idea into her head that you have been having an affair with Lilith for years. That bloody Leona Vesey told her so the other night at Lady Tarleton's soiree. Of course I told her it wasn't true, but…well, you know I'm not that good at lying, and it took me so by surprise when Leona said Mrs. Neeley's name that I am sure something showed on my face. I denied it, but I can tell Rachel didn't believe me.''

''I know. She came to Lilith's house.''

''What!'' Perry's eyes bulged in alarm. ''How the devil did she know where she lived? I swear to you, I didn't give Rachel the address. She asked me, but I never told her.''

''I think someone else did,'' Michael said, looking grim.

''Well, now, that puts the fat in the fire, don't it? What did Lilith say? What are you going to do?''

Michael waved a hand. ''Never mind. I think Lilith managed to cover it up. It's deuced inconvenient, but…''

''Why don't you just tell Rachel the truth?'' Perry asked. ''Save you a lot of problems, if you ask me.''

''Yes, I know, so everyone keeps telling me. Believe me, I would, except that now it would cause such a dustup if I revealed it. And if Rachel should happen to say anything, don't let on that I know about Lilith and that I do not have an illegitimate half brother.''

Overhill's eyes grew even bigger, and his voice rose as he gasped, ''What! Michael, are you mad!''

''Sometimes I think I am. Or I soon shall be.'' He

sighed and ran his hand through his hair. "But that isn't why I came here." Michael sat forward in his seat, looking intently at his friend's face. "Perry... what do you know of Anthony Birkshaw?"

"Birkshaw? I'm not sure I—oh, the chap who married that heiress from...Birmingham, was it? No, maybe it was York. Moved there, didn't he?"

"Yes. Some years ago. But apparently he is in London now."

"Oh, wait! I did hear something about him. What was it? Let me think, now." Overhill closed his eyes in thought. "Was it Fitzhugh who said something about him? No, Charles Wardlaw. That's who it was, last week at the club. He said Birkshaw had returned to the city. Wife died. That's what it was." Perry grinned, pleased at his powers of recollection.

"His wife died?" Michael stiffened. "When? How?"

"Good God, man, I don't know. I was lucky to remember that much. You know how Charlie Wardlaw goes on. Don't pay attention much to what he says. Why?"

Michael forced a smile. "Oh, probably nothing..."

So Birkshaw's wife had died, and now he was hanging about Rachel.... The jealousy that had stabbed Michael earlier twisted even deeper inside him.

"Convenient that his wife died young and left him a great deal of money, no doubt."

Overhill raised his eyebrows in astonishment.

"What the devil are you saying, Michael? That Birk-shaw killed her? Why, he's a gentleman."

Michael cast him a sardonic look, and Perry shook his head.

"I say, old man, I think you have been hanging out amongst criminals for too long."

"I daresay you are right," Michael replied mildly, rising. "However, I think that I just may pay a visit to my friend Cooper."

"The Bow Street Runner?" Perry's eyes grew wider. "I say, Westhampton, don't you think—"

Perry stopped, realizing that he was talking to himself. Michael was already striding out the door.

11

Rachel spent the evening in her bedroom, even taking supper there. Her maid fussed over her, certain that her ladyship was ill, until finally Rachel in exasperation sent her away. All she wanted was to be by herself to think about what had happened this evening.

She had kissed Michael's brother—a man she had met only minutes before. Of course, it had been he who had actually kissed her, but Rachel was too honest not to admit that she had enjoyed the moment thoroughly and had, perhaps, even kissed him back. She had kissed a man she barely knew, a man who was not her husband, an act which was highly inappropriate, improper, immoral—and, she was sure, a hundred other not-right words she could not think of.

And the worst of it was, it had been glorious. It had been the most intense, acute moment of pleasure she had ever experienced. It had shaken and disturbed her; it had set her on fire. And it had left her in turmoil.

She was certain of one thing—that it must not ever happen again. No, she corrected herself, she was certain of another thing, as well, and that was that there was nothing she wanted more than to have it happen again.

Rachel raised her hands to her head, hardly able to believe the thoughts that were pounding there. How could she suddenly be so lost to propriety? So dead to virtue?

It was utterly ridiculous, she reminded herself. The man was a boor—impolite, rough, common. It was absurd that the kiss of a man like that should arouse her. It was also utterly wrong! He was the illegitimate half brother of her own husband. It embarrassed her even to admit how much she had enjoyed his kiss, how little she could stop thinking about it.

Only two other men had ever kissed her. There had been the two soft, worshipful kisses that Anthony had bestowed on her before she became engaged to Michael, and they had felt nothing like that. Heat had not slammed through her as it had this evening, wild and stunning.

The other man had been Michael, just two nights before their wedding. His kiss had been more like this one, hard and demanding, although it had been so long ago that she had trouble remembering the exact sensations she had felt. The main thing that she remembered was the panic she had been feeling that day, both before the kiss and even more afterward. She remembered, too, that something had stirred in her, odd and scary, but it had not been this powerful, this delightful. Her whole being had not risen up in response to it.

Rachel wondered what it would be like if Michael kissed her today. Was the difference not in the men but in herself? Was it because she was older, not scared, not in love with another man as she had been then? She tried to imagine Michael pulling her to him as his half brother had. They looked so much alike that it was difficult to separate the two of them. Michael, of course, would not be so rough; there would not be the scratch of a day's growth of beard. His lips, she was sure, would be gentler, softer. He could kiss her, touch her, and anything she felt would be all right. There would be no moral quandary, only passion and hunger....

Rachel realized that she was tracing her lips with her forefinger as she thought, and that her lips were curved up in a dreamy smile. A sensation stirred deep in her abdomen, warm and achy.

What nonsense!

She grimaced, clasping her hands together in her lap. It was foolish to think of the possibility of Michael's kisses, she told herself. He was not here, and he would not be kissing her. He would rather, she thought with some bitterness, be up on his stupid estate, planting things and corresponding with strangers, than be here in his wife's arms.

She realized that she was being unfair. This was, after all, how their lives had always been. How she liked it. It was only recently that she kept thinking about changing their arrangement.

It was because she wanted a child. Rachel was certain that was it. Ever since she had found out that Miranda was carrying a child, she had been thinking about babies, wanting a baby herself. It was that desire that had spurred her to start thinking about Michael in that way. And now that she thought about it, she could see that it was probably her wish for a baby that had made her react to James Hobson's kiss today. She had been thinking about a baby so much, debating whether she would be able to persuade Michael to change their marital arrangement for the sake of having a child, that she was much closer to her basic instincts right now than she usually was.

When she said it straight out like that, it did not sound very reasonable, she supposed, but emotionally, somehow it made sense to her. It had not been desire for a man, especially not desire for that particular man, that had caused such searing passion to explode in her. It had been the natural, normal, female longing to bear a child.

Having set up the frail argument, Rachel quickly moved away from it. It was best not to think about it, she told herself. Far better to think of something else. Anthony's problem, for instance.

She could not ask Michael to help Anthony now that she had discovered that it was not he who had been working with Bow Street but his brother James. She could tell Anthony about James, she supposed, but she did not want to expose Michael's family secrets to anyone, especially to a man whom Michael disliked as much as Anthony. There was, of course, the possibility of going to James herself and asking him to look into the matter, but that, she knew, was a bad idea. Whatever had sparked the feeling in her during the kiss this evening, it would be far safer for her to stay away from Hobson. If she was not around him, there would be no possibility of it happening again—and she had to make certain that it would not. Her very honor—and Michael's—depended upon it.

She supposed that she would simply have to tell Anthony that Michael could not investigate the matter for him. But she hated to say anything that would make Michael appear petty or mean.

Rachel sighed and leaned her head back against the chair, closing her eyes. Why couldn't she look into the matter herself?

This startling thought brought her back upright in her chair, eyes wide-open. It was absurd, of course. It would have been strange if Michael had been investigating criminal activities, but for a lady to do so would be considered not only ridiculous but scandalous, as well. A year ago she would not even have thought of it, she knew.

But she could not help but think about what Miranda would do in a similar situation. If she wanted to solve something, she would wade right into it. And had Rachel herself not been right there at Richard's home at Christmas, when Jessica very capably aided him in solving the mystery of who had killed one of their guests? It seemed to Rachel that she ought to be able to do something, just as Jessica had.

She pushed aside the niggling thought that Jessica

had very nearly been killed during the course of the investigation. After all, Rachel knew that she would exercise the greatest care…and there probably was not even a killer, anyway. No doubt Mrs. Birkshaw's death had been an accident, and it was merely Anthony's grief that had led him to suspect something like that—although, of course, he had not been exactly grief-stricken.

Rachel wondered how one went about investigating a death. The prospect seemed a little daunting when she considered the fact that the death had taken place in another city entirely. She thought for a moment.

If Anthony was here in London, then he had probably brought at least some of his servants, and servants were the people most likely to know what went on in a household for good or bad. Certainly talking to them seemed a logical place to start. Mrs. Birkshaw's personal maid would have been the one most likely to know everything about her mistress and the poor woman's last illness.

Therefore, the next morning, she sent a note over first thing to Anthony's residence, telling him that she would need to speak to his wife's personal maid and the other servants. An hour later, Anthony himself came to the house.

"Then Michael will take on this task for me?" he asked, looking so hopeful that Rachel hated to disappoint him. "How have you had time to contact him? I thought he was at his estate."

"Oh, he is. I just thought that it would be a good

idea if I could send him some basic information. He might be more inclined to take on the job if he knew a bit more. I thought that if I could speak with your wife's personal maid and learn the details of her illness…''

"Of course, of course. That would be extremely kind of you," Anthony said, beaming. "You are so good to offer. However, her maid no longer is in my employ. She was an accomplished lady's maid, and with Doreen gone, well, there was really no work for her appropriate to her skills and station, so she left our house."

"Oh."

"But I have her address. She was from London, and she moved back here right after Doreen's death. I got her address from Jameson, the butler. I could send her a note asking her to come see you. I am sure she would be willing."

"No, don't bother. If you have her address, just give it to me, and I will contact her. And if I want to talk to any of the other servants…?"

"Just let me know, and I will instruct them to tell you whatever you ask."

Anthony finally left after a round of profuse thanks, and Rachel breathed a sigh of relief. Had he always talked so much and to so little purpose?

Now that she had the address for Doreen Birkshaw's personal maid, she intended to visit the woman. No doubt it would be more proper to send her a note and wait for her to come to Rachel's house than it would be to venture to wherever the woman lived, but Rachel had no interest in waiting. She had gone to where Lilith Neeley lived; surely she would be able to manage this just as easily.

Dressed in her plainest and least expensive day dress, she ventured forth, once again hailing a hansom cab a few blocks from her home. Giving the driver the address, she settled back in the vehicle, congratulating herself on taking matters into her own hands. It was rather enjoyable, she thought; no wonder Miranda was given to running things. It was much easier and more interesting than waiting for a man to do something for one, and there was a certain sense of adventure about it that was invigorating.

It was somewhat less intriguing a few minutes later when the hansom set her down and Rachel looked around to find herself in an area that was older, dirtier and more crowded than that where Mrs. Neeley's gambling establishment had been located. Grasping the slip of paper with the maid's address on it, she started up the street, looking for a number. She was aware of the eyes of everyone else on the street, watching her.

A frowsy woman stood in the doorway of one narrow house that looked as if it had been there since the Great Fire, watching Rachel walk toward her. As Rachel neared her, she called out something that Rachel could not understand, given the woman's thick accent. However, it was enough to make Rachel stop and turn to her for help.

"Excuse me. I cannot seem to find this address. I wonder if you could help me."

"Eh?" The woman seemed to find Rachel's question amusing, for she began to cackle, slapping her hand against her thigh. "'Elp you, can I? I 'spect so, me lady." She made a wobbly mock curtsey.

Rachel moved somewhat cautiously toward her. The woman reeked of something it took Rachel a moment to identify, but as the woman laughed again and mumbled something, shaking her head, Rachel realized that it was the same smell that had hovered around the head groom when she was a child. Gin, she had heard the servants say when they did not realize she was around. It was an abundance of this drink in the woman, she assumed, that accounted for the woman's mirth and for some of the difficulty Rachel had in understanding her.

"I am looking for this address," Rachel said, reading out the address written on the slip of paper.

This sent the woman off into further laughter. Rachel sighed and started to turn away, but then the woman said, "'is ain't Poppin's Way, lady. Free streets over now, ain't it?"

"Pardon me?" Rachel turned back to her. "Are you saying that I am on the wrong street?"

"Just so," the woman agreed, nodding. "Ever'body knows the Popper's over there." She pointed behind her. "Free," she added, helpfully holding up three fingers.

"Thank you." Rachel reached in her reticule and pulled out a few pence and handed them to the woman, doing her best not to breathe in the rank odor that hung about her.

She started up the street briskly and took a right at the next corner, looking somewhat anxiously for some sort of street sign. There were none on any of the twisting, narrow lanes, some of which looked too narrow to even admit a carriage. She also noticed to her dismay that she had attracted a small tail of children behind her, calling out to her for coins. It had been a mistake, she supposed, to pull out the coins and give them to the woman. Turning, she shooed the children away, and they fell back a little, laughing, then followed as soon as she began to walk again.

She took the third street, hoping that her benefactress had not been too steeped in alcohol to know what she was saying. She could not find a number "8" anywhere, but after two or three passes, she located an eight scratched on the wall of one building, so she knocked tentatively on the door.

It opened a crack, and an eye appeared halfway down the crack, glaring at her. Rachel tried a smile and bent down to say, "I am looking for number 8, Poppin's Way. Is this it?"

"Eh?" came the scratchy voice of an old woman.

"Number 8," Rachel repeated.

"What ye be wantin' with 'em, then?" the woman demanded.

"I want to talk to Martha Denton," Rachel said, trying to look reassuring, although she was not quite sure what would make this woman feel reassured. "I am interested in obtaining a lady's maid," she lied, for she would never give up her own Polly. "I understand that she is an accomplished lady's maid."

The woman continued to look at her for a long moment. Conscious of the children grouped behind her, Rachel was reluctant to dip into her purse again, but she decided that she had little choice. She opened it and began to search through it for coins, not sure exactly what such information was worth. She had given the other woman three or four pence. Should she pay this one more? A shilling, perhaps? She could find nothing but a couple of florins and several ha'pennies, and she contemplated giving the woman as much as a florin. If she had known that she was going to have to hand out coins, she thought, she would have brought more of them and a better variety.

Suddenly a male voice burst out behind her, "Good God!"

She whirled to see a man striding toward her, weaving through the children. Her first thought was that it was Michael, but of course it was not. It was James Hobson. She squared her shoulders and looked at him coolly.

"What the devil are you doing here?" he exploded, scowling.

Rachel raised her brows. "I fail to see that that is any of your business."

He looked nonplussed for a moment, then went on, "No, it is your husband's, and a wretched job he's makin' of it, I must say. Have you no sense of propriety?"

"*You* are going to lecture me on propriety?" Rachel huffed, her usually calm temper rising.

"Somebody ought to," he responded. "Clearly you don't know enough about it."

"I have been taught propriety from the day I was born, Mr. Hobson, and I think I am well able to decide what I should or should not do. What are you doing here, I might ask?"

Her question pulled Michael up short. He had been so astounded by seeing Rachel in this place that he had charged in without any thought to his story. It was fortunate that he had dressed in his scruffy attire today to visit the late Mrs. Birkshaw's personal maid, so that Rachel assumed once again that he was James Hobson.

"Well, as you said afore, that would be none of your business, my lady."

Last night Michael had visited the Bow Street Runner whom he often assisted and had asked Cooper if he had heard anything at Bow Street about the death a few months before of Mrs. Anthony Birkshaw. Michael knew, with some shame, that he was acting as much at the spur of jealousy as anything else, and that probably the woman's death had been perfectly natural, but he could not keep himself from inquiring into it. The death of a woman her age was unusual, and the fact that her husband, still in mourning, was paying calls on the woman he had once aspired to marry was enough to arouse suspicions— even in someone else besides the husband of that woman.

Cooper, looking thoughtful, had said that the name sounded familiar to him, but he did not know why and had offered to check into it. This afternoon Cooper had come around to Lilith's house and told him that the case had, indeed, come under the investigation of one of the other Runners.

"Ben Mowbray, it were, sir," Cooper had said. "One of the dead woman's cousins 'ired 'im to look into it. 'E were suspicious, the cousin, of the 'usband, 'count of 'e inherited so much." He shrugged. "'Course, it were the cousin who would get it if the 'usband 'ad done her in. Anyway, Mowbray couldn't find nothin' to say 'e did it. 'E weren't even 'ome when she come down sick. Come back a week later, when 'e learned 'ow ill she was. Mowbray talked to all the servants and such, and the doctor. Doctor didn't think it were odd, much. Seems she was allus given to ailments like that. Spent several weeks dyin'. Doesn't sound like poison. And none of the servants thought it were anything but a regular death. Did you 'ave some reason for thinkin' otherwise, sir?"

Michael had had to admit that he did not, that he had asked merely out of curiosity. Cooper had given him the address of the late Mrs. Birkshaw's maid, who had left Birkshaw's employ shortly after the death, and Michael had decided that he would at least interview the woman, and maybe the other servants, as well. So he had set out to find Martha Denton and had been shocked down to his toes to see Rachel standing amidst a crowd of dirty urchins in the middle of a part of town that he would have thought she didn't know existed, talking to an old crone hiding inside a wretched house.

He started to go around her to speak to the old woman, who had grown interested enough in the spectacle on the street that she had opened the door another four inches, revealing her whole face.

"Excuse me!" Rachel exclaimed, stepping to the side to block him. "I think I was here first. Please, if you will stand aside while I continue my conversation with this good woman..."

She whipped out the florin—Hobson's presence had goaded her into making certain that she got the information she wanted—and held it up for the woman to see. "You were about to tell me where Martha Denton lives—8 Poppin's Way?"

"Aye." The woman eyed the silver coin avidly, then jerked her thumb toward the narrow stairs leading up to the second floor of the next building. "'At's number 8 there." She reached for the coin.

Rachel started to give it to her, then stopped, her eyes narrowing at the way the woman had phrased her answer. "And is that where Martha Denton lives?"

"Used ter," the woman admitted.

"And where is she now? I think this coin is worth better information than that, don't you?"

"Aw right," the woman whined. "I don't know where she be 'xactly, but she said she 's goin' to work for a lady. Lady Easter sommat, I don't know what."

"Esterbrook?" Rachel hazarded. "Was it Lady Esterbrook?"

"Aye, that be the name." The old woman nodded eagerly, holding out her hand, and Rachel dropped the coin into her palm.

Rachel turned and gave Mr. Hobson a brilliant smile. "Now, if you will excuse me..."

"I hope you don't intend to go flashin' coins all over the neigborhood, my lady, or you're like to find yourself set upon by thieves."

"Indeed." Rachel stopped and rooted in her reticule for the penny and ha'penny coins in it, then tossed them all out to the children, flashing Hobson a look of defiance.

She started off down the street. He turned and caught up with her. "This is scarcely the sort of place for a woman like you. You might have some thought to your safety, you know. There might be a few who would mourn your death."

"How kind of you. But I assure you that I can handle things quite well myself."

"Oh, really." His voice dripped sarcasm. "And exactly how are you plannin' to find your way out of here, may I ask? Where will you find a hansom?"

Rachel faltered. Much as she disliked it, she had to admit the truth of his words. She hadn't the slightest idea how to find her way out of this place, and she did not much relish the idea of trying. And, frankly, despite his boorishness, she felt much safer now that Hobson was with her.

"What are you doing here?" he asked again, this

time in a calmer tone. "Why are you paying people to find out where Martha Denton is?"

Rachel glanced at him. "Well, I could say that I was in need of a good lady's maid."

"You could, but we would both know that was a lie." He cast her a sideways glance.

It occurred to Rachel that his eyes were a beautiful color, the palest of grays in the sunlight, almost silver. Yesterday evening, in the carriage, they had been dark, filled with emotion. She stumbled a little, and he whipped out a hand to steady her. Rachel blushed, for she knew that she had stumbled because she had been thinking about his eyes—and also because that brief touch of his fingers on her arm had sent a thrill all through her.

She cleared her throat and turned to look ahead. "I want to talk to the woman. I am trying to help…a friend. Martha Denton was lady's maid to his wife, who died, and he—he has some suspicion that she was murdered."

"So he asked you to look into it for him?" Michael blurted out, his voice rising.

"No, of course not. He would not have asked me. No one would have asked me to do anything useful."

His eyebrows sailed up at her last rather bitter statement, but he said nothing.

"He wanted me to ask Michael to look into it. I told you that he thought Michael was the one who investigated things for Bow Street. He did not realize that it was you. I told him I would ask Michael, but obviously I cannot, since he does not do such things.

But I—well, my friend seemed so upset that I hated to tell him that Michael refused to do it, and besides, Michael has reason not to like him, and Mr. Birkshaw would think it was because of that. And I did not want him to think that Michael would be petty.''

He glanced at her in surprise. "Why not?"

The gaze she returned to him was also surprised. "Why, because Michael is *not* petty. Not at all. I am sure that, had he known about it and been able to, he would have tried to help Mr. Birkshaw."

Her companion snorted inelegantly. "I find your faith in your husband touching, my lady. Very few men are eager to help a man whom their wife… befriends."

"You make it sound as if it were something it's not!" Rachel snapped. "I cannot conceive why you are so determined to think the worst of everyone— me, Michael, Anthony—when you don't even know us."

"I know the aristocracy," he answered gruffly, continuing in the rather bitter persona he had established for his alter ego.

"I understand why you feel the way you do," Rachel said, "but I can promise you that Michael is nothing like his father."

"Really?"

"Yes, really. And you needn't sound so scornful. Michael is a very fair man."

"And you think he is so fair that he would be happy for you to be out here tramping about the East

End, mingling with people like me and worse, looking into a murder?''

"Well, no.'' Rachel was too fair herself to pretend otherwise. "He probably would not. He would doubtless be afraid that I would get into some sort of trouble. I am not generally considered someone who is capable of doing things, you see.''

He turned to look at her, his brows drawing together in a frown. "I don't think—'' He paused and cleared his throat, then continued. "I don't think Lord Westhampton would look at it that way.''

She cast him a quizzical glance. "This from the man who was just disparaging Lord Westhampton and all the aristocracy?''

Michael made a face. "I'm just sayin' a man would want to protect you—if you belonged to him, I mean. He would worry about you and want you to be safe, and that's why he wouldn't want you wandering about here by yourself. Not because he thinks you cannot do things. What sort of things? You look quite capable to me.''

Rachel chuckled. "No, I don't. I probably seem even more useless to you than I do to Michael. I am, after all, like most of the women of my station—bred for pouring tea and stitching pretty things, but not for thinking or doing anything important. My brother married a woman who runs her own business. Her father used to take her into the wilds with him when he traded with fur trappers. She can shoot a gun and even use a knife.''

"Your sister-in-law sounds like a rum 'un to me.''

Rachel laughed, a silvery sound that snaked down through Michael's gut. "No, she is not a 'rum 'un.' She is from America."

"There you go, then."

"But my other—well, I guess he is not really a relative anymore, but my friend—anyway, his wife is a well-bred Englishwoman, but she is capable, as well. She worked as a governess for years, and she helped Richard solve a mystery at his estate at Christmas. And—and, well, she speaks her mind, and Richard respects her opinion."

"I am sure your husband respects you."

"Oh, he respects me, as any gentleman would respect his wife, but that isn't the same thing as respecting my opinion—thinking that what I say has worth and—"

"You think he discounts you?"

She looked at him, considering his question. It surprised her that she was discussing such things so freely with this man, whom she hardly knew. But there was something freeing about talking to a man who did not really know her, who had no concern with how she should act or talk. James Hobson would not care if what she said was unladylike or did not reflect well on her husband or her family. Yet at the same time, because of his similarity in looks to Michael, he seemed familiar to her. It was almost like talking to Michael, but without any worry about how he would take what she said, given the events of their past.

"No," she said after a moment. "Michael would

not act like that. But I do not think he would assume that I could do anything difficult, either. I never have, so I cannot see why he would think I could. But, you see, I can do this," Rachel told him earnestly. "I can talk to Martha Denton. Better than you can, I warrant, for I can manage to see her at her new place of employment, but I doubt Lady Esterbrook would give you permission to speak to her."

"No. I imagine you are right about that."

They walked on in silence for a moment. Michael glanced at Rachel thoughtfully, then said, "I know where there is an inn not far from here. We could go there and get a bite to eat, mayhap."

Rachel had to admit that she had worked up a hunger, but she hesitated. "But I cannot—what would people say if I went into an inn with a strange man?"

His brows rose comically. "You think you are going to see anyone you know going into an inn anywhere around here?"

"Well, no." Rachel smiled. "Probably not, but…"

"Besides, you know how much I resemble Lord Westhampton. Anyone who saw you would assume that you are with your husband."

"Yes, I suppose you are right. Although they would wonder why you were dressed so oddly."

"We can discuss this investigation further over luncheon."

Rachel looked at him warily. "What do you mean? You are going to try further to convince me not to do it?"

A smile quirked up his mouth, lighting his face in a way that reminded Rachel forcibly of Michael. "No. I mean, perhaps we could, um, work on it together. Perhaps you could do the sort of things that you are better at, like speaking to Lady Esterbrook's new maid, and I could talk to the men who work for Birkshaw—as an equal, see, 'cause they'll tell me things they would not tell a toff. And we could tell each other what we found out, and talk about it and what it means. After all, we are trying to find out the same thing."

"All right," Rachel replied, feeling rather daring. After all, there was, she told herself, nothing intrinsically wrong with dining with this man.

She remembered what had happened the last time she had been alone with James Hobson, but she immediately dismissed the thought. It had been an aberration, she told herself, something that had been brought about by that particular situation. Their emotions had been aroused, and even if it had been anger that she was feeling, somehow it had made it easier for her to slip into an unaccustomed passion. Being together in a public place like an inn, talking about working together on this case, would be an entirely different thing.

It took only a few minutes to arrive at the inn, named The Red Boar, a large, busy stopover for travelers. Hobson was able to procure them a private room in which to dine, and they were waited on by the innkeeper himself, who, Rachel noticed, addressed them as my lord and lady.

After he had bowed out, leaving them alone, Rachel turned to her companion, saying accusingly, "You told him you were Michael, didn't you?"

Hobson shrugged. "I told you no one would think it odd to see you dining with your husband. Besides, it got us a private room. You wouldn't want to be stared at by the common mob, would you?"

"I doubt there is a mob in this inn," Rachel pointed out, then admitted, "But no, I would prefer to dine alone." She paused, looking at him thoughtfully. "How often do you do that? Pretend you are Michael, I mean?"

He grinned, his eyes dancing with merriment. "Only as often as it helps me—and I can get away with it."

"You are utterly shameless," Rachel scolded, although it was all she could do not to return his grin, there was something so engaging about it. "Doesn't it bother you at all that you profess to disdain the man, then use his identity whenever it will get you something you want?"

He shrugged. "It isn't as if I steal anything from him. I don't even do anything that would reflect badly on him: I always pay my shot. I just use his name to get me the things that it gets him. He got that name from his father, didn't he? It isn't as if it was somethin' he earned, now, is it? He was born to it. And since his father is my father, it seems to me that there's nothing wrong with me getting a little bit of that, even if I didn't happen to get the name."

"You have a way of making things sound very reasonable," Rachel replied.

"That is because I am a reasonable man." He picked up the bottle of wine the innkeeper had brought to them and held it over her glass, raising his brows in question.

Rachel hesitated. It was also not proper for a well-bred lady to be drinking wine, especially so early in the day, and even more especially with a strange man. But who would know? And she felt so invigorated by her activities this morning, so much freer and more daring, that she could not resist trying something else that was not proper.

She nodded, and he poured her half a glass. Rachel took a sip. It was not very good wine, rather sour, actually, but she drank a few sips, just to do it.

Rachel leaned back in her chair, leveled a serious gaze on Hobson, and said, "Now, then, tell me why you are wanting to talk to Mrs. Birkshaw's maid."

When he hesitated, she prodded, "It's only fair—I told you why I was there. And if we are to work together…"

"Yes. Of course, you are right." Except, of course, Michael thought, that he could not tell her the truth—that the husband she thought incapable of pettiness was so jealous and suspicious that he saw the possibilities of murder in what had in all probability been a simple, natural death.

"I was hired," he said, using Cooper's explanation of Bow Street's involvement, "by a cousin of the late

Mrs. Birkshaw, who thought that her death was suspicious.''

"But Anthony was not even at home when she became ill, isn't that true?''

Michael nodded, watching her with narrowed eyes. "Still, there is always some suspicion when a person dies at a young age…and when the spouse stands to inherit a great deal of money.''

"And who would inherit the money if Anthony Birkshaw were to be found to have killed his wife?'' Rachel asked shrewdly.

"You are right, of course. The cousin would inherit, so there is self-interest behind his request.''

"I wonder if we could work together, then,'' Rachel went on. "Would we not be working at cross-purposes—you to prove that Mr. Birkshaw did it and I to—''

"I would hope,'' he put in, leaning forward and looking earnestly into Rachel's eyes, "that we would both be looking for the same thing—the truth.''

Rachel felt as if it were suddenly difficult to breathe. She could not move her eyes from his, and she was unaccountably warm all over. They were talking about Anthony and a murder, but her wayward mind seemed to want to turn only to the kiss she had shared with this man yesterday.

"Yes, of course,'' she said, scarcely noticing what she was saying.

His hand lay on the table, palm up, and she reached slowly across the table and touched the tips of his fingers with her own. His eyes, still locked on hers, darkened. He turned his hand so that their palms faced each other and slid his fingers through hers, interlacing them. His skin was searing. His eyes drew her in. Rachel leaned forward, too, stretching instinctively toward him.

12

The handle of the door turned noisily, and both of them jumped at the sound. Rachel sat back in her chair, clasping her hands together in her lap as the innkeeper backed into the room, carrying a large tray. After him came a lad carrying another tray.

They busied themselves setting the trays down on a sideboard and bustling over to set the dishes of food on the table before them. Rachel looked away from Hobson, seizing the opportunity to bring her breathing—and her thinking—back under control. What had she been about to do! If the innkeeper had not barged in, what would have happened? Was she so weak, Rachel wondered, so unable to control her baser impulses, that she would have kissed Michael's brother again? She could scarcely believe that she would have, yet neither would she have believed she would have reached out and taken his hand!

By the time the innkeeper had laid out their lunch and retired from the room, Rachel had her face set in calm lines again. She did not look at James as she dished out food onto her plate, but chattered in an aimless manner about how good the food looked, how delicious it smelled, how little she would have guessed that such an unassuming inn would turn out such fare.

It was a relief to her to stop talking and begin eating. She thought, with an inner spurt of amusement that it was probably a relief to Mr. Hobson, as well.

By the time they had finished eating, Rachel was able to look Hobson in the face again. She knew that she should not work with the man on the investigation any longer. Obviously, she thought, she had some sort of bizarre reaction to Michael's half brother, some sort of…attraction, though she could hardly bring herself to think the word.

For his part, Michael was wondering what sort of insanity had prompted him to offer to let Rachel work on the case with him. There would be so much more possibility of his identity being discovered, not to mention the fact that he would be putting his gently bred wife into situations and places that were far from anything she had ever experienced in her sheltered life, even, perhaps, into possible danger, should it turn out that Birkshaw's wife actually had been murdered.

But there had been such unhappiness in Rachel's voice when she had talked about the way she thought people viewed her, about the boredom and lack of purpose in her life. He had wanted to protest that he did not think her useless or incapable at all, that yes, he wanted to protect her, but only because she was the dearest thing in life to him. But of course he could not tell her those things. And, wanting to lift her spirits—and, yes, wanting to be with her, he had to admit that, too—he had offered her this chance of working together. It was another symptom of the pure idiocy that seemed to afflict him every time he was around her.

"About our working together..." he began.

His words sent a chill through Rachel. She was certain that he was about to rescind his offer, so she jumped in before he could say anything more.

"Yes, I suppose we had better divide our duties, hadn't we? Well, I will talk to Mrs. Birkshaw's maid. I do not know Lady Esterbrook well, but I am sure that she will permit me to question the maid," she said, presenting him with the thing that made her participation useful—a personal lady's maid was the person who a man, either genteel or common, would have the most difficulty getting to interview. "I shall start to work on it tomorrow. What will you do?"

He hesitated for a moment, then said, "I shall drop by the tavern most likely to be frequented by the servants from Birkshaw's house and engage one of them in conversation."

"And what if they don't imbibe?" Rachel asked.

"Then I will have to find some way to approach them at his house. Confusion over a delivery is often a good way."

"This could take some time, I suppose. How will we…communicate whatever we learn?"

"Send me a note and I'll come around—no, that wouldn't work."

"No. I think my servants might find it a bit odd to see Michael dressed that way coming to pay a call on me. When I find out anything, I shall go to your sister's house and tell you."

"All right." Michael knew that he should tell her not to come, to simply send a note with her news, but he could not. He wanted to see her again, wanted the chance to spend a few more moments with her. It was odd, but there was something freeing about being with Rachel like this, all the constraints that seemed to bind them as man and wife suddenly gone. She had talked to "James" with an ease that was both a joy and a stab of pain. Why had she never told him—*Michael*—about her feeling that others viewed her as useless and incompetent? Was he so remote? So difficult to approach? So unlikeable?

The meal was over, their business done, but Rachel felt a curious reluctance to leave. It was pleasant to have someone to whom she could talk this freely without worrying over what he thought of her or if she had said the wrong thing, as she often did with Michael.

"Well, I guess it is time to go…."

"Yes."

Neither of them made a move to get up, however. Rachel thought of the things she had waiting for her to do at home. There were calls she ought to return, but it would probably be too late for that, fortunately. There was the cunning little baby cap that she was making for Miranda's and Dev's child. There might be some household matter she had to resolve, and then later she would have to choose a gown and dress for dinner at the Mannings'. Her life, she thought, was unfailingly boring. She wondered exactly when she had grown tired of having nothing to do but dress and eat and attend social events, when the round of parties and plays and operas had taken on a dull routine.

Today had been much more interesting.

Resolutely, she pushed that thought aside, for life was rarely like today, and rose from her chair. "I had better find a hansom."

"I will escort you." Michael stood up and walked with her out of the room, holding the door for her and walking out after her, his hand going naturally for an instant to her elbow in a courteous gesture.

Rachel felt his touch all through her. She kept her eyes carefully in front of her, afraid that if she glanced at him, she would blush. Did he feel it, too, this explosive sizzle that ran through her at the merest touch? Or was it merely some mad reaction that belonged to her alone?

Whatever it was, Rachel knew that the best thing for her to do was to go home and never see this man again. She also knew that she would not heed her own advice.

Rachel laid her plans for approaching the late Mrs. Birkshaw's lady's maid. She thought that Lady Esterbrook would probably allow her to interview her new maid, although she would find it an odd request. However, Rachel thought that the resulting conversation with the maid would be awkward and stilted. She would get a far more honest reaction from the woman about her former mistress and that lady's death if she could approach her more naturally.

By happy coincidence, Lady Esterbrook lived on the street that ran along the other side of the park across from Rachel's own home, little over a block away. Therefore Rachel took a pad and charcoal and, donning a bonnet, went into the park and took up a position on a bench from which she could observe the Esterbrooks' front door. For a day and a half she drew, or pretended to, all the while keeping a sharp eye on the Esterbrook door. On the second afternoon she was rewarded by Lady Esterbrook leaving the house, a neatly and much more inexpensively dressed woman trailing a step or two behind Lady Esterbrook's stout figure. With any luck, Lady Esterbrook was being accompanied on her walk by her maid.

Excited, Rachel leaped to her feet, dumping the pad and charcoal pencil onto the ground. Leaving them there, she walked quickly through the park in the same direction in which the other two women were going. She had to make a detour to leave the park by its main entrance and then cut back over to their street, by which time they were half a block ahead of her. However, it was easy enough to keep them in sight, and she did not want to get close enough for either of them to notice her, anyway.

Lady Esterbrook dawdled in front of a millinery shop, looking in the front window at a display of hats, so Rachel had to idle where she was to keep far enough behind them. Since there were no store windows in which to look beside her, she fiddled with the buttons of her glove as if there was something wrong with it, glancing up now and then to see if they had moved on. When they did, she started forward once more. A few minutes later Lady Esterbrook stopped again to look into a window, and Rachel felt a twinge of impatience.

But then Lady Esterbrook said something to the other woman and went into the store, leaving the other woman waiting idly on the sidewalk. Rachel was certain now that the other woman was her maid. She would not have made a friend or even a hired companion loiter on the street instead of going inside the store with her. Rachel quickened her pace until she drew level with the woman. She glanced at the maid and took a step past her, then stopped and turned and came back to her.

"Martha?" Rachel asked in a tentative voice.

The maid glanced at her in surprise. "Yes, miss?"

Rachel smiled. "You are—I mean, you were Mrs. Birkshaw's lady's maid, were you not?"

The woman, who looked to be a few years younger than Rachel, beamed. "Why, yes, miss. How did you know?"

"I knew your mistress," Rachel said, telling her the story she had concocted last night. "I saw you once at her house. Perhaps you don't remember me. I am Mrs. Glendenning."

"Oh, yes, ma'am," the maid said a little blankly.

Rachel was counting on the woman's not contradicting a lady of quality. She went on quickly. "Poor Doreen. I was so sad to hear about her death."

"Oh, yes, ma'am. Such a dear, dear lady." Martha's eyes filled with tears, which made Rachel feel somewhat ashamed of herself.

However, she reminded herself that she was trying to discover if the woman had been murdered, surely a project worthy of a bit of lying. "I can see you were very close to your mistress."

"Oh, yes, I was. She was so good to me. Give me all her cast-off clothes, she did. Some of them were much too fine for me, but I cut them up and used the material for curtains and pillows and such." She heaved a sigh.

"I hope she did not suffer much."

Again the maid's eyes filled with ready tears. "She was powerful sick, ma'am. Her stomach, you know. I felt so sorry for her. But there weren't nothing I could do for her. She couldn't hardly keep nothing down, poor thing, and it got to where I had to feed her her soup and all." She shook her head.

"It must have been devastating for Mr. Birkshaw."

"Oh, aye. Now, there is a gentleman. And handsome!" The starry look that came into Martha's eyes bespoke volumes about how she had viewed her mistress's husband. "The missus, she loved him something terrible. She thought the sun rose and set on that man. And he was good to her. As soon as they sent word to him that she was sickly, he came home right away. And he sat by her bed every day, he did. I remember, even there at the end, her sayin' to me, 'Martha, he's the best husband in the world. He means everything to me.' It made her real happy, even feelin' so sick like she was, that he visited her.''

Rachel felt tears sting her own eyes at the maid's simple words. They had brought home to her the reality of Doreen Birkshaw's death, the pain and sorrow of those who loved her. Her life had ended far sooner than it should have, and if, as Anthony suspected, it had been murder, then whoever had done it had acted in a manner so wicked that Rachel could hardly conceive of it. She could not help but feel a further pang at hearing how deeply the woman had loved Anthony, knowing that he had not loved her in return.

"I am so sorry," Rachel told the maid sincerely. "It doesn't seem fair that her life should end so quickly."

"I know—when there are so many others in the world that don't hardly deserve to live." A quick glance from her toward the store gave a clear indication in which group she was inclined to place her present employer. "Oh, there's my lady now."

"Well, I won't keep you, Martha. It was so nice to see you. Mrs. Birkshaw was truly lucky to have had you."

Martha smiled and bobbed a quick curtsey to her. "Thank you, ma'am. That's very kind of you."

Rachel could see the door to the shop opening to her side, and she nodded to the maid one last time and walked away. It would not do to meet Lady Esterbrook and have her call her by her true name right in front of Martha. She should have thought of that before, she told herself; she had thought the situation only partway through, knowing that it was unlikely that Mrs. Birkshaw in York would have been friends with a titled London woman. If she was going to continue to investigate, she was going to have to learn to be more thorough.

She started walking back to her house, crossing over to the next street to avoid running into Lady Esterbrook and Martha. As she walked, she mulled over what Doreen Birkshaw's maid had told her. Before she reached her house, she stopped, then turned and hailed a hansom cab. She called out Lilith's Neeley's address to the driver and climbed in.

When Rachel arrived at Lilith's house, a maid showed her into the drawing room, where Lilith was sitting with a well-dressed gentleman. She sprang to her feet when the girl announced Rachel.

"Oh! My! Lady Westhampton...I, uh..." She cast a glance back at the gentleman, who had also risen to his feet. He was a dark man who looked faintly familiar to Rachel. "Lady Westhampton, I'm not sure if you know Sir Robert Blount."

"I don't believe we have actually met," Rachel replied with a smile that hid her racing thoughts.

She had heard Sir Robert Blount's name a time or two, she thought, and she was rather sure that she must have seen him sometimes at parties, though he was not someone who moved in exactly the same circle she did. However, he was obviously someone of the aristocracy, and his presence here in Lilith's house, as well as his casual state of dress, his coat off and folded over the back of the couch, sent her leaping to the obvious conclusion that he was Lilith's lover.

Rachel hardly knew what to say. She had never been in such a situation before. Her mother or Araminta would doubtless have lifted her nose, turned and walked out. However, Rachel found it difficult to snub anyone—other than Leona Vesey, of course—and, besides, she rather liked Lilith. So she walked across the room, extending her hand to the man.

"How do you do, Sir Robert?"

"Very well. And you, my lady?" There was, Rachel thought, a definite twinkle in the man's dark eyes.

"Quite well, thank you." Rachel turned to extend her hand to Lilith. "Good day, Mrs. Neeley."

Lilith murmured something, her cheeks turning pink, and gestured vaguely toward a chair. "Won't you sit down, my lady?"

"I am sure you ladies must want to talk alone,"

Sir Robert went on smoothly. "So I will be on my way. Lilith?"

She shot him a grateful look and a parting nod, and he picked up his jacket, draping it over his arm, and walked out the door.

"I—uh, forgive me, Lady Westhampton," Lilith began apologetically.

"There is no need to apologize," Rachel told her firmly. "I should apologize for coming here unannounced and chasing off your other guest."

Lilith smiled. "You are very kind, my lady."

"It seems to me," Rachel went on, "that as you are my husband's sister, we could dispense with 'Lady Westhampton.' I wish you would call me Rachel."

Mrs. Neeley looked shocked. "Oh, no, my lady, I couldn't!"

"Please? As a favor to me? I feel most dreadfully out of place, you see, with you using my title all the time. Here I am, imposing on your hospitality, and you are calling me 'my lady this' and 'my lady that.' It makes me feel even worse."

Lilith smiled. "All right…Rachel. You are very nice." She hesitated for a moment, then said, "I, um, are you here to see, um…"

"Mr. Hobson? Yes. I am sorry to intrude, but I had something I wanted to tell him."

"I'm afraid that he is out right now. He has been all afternoon. If you want to wait for him, you are welcome, but I don't know when he will return."

"If it would not be a bother to you," Rachel said

tentatively. "I would like to speak with him, but I don't wish to impose on you."

Lilith smiled. "It is no bother, I assure you. But, if you don't mind, there are some things I have to attend to, um, next door. So if you are all right just sitting here...I will tell the maid to bring you some tea."

"That is most kind of you," Rachel assured her. "I shall be perfectly fine here."

"Very well, then." Lilith started toward the door, then turned and said to her, a little wonderingly, "You are not what I expected, my—I mean, Rachel."

Rachel grinned, saying, "Did you expect me to be another Araminta?"

"Ara—oh! Michael's sister! I have never met her, either."

"She is your sister, too, is she not?" Rachel pointed out.

"Yes, I suppose so, but I, well, I do not really think of her—of either of them, really—as my siblings."

"I can tell you without fear of contradiction that you would prefer not to make Araminta's acquaintance," Rachel assured her. "I often wish I had not."

A laugh escaped Lilith at Rachel's words. "I will not pine over it, then," she replied gaily and left the room.

Rachel did not have to wait long. The maid had just brought her tea and she had barely begun to sip it when the front door closed and there came the sound of someone striding down the hall. Michael glanced into the drawing room and stopped abruptly, seeing Rachel sitting there.

"Rachel!" His eyebrows went up, and he hurried into the room. "Is something the matter? Where is Lilith?"

He did not even seem to notice, Rachel thought, that he had addressed her by her given name. For some reason, the sound of her name on his tongue warmed her. She stood up, aware that the world seemed suddenly brighter, warmer, more exciting. She smiled because she could not keep herself from doing so.

"Hello. Lilith is next door. She had something to do there. There is nothing the matter. I just came to tell you what I found out from Mrs. Birkshaw's maid."

"Oh! Oh, yes. I suppose I did not expect you to come up with anything so soon."

"I was lucky," Rachel admitted. "I was able to arrange a 'chance' meeting today."

"Mmm. Sounds less like luck than good planning," he replied.

"Perhaps a little of both." Rachel was aware, with a combination of embarrassment and astonishment, that she wished very much at the moment that James would take her hand. Or kiss her again.

She turned aside, gesturing in the general direction of the teapot sitting on the tray. "Would you care for a cup of tea? The maid brought two cups."

"Yes, that would be very pleasant, thank you."

Rachel sat back down on the sofa and busied herself with the ritual of pouring tea. She could see the faint trembling of her hand as she handed him his cup. She hoped he did not notice it.

"What did you find out?" he asked, taking a sip of tea.

"That the maid saw nothing out of the ordinary in her death. She seemed to think it was an intestinal disorder. She said Mrs. Birkshaw was very sick, could keep nothing down."

"Could be almost anything."

"Yes. The girl seemed quite fond of her mistress. I think she would have been more outspoken about it if she had had any doubt that Mrs. Birkshaw's death was natural. She said, as Mr. Birkshaw had told me, that he was not there when Mrs. Birkshaw first became ill but came home as soon as he learned of it. She seemed to hold him in the highest regard, too. She believed that they loved one another devotedly."

Her companion raised one eyebrow. "Do I detect a note of reserve about that statement? Were they not devoted?"

"I believe that Mrs. Birkshaw loved him, and apparently he was good to her. From what he said to me, I do not think he loved her. He characterized their marriage as an arranged one."

"He does not mourn his wife?"

"Now don't get that look in your eyes," Rachel said firmly. "He was fond of her, and both he and the maid certainly indicated that he was a good hus-

band. But I do not think he loved her.'' She sighed.
''It seems rather sad, such an inequity of feeling.''

''Perhaps it is always so—the feelings of one side
stronger than those of the other.''

Rachel looked at him. His eyes were so intent upon
her face that she could almost feel their touch. ''That
would be even sadder, wouldn't it?''

''Love is often unkind,'' he said abruptly, turning
aside to set down his cup, then rising to his feet. He
began to pace about the room. ''I chatted up one of
Birkshaw's footmen today. He, too, had no suspicions about the woman's death. But he did say one
interesting thing. One of the footmen quit his job
three months ago and moved to London. My bloke
saw him not long ago in a tavern. The fellow gave
him his address, which he was happy to sell me. I
asked him why the other footman left, and he said
the man didn't like living in York, as he was from
London originally. He'd worked for them for only
six months—three months before Mrs. Birkshaw's
death.''

''And he left the Birkshaw residence about three
months after her death?''

''Yes.'' He turned and looked Rachel in the eyes.
''Even more interesting, this footman carried Mrs.
Birkshaw's tray to her room after she grew ill.''

''Always?''

''Almost every single meal. It was not a task the
others liked—climbing two flights of stairs carrying
a heavy tray without spilling any of the soup in the
bowl. And they had a fear of the sickroom. So this

bloke was given the task. Once, when the butler gave the job to someone else, he offered to do it for them.''

"That is interesting. He would certainly have had the opportunity to poison Mrs. Birkshaw's food, if in fact that is how she died.''

He nodded. "Yes, and he came and went rather conveniently.''

"But if this footman did in fact poison her, then surely it would mean that someone else paid him to do so.''

He nodded. "In all likelihood the poor woman's husband.''

"It was not Anthony," Rachel said flatly. "Why do you assume it was Anthony?''

"In murder, you look to who would benefit. In this case, the husband.''

"But why would he pay someone to do it when he could easily do it himself? He was right there in the same house.''

"Yes. But not the first week, when she became ill, if you will remember. It gave him something of an alibi. Of course, once he knew she was ill, he had to come home to play the part of the concerned husband.''

"I cannot believe it," Rachel said, shaking her head.

"You just told me that he did not love her.''

"Yes, but there is a great deal of difference between not loving a spouse and putting her to death!''

"To begin with, we do not even know if the

woman was done in and, if so, whether this chap had anything to do with it. That is why I intend to visit him.''

"Now?'' Rachel asked, rising from her chair. "I want to go with you.''

"You? No. Absolutely not.''

"Why not?'' Rachel cried. "You said that we were going to work on it together. Surely it would be better if two people were there to judge whether this man is telling you the truth when you question him.''

"You are talking about a man who may have killed a woman. I am not putting you in the same room with him.''

Rachel shot him a disgusted look. "He poisoned her. I promise I will not eat or drink anything he offers me.''

"I'm serious.''

"So am I! What is he going to do to me with you right there? Surely he is not going to pull out pistols and shoot us both because you ask him a few questions. And if he is dangerous, two people would be better than one.''

"Do you plan to wrestle him to the ground if he proves a danger?'' he asked, raising an eyebrow pointedly.

"If I had to, I would,'' Rachel shot back. "However, if you have a small gun, I could conceal it in my reticule and use it if anything happened.''

"I don't know about him, but you are certainly frightening me.''

"If you are not serious about our investigating this thing together, then I shall simply go on my own," Rachel told him.

"Dammit, I will not allow you to—"

Rachel crossed her arms and looked at him, brows raised. "Excuse me? I don't believe that there is any question of your allowing or not allowing me to do anything."

He set his jaw, then said grudgingly. "Of course not, Lady Westhampton. If you wish to endanger yourself, there is nothing I can do about it."

"I will not endanger myself," Rachel retorted. "Don't be foolish. I can take a footman with me. Or Anthony could accompany me." Of course she would not do that, Rachel knew. She had no intention of seeing Anthony again because of her long-ago promise to Michael, but this man did not know it. There was no reason for him not to believe that she would carry on the investigation without him.

His eyes flashed and he began "You will not—"

He broke off and slammed his hand down on a nearby mahogany dropleaf table, making the array of delicate porcelain figurines on it rattle. "Bloody hell! You are the most aggravating female I have ever had the misfortune to meet."

"Then I presume you must have lived a life very much to yourself," Rachel retorted amiably. She could sense that she had won the argument.

"No one but you would suggest taking a possible murderer with you as protection."

"Oh, Anthony Birkshaw is no more a murderer

than I am. Are we going to interview the footman or not?"

"You cannot go dressed like that," he protested, looking her up and down with a critical eye. "It is obvious that you are a lady. He would never talk honestly in front of you."

Rachel looked down at her dress, frowning. She had been rather obvious the other day in the East End, she thought, remembering the ragtag collection of children that had followed her.

"I will get a change of clothes from my maid," she said.

"That will take too long. I have little desire to be trudging about with you late at night, inviting thieves—or worse—to attack us."

"Oh, you are just trying to be obstructive," Rachel replied crossly.

A grin crossed his face. "Am I succeeding?"

"Yes. You are exceptionally good at it."

He sighed, giving in. "All right. You can borrow something of Lilith's."

"She isn't here. She went next door."

"That's all right. I shall get a maid to find something. Lilith won't mind."

Rachel was not so sure about that, but she wanted to go too much to protest. Hobson rang for Lilith's maid and explained what he wanted, so the maid led Rachel upstairs to Lilith's room and after the woman sorted through the dresses in her mistress's wardrobe for a while, she brought out two, one bright red and the other an equally vivid peacock blue. Rachel, feeling daring, chose the scarlet one and let the maid help her out of her own dress and into that one.

She inspected herself in the mirror, feeling a mixture of delight and trepidation. It was not a dress any lady would wear. The low-cut top exposed more of her breasts than anything Rachel had ever worn, and the fact that Lilith was slightly smaller than herself meant that the material was stretched tautly across them. But the vivid color sang against her coloring, and excitement made her eyes sparkle and her face glow, and she looked, she thought, more dashing than she ever had before.

Rachel left the room and descended the stairs, her nerves jumping a little as she wondered what James's reaction would be. She had her answer soon enough in the way his eyes widened and his jaw dropped as he looked up at her from the bottom of the stairs. He drew a quick breath, then opened his mouth and immediately shut it.

"I can see I shall have my work cut out for me if I am to keep you safe in that," was all he said.

But Rachel had seen the fire that had lit up in his eyes when he saw her, and the tightening of his face. She knew as surely as she knew anything that he wanted her. The rather frightening thing was the fact that his obvious hunger had awakened a similar response deep inside her. Feeling rather too warm and breathless, Rachel gripped the stair rail and continued down the last few steps to the bottom of the stairs.

They stood for a moment facing each other. His eyes went to her mouth, and Rachel wondered if he was going to kiss her. She knew, guiltily, that she wanted him to.

He cleared his throat and called up the stairs to Lilith's maid, "Fetch us one of Mrs. Neeley's cloaks, too."

Rachel said nothing, merely raised a sardonic eyebrow at him. His fair skin colored a little, and he stepped back, turning away from her to the door. "I am going to get us a cab while she does that."

He stepped out and started down the three steps leading to the street. Rachel walked over to the door to look out after him. Just as he reached the street, there was a sharp crack, something hit the stone steps in front of Rachel, sending up a spurt of stone dust, and James spun half around and fell.

13

Rachel let out a shriek and ran toward him.

"No! Go back!" Hobson stumbled to his feet, clutching his arm, and started up the steps.

Rachel ignored his words and met him, grabbing his unhurt arm with both hands, and pulled him with her back up the stairs and into the house. Slamming the door with her foot, she helped him over to the stairs, where he sank down onto the bottom riser. He was still clutching his arm with his other hand, and he looked down at it now. Red was seeping through the sleeve of his jacket.

Rachel's eyes followed his, and she swallowed, feeling suddenly queasy. "Oh. Oh, my."

She sat down quickly on the step beside him and rested her head on her hands, elbows propped on her knees. "You have been shot, haven't you?" she managed to say.

"It appears so."

"Why? Who?"

"I have no idea. Here, help me out of my jacket."

"But—"

"Rachel—"

"All right. You're right. That's not important right now." She took a deep breath, then gingerly took hold of the lapels of his jacket. She eased the coat back off his shoulders, but her care did not keep him from sucking in his breath sharply and later emitting a soft groan. Finally she got the jacket off his good shoulder and managed to gently tug the other sleeve slowly down from his wounded arm. The shirt underneath looked even worse, much of the arm soaked red with blood, and with a dark hole in it where the ball had gone in.

"Let's cut off that sleeve," Rachel suggested quickly. "Come on. Where is the study?"

He nodded toward the rear of the house, and she took his good arm and helped him to his feet. They made their way down the center hall to a room on the left, a small study.

"There's liquor in that cabinet," Hobson said, nodding toward a chest-high mahogany cabinet.

Rachel hurried over to it and pulled out a decanter of brown liquid and a glass, and brought them back to the desk, where Hobson sat on the edge, legs braced against the floor. She poured a half glass of whiskey, her hands trembling so that crystal clanked against crystal. She handed the drink to Hobson, who took a large swallow.

"Scissors," he said, pointing to the top desk drawer.

Rachel opened the drawer and pulled out the scissors, then turned back and began to carefully cut away the sleeve at the shoulder. She peeled the sleeve downward, having to tug a little where it was stuck to the wound. Hobson winced but said nothing, and she pulled it the rest of the way off, exposing the raw, bloody wound.

She reached over and took the glass from his hand, downing a quick gulp. Rachel let out a gasp as the fiery liquid tore down her throat and crashed in her stomach, making her eyes water. Hobson let out a soft laugh at her expression and took back the glass.

"Can you see the back of my arm?" he asked. "Did it go all the way through?"

Carefully Rachel craned her head around to look at the opposite side of his arm, where there was, indeed, another hole in his flesh. "Yes. It looks like it went through. I'll send one of the servants for a doctor."

"No. Never mind that. I don't need one if the ball is gone. We'll just clean the wound."

Rachel suppressed a small moan at that thought. "I really don't think—"

She straightened, squaring her shoulders. She was not going to give way to useless ladylike vapors now. "All right."

He finished off the glass, and she poured him another long drink of whiskey, then rang for the maid and requested water and rags. Hobson continued to drink as she got together her supplies, then began to carefully dab at the wound with a wet cloth.

He drew in his breath in a hiss, and Rachel stopped, looking at him uncertainly. "Shall I stop?"

He shook his head. "No. Go on. Just ignore me and get it done." He swallowed another stiff gulp of whiskey.

Rachel did her best to follow his advice and ignore him as she gently washed away the blood from the wound. But it was difficult to do when she was standing so close to him. It was very unusual for her to be this close to a man, even her own husband; she could smell the whiskey on his breath and feel the warmth of his body. When he turned his head and looked straight into her eyes, she was suddenly breathless.

"You are so beautiful," he murmured, his voice slurred.

"And you are drunk," she responded tartly, ignoring the little quiver in her abdomen.

He chuckled, his eyes crinkling up in a way that struck her as charming. It was absurd, she thought, that he was flirting with her when he was sitting there with a hole in his arm.

"You need to pour some of this whiskey on the wound," he told her.

"What? Are you mad? I will not! That will burn horribly."

"I know. And while I am grateful for your concern, it is what you must do. It will help."

Rachel looked at him for a long moment, then sighed and nodded her head. "Clearly this sort of thing is quite commonplace for you."

Holding a cloth beneath his arm, she lifted it with one hand and poured whiskey directly on the wound. He made a muffled sound and stiffened all over, and Rachel glanced at him anxiously. His face had paled considerably.

"Are you all right?" she whispered.

He opened his eyes and looked at her. Humor glinted in his gaze. "Why are we whispering?" he whispered back.

"I don't know," she said aloud, releasing his arm with an exasperated noise. "I was afraid I had hurt you. But I can see that nothing would do that."

"You'd be surprised."

"I would indeed."

Rachel pressed a small pad to each side of his wound and began to wrap a long strip of linen around them. "Do you think someone shot you because of your investigating this—Mrs. Birkshaw's death, I mean?"

"I have no idea. There have been other things I have been working on. And there are people who don't like me from the past."

"You know, someone told Michael that he should be careful, that someone didn't like what he was doing. Of course, it was really you he was talking about. I should have told you: I didn't think about it."

He shook his head. "Don't worry. A man can hardly guard against a man lying in wait and firing at you when you come out the front door." He paused, then added, with a touch of humor, "However, I do believe that, in the future, I will exit by the rear door.''

''Did you see them?''

He shook his head. ''No. There was no one directly across the street from me. They were hidden from sight. I—I think the shot came from above, perhaps from the building facing this or even on its roof.'' He glanced down at his wounded arm, where she was now tying a neat knot in the ends of the bandage. ''What was the path of the bullet? It came out below where it entered, didn't it?''

''Yes. Oh, I see. That means they must have fired down on you.''

Picking up the scissors, she snipped off the ends of the bandage and tucked them neatly in. ''There. You are done.''

She started to step back, but he wrapped his other hand around her wrist and held her in place. ''Thank you.''

Rachel looked into his face. The laughter was gone now, his gray eyes serious. ''You're welcome.''

He released her wrist, raising his hand to her face and gliding his knuckles lightly over her cheek. ''You were very gentle.''

''I—I tried to be.'' Rachel's flesh tingled where he touched it, and she could feel heat suffusing her cheeks.

His eyes dropped to her lips, then traveled downward to the swell of her creamy breasts above the blazing red dress. He traced her upper lip with his forefinger, then trailed his fingers down along her throat, following the path his eyes had taken, until they came to rest on the quivering white top of her breast.

Rachel shivered. Every inch of her was blazingly alive. She could not tear her eyes away from his. And much as she tried, she could not regulate her breath, which came faster and harder. His hand curved over the satiny skin and slid slowly across her chest to the other breast. A shudder ran through Rachel.

"This—you—" she began, unable to bring out a coherent thought. "I—I am married."

"Your husband does not deserve you," he told her hoarsely, watching his hand as it caressed the tops of her breasts and spread out over her chest.

"He—yes, of course he—he is a very worthy man." Rachel was finding it hard to think, her brain was so bombarded with the pleasant sensations he was creating.

"He does not satisfy you," he went on, his voice rough. "I can tell. You have the look of a woman who—" his fingers slipped down beneath the top of her dress, caressing the soft skin and coming to rest upon the hard button of her nipple "—does not belong to a man."

A small noise escaped Rachel at the touch of his finger, faintly roughened, on the sensitive flesh of her nipple. She had never felt anything so daring, so ungentlemanly and... Her teeth sank into her lower lip as his finger began to move on the bud.

She closed her eyes in pleasure, and her hands tightened into fists at her sides.

Michael watched her, shaken himself by the clear desire on her face. Impatiently, he shoved the neckline of the dress down and cupped her breast in his hand. A shudder ran through Rachel, and she swayed a little. Gently he squeezed the soft orb, his thumb tracing her nipple, now hard and pointing.

He was vaguely aware that he was very drunk and that he would probably regret this in the morning, but right now he did not care. The woman he had yearned for for years was in front of him now, enjoying his intimate caresses, and he had no desire to stop. He was not sure he even could stop. At the moment he did not care if Rachel was enjoying the caresses of another man in her mind. All he wanted was to taste her.

He bent and brushed his lips against hers. She drew in a little breath of surprise, but then her arms were sliding around his neck and she was kissing him back, her soft lips pressing into his, her mouth opening gently, naturally. With a groan, he wrapped his arm around her back, pulling her up into him, pressing her body flush against his.

Desire roared through Rachel, stunning her. She had never before felt the force of it, the driving need that pushed aside all else. Her thoughts scattered, and she knew only the hunger, the eagerness that burgeoned inside her. She clung tightly to him, kissing him back, her tongue twining eagerly with his. Her breasts felt tender and swollen, aching for the feel of his hands again. She moaned deep in her throat, rubbing her body instinctively against him.

His groan acknowledged her movement, and his arm slid down her back to her hips, pressing them into him. She could feel him hard and pulsing against her, and his hand caressing the curve of her buttocks aroused her even more. There was an ache deep in her abdomen, a blossoming of moist heat between her legs. The things that her mother had related to her years ago of what a man did to a woman seemed not frightening at all at this moment, only exciting and desirable. The ache inside her wanted filling, completion, wanted...him.

His hand went to the back of her dress, fumbling with the buttons, handicapped by the present uselessness of his wounded arm. Instinctively he started to move his wounded arm up to help, but he was stopped by an immediate and fiery stab of pain. He continued working at the buttons with one hand, but given his state of inebriation and his lack of practice at using just one hand, he moved slowly and clumsily.

Rachel stepped back, moving her hands behind her to help him with the buttons, but that act disconnected her from the moment, bringing her with a crash back to reality. They were in the study of Lilith Neeley's house, and she was about to give herself to James Hobson!

She froze, horror at what she was doing dawning on her face. "Oh! Oh, my God! What am I—you— you should be in bed." She blushed red to the roots of her hair. "That is—I mean—I cannot do this. This is insane. You are drunk, and I—I am mad, I think."

"Rachel! No!" He grabbed for her as she whirled and ran to the door. "Don't go."

"I must! I cannot stay! This is terrible. We cannot—I don't know what came over me. I—please. I am going upstairs and changing back into my own clothes. Will you send a servant to fetch a hansom for me? Please..." she added when he hesitated.

"Yes."

Rachel hurried from the room and dashed up the stairs. Lilith's maid was there, and helped her out of her clothes and into Rachel's own dress. When Rachel went back down the stairs, James Hobson was standing there, looking so much like Michael that it sent a fresh wave of guilt through her.

"Rachel..."

"No," she said quickly, raising her hand. "Nothing like that must ever happen again. We cannot do this. I know it must not seem like it to you, but I am a woman of morals. I have a husband: I will not betray him in this way. You must understand."

He did not answer, his eyes blazing.

"Promise me you will not—that this will not happen again. I cannot work with you anymore if we do not maintain our distance."

"You want me," he said in a low voice that sent a shiver through her. "I know you do. I can feel it in you."

"That does not mean that I have to give in to it," Rachel replied firmly.

He looked away, then said, "All right. I understand. You will not make love with any man but your husband.''

"Yes. That's right. You have to agree to that."

"I agree."

"Very well. Then...goodbye.'' She hesitated, then walked around him and out the front door.

Rachel stayed in her house the next day, not at home to anyone. There was no one she wanted to see except James Hobson, nothing she wanted to do except be with him. It was insanity, she told herself; if she continued seeing him, it would be sure to lead to disaster. For the first time since her wedding, she was under Eros's spell, and it shook her to the core. She had always thought of herself as a loyal, trustworthy, honest woman, one who would never think of being unfaithful. Yet last night, she had been only a hairbreadth away from going to bed with her husband's brother!

Hobson had had some excuse; he had been inebriated. She, on the other hand, had been clearheaded—well, no, she thought, she had not been clearheaded at all, but her mind had not been fogged by alcohol. It had been made hazy only by her own passions. She could scarcely believe that she had done what she had done, felt the way she had felt.

It was only after much cogitation that she arrived at what she thought must be the answer: the excitement and fear that had sprung into being at Hobson's close brush with death, the worry and tension of tending to his wound, had upset her so that she simply had not been herself. They had caused her to act in a way that was completely unlike her.

In the normal course of events, she would not have done that, she decided. Therefore, it was not something that would occur again, because they would not again be put into such a situation. Surely Mr. Hobson was not shot at every day of his life.

Besides, she had faced the fact of her attraction to James Hobson and had told him that she would not sleep with him. He had accepted what she said and had agreed to their not acting on their desire, either last night or in the future. With both of them avowed to it, there would be no giving in to the highly inappropriate lust they felt.

Therefore, the next day, when she received a note from James Hobson stating that he planned to visit the footman that afternoon, she was able to send back a reply that she would come to his sister's house at one o'clock. There would not, she told herself, be any chance of what had happened the other night happening again.

"How is your arm?" she asked James politely as he swung up into the hansom and settled in the seat across from her. Sternly she ignored the little leap of pleasure she had felt when she saw him.

"It's all right," he assured her, although she knew he was lying from the grimace of pain he made as he sat down in the carriage and from the awkward way in which he carried the arm. "Fortunately, it is my left arm, so it should not hamper me much."

"Have you any better idea who did it? Or why?"

He shook his head. "Sir Robert went across the street and managed to get onto the roof. There is a handy place to hide and brace oneself behind the chimney, and the tiles there are scuffed and one broken. He thinks the assailant must have fired from there. It is of little help, however. Everyone we questioned in the buildings around here disclaimed all knowledge of the shooting or anything connected to it. There is little I can do to protect myself except resolve this mystery."

"Or the others you are working on."

"Yes. Or the others."

His eyes swept over Rachel's figure, and a faint smile touched his lips. "I see you must have raided your maid's closet."

Rachel had, indeed, worn a dress borrowed from her maid, a brown gabardine with a plain round collar and equally plain buttons all the way up the front to her throat. "Yes, and she clearly thought I was quite mad to ask her for it."

He grinned, a twinkle in his eyes, as he said, "I liked the other one better."

She colored at his reference to the much more revealing scarlet dress she had put on the other day, but she could not suppress an answering smile. Rachel had been afraid that things would be terribly awkward between them after their lustful kisses two days before, but his teasing remark had broken the ice. She could not help but wish that it was as simple to feel at ease around his brother.

It was not as difficult to find the footman's address

as it had been to find Martha's the other day, and the hansom dropped them off almost in front of his door. His room lay around on the side of the building and up a narrow staircase, and he opened the door quickly at James's knock.

It seemed as if he were expecting someone else, for he frowned when he saw the two of them standing on his doorstep. "'Ere now, 'oo are you?"

"My name is really not important," Hobson said, putting his arm firmly against the door to prevent the man from closing it, then stepping into the room. Rachel followed right on his heels.

The other man glowered but stepped aside and allowed them to enter, closing the door after them. Rachel glanced around the room. It was dark, for there was but one window and its shutters were only partway open, but there was enough light to see that it was a fairly large room with a sturdy if small bed, as well as a table and two chairs, and a small oak chest of drawers. It was not, however, a clean room; it was clear the occupant had not dusted in weeks or swept the floor, either, and the bed was an untidy pile of bed linens.

Hobson pulled out one of the straight-back chairs for her to sit in, bending down first to dust it off with his handkerchief. She sat down, and he stood beside her, both of them turned to face the other man.

"Ben Hargreaves?" James asked.

"An' wot if I was?" the other man retorted sullenly.

"Then you would be the man I was looking for,"

James replied easily, reaching into his pocket and taking out a crown. Idly he flipped the gold coin in his hand, steadily watching Hargreaves.

Hargreaves looked from James to the coin and back. "I'm Hargreaves. Wot you want from me?"

"A little information, that's all. I understand that you once worked for a Mr. Anthony Birkshaw. Is that correct?"

The other man stiffened and looked at James warily. "Aye—an' if I did?"

"I also understand that you were working for him at the time that Mrs. Birkshaw took ill and died," James went on.

"Aye."

"And that you brought her food on a tray every day while she was ill."

"Wot of it?" Hargreaves retorted somewhat defiantly.

"Nothing. I merely wanted to establish that you are the right man."

"Wot are you talkin' about?" the man growled. "The right man for wot?"

"For this gold coin," James said, flipping the coin in the air and catching it neatly. "I want you to tell me about Mrs. Birkshaw's death. How did it happen?"

"'Ow?" the former footman replied blankly. "She took sick, like, and died, that's 'ow."

"I was hoping for a trifle more detail."

The man sighed. "She must of ate something wot made 'er feel bad. She just started sickin' up 'er food one night. Wasn't the first time, I can tell you. She took bad like that often enough. Only that time she didn't stop. That's when they started sending 'er food on trays. She didn't feel like getting out o' bed, see.''

"Do you remember what you took her?"

"Soup, mostly. It was covered up, like. I didn't take off the covers and look." He shrugged.

"And did you carry it to her door and leave it there, or did you carry it into the room?"

"Usually knocked on the door and that snooty maid of 'ers took it from me."

"And this was both before and after Mr. Birkshaw returned home?"

"Yeah. Wot of it? I didn't do nothin' wrong, just carried it to her door."

"Right, then, let's say you didn't do nothing wrong." Rachel noticed that Hobson's speech was rougher and more heavily accented when he talked to this man than it was with her. Now that she thought about it, it occurred to her that his speech had been rougher when she first met him. He was, she thought, something of a reverse snob, wanting others to think that he was harder and more unrefined than he was. "What about the others? Maybe you saw somebody else put something into Mrs. Birkshaw's food. Downstairs, maybe, before you took the tray, or upstairs after you handed the soup over to Martha."

"No. Course not," he replied, his face set. "Oo'd be puttin' somethin' in the missus' food?"

"It could have been medicine," Rachel suggested.

"Someone could have poured something out of a little vial or scattered something atop her food."

Hargreaves narrowed his eyes at her. "Now, why would anybody do that?"

Rachel did not answer, merely raised her eyebrows and looked at him until he shifted nervously and turned away.

"Who you workin' for now?" Hobson asked.

"Nobody." The man seemed relieved to change the subject. "I'm me own man."

"Mmm." James glanced around the room. "Nice room you got. Big."

"I like it." He crossed his arms and glared at James. "Wot's it to you?"

"Nothin'." James shrugged and touched Rachel lightly on the shoulder. "I guess we'll go now."

Hargreaves frowned. "'Oo are you, anyway? Wot you doin' 'ere?"

"Earnin' a livin', same as you," Hobson replied.

Rachel walked with James out of the room, but once the door was closed behind them, she turned to him, saying in protest, "Why did we leave? Why didn't you ask him anything else?"

"Such as what? 'Did you kill Mrs. Birkshaw?'" James suggested. "He would not have told us." They had reached the bottom of the stairs, and he turned right.

"You could have asked where he got the money to live, since he is not employed," Rachel suggested.

He shrugged. "He would not have told us the truth."

"What shall we do now then?"

"Well, I thought we might go back to the inn we visited the other day for some luncheon."

Rachel chuckled. "That sounds very nice," she said, ignoring the little voice inside her that warned that another secluded luncheon in a private room with this man was not the wisest course she could take. "But what I meant was what was the next stop in the investigation?"

"Oh. Well, I shall come back here and spend a few evenings in that tavern down the street, see what his neighbors have to say about him, find out how freely he has been spending money and for how long. Then, I think, Bow Street might be interested in talking to him."

Rachel started to speak, but he forestalled her, holding up a hand and saying, "No."

"You didn't even let me say anything."

"The answer is still no. You cannot go to the tavern with me. It would inhibit everyone, including me, to have a woman with me while I am drinking with the people there. I don't care how you dressed. I would find out nothing."

Rachel grimaced, knowing that he was right, but feeling left out anyway. "It's not fair."

"No," he agreed placidly. "The world seldom is."

There was something about the way he said the words that reminded Rachel suddenly and so intensely of Michael that it made her chest squeeze in pain. What was she doing here? It was wrong, no matter what she said to herself about it.

"However," he went on, not noticing the change in her expression, "you can go with me to interview someone else. In fact, I imagine your presence is necessary."

"Who?" Rachel asked, her curiosity piqued.

"Your friend Mr. Birkshaw."

"Anthony?" Rachel repeated in surprise. "Why?"

"I have been wondering about some things. Why did he tell you this story about his wife's death now?"

"I told you—he thought that Michael could help him."

"No. I mean, why now? Why at this particular time, six or seven months after she died, did he suddenly decide to investigate her death? What made him wonder if it was murder, given the fact that everyone at the time seemed to have assumed that it was merely an illness?"

"I don't know. Why did Mrs. Birkshaw's relatives hire you right now?"

"What? Oh. They, um, hired a Bow Street Runner some time ago. He found nothing, so finally he told them that I might be willin' to do it. I've had some luck with a few things."

"I see." Rachel nodded. "I guess it is a trifle strange, isn't it? After all this time…"

"It occurs to me, maybe this fellow Birkshaw knows something else."

"All right. Let's go see Mr. Birkshaw," Rachel agreed.

Michael glanced at her in some surprise. Jealousy had been roiling deep inside him from the moment he learned she had talked to Anthony Birkshaw, and it had only increased the other night when she had taken Anthony's side, arguing that it could not be he who had killed his wife. He would have expected her to protest the two of them going to see the man.

She frowned. "But how are we to explain you?"

"What do you mean?"

"I mean, your resemblance to Michael. He will be certain to notice."

He shrugged. "What does it matter? Tell him I am Westhampton's half brother." Even as he said it, he realized how much it would further entangle him in this nonsensical story of Lilith's; the existence of this phantom bastard brother would be all over the *Ton*.

"Oh, no," Rachel protested quickly. "It would be bound to get out somehow, and then Michael would be embarrassed. He doesn't even know about you. I could not possibly give Mr. Birkshaw that knowledge when Michael doesn't even know."

He looked at her, oddly touched. "Well, then, I shall simply pretend to be Michael."

"What?" She stared at him.

"Yes. You bring me a suit of his clothes, and I shall put it on. I can seem quite the aristocrat if I choose." He assumed a haughty expression, raising his chin and looking down his nose. "Here. You. Bring around my carriage, there's a good fellow."

He whipped his handkerchief out of his pocket and held it delicately to his nose. "Egad, how the masses smell. 'Tis positively ghastly."

Rachel chuckled at his performance. "You cannot act like that if you expect him to believe you are Michael."

He smiled. "I shall moderate it a bit, then."

"What about your hair?"

He shrugged. "Does he know Lord Westhampton that well? Will he not just think that he was mistaken as to the color of his hair?"

"Yes, you are probably right. That would be much more likely, of course."

They reached the The Red Boar, the inn where they had eaten the other day, and were once again ushered into the private dining room.

"I thought it would be better if we talked here," he explained. "I dislike imposing on my sister any more than I have to, and, well, it isn't exactly a proper place for a lady like you—especially when Sir Robert is there."

Rachel raised an eyebrow. "You need not protect me, Mr. Hobson. I am a grown woman—and married."

"Still...it is an awkward situation."

"I am surprised—" Rachel began, then stopped, aware that what she had been about to say might sound rude.

"You are surprised by what?"

She shifted a little uncomfortably in her chair.

"Well, I am just a bit surprised that you take Mrs. Neeley's...relationship with Sir Robert so equably."

He smiled faintly. "Truth is, I have little to say about the matter. She is, as you pointed out about yourself, a grown woman."

"That would scarcely stop my brother," Rachel commented wryly.

"No, I am sure not," Michael agreed, with a grin.

"What did you say?" Rachel looked at him oddly.

Michael realized that he had made a slip. He should not know what Devin Aincourt was like. "I, uh, I mean, he is an aristocrat, and I cannot imagine one of them not having the arrogance to run your life."

"Well, Dev is not arrogant," Rachel defended her brother. "But he would feel he had to protect me."

"Lilith does not need protection from Rob. He is— I know him well. We worked together during the war. The fact is, he loves my sister very much. I am sure that he would, in fact, defy all the social rules and marry her if he were free to do so."

"He is married?"

He nodded. "It is a terrible situation."

"An arranged marriage?"

"No. They married for love, actually. She was young, only seventeen, but her parents were happy for her to marry. They neglected to inform Sir Robert that she was not stable in her mind."

"What?"

"She was subject to peculiar fancies. At first Rob wrote them off as girlish silliness. But when she conceived a child, she grew far worse, and he began to realize that her mind was…disordered. After she bore the child, she became quite mad. One night she even tried to harm the baby. Sir Robert took her to doctors, but they all offered no hope for her. All he could do was keep her as comfortable as he could and make sure that she was never around the child. Her room had to be stripped of anything she could use to harm herself or others, and there are bars on the windows and a stout lock on the door. Most of the time she is harmless. She carries on conversations with people who are not there, but then she will suddenly turn on her keeper and attack her, claiming that God or the archangel Michael told her to.''

"How awful," Rachel said, shocked.

"Yes, it is. He has borne it for many years now. He makes sure she is well taken care of, but of course he can have no real life with her. Then he met Lilith. He loves her truly, but he cannot marry her. And Lilith loves him. She wants no other. Who am I to tell her that she cannot live the way she chooses? Have the love she wants?''

"What a sad story." Tears glistened in Rachel's eyes. "I cannot blame either one of them for what they have chosen."

He reached out and touched her cheek, where a tear had rolled from her eye. "You cry for them, even though you scarcely know them."

"Their story is sad," Rachel said. "And yet, there is also a beauty in it. It must be sweet to know that the one you love, loves you in the face of society's strictures, that he stays with you even though nothing binds him but love. I have to think it must be even sadder to live without love.''

''There are those who would call them sinful.''

Rachel looked up to find his eyes fixed on her face as though he could read what lay inside her. She hoped he could not, for at the moment, what was uppermost in her mind was the desire to feel his lips on hers again. ''I—I don't know. Is love a sin?''

''Some would say 'tis only desire.''

She could not look away from him. ''And is desire so separated from love?''

''Rachel...'' He stood up abruptly and came around the table, reaching down to pull Rachel to her feet.

Her hands went up to his arms. She thought to hold him away from her, but as if of their own volition, her hands slid up his arms. She felt the hard curve of his muscle beneath his sleeve, the strength of him, and her abdomen fluttered in response.

''I should not,'' she murmured, but the warmth in her eyes did not speak of denial.

''No,'' he agreed as his hands went around her waist, pulling her closer. He bent to kiss her, and her eyelids closed, her face tilting up to his.

14

Michael paused for an instant, taking in the beauty of her face, the arch of fine dark brows above her closed eyes, lashes fanning across her cheeks, the straight line of her nose and curve of her lips. He wanted her so much in that moment that he could hardly breathe, so much that he ignored the sting of hurt in knowing that it was not him she wanted, but the man who was a figment of his imagination.

Then his lips were on hers, and he forgot all else. Her mouth was soft and yielding beneath his; her body pressed up to meet him. Passion thrummed between them, and they kissed again and again, their desperate hunger growing with each moment.

Rachel was on fire, trembling with the force of her passion. She wanted him, needed him, ached for his touch. She moaned, her hands roaming over his shoulders and arms. She wanted to feel his naked skin beneath her fingertips, wanted to be immersed in his heat. A few weeks earlier, she had wondered what it would be like to feel desire. Now she knew the molten clutch of it in her abdomen, the breathless, thundering gallop of her pulse.

They clung to each other, their bodies hungering for completion. His hands swept down her back and over her hips, then back up her sides to the soft swell of her breasts.

He broke their kiss, trailing his lips down the side of her throat, tasting the soft flesh there with lips and tongue, sending shivers through her when he nibbled gently at the cord of her neck. His hand cupped her breast, kneading it gently and caressing her nipple until it hardened, pressing against the cloth of her dress. She moaned softly, sagging against him. He slid his hand beneath the neckline of her dress, slipping down under the lace-trimmed edge of her camisole onto the soft, trembling flesh of her breast. Lightly his fingers curved over the lush orb, finding the hard bud of her nipple and teasing it. Rachel caught her breath at the ripple of pleasure that moved down through her, and a hot yearning blossomed between her legs. She squeezed her legs together, aware of a shocking urge to feel his hand there.

"James," she murmured, her hand clenching in the front of his shirt.

Michael froze, the sound of his alter ego's name shocking him back into reality. Rachel, feeling his hesitation, was suddenly aware as well of where she was and what she was doing.

"Oh, God," she whispered and pulled away. Shame flooded her cheeks, and she turned away from him, straightening the front of her dress. "This is wrong—so wrong!"

"I know. I am sorry," he replied inadequately, also turning away. Passion was coursing in him, mingling with a bitter jealousy that would have been laughable if it had not seared so much.

"I cannot do this. I cannot betray Michael. I—" She looked around dazedly and began picking up her pelisse and reticule. "I must leave."

She started toward the door, and Michael turned, saying, "No. Let me get you a carriage."

"No!" Rachel paused. "I mean—it isn't necessary. I saw several outside the inn. I will be perfectly all right." She half turned toward him, unable to bring herself to look into his face. "I am sorry. It is clear that I should not be around you. I cannot—" Her voice broke, and she pressed her lips together, willing her voice into calm. "I cannot see you anymore. You will have to continue this investigation alone." She gave a little watery chuckle. "No doubt you will work much better that way. Thank you for—for letting me help. I— Goodbye."

"Rachel!" Michael started after her, the truth ready to tumble out of his mouth. He did not want her to go; he wanted to tell her who he really was, to show her that she could continue to work with him in the same easy way they had been.

But reason and caution stopped him. He knew that if he told her the truth, things would not continue in the same way. She would be furious; she would hate him for the way he had deceived her. And he knew that she would have every right to. There would be nothing he could say or do that would excuse the fact that he had been pretending to her for days. It would probably be the end of any chance he had of ever winning her love as himself.

All he could do was stand and watch her leave.

Rachel went home and spent the rest of the day on her bed, curled up in a ball of woe. She was certain that she had done the right thing—the only thing, really. But why did it have to hurt so much? She cried for a while and then lay dully, thinking about the empty days in front of her. The prospect of attending balls and routs, of spending long afternoons shopping with Sylvia or paying calls on her large circle of friends and acquaintances—all filled her with acute boredom. She tried to remember exactly why she had thought she enjoyed that life; it paled in comparison to what she had done the past few days.

It was not just the excitement of the possible danger or the freedom of going where she pleased, or the unaccustomed pleasure of actually doing something useful. It was not even just the fiery explosion of passion that she ached to feel again. What she would miss most was…simply him. She thought about no longer talking with James Hobson—no more of the laughter or heated discussions or easy chat—and her eyes welled with tears once more. And it was then that she realized that not only did she desire a man who was not her husband, she was coming dangerously close to loving him.

That fact, of course, made it even more imperative that she stay away from him. Even if she could control her passion—which, she had to admit, she had already proved she could not do—merely being around him would push her closer and closer to loving him.

She spent the next few days trying to occupy herself with her usual pursuits. She called on her mother; she called on Sylvia and several of her other friends; she even paid a dutiful visit to Miranda's father and stepmother to relate to them how Miranda was doing. She allowed Perry Overhill to escort her to the opera; she went to Lady Evesham's ball and Lydia Farnham's soiree. She danced, she gossiped, she spent an entire afternoon at the milliner's and bought three new hats.

And through all of it, her thoughts returned again and again to James Hobson. She wondered what he was doing and what progress he had made with the case. She did not know what she was going to tell Anthony Birkshaw, and she considered making one last visit with James to see Anthony. Only the firmest use of her self-control kept her from doing so.

One evening, four days after she had decided never to see James Hobson again, she was alone in her sitting room. She had been unable to build up any interest in going to a party, although there were invitations to three of them sitting on her desk upstairs. It occurred to her that she might leave London altogether. She could go back to Darkwater early to be with Miranda while she waited out these last months of pregnancy. Or she might even go on to Westhampton. It was reported to be beautiful there this time of year. And she could see Michael.

She knew it must be wrong to want to see her husband because he reminded her of another man. But no one would know it except her, and...well, what if she and Michael could get to know one another better? Perhaps he could grow to love her again, and she could perhaps come to feel for him something of what she felt with his half brother.

She was sitting there, frowning down at the pattern in the Turkish rug, wondering if what she was thinking was normal and reasonable or if her thoughts showed that she was a wicked and wanton woman, when the sound of footsteps coming down the hall startled her. She looked up just as Michael appeared in the doorway.

Rachel stared at him, for a moment thinking crazily that her thoughts had somehow conjured him up. Then she jumped to her feet, pleasure replacing the surprise in her face. "Michael!"

She knew that the smile on her face was too broad. He would probably wonder what was the matter with her. But she could not seem to control it as she hurried to him, arms outstretched. At the last moment she realized that to hug him, as she had been about to do, would strike him as odd, so she dropped her arms and came to an abrupt halt in front of him.

Awkwardly, she extended her hand to him. "How

re you? Whatever are you doing here? I had thought
ou were back on the estate these last two weeks or
nore.''

He looked different, she thought, his hair a lighter
lond and shorter—or, no, perhaps it was just that he
ooked different from James Hobson.

''I was,'' he replied, taking her hand and raising
t to his lips.

A shiver ran through her as his lips grazed the back
f her hand. She hoped he did not see her response.
Vas she so lustful now that any man aroused her
asest instincts? But she knew that that was not the
eason. She had felt that little thrill of desire because
e looked like his half brother. That was no doubt a
errible thing, she told herself, to feel something for
ne's husband because he looked like someone else,
omeone she could not have. Yet was it really so
vrong? What had been a sin with James would not
e with Michael. Would it really be so awful if she
ould find pleasure with her own husband?

''I worried about you,'' Michael went on, releasing
er hand. ''It came to me that it was worse than fool-
sh to rush back to my lands. The estate manager can
andle that. And I would never forgive myself if
omething happened to you. So I came back to Lon-
on.''

''Why, thank you. That is very kind of you.''

They sat down, and silence fell upon them. Then
hey both rushed to talk, their words coming out at
he same time, and they stopped, smiling in an em-
arrassed way.

"You first," Rachel said.

"I was merely going to ask what you had been doing. If you were busy."

"Oh, yes. Balls and parties and such." Rachel hoped she did not begin to blush. "The other day Perry and I went to the opera."

"How is Perry?"

"Oh, as always."

"And Lady Sylvia?"

"She is much the same, as well." Rachel wanted to tell him about what she had been doing and discuss it with him—Anthony's wife's death and her investigating it with James Hobson, the shot that had been fired at James, the suspicious behavior of the Birkshaws' footman. She wanted to tell him about Lilith, his half sister, and her affair with Sir Robert Blount. She wondered if he knew Sir Robert.

Yet she could say nothing of any of it. She doubted that any aristocratic husband, even one as kind and tolerant as Michael, would approve of her traipsing about the East End, looking for Birkshaw's ex-servants and asking them questions. Dining at an inn with a man she barely knew. Dodging bullets and frequenting a gaming house, conversing with a woman who was someone's mistress. No, she felt sure that such things would be enough to send even Michael into a fury. He would not like that she had conversed with Anthony, let alone all the rest of it.

"Well," she said finally, "I suppose, um, no doubt you would like to go up to your room to freshen up after your journey. I shall make sure that Cook knows you are here.''

"Yes, of course," he said, his tone a little weary.

She walked up the stairs with him, even though there was really no reason to. They lingered for a moment outside his door.

"I trust that you will find everything as you want it," Rachel said, nodding toward his room.

"I am sure I will."

She nodded and, having nothing else to say, walked on to the door of her own room, which lay next down the hall. She went inside and glanced over at the door that led to Michael's room. It was, as always, closed.

After informing Cook of Michael's arrival, Rachel rang for her maid and began to dress for dinner, taking extra care tonight to look her best. She told herself it was foolish to feel excited and hopeful. Just because something in her had changed, it did not mean that Michael had changed in any way. The fact that her foolish infatuation with James Hobson seemed to be seeping into her feelings for Michael would only rouse Michael's ire, she was sure.

Still, she could not help but think about the fact that Michael had loved her once, had desired her, and even if it had been many years ago, and even though she had ruined the feeling by her actions, surely there might still be a spark lying buried somewhere inside him, some small flicker that could be brought into life again.

So she wore her pearls and her favorite green silk

gown, and she had her maid fix her hair up into a fetching style, with curls caught to the side and cascading down to her white shoulder. She looked, she thought, alluring, and she thought that when she walked into the dining room later, a spark flashed for an instant in Michael's eyes, although it was hard to tell in the soft light of the candles.

The setting was scarcely intimate, for even though they ate in the smaller of the two dining rooms, they were seated at opposite ends of the table, with a silver epergne filled with fruit in the center between them, and two footmen to serve their meal. Whatever thought Rachel had had of flirting with her husband died quickly.

After the meal, Michael excused himself, saying that he thought he would drop by his club. In fact, he had an appointment with one of his informers in a tavern, but, of course, he could not tell Rachel that, and he cursed inwardly when he saw the look of hurt flash across her face.

He had been a fool to come home, he thought, striding down the street and looking for a hansom to take him to his sister's house, where he would change clothes for his appointment with a pickpocket. He should have realized how it would be, how awkward and unworkable.

All he had thought about was how much he missed Rachel and how good it would be to be with her, able to talk and laugh together as they had the past few days during their investigation. So he had decided that he would change back into himself and go

to live at his house with her, and had to that end
leached the color from his hair and had Lilith cut it
to make him look as different from James Hobson as
he could.

He had ignored the problems inherent in operating
in secrecy out of his own home, the lies that would
be necessary to explain his absences, the logistical
problems of having to turn into a different person
from the man Rachel and his servants saw in his
house. Nor had he thought of how it would be to be
with Rachel as himself.

He could not give himself away, he knew. It would
be disastrous if Rachel realized that he had been playing the role of his half brother. She would be furious
with him for playing such a trick on her, and she
would have every right to be. There would be nothing
he could say to excuse himself.

Therefore, he could not conduct himself in the easy
manner that he had adopted as James Hobson, so he
found himself trapped in the same stiff, distant relationship with her that he had always had. Having
known that ease with her, it was now even worse to
be condemned to their old habits.

He should have gritted his teeth and borne it, he
told himself. It was, after all, what he deserved for
ever having entered into that ludicrous charade. He
should have remained apart from her until he was
through with this investigation, given her time for
James Hobson's image to blur. He had been a fool
to rush his fences, and it would be a miracle if he
did not come a cropper.

* * *

Disgruntled, Rachel went to bed early. She did not want to give the appearance of having waited up for Michael to return from his club. After all, if he preferred his club to her company...well, she didn't know what, but she was sure that she would be foolish in the extreme to let him see that she had missed him.

It took some time for her to go to sleep, however. She tossed and turned, thinking about James Hobson and Michael, and listening for sounds in his room next door that would indicate he had come home. That did not happen until well after midnight, and when she did hear him moving about, she waited, her whole body taut, listening for the sound of the knob turning on the door between their rooms.

It did not come, and finally, much later, she fell asleep.

The next morning she awoke in a better frame of mind. Sylvia was having a party tonight, and Rachel thought she would ask Michael to accompany her. Perhaps if they spent the evening together...well, who knew what might happen? She felt a twinge of guilt, knowing deep down that she was using him as a substitute for James Hobson.

But she pushed that thought away. If she could, somehow, work out some semblance of a real marriage with Michael, then that would be good, would it not? Life was not always perfect; *people* were not always perfect, least of all herself.

When she heard the sounds of him moving about

in his room next door, she went down the hall to his door and knocked. At the sound of his voice, she turned the knob and opened the door, stepping into his room. Michael was standing before his shaving mirror, shirtless, a towel draped over one shoulder and a shaving mug in his hand. He was in the process of stirring up the shaving soap into a foam, and he half turned toward the door. He looked startled when he saw her, and a red flush crept up his face.

"Oh! Rachel! I thought it was the footman with hot water."

Rachel flushed, too, very aware of his semi-nakedness and of the jolt it sent through her loins. Whatever was the matter with her? Why had she turned into this wanton creature who seemed always on the edge of lust?

She quickly averted her gaze, turning to her right, as Michael scrambled for his shirt. She discovered, however, that turned as she was, she was now looking directly into the mirror over his dresser, and it reflected Michael's image across the room. He was turned to the side, so that his right side was toward her, but by a trick of the mirrors, she could see in the dresser mirror the reflection of his shaving mirror, and in it his left arm was clearly visible.

Rachel frowned, looking more intently into the mirror as Michael picked up a shirt and began to slip it on. There was a red welt on the back of his left arm. He turned to put his left arm in its sleeve, moving a little awkwardly, and she saw that there was a red welt on the front of that arm, as well.

Suddenly, in a blinding flash of knowledge, she realized what the welts were—the newly healing scars where the ball had gone through James Hobson's arm. *Michael was James Hobson!*

"There," he said, walking over to her as he buttoned his shirt.

Rachel turned back to him, hoping her shock did not register on her face. She forced a smile. "I am sorry. I should not have barged in on you like that."

"It's not a problem," he assured her with a smile. "Did you need something?"

"Oh! Yes…I, um, just wanted to say that I had planned to go to a party at Sylvia's tonight. I hope that is all right."

"Shall I escort you?"

"Oh, no. No. It is to be a musicale. Dreadfully boring, I'm sure. I would not drag you to that. I would not go myself if I had not promised Sylvia. I just wanted to make sure that you did not, that is, had not made other plans for us."

"No," Michael replied quietly. "I was—I shall go round to my club, no doubt."

"I see. Well, then…that's good." Rachel turned toward the door, saying, "Perhaps I will see you later. No doubt you are busy today."

"I had planned to go out, see a few friends."

Rachel nodded. "Good. I will be doing the same." She gave him another false smile and walked out the door.

She managed to make it to her bedroom before her knees gave way beneath her. She sank down onto the floor, heedless of her dress or anything else. *Michael was James Hobson!*

For a moment she wondered if James had decided to pretend to be Michael and gain entrance to the house; he was able to imitate Michael, after all. But, no, she reminded herself, that could not be it, for Michael had talked about her family yesterday, about the estate and their servants, things his illegitimate half brother would not know.

Of course he would not know those things, she thought, letting out a faintly hysterical little laugh. How could he know them when *he did not exist?*

It was clear to her now. Michael had been pretending the entire time. He and Lilith Neeley had carried out this elaborate charade, fooling her into believing that Michael was really his own half brother. Chagrin swept her as she realized how the two of them had made an utter fool of her. She thought back, cheeks burning, to all the time she had spent with him, the way she had swallowed their entire story. What an idiot they must think her. What a silly, naive fool!

She remembered the way he had kissed her, all the time knowing that she was really his wife, yet allowing her—no, encouraging her—to feel the pangs of guilt at betraying her husband! Pain sliced through her, followed immediately by an equal storm of rage. How could he? Did Michael hate her this much?

But it was all right, she thought. She didn't care. Because she now hated him!

An idea flashed into her head, so sudden, so forceful, so brilliant, that she jumped to her feet in response. *Would it work?* She strolled over to the window and looked out, her mind racing, considering all the factors. It might work, she thought. It just might work. She smiled tightly, her eyes bright with fury, and crossed the room to yank at the bellpull.

When a maid appeared at her door, she said, "Have the carriage brought round. I am going out."

She went first to The Red Boar, the inn where she and James Hobson had twice eaten lunch. With ingratiating courtesy, the landlord showed her the nicest bedchambers in the inn, and she saw that the place was even better for her purposes than she had hoped, having a suite of two rooms with a door between them in the connecting wall, and both of them having outer doors into the hall, as well.

She quickly rented both rooms, then sat down and penned a note to James Hobson. She paid a lad to deliver it to Lilith Neeley's house, hoping that Michael would in the course of his day drop by there to assume one of his disguises, or that Lilith would let him know he had a message there. It was the only part of the plan over which she had no control. She considered putting it off for a day to give him adequate time to receive the message, but she realized she could not bear to do that. Her bitter pain and anger thirsted for immediate revenge. She could not wait, could not allow herself to pause or think, or the hurt that clamored inside her would swallow her up.

Afterward, she went home and started setting up the rest of her scheme. Searching through her wardrobe, she finally settled on an emerald-green gown that deepened the green of her eyes. It was a dress she rarely wore, for its neckline was a trifle lower than she liked. It would be perfect for tonight, however.

She pulled it out and sat down to carefully remove the stitches that held in place the lace ruffle that decorated the neckline, making it even lower. Then she took in the seams a little on both sides, rendering it quite a bit tighter. When she tried it on after her alterations, her eyes widened at the way the tops of her breasts swelled above the neckline, and for a moment she considered not wearing it, but then she squared her shoulders, reminding herself not to be an idiot. This was precisely the effect she was looking for.

Next in order were a bath and shampoo and the long, tedious process of brushing her long, thick hair dry in front of the fire. That was followed by a beauty treatment for her face that left it soft and glowing. Finally she did her hair up in a simple arrangement. She did not want to have her maid do it, for then she would have expected to help her into her dress, as well, and Rachel had no intention of anyone in this house seeing that dress.

When she had struggled into her dress—tight as its bodice was, she had a good deal of difficulty in fastening the buttons in the back—she inspected herself in her mirror. What she saw shocked her a little. She looked as lovely as she had ever seen herself— the prospect of battle had put a light in her eyes and a glow in her cheeks that were quite attractive—and the dress had actually turned out to exceed her expectations. It was so tight across the bosom that she could see the small buttons of her nipples, and the neckline was cut almost down to that level, as well, with the creamy white tops of her breasts looking as if they might spill out at any moment.

It was what she had wanted, of course, but she felt a certain trepidation at facing Michael like this. For a moment she wondered whether she would be able to carry it off. But then she thought once more of how he had callously tricked her and a saving anger swept through her. She would have her revenge. She would not allow herself to act the coward.

Wrapping her black velvet mantle about her, she left the house.

Michael found it difficult to keep his mind on his work. It was all beginning to seem pointless, anyway. He was working his way back through his various contacts, asking for information that no one seemed to be able—or willing—to supply, no matter how he tried to bribe, threaten or reason with them. It did not help that his mind kept returning to his encounter with Rachel that morning.

He had been hoping that he would spend the evening with her, that they might go to a play or party together, that he might manage to work his way around to talking to her with less constraint. His heart had leaped in hope when she entered his room. But then he had acted like an embarrassed schoolboy, and their conversation had taken its usual stilted course.

Thank heaven he had at least been turned away from her so that she had not seen his bare left arm. The scars would have been a dead giveaway that he was James Hobson.

It had been obvious that she had not wanted him to accompany her to Sylvia's party. She had even seemed a trifle nervous about it, as if she were afraid he might insist on going. He told himself that he was just being suspicious, but when he dropped by his sister's house to see if any of his informers had come by, he discovered that he had good reason to be suspicious.

There was a note from Rachel waiting for him, addressed to James Hobson. He opened it and read it, his heart sinking as he did so. She was asking James to meet her tonight at The Red Boar. That, of course, was why she had refused his offer to accompany her to Sylvia's party. He did not think she wanted to discuss Birkshaw's case. She was planning to be unfaithful to him tonight.

He did not miss the irony that if he went to her, he would be cuckolding himself. He also knew that even though the knowledge cut him to the core, he would be at The Red Boar as she requested. Hurt and disappointment tangled with desire inside him.

He thought of kissing Rachel, touching her, losing himself within her, and he knew that he could not stay away, no matter how much it hurt to know that she was—in her mind, anyway—breaking her marriage vows. He could not miss this opportunity to taste her love—even if she intended it for another man.

15

Rachel sat on the edge of the small couch, waiting. Her stomach was a mass of nerves, and it was so difficult to breathe in the tight dress that she felt a trifle faint. A dozen times since she had arrived at the inn, she had thought of throwing her mantle around her and running, but she had forced herself to stay. She was determined to do this.

The room was lit with a dozen candles, giving the room a warm, golden glow. The landlord had brought a feast of food, as well, though she did not intend to let the evening get that far. He had also brought a bottle of wine, and she had drunk a glass of it for courage, with the result that she was slightly unsteady.

It was almost the time she had designated for their rendezvous. What if he did not appear? Rachel had not really considered that possibility, and it was a curiously lowering thought.

Then there was the sound of feet in the hallway

outside, and Rachel rose to her feet, facing the door. The door opened, and Michael came in, dressed as James Hobson. His hair was brown again, and she felt a little flicker of doubt. But then she saw that it was the same length as Michael's new haircut, though he had tried to comb it differently.

He stopped dead still, his face stunned. His eyes ran down her body, then back up to her face. Rachel, watching him, smiled. The dress had brought out exactly the reaction she had hoped for. She strolled across the room toward him, her hips swaying lazily.

"Hello, James," she said, her voice low and provocative.

He cleared his throat. "Rachel."

"I was beginning to think you were not going to come," she said, coming to stand only inches away from him and gazing up into his face.

"How do you think I could stay away?" he asked. His eyes were dark with hunger, the heavy gray of storm clouds.

Rachel smiled teasingly and walked her fingers up his chest. "I was hoping you could not."

"Although, I must admit, I was a little surprised. I thought you had decided to remain faithful to your husband." His accent slipped a little on the last few words, and the slip strengthened Rachel's resolve.

"Like you," she said, "I found that I could not stay away. Lord Westhampton may be my husband, but you are the man I want. It is you who takes my breath away, who makes me feel as if—"

Her last words were cut off as he clamped his

hands around her arms and jerked her to him, his
mouth swooping down to claim hers. His kiss shook
her, turning her loins to molten wax and making her
legs tremble so that she was not sure she could have
stood without his support. Rachel pressed up into his
hard body, giving in to the pleasure for a moment,
letting herself feel what she never would again.

His hands roamed her body, caressing her through
her clothes, and she clenched her fingers in his hair,
moaning softly at the sensations his fingers aroused
in her. In that instant, she was lost in her passion, her
body alive and tingling with desire. She wanted to
let go, to give in to the yearning in her loins, to experience the pleasure she had never known.

But then, with an almost forcible yank, she pulled
herself back from that precipice. She would not be
weak. For once, she reminded herself, she was going
to be strong; she would take charge of her life. She
would not be moved about at her father's whim or
Michael's; she would not be dictated to or manipu-
lated or tricked anymore. She, and she alone, would
decide what her life would be.

With her resolve firmed, she distanced herself
mentally from the physical pleasure coursing through
her. Giving a little moan, she ran her hands down his
front and back up, caressing him through the rough
work shirt he wore in his Hobson role. She felt his
flesh quiver beneath her touch, even through the shirt,
and the sense of power over him was sweet.

Her fingers dug into his shirt, bunching it in her
hands, and she pulled and tugged, sliding her hands

around to his back beneath his jacket to pull his shirt out from his waistband. His breath grew hard and rasping as she worked at his shirt, and he shuddered, letting out a groan, when her fingers went to the top button and began to unfasten it.

His hands started toward the buttons down the back of her dress, but Rachel forestalled him by taking his hands and sliding them back to her breasts. He quickly lost interest in the fastenings of her dress as his fingers kneaded and caressed the soft orbs of her breasts, slipping beneath the low neckline to explore.

Rachel finished unbuttoning his shirt and moved her hand beneath it to the bare skin of his chest. She caressed his flesh, teasing his flat masculine nipples with her fingers until they were hard and eager. Then she swept her hands up to his shoulders and outward, pushing both his shirt and the jacket atop it down and off his shoulders. They fell in a heap on the floor at his feet, and she roamed his chest and back freely with her hands.

They kissed again and again, turning and moving, walking slowly backward. In small increments, she moved him in the direction of the door into the hallway, and as she did so, she reached down to his belt and unbuckled it, then started on the buttons of his trousers. He stopped and hastily stepped out of his shoes. Rachel hooked her thumbs inside the waistband of his breeches and pushed them down over his hips until they fell to the floor and he was naked against her.

He made a noise deep in his throat, and his hands dug into her buttocks, pressing her against him. She could hear the slamming of his heart against his chest, the harsh rasp of his breath in his throat.

Their kisses intensified as she backed slowly up until her back was against the door. Rachel reached behind herself and found the doorknob, turning it silently. Then she put her other hand at Michael's waist, pushing him gently back and to the side, not breaking their kiss. Quietly she opened the door, maneuvering him until he was squarely in the middle of the open strip of doorway.

Quickly she slid her hands between them, bracing them on his chest, and pulled her head back. He opened his eyes and looked at her in confusion, his face heavy and blank with passion.

"Wha—" He seemed to sense something behind his back and started to turn his head around to look, but Rachel seized his face between her hands.

"Do you want me?" she asked, breathless from the kisses and the tension of the game she was playing.

"Yes." His eyes darkened, and he bent kiss her.

Rachel moved forward, but instead of arching up to kiss him, she planted both hands firmly on his chest and shoved with all her might. Taken by surprise, he stumbled back into the hallway.

"What the—" he began.

"Well, I don't want you!" she shot back, her controlled fury springing forth now in a blaze. "Michael!"

She stepped back and slammed the door shut, then turned the lock.

"Rachel!" he roared, and an instant later he began to thunder against the door with his fists. "What the devil do you mean! Let me in!"

Rachel hurried across the room and threw her mantle around her shoulders, then scooped up his clothes. Outside she heard a woman's shriek while Michael cursed loudly and continued to bang on the door. Allowing herself a small, wicked smile, she opened the connecting door between the two rooms she had rented and strode over to that room's outside door.

She opened the door and stepped out into the hall, looking back down the hallway to where Michael, as bare as the day he was born, was pounding on the door and shouting her name. Doors had opened up and down the hall, and heads had popped out. In the doorway across the hall from Michael a woman was standing, hands over her eyes, babbling in a high-pitched voice while beside her a man ranted at Michael.

"Oh, Michael!" Rachel raised her voice.

He swung around and started toward her. "I suggest you spend the night at your 'sister's,'" she said, holding up his clothes and tossing them into the room behind her. Then she whirled and ran down the stairs.

Behind her, she heard Michael bellow and start to run, then stop. He would have to go into the room and dress before he could pursue her, which she had counted on.

Rachel flew out the front door and ran straight to

one of the hansom cabs that waited there. She called out her address and jumped inside the carriage, leaving Michael behind.

Her anger propelled her up the stairs of the house to her room, where she tore off her dress and threw it into the fire. She pulled out a serviceable brown traveling dress and put it on, then dug out a soft-sided bag from the back of her dressing room and laid it open on her bed. She pulled open drawers and dug out undergarments and nightgowns, tossing them onto the bed.

And all the time, she was listening, waiting for the sound of Michael's return. He would not come, she told herself. Now that he realized she knew about his masquerade, he would not bother pursuing her—or, at least, not once he calmed down. Why should he? There would be no more fun now to be had from fooling her.

She wadded up a nightgown and stuffed it into the bag, following it with a handful of stockings and garters. There was the sound of running footsteps in the hall outside, and Rachel whirled to face the door, her heart hammering in her chest. The door was flung open, crashing against the wall. Michael stood in the doorway.

He was not his usual sartorially neat self. He had no coat or hat, and he wore the rough trousers and shirt of James Hobson. His shirt was buttoned only halfway up and hung loose outside his trousers. A ridge of red flamed along his cheekbones, and his hair was tousled. He paused, his chest heaving.

Rachel looked at him coolly, then said, "I am surprised to see you here. I would have thought you would go to your lover to soothe your wounded pride."

"Lover!" He gaped at her. "What the devil are you talking about?"

"Really, Michael, it's a little late for that innocent air, isn't it?"

Rachel turned her back on him and began folding another nightgown and putting it into the bag.

"I have no lover!" he snapped and strode farther into the room. "What are you doing?"

"I should think it's obvious."

"You're packing?" There was a faint note of panic in his voice. "Where are you going?"

"That is scarcely any of your concern," Rachel retorted, continuing with her job, not looking at him.

"Dammit! It is very much my concern!" he shot back. "I am your husband!"

"Oh, are you?" Rachel asked with heavy sarcasm, not turning to look at him. "And here I thought you were James Hobson, investigator *extraordinaire* and illegitimate brother of Michael, Lord Westhampton."

"Rachel…let me explain."

"Explain?" She whirled around, fairly vibrating with barely contained fury. "You want to explain? Yes, I rather wish you would! Explain why my husband saw fit to deceive and ridicule me! Did everyone in London know about you and your mistress?

Everyone except me, of course! Did you tell all your friends how I was even so horrendously naive and foolish that I actually believed you when you handed me that cock-and-bull story that you were your own bastard brother? Or was that juicy little item something you kept between you and Lilith, so that you could laugh at me and all my foolish—''

She broke off, tears choking her voice, and whipped back around. She refused to let him see that he had brought her to tears. She picked up another bunch of clothes and stuffed them into the bag.

''No! Rachel, my God! I never laughed at you! I never wanted to hurt or ridicule you.''

''Well, you succeeded well enough anyway. Congratulations!''

''Rachel, listen to me....'' Michael grasped her shoulders and turned her around, but Rachel jerked away from him, her eyes blazing.

''Don't touch me! Don't you dare touch me again. Why did you pretend to—'' She broke off again as her treacherous voice thickened. ''No. I understand why you lied to me. It was the easiest way to get out of it when I confronted you and...her. And, of course, I was so gullible, such an idiot, that I believed it! But why did you pretend to—to like me? Why did she act as if she were my friend? Do you hate me that much? Are you that cruel?''

''No!'' Michael paled as if she had struck him. ''God in heaven, no! Rachel, I would never try to hurt you. Lilith is not my mistress!''

''How foolish do you think I am!'' Rachel cried.

"You are going to make up some other story now, and you think that I will swallow it, too?"

"I am not making anything up. I swear it! Lilith *is* my sister. My illegitimate half sister. There is no other sibling, or at least, none that I know of. There is no James Hobson. But Lilith truly is my father's daughter, born to the daughter of a farmer near one of his friend's hunting lodge. I did not know of her existence until a few years ago. Rob told me about her. He met her first. He was in love with her, and she told him her story, and he knew that I— There! That's it! You have seen Sir Robert there. You know he is Lilith's lover. You cannot believe that he would stand by and let her have another man, as well. Right there, beneath the roof that he paid for?"

Rachel looked at him. His words made sense, she had to admit. She did not know Sir Robert, but he had not struck her as a man who would be inclined to share.

Michael saw her thinking over his words, and he pressed his advantage. "I never intended to tell you that story. Lilith made it up on the spur of the moment, and I—I didn't know what to do."

"So you continued to act out the lie?" Rachel asked scornfully.

"Well…yes. All right, obviously it was an idiotic thing to do. She should never have made it up, but she was only trying to help me, to keep you from being angry with me. And I did not deny it. I didn't know what to do, and once she had said that, it would have seemed even more idiotic if I had denied her words. I took the coward's way out. I said nothing. I thought it would not matter, that I would never see you again.''

"And what about when you did?" Rachel asked, crossing her arms over her chest and raising her brows at him. "What stopped you then?"

"I—oh, bloody hell!" He swung away, smashing his hand into the wall. "I was a bloody fool! There! I have no other explanation! I…wanted to be with you.''

"You are my husband! You could have been with me at any time," Rachel pointed out.

"Not in the same way."

"No, clearly not. Then you would not have had the fun of deceiving me, of wooing me—of making me sick with guilt and remorse, thinking that I was breaking my marriage vows, when all the time… ohhh!" She ground out the last word, swinging around and stalking away. "When I think of the things I did. The things I said. And all the time you were laughing up your sleeve at me!"

"I never laughed at you! My God, do you think I enjoyed deceiving you?"

"It certainly appears so," Rachel retorted. "You obviously thrive on deception. You have deceived me from the moment we got married. You have had an entire life that I knew absolutely nothing about. You had a sister whom you kept secret from me. You had all these investigations, which you also kept secret from me. Even when that man stopped my carriage to warn you about the danger you were in, you lied to me. You pretended that you did not know who he was or what he was talking about. I was your wife, yet clearly that highwayman knew you better than I did!''

Michael let out a groan, plunging his hands into his hair and tugging at it. "I did not mean any wrong! I never intended to hurt you. I didn't set out to deceive you. I—it seemed foolish. I would have felt like a braggart, a crowing, swaggering cock o' the walk trying to impress a girl.''

"So you thought it was better to be a liar, instead?''

"I did not lie to you!'' He paused, then added fairly, "Well, not until the highwayman stopped you.''

"Oh, so you didn't lie to me. You just neglected to tell me anything of importance about your life.''

"I—it never came up. We were rarely around one another. It was part of the life I lived at Westhampton. I—we were not close.''

"No. How could we be, when I did not know you at all?'' Rachel shot back.

"You lived the life you wanted in London,'' Michael retorted, old anger and resentment roughening his voice. "You did not care to be a part of my life.''

"Are you saying that your deception was my fault?''

"No, of course not. But, dammit! It isn't as if we shared a life. It isn't as if you were truly my wife or cared anything for me. And since we are speaking of deception, you are not entirely blameless, now, are you? You have been seeing Anthony Birkshaw! You swore to me that you would not, but you—"

"Twice! I saw him only twice! Just a week ago, when he came to me, begging me to let him talk to me, saying it was urgent. So I spoke with him. I did not turn him away. I listened to his problem and told him I would speak to you about it. And had you been here, I would have told you immediately. And then once more to find out more about his case. I did not try to hide anything from you. I have never tried to hide anything from you. I made one foolish mistake, and I have spent the last seven years trying to atone for it. But obviously you will never forgive me."

"Forgive you? What do you mean? I forgave you long ago.'

"No. You tolerated me." Rachel turned and walked back to the bed, beginning again to fill the bag with her garments. She felt suddenly weary to the bone, and so sad that she was afraid she would begin to weep.

Behind her, Michael groaned and said, "Oh, God! I've made a mess of everything."

"We both have," Rachel responded listlessly. "I—I am going to leave tomorrow morning. I am too tired tonight, after all."

"Where will you go?" he asked in a voice as dead as hers.

"To Darkwater, I think. It is home, after all, and Miranda will need me before too much longer."

"I see."

"Please...if you don't mind, I am rather tired. I would like to go to sleep now."

"Yes. Of course."

Rachel did not turn around as Michael walked out of the room, closing the door behind him.

Even as tired as she was, Rachel had trouble going to sleep, and once she finally did, she spent a restless night, waking often and lying in the dark staring up at the tester of her bed.

The next morning, when she awoke, the prospect of journeying to Darkwater filled her with little joy. Her life, she thought, would be as empty there as it was here. The impetus for her anger had dried up. She felt tired, bored and sad, and none of those conditions seemed as if they would improve with a long journey.

She put off ringing her maid to start packing her trunks and went downstairs to breakfast. Michael was there waiting for her, and only the presence of one of the footmen kept her from turning around and beating a hasty retreat.

"Good morning, Rachel," Michael said levelly. He was as neatly and soberly dressed as ever, but the blue shadows beneath his eyes and the drawn quality of his face bespoke a night as unfulfilling as Rachel's own.

"Michael." Rachel sat down in her chair, and the footman poured her a cup of coffee.

"That will be all, Deavers," Michael told the footman. "Lady Westhampton and I will serve ourselves.'' He nodded toward the sideboard loaded with dishes.

The footman left and Rachel set down her cup. "I—I think I will go back up to my room. I am not very hungry, I find."

"No, please, don't go. I have something I want to talk to you about."

Rachel remained, her eyes fixed on her plate.

"I realize that you are very angry with me right now," Michael went on. "And you have every right to be. I—I will not be so impertinent as to ask you to give me another chance. But I would point out to you that Mr. Birkshaw is relying on you."

"What?" Rachel was so startled that she raised her eyes to Michael's face. His statement was the last thing she would have expected him to say.

"There is the unresolved matter of his wife's death. I have been continuing to investigate it. I spent two or three evenings talking to some of the male servants in a tavern, but none of them offered anything particularly interesting, other than an indication that few people liked that chap Hargreaves and that he had not worked for the Birkshaws long before Mrs. Birkshaw was taken ill."

"I see. What will you do next?" Rachel asked, interested despite herself.

"Well, you and I had discussed visiting Anthony Birkshaw. I thought perhaps we might do that to-day…if you were still in town, that is."

Rachel looked at him for a long moment. "Are

you saying that you and I should continue to work together on this investigation?''

He shrugged. ''I see no reason why we cannot. I would think that you would have an interest in seeing that the truth is found out about Mrs. Birkshaw's death. You have in the past expressed a belief that I would not be entirely fair to Mr. Birkshaw. I presume your presence during the investigation and your influence upon it would ensure that he received fair treatment.''

''Are you bribing me to stay here by offering me a chance to work with you on this investigation?''

''Yes.''

A startled laugh escaped Rachel. ''Well, you are very blunt this morning.''

''I am trying to be completely truthful with you,'' Michael responded, and his gray eyes warmed a little with humor. ''I found it much more enjoyable working with you than by myself, and our discussions were…not only pleasant but enlightening.''

He looked down at the table, seemingly finding something engrossing in the pattern of the cloth. ''Please stay. Give me a chance to redeem myself.''

Rachel ignored the little flutter in her stomach. ''All right,'' she agreed. ''I will stay to help Mr. Birkshaw.''

''Of course.'' Michael raised his head and smiled at her.

Rachel stood up and went to the sideboard to fill her plate. Her appetite, she discovered, had returned.

16

Rachel and Michael walked to Anthony Birkshaw's house. They said little, the awkwardness that was so common to them even more pronounced than usual. Rachel glanced over at him as they walked. She wished that she could still feel the burning anger at him that she had felt last night. Then she had felt powerful. Righteous. Now all that was left of that fire was a sad ache.

At Michael's request, Rachel had not sent a note to Anthony to say that they would be calling on him. He wanted to surprise the man, Michael had explained, feeling that they would get the most honest response from him in that manner. It was clear from Anthony's expression as he came forward to greet them that they had indeed succeeded in surprising him.

"Lord Westhampton. Lady Westhampton. I—it is very good of you to visit me. Please, sit down." He gestured vaguely toward a grouping of chairs. Would you care for some refreshment?"

At their negative response, Anthony closed the doors of the drawing room and came back to sit across from them. "Does this mean that you have learned something? Have you found out if Doreen was…?" He hesitated.

Michael shook his head. "We have learned a little. But not enough to know whether her death was by misadventure. Everyone involved at the time seems to think that it was illness."

"Yes. So did I," Anthony agreed.

"Then why did you approach my wife about it?" Michael asked coolly.

"Oh. I, ah…well, I just began to wonder about it. It—it seemed odd in retrospect, her dying like that. And so young." Birkshaw broke off, glancing at Michael.

Michael gazed back at him without saying anything, his disbelief clear. Anthony looked toward Rachel as if for help, but she simply watched him, too. Anthony shifted in his chair, appearing very much as if he wanted to be elsewhere.

Finally he said, "Very well. I see I must tell it. It…is so odd, I could not bring myself to say anything before. But I—well, a few weeks ago, I received a letter, and inside it was a piece of metal."

"Metal?" Rachel repeated, surprised.

Birkshaw nodded. "Yes, obviously snipped from a tin of rat poison. It had enough writing that I could tell as much. Arsenic, you see. Well, I had no idea what to make of that. It was disturbing. I— Was someone threatening me? Why? But then, later, I got a second letter. It had printing inside, large and awkward-looking, like a child's writing. It said, 'Favor for favor.'''

"What?" Rachel asked. "What does that mean?"

Michael said nothing, merely watched Anthony.

"I don't know!" Anthony cried, lifting his hands. "I couldn't understand. But...but it also said, 'Arsenic remains in the body after death.'''

He turned to Michael, his face pale and sick-looking. "I think they were talking about Doreen."

"Why do you think so?"

"What else could it mean? I racked my brain trying to think of something. But, I mean, obviously Doreen had died of the sort of illness that could have been poison. Couldn't it?"

Michael nodded, his eyes never leaving Anthony's face. "Some poisons, certainly. Arsenic, for instance, builds up in the body. Given in small doses, it makes the person sick but doesn't kill until enough of it has built up to do so. And it does remain in the body after death—in the hair and nails."

"It was as if they were threatening me," Anthony said, fear in his eyes. "As though they were telling me that they could make everyone believe that _I_ had killed my wife. It's absurd! But then I began to think—how can one prove that one did _not_ do something?"

"Why would someone want to do that?" Michael asked. "Make it appear that you killed Mrs. Birkshaw?"

"I think—I think it must be that they want me to

do something for them. This 'favor for favor' bit. All can think is that they are going to ask me to do something I wouldn't want to or—or, I don't know, pay them money or something, with the threat that if I do not, they will tell everyone I did it.''

Michael gave him a long look. "So you are saying that someone whom you don't know decided to kill your wife in the hopes that a few months later they could blackmail you into doing them a favor?"

"I know it sounds bizarre," Anthony protested stiffly.

"That is something of an understatement," Michael replied.

"But what else could it be?" Anthony's expression was frantic. "Why are they plaguing me with these things? Won't you please find out what happened? I know I have no right to ask anything of you—"

"You are correct in that."

"But I am a desperate man. I cannot imagine what I will do if—"

"Of course we are going to help you, Mr. Birkshaw," Rachel put in. "Why, we—he, I mean, is already working on it. Aren't you, Michael?"

"I am looking into it," Michael agreed shortly. "My dear, I think it is time we left. Birkshaw." He rose, nodding toward Anthony, and held out his hand to Rachel.

She took his hand and walked with him out of the room, leaving Anthony looking after them. They had barely gotten out the front door when Michael whipped around to look at her, exploding, "It's an idiot's tale! Surely he cannot expect me to believe that!"

"It is exceedingly odd," Rachel admitted. "But does it not make you wonder why he would make up something so silly?"

"Because he has cotton batting for brains, that's why."

Rachel could not suppress a giggle. "Perhaps. But let us look at this logically."

"I'm not sure that is possible," Michael retorted.

"Try," Rachel replied firmly. She felt much better suddenly, and she realized that the reason was that the constraint between her and Michael had vanished. It was like being with James again, words flowing between them freely.

"There are only two possibilities," she went on. "Anthony either killed his wife or he did not."

"Agreed."

"Now, if he killed his wife and everyone assumed she died of an illness, if even Bow Street had investigated it and come up with nothing to show that she was murdered—then why, six months later, would he start the whole thing up again by asking you to investigate her death? What could he possibly hope to accomplish by setting a man known to be superior at investigating things on his own trail? And if, for some reason we cannot fathom, he did do this, why would he then make up an idiotic story as some sort of...I'm not sure what. Alibi, I suppose? A note and a bit of a tin of rat poison are scarcely proof of innocence,'' Rachel pointed out.

"I agree. It makes no sense."

"But if he did not murder his wife, you have the same questions. Why ask you to investigate? Why give this foolish story as the reason? I cannot see why anyone would...unless it was the truth."

Michael cast her a caustic glance. "Killing her in the hope that Mr. Birkshaw would do them a favor?"

Rachel shrugged. "I admit that it does seem a rather iffy proposition. But perhaps there is something more to it. Something we simply don't see." She paused, then went on. "The other thing that struck me was that the fear on Anthony's face was quite real. I don't think he is pretending."

Michael sighed. "No. I saw that, too. But perhaps the fear is that he will be caught. It is a given, you know, that it is commonly the person who benefits who is the murderer," Michael stated firmly.

"But surely there are times when it is not so," Rachel argued. In the heat of her argument, she unconsciously laid her hand on Michael's arm. "When someone else murders them."

"Yes, of course." Michael wanted to clamp his hand over hers and hold it there. It took all his willpower to continue walking and talking as if nothing had happened. "I have been working on a case where the most obvious suspects are all clearly not involved in the crime. It's been bloody hard to solve, too." He told her the story of the Earl of Setworth's stolen illuminated manuscript, adding, "I assume that case is the one which Red Geordie went to such great lengths to warn me off from. But I cannot imagine why anyone would have been concerned about my getting too close to the truth. I was not close to anything. It was an utter failure, just like another case about a year ago. My last few cases have been rife with failure."

"What was that one concerning?" Rachel asked. "The one a year ago."

"A wealthy goldsmith was attacked one night after he left his shop," Michael told her. They had reached the park across the street from their house, and he walked into it, leading her to a bench and sitting down to finish his story.

"The man was knocked over the head and killed. The assailant took his gold pocket watch and the coins that were in his pockets. Straightforward enough, one would think. Killed by a thief. Now, in those same pockets was a key that opened the door to his shop, yet the thief, who robbed him right outside the store, did not take the key and open the store and steal a great deal of very valuable gold items and money."

"That seems very careless of him," Rachel commented. It was so pleasant to sit there, watching Michael talk, his face animated. How was it, she wondered, that she had never before noticed how very handsome her husband was?

"The store belonged to the man who died and to his partner, a less talented fellow and one, moreover, who lived beyond his means," Michael went on.

"The partner inherited the dead man's half of the store, for he had no family, and such was their agreement. It aroused my suspicions immediately. How handy for his partner that the thief had happened to kill him in the course of stealing a few pounds worth of things. But I could find nothing to connect the partner to the death. He was at a dinner party at the time it happened. The man's watch never turned up at a pawn shop. None of the usual thieves' dives yielded any tales of a thief in his cups confessing."

"Then how can you say that a murder done by someone other than the person who benefits is not common? You have had three like that, counting Mr. Birkshaw's case."

"Yes, but, you see, it is normally rare. When I consider all the other investigations I have had where—" He stopped and frowned thoughtfully. "That *is* odd. They *are* rather alike."

"What are you thinking?" Rachel asked, excitement rising in her. "I can see that you are putting something together."

"I'm not sure. But it is a pattern of sorts. One always looks for patterns in crimes. Thieves who follow a certain method. Killers who use the same instrument. Normally the pattern is that murders are done by the person who would benefit from the crime. But here, there is a pattern that the person who benefits could *not* have done it. So when I see a pattern that is very much unlike the normal pattern— well, it makes me wonder."

"If the the three cases are connected somehow...?"

"It seems unlikely. And yet...it would be odd if
they were random, don't you think?"

"Could the same person have done all three?"

"That, too, seems unlikely. One crime took a very
accomplished thief, one a poisoner who must have
gotten inside the house—or paid someone to do it for
him—and the other a killer who caved in someone's
skull. They were in separate parts of the country. The
house party was in Dorset, the goldsmith in London,
Mrs. Birkshaw in York. Still...I think it might be of
benefit to pay a visit to Bow Street."

In point of fact, they did not go to Bow Street,
where the presence of a lady would have caused great
consternation. Instead they met John Cooper, the
Runner with whom Michael often worked, at an inn
not far from headquarters. If Cooper, a large, slow-
moving man with sleepy brown eyes, found it odd to
be meeting Michael with an aristocratic woman
along, he gave no evidence of it, merely tipped his
hat to Rachel gravely.

"Now, what's this that's so important, guv'nor?"
he asked. "You found out anything for me?"

"I'm not sure. All I have at the moment are questions," Michael replied.

"Well, that's typical, ain't it?" Cooper responded
good-naturedly. "Now, what would you be wantin'?"

"I am interested in unsolved cases," Michael began.

"Well, we've got a might of them," Cooper said. "Seems like more than ever, these days."

"Does it?"

"Aye, there's allus a lot of things you can't find no one to blame for, or, leastways, no proof of it. Well, you know that well enough. It's why I come to you so often. But the last couple of years seems like much more."

"What I am interested in particularly are ones in which the person who would benefit the most could not have committed the crime."

Cooper's eyes narrowed thoughtfully. "You *are* on to something, aren't you?"

"I may be. But I need a lot of information first. Can you get that for me?"

"Aye, I 'spect I can do that. Long as you'll let me know what you figure out."

"Of course."

The Runner looked at Rachel, giving her a slow smile. "He's a downy one, he is."

"Yes," Rachel agreed. "I have found that he is very crafty."

Michael looked at her narrowly, but Cooper seemed happily unaware of any undertone to their conversation. "Aye. He is that."

"And very good at deception," Rachel added.

"Oh, yes. The guv'nor's the best."

Rachel cast Michael a significant look, one eyebrow raised.

"Well, Cooper, thank you for that encomium," Michael commented dryly.

"You're welcome, sir." The twinkle in Cooper's eyes told Rachel that perhaps the man was more aware of the undercurrents of their conversation than he let on.

That next afternoon Cooper came to their house. Michael and Rachel met him in Michael's study, where Cooper set a large box down on Michael's desk.

Michael cast a wary eye at the box. "What have you got for me? It looks like quite a bit."

"Aye, that it is, sir," Cooper agreed cheerfully as he laid a list of names on top of the box. "This list is of all the cases of the sort you wanted that we could remember. No doubt there's more of 'em, but I reasoned this'd be enough to start you off."

"I believe so," Michael replied dryly, casting an eye at the large stack of paperwork.

"I brought the Runner's report on some of 'em, ones that seemed most like what you wrote me about. Hope you can figure something out about them. If anybody could, it'd be you, I'd wager."

"Thank you for your confidence, Cooper," Michael replied, adding, "I am afraid I feel rather less sanguine about my abilities at the moment."

Cooper took his leave, nodding again to Rachel, then turning and striding out of the room like a man relieved of a great burden. Rachel walked over to Michael's desk.

"I would say you have your work cut out for you," she commented.

"*We* have, my dear, *we* have."

Rachel sat down in front of the desk. She did not like to admit how much she wanted to help him with the files. The cases would be far more interesting than calling on anyone or receiving calls, but more than that, she knew that she wanted to spend the afternoon with Michael. It was humiliating, she told herself, that she could still want to be with him after what he had done.

Even if, in the calmer state of mind she was in today, she no longer believed that Michael had perpetrated his charade on her because he wanted to ridicule or humiliate her, she could not overlook the fact that he had kept a large part of his life secret from her almost the entire time they had been married. Clearly she was not someone he trusted, certainly not someone he loved. He was a stranger to her, and six years of marriage had not changed that.

That fact made it even more humiliating that she felt as she did about Michael. Or James. Or whoever it was for whom she had these muddled, yearning emotions! All she knew was that she felt a simmering excitement around him and, at the same time, a quiet contentment...not to mention a hundred other conflicting feelings that made being around him so pleasurable and torturous all at the same time. Yesterday, after going to see Cooper, they had spent the evening discussing the oddities of the case and Michael's other cases, and she had enjoyed it far more than she would have a party. And when, later, Michael went out to visit the sort of informants whom he could meet only at night in dark and secret places, Rachel had been distinctly disappointed and lonely as she put on her nightgown and climbed into her big, empty bed to sleep.

She knew, deep down, that it was these feelings, more than any concern about helping Anthony, that had really made her agree to stay here—just as, now, they impelled her to sit down across the desk from Michael and agree to help him with the files.

"Shall I read some of them and you others?" she asked.

"Let's go through them together," he suggested. "It will be slower, I know, but I think it would be better if we had two minds working on the problem. Here, come sit here beside me." He pulled up another straight-back chair next to his and placed the files on the desk between the two chairs.

"What are we looking for?" Rachel asked, going around the desk and sitting down beside him. Her pulse quickened, though she managed to keep her voice and face cool and calm.

"I'm not sure," he replied. "Some connection. A pattern."

"We already know that they have one thing in common, right? The person who stood to benefit the most in each could not have committed the crime."

He nodded. "That, and none of them have been solved." Michael ran his finger down the list on top of the stack. Ah, here is my most recent, Lord Setworth's illuminated manuscript. And, yes, further down here is the goldsmith that I told you about. All right, let's see what else we have."

Michael set the list aside. "First, we have Harold Benton. Murdered. Hmm." He scanned down the report, saying, "He was to be a witness in a trial against his former partner in crime, one Bart Mansfield. This Mansfield sounds like a piece of work." He read down a list of crimes of which the man was accused or suspected.

"My goodness. He seems to be the complete criminal," Rachel commented. "My guess would be that he was the one who did poor Mr. Benton in, so that he could not testify against him."

"That would have been Bow Street's opinion, too, except for the fact that the man was in Newgate, awaiting trial for his misdeeds, when Benton was struck down. So Mansfield could not have done it." He read some more of the particulars, then added, "Seems the Runner in charge suspects that Mansfield got someone else to do the job for him, but they were unable to prove it."

He continued to read through the string of investigations—a seemingly endless series of robberies, thefts and homicides, none of them alike except in the fact that they had baffled their investigators.

"Now," Michael said, picking up the fifth report. "This concerns one Dutton Parkhurst, Esquire. He was stabbed to death one evening as he was walking home from his club. One of his servants went out to look for him when he did not return home, as he was a man of very regular habits, and found him slumped in a doorway. He thought at first that he was drunk, though that was not like him, but then he saw the blood all over the front of his coat. There were no witnesses. Nothing was stolen from his body. His nephew, who inherited his fortune, was with a group of friends all evening. They went first to a play and finished up the evening gambling. There were numerous witnesses to his presence there, and..." He paused, frowning.

"What is it? Did you find something?" Rachel, watching him, sat up straighter.

"No. It's just...the name of this nephew. It sounds familiar. Roland Ellerby."

He straightened suddenly. "Wait. I think—"

Michael thumbed rapidly through the papers remaining in the stack, stopping at one of them and scanning down it. "Yes! I thought I had heard his name. Roland Ellerby was one of the guests at Lord Setworth's estate party two weeks before his illuminated manuscript was stolen!"

He looked up at Rachel triumphantly.

She leaned forward. "Michael, that must mean something! Surely that could not be coincidence."

"I am beginning to think that none of this is coincidence. Rather, it is all very well planned and carried out."

"Do you think there is someone who goes about doing what Anthony said? Committing a murder or a theft and then forcing the person who benefitted from it to do them a favor?" Rachel asked.

"That still sounds absurd," Michael said, shaking his head.

"Surely all these people who benefitted could not have just banded together and decided to carry out the various crimes."

"I wouldn't think so. It would be too unwieldy. There would be too much danger of one of them developing a conscience and turning the others in," Michael said. He put his elbows on the desk and steepled his fingers together, staring thoughtfully into space. "But what if there was one person, someone entirely unconnected to the beneficiary of the crime, who knew how much that person would like it if some crime or other were done, in this instance getting rid of a rich uncle. And say the criminal, the mastermind of this scheme, went to this nephew and offered to do away with the uncle, told him when it would happen so that the nephew could provide himself with an unassailable alibi. And all our mastermind asked in return was that in the future the nephew—or whoever benefited—would do a favor for him. In this case, the favor turned out to be going to an estate party and learning the whereabouts of a valuable object that the criminal wants to steal. Then the criminal goes in or hires a thief to go in and remove the valuable object, and the money he makes off it is his payment for doing away with the uncle."

"Or, in some cases, he could ask for direct payment, I suppose—or blackmail someone, as he is doing to Mr. Birkshaw now. 'If you don't do as I tell you, I will make it appear that you committed the crime.'"

"Exactly."

"But who could it be?" Rachel mused. "It would have to be someone who knew a great deal about people who had money or valuable possessions, as well as about who would benefit most from, say, a wealthy relative dying."

"Yes." Michael looked at her thoughtfully. "It would almost seem as if it would be someone of the *Ton*."

"Michael!" Rachel stared at him, shocked. "You are saying that—that it is a peer? Even someone we know?"

He shrugged. "I am sure there are a fair number of larcenous peers. Now, whether there are many who are clever enough to have thought of this, that is another matter altogether," he said dryly.

Rachel chuckled. "You are dreadfully unkind."

"Mmm. Or too truthful."

"There are others it could be," Rachel suggested. "Servants hear a great deal of gossip, not only upstairs, but also from other servants at other houses. One can often get the most up-to-date gossip from one's lady's maid. Dressmakers, milliners…and I'll warrant men exchange a great deal of information in front of their tailors or boot makers, as well."

"Yes, and there are secretaries to men of wealth and power," Michael added. "That would seem a good field for a possible mastermind—a man of intelligence, even good social standing, perhaps, and lacking in money, or he would not have had to take the position.''

"Yes. You are right. Or perhaps there is more than one person—two, say, one who knows the criminal world and another who knows the wealthy world.''

Michael nodded. "That's a good thought. Thank you, Rachel." He smiled at her as he stood up. "I think I should go talk this over with Sir Robert.''

"Blount?" Rachel asked, surprised and, she realized, disappointed, that he was leaving. "But why?''

"He has the best mind I know for this type of thing," he answered.

"Oh, yes. That's right. He is the one who got you into investigating such things," Rachel said. She remembered now his telling her about Sir Robert's bringing him into the business during the war and later introducing him to Bow Street. Of course, it had been James Hobson who had been telling her the story at the time....

She rose, the ease she had felt with Michael gone now, chased away by the memory of his deception.

Michael, watching her, felt his heart sink. He wished he had not mentioned Blount. Things had been going well until then. Now Rachel looked as aloof as she had yesterday morning when they set out. It seemed as if their conversations were filled with hidden traps, ready to snap to at the first unwary move he made.

"I suppose I will go to the Wilkinson soiree tonight," Rachel said. She did not really wish to, but it would be a way to fill an empty evening. "I presume you will be with Sir Robert all evening?"

"I'm not sure—yes, perhaps." There would be little point in his coming home early, he thought. Rachel would not be there.

Michael hesitated, wishing, once again, that he could redo the last few minutes. Then, with an awkward nod, he picked up the list and left the room.

Rachel plopped back down in her chair. She thought about going up and dressing for dinner. It seemed pointless, with Michael being gone. Perhaps she would just have her supper brought to her on a tray in her room. She knew she had no interest in going to the Wilkinson soiree, either.

She ate an early supper and spent most of the evening reading. The whole time there was a niggling little hope inside her that Michael might come home earlier than he had said, though she tried time and again to quell it.

Finally, around ten, she went up to her bedchamber and rang for her maid. She did not want to appear to be waiting up for Michael, so she put on her nightgown and dressing gown and took down her hair. Turning the lamp down low, she sat down on the window seat in her room, gazing out into the dark night and brushing her hair.

The moon was only a sliver, providing little light on the landscape, but street lamps at the end of the block provided two circles of illumination in the blackness. Outside the glow of the lamps, one could see little other than the looming bulk of buildings.

Rachel brushed her hair, the long even strokes soothing, almost hypnotic, her gaze on the street. She would not have admitted, even to herself, that she was watching for Michael, but when the dark figure of a man came walking into view in the distance, she straightened, leaning forward to focus on it. As he strode into the light of the street lamp, she saw that it was indeed Michael, and her pulse speeded up a little.

She continued to watch as she tried to decide what she should do. Go to bed and pretend that she did not care what time he came in? Or perhaps she could go down to the library and look for a book, act surprised when he walked in the door. The last thing she wanted was for him to think she was waiting for him. She was *not*. Yet she would like to hear what he and Sir Robert had discussed.

All such thoughts flew out of her head, however, for as she watched Michael leave the circle of light and step into the dark again, suddenly, seemingly from nowhere, three men rushed out from the darkness at him and set upon him with their fists.

17

❦

"Michael!" Rachel shrieked, jumping to her feet.

She whirled and ran from the room, pelting down the stairs, calling for the servants at the top of her lungs. "Westhampton is being attacked. Help! Help!"

By the time she reached the front door, footmen, maids, Michael's valet and even the dignified butler were rushing toward her. Rachel flung open the door, then, seeing a potential weapon in the umbrellas stuck into the umbrella stand beside it, she grabbed the stoutest-handled one and ran out into the night, brandishing the umbrella in her hand and screaming Michael's name.

Michael had stayed longer with Sir Robert than he had intended to, but even after they had gone over the facts of the cases, as well as the possibilities, in great detail, he found himself reluctant to return to his house, knowing that Rachel would not be there.

He tried not to think about her at a party somewhere, laughing and talking with her friends, thinking not at all of him. So it had taken little urging on his friend's part to get him to have a drink, and then another, before he set out for home again.

He had almost reached the house when suddenly three men darted out from behind the bushes and came straight at him. Caught by surprise, he did not manage to completely dodge the first fist aimed at him, and it caught him on the side of his head. Michael turned and swung at his attacker, landing a flush hit on the man's jaw that sent him staggering backward. But the other two men jumped on him, and though he kicked and punched, he was no match for the two of them, especially after the man he had hit staggered to his feet and waded into the fight again.

Michael was knocked to the ground, and as he struggled to stand, fists and feet thudding into him, he saw the astonishing sight of Rachel running down the street toward him, holding aloft an umbrella, hard, hooked handle upward, and screaming like a banshee. Behind her came the rest of his household, from the hardiest footman to the lowly potboy, shouting and carrying torches and assorted weapons such as pokers, mops and iron skillets.

"Jaysus, Mary, and Joseph!" exclaimed one of his attackers, with the distinct sound of Ireland in his voice, as he looked up and saw the group bearing down on them.

The three men hesitated for an instant, then took to their heels, leaving Michael where he lay.

"Michael!" Rachel reached him and dropped down beside him on her knees.

Her robe had come undone as she ran and now hung open; her hair was loose and tumbled down around her shoulders in a thick black fall. She was, Michael thought, the loveliest sight he had ever seen.

"Rachel..." Michael said and smiled. "You came to my rescue."

"Of course! I was at my window, and I saw those men set upon you."

"My lord! Are you all right?" Garson, Michael's valet, squatted down on the pavement beside Michael and reached out to help him rise, while the butler hovered over him anxiously.

Several of the footmen kept after the attackers, chasing them down the block, but most of the servants stopped when they reached Michael, forming a gawking semicircle around Michael and Rachel on the ground.

"I am fine," Michael assured them, ignoring the pain in his side as well as the throbbing in his head.

Rachel reached out to take his other arm, and between them, she and the valet helped Michael to his feet. Solicitously, Rachel slipped her arm around Michael's waist, and he put his arm around her shoulder, leaning slightly against her as they walked back to the house, the crowd of servants trailing along after them. The truth was that, though he was feeling various aches throughout his body, he could have walked without assistance, but Michael enjoyed the feeling of Rachel's body close against his side too much to tell her that.

Once inside the house, the butler took charge of the servants once again, sending a maid to bring cold water and cloths up to Michael's room

Garson escorted Michael up the stairs, solicitously hovering at his side, ready to reach out and give him an assist. Once inside him bedchamber, Rachel guided Michael over to the side of his bed, where he sat down.

Garson bustled up, saying, "Let me help you out of that coat, my lord, so that we can see to your injuries."

"I'm all right, Garson. No need to hover. Lady Westhampton can tend to me."

Garson looked startled. He cast a quick glance at Rachel, then looked back at Michael. "Very well, my lord. If you are sure."

"I am."

Looking somewhat affronted, the valet bowed and left the room. Rachel helped Michael off with his coat and laid it aside, then started to unbutton his shirt. She was bending down, her head close to his, and her perfume filled his nostrils. He was very aware of her fingers on the buttons of his shirt, and he could not help but think of the other day, when Rachel had seduced him as part of her revenge, unbuttoning his shirt and peeling it off his body.

Rachel's mind, too, turned to the other day and the way she had so brazenly undressed him. It amazed

her a little that she had had the courage. It also occurred to her to wonder how she had been able to
stop and play out her joke on him, for right now, this
close to him, in this intimate setting, all she was able
to think of was how much she would like for him to
take her in his arms.

The maid knocked, and Rachel jumped at the
sound. Quickly she took a step backward as the maid
bustled in and put a bowl of water on the bedside
table, laying a small stack of cloths down beside it.
After the girl left, closing the door behind her, Rachel
went to the bowl and soaked one of the rags in it,
then squeezed it out.

Turning back to Michael, she held the cold com-
press against his cheekbone, where there was a raw,
red patch. Michael finished taking off his shirt, winc-
ing a little, and tossed it aside. There were red
splotches on his chest and stomach, one already starting to purple.

Rachel sucked in her breath when she saw them.
"Lie down," she ordered, and took his hand, putting
it against the cloth to hold it to his face while she
went to wet another rag and bring it back to lay on
the injuries on his chest. Again and again, she wet
the rags and squeezed them out, then folded them up
and placed them against each sore spot.

Michael lay, his eyes closed, luxuriating in the
gentle touch of Rachel's fingers, the coolness of the
cloth. He scarcely noticed now the soreness of his
bruises, so sweet was the sensation of Rachel caring
for him.

Rachel was sure that she must be a thoroughly wanton woman, for as she looked at his naked chest, her mind kept turning to lustful thoughts. He was hurt, yet all she could think of was how it felt to touch his skin, how much she wanted to stroke her hands across his chest, to bend down and kiss the smooth flesh.

She glanced up at his face. His eyes were closed, lashes fanning his cheeks, giving him a vulnerable look that somehow stirred her desires even more. Without stopping to think, Rachel raised her hand and lightly brushed her fingertips across his cheek.

Michael opened his eyes and looked at her, and there was in his gaze the same hot hunger that she had seen in his eyes before, when he was pretending to be James Hobson. She drew a quick, uneven breath, heat rising up her throat and into her face. She hardly dared to move, for fear it would break the fragile moment and throw them back into their stiff separation.

He reached out to her other hand, which rested atop the cool cloth on his chest, covering her hand with his. Slowly, lightly, he slid his fingers up her arm, then just as slowly back down to her hand. Her skin tingled, suddenly intensely alive wherever he touched it.

Tentatively, without speaking or even daring to look into Michael's face, Rachel trailed her other hand down from his face onto the hard plane of his chest. Fingers spread out, she drifted across his chest, exploring the differing textures of smooth skin overlaying muscle and bone. She could feel his response in the quiver of his skin, in the quickening of his breath, and it emboldened her to glide her hand lower, onto his stomach.

"Rachel..." Michael sat up and took her face between his hands.

Rachel looked up at him. His eyes burned into her, and desire softened his mouth. He gazed at her for a long moment and seemingly found the answer he sought in her face, for he leaned forward, and his mouth met hers. They kissed softly at first; then their mouths deepened with passion, their tongues meeting and twining in an intricate, intimate dance.

Michael groaned, and his arms went around her tightly, pulling her against his chest. He lay back down, taking her with him. Arms and legs wrapping around her, he pressed her body into his, and Rachel strained to be even closer, yearning to somehow melt into him. They rolled across the bed, kissing and caressing, the bonds of restraint that had been in place for years snapping one after another.

Frantically, heatedly, they kissed, their hands roaming each other's bodies. Tasting, touching, they explored with all the ardor they had denied themselves for so long.

His hands were beneath her open dressing gown, moving all over her body, with only the thin material of her nightgown between his skin and hers. He bunched the material in his hands, pulling it up until his fingers touched the bare skin of her thighs. He moved up beneath her gown, exploring the petal-like softness of her flesh. His breath rasped harshly in his throat. His senses were filled with her—the scent, the feel, the taste. He longed to sink into her, to rush to the fulfillment he had waited so long for, yet at the same time he wanted to savor each exquisite sensation, to feel as much and as intensely as he could.

Rachel quivered and dug her fingers into his shoulders, bombarded with such a dizzying rush of pleasurable sensations that she felt as if she might simply break up and fly apart at any second. The faintly roughened skin of his fingertips teased her delicate flesh, roaming her thighs and moving up onto her hips. She moaned as his hand moved onto the soft, flat plane of her stomach, then up until finally, satisfyingly, it curved around the soft orb of her breast. He cupped and caressed it, teasing the nipple into aching hardness.

She dug her heels into the bed, arching up against him as he stroked her breast, then took the nipple between his thumb and forefinger and squeezed gently. Desire shot through her, and she pulled away, shrugging out of her dressing gown and shoving it aside. Eagerly he helped her take the nightgown off over her head and tossed it off the bed.

Letting out a long breath, Michael looked at her, his gaze roaming down over her naked white body. She was as beautiful as he had always dreamed she was, smooth and alabaster-skinned, the soft, full orbs of her breasts centered by pink-brown nipples.

Rachel lay back down upon the bed, stretching her arms up over her head. She realized that she loved the way he looked at her, that the touch of his heated gaze was almost as pleasurable as the touch of his hand.

Still gazing at her, Michael stood and quickly skinned out of the remainder of his clothes, letting them drop to the floor, then returned to the bed. Leaning on his elbow, he placed his other hand on her chest, moving slowly down over her breasts and onto her stomach, desire burgeoning in him as he watched his hand on her skin and saw her move in response to his caresses.

His fingers delved down between her legs, and Rachel jerked in surprise, her eyes flying open. But the pleasure he evoked in her did not leave room for modesty; she gasped, catching her lower lip with her teeth, and began to move with the thrilling sensation. His fingers opened and explored her soft, secret femininity, stroking and caressing until passion was thundering in both of them.

Then he bent and touched his tongue to her nipple, and Rachel let out a strangled noise of pleasure, her fingers digging into the sheets as if to keep herself anchored to the bed. Lips and tongue loved her nipple, turning it into a hard, aching bud, while he continued to stroke and caress her nether lips, until she was moaning and desperate, her hips moving on the bed, her fingers digging into his shoulders and arms.

She wanted him inside her, but she could do no more than gasp out his name like a plea.

He moved between her legs then and slid into her. She tightened at the bright flash of pain, and he paused, kissing her neck and murmuring soothing sounds as he stroked her legs and sides. She relaxed, and he sank deep within her, and then there was no more pain, but only a deep satisfaction, mingled with a throbbing, urgent need. He moved inside her, thrusting in and out in a deep, primal rhythm, and Rachel matched him, wrapping her legs and arms around him.

Pleasure built inside her, swelling and pulsing, aching for release, until finally it exploded inside her, sweeping up through her so that she cried out, trembling under the force of it. Michael shuddered, groaning, as his own release took him. He collapsed against her, and they lay tangled together, damp and hot and, at last, at peace.

The world seemed a brighter place the next morning. Rachel hummed as she went through her morning toilette. The connecting door stood open between their rooms, and she could look through into Michael's room, where he stood, shaving. She watched him, a small, secret smile hovering about her lips.

They had made love again this morning, waking in the pale predawn to the uncommon pleasure of lying in each other's arms. This time their lovemaking had been slow and dreamy, culminating in the same shattering burst of passion. And Rachel had known that somehow, after all this time, with all that lay between them, she had fallen in love with her husband. She was not sure how it had happened or when, whether it had happened gradually during the years of their marriage or had bloomed only recently within her when she had looked at him as a different person instead of the familiar man she had known all this time.

It didn't matter, really, she thought. All that mattered was that she loved him. She did not know if he loved her still, or if it had died during the long, barren years of their marriage. But she was certain now that he wanted her, and that was enough for the moment. He would come to love her again; she would make sure of it. And for right now, the pleasure of their lovemaking was enough.

Michael came to the doorway between their rooms, wiping away the remains of his shaving soap from his chin and smiling at her.

"I think the best thing to do now is to talk to that footman again," he said. "Hargreaves. He is our best link to the person who is behind all this. If, as we surmise, our unknown criminal hired him to poison Birkshaw's wife, he must have contacted Hargreaves in some way. He might even have spoken to him directly."

So, a short while later, yet another hansom was setting them down in front of the former footman's residence. They climbed the outside set of stairs, and Michael rapped sharply on the door. To their surprise, the door moved beneath his touch, opening a few inches. It had not been completely shut, only pulled to. Michael and Rachel glanced at each other, a sense of alarm growing in them.

"Stay back," Michael warned, putting out an arm

to shield Rachel and hold her back as he pushed open the door and stepped cautiously inside. "Hargreaves?"

Rachel, now behind Michael's back, could see nothing, but she heard his sudden sharp intake of breath. Then Michael rushed forward quickly and dropped down on one knee on the floor. Rachel started in after him and stopped abruptly as she realized that Michael was kneeling beside a man on the floor. Michael's body blocked the man's chest, but she could see his legs splayed out limply on the floor and his head, turned toward her, eyes open and staring lifelessly. Blood smeared the side of his face.

A small, shrill cry escaped her. "Michael! Is he—"

"Yes," he replied tersely. "Hargreaves is dead. Go back outside, Rachel. There is no need for you to see this."

Rachel was not inclined to argue with him. She turned and walked back out the door and plopped down on the top step. She leaned her head forward, fighting the rush of dizziness. She had never seen anything as horrible as the sight of that man's eyes, pale and devoid of life. She swallowed hard and drew a ragged breath.

There was the sound of footsteps behind her, and she turned to see Michael step out onto the landing. He glanced around, then trotted down the stairs and called to a boy playing in the street, promising him a shilling if he returned with a constable. He returned to where Rachel sat.

"Are you all right? I cannot leave here until the constable comes, but I could hail you a cab and send you home," he told her, leaning over her in concern.

Rachel turned up her face to him and smiled wanly. "No. I will be fine. I felt a little light-headed for a moment, but it has passed."

"Good." He sat down beside her on the step and took her hand. "I am sorry you saw that."

Rachel nodded, saying candidly, "So am I. Oh, Michael, did someone shoot that man?"

He frowned. "It doesn't look like it. There was a pistol on the floor beside him, and he left a note."

"A note? You mean…are you saying he committed suicide?"

"It appears so."

"What did the note say?"

"That he poisoned Mrs. Birkshaw with arsenic, day by day, in the food he carried to her room." Michael pulled the piece of paper out of his pocket and unfolded it, handing it to her. "But, as you can see, he also says that Mr. Birkshaw paid him a healthy sum to do it. He was supposed to do it while Birkshaw was out of town, but he felt too guilty and could not finish what he started."

Rachel's eyes ran quickly down the page, reading, "'So Mr. Birkshaw himself came back and did it. I cannot keep silent. I cannot live with the guilt any longer.'"

She stopped and looked at Michael numbly. He took the piece of paper from her fingers and folded it back up.

"I don't believe it," Rachel said flatly. "I cannot believe that Anthony killed her."

"A deathbed confession is a pretty powerful piece of evidence," Michael pointed out.

"Yes, and it is very convenient, too," Rachel replied tartly. "Just as we are about to question the man, he writes a note implicating Anthony in the crime, then shoots himself, rendering it impossible to question him about his confession."

"Still, it seems rather unlikely that he killed himself simply to implicate Birkshaw in the crime."

"And do you know for sure that he killed himself? Could not someone else have shot him and left the gun there to make it look as if he shot himself? Do you know that the gun was even his?"

"No. But there is the note."

"Which anyone could have written. I am not familiar with the man's hand. Are you?"

"No, of course not." Michael pulled out the note and looked at it again. "It is full of misspellings, as if an uneducated person wrote it."

Rachel cast her eye over the clumsy, uneven printing. "Or as if someone was clever enough to make it appear that an uneducated person wrote it. We don't even know whether or not Hargreaves could read and write."

"You're right." He sighed. "It does tie everything up rather neatly. In my experience, life is seldom that neat. But why would anyone kill the man and go to so much trouble in order to implicate Birkshaw? Who hates him? Besides me, of course."

"I don't know. Maybe they are doing it to throw you off, give you a false scent. So that you will go haring off after Anthony and not pursue the real killer." Rachel reached out and took Michael's arm as a thought struck her. "What if the man who is behind all those crimes is alarmed because you are investigating some of them? What if he set up this entire thing to throw you off? To distract you from the crime you were working on? To set you looking into something that really had nothing to do with the rest of it but that you would be bound to investigate? Suppose someone knew that you would be ready to believe the worst of Anthony, and they used that?"

He looked at her for a long moment. "But who would know that? No one knows how much I dislike Anthony or why. No one was privy to what happened that night except the three of us and your father. Ravenscar would not have told anyone."

"No. But perhaps whoever did this would not have to know the details. Perhaps someone saw that, well, that Anthony and I seemed to…have a partiality for each other before you and I were engaged. It would not be a great leap of thinking to assume that you might carry some jealousy toward the man. Perhaps Anthony even told someone or other what happened, or part of it. Or this man knew Anthony and knew that he disliked you and suspected the feeling was mutual."

Rachel could see that Michael was considering her reasoning, and she pressed her point. "Why would Anthony have come to ask you to find out what happened to his wife if he were the one who killed her? That would be the last thing he would want. And if this is all part of some larger conspiracy, as it seems to be, do you honestly think that Anthony is orchestrating it?''

Michael looked at her consideringly. Tendrils of jealousy still twisted within him a little at Rachel's championing of the fellow, but he knew that they were the result of emotion, not reason. Rachel had never been unfaithful to him; he knew that beyond a shadow of a doubt after last night. It had been years since what had happened between Rachel and Birkshaw, and they had not even seen one another until recently, when he came to her for help. Michael believed implicitly in Rachel's honor and integrity.

"No," he admitted finally. "I don't."

"I have no interest in Mr. Birkshaw," Rachel told him seriously. "I do not plead his case because of any feeling for him but because of what I think. I don't want you to make a mistake because you are affected by emotion, for I know that then you would bitterly regret it.''

Michael smiled faintly and raised her hand to his lips. "As soon as the constable arrives," he said, "we will go visit Birkshaw and see what light he can shed on this. There is something about all this that seems planned."

The constable arrived not long after, and Michael left him with the letter and the body, pleading a need to take his wife home from such a grotesque and upsetting scene. As soon as they were able to hail a hansom, they drove to Birkshaw's house.

The butler showed them into the drawing room, and a moment later Anthony hurried in, looking eager. "Lord Westhampton. Lady Westhampton. This is an unexpected pleasure. Can I take from this that you have discovered anything?"

"Yes. We have found a dead body," Michael told him bluntly.

Rachel let Michael take the lead, setting herself to closely watch Anthony for his reactions. He paled now at Michael's words, his eyes widening. "Good Gad, man. Who?"

"Your former footman. The one who brought your wife her meal tray."

"Someone killed him?"

"Why would you assume that?"

"I don't know. Because he was not ill or old, I guess. Was it an accident, then?"

"It appears to be suicide."

"He killed himself! But why? Not because—was he responsible for Doreen's death?"

"The note he left says that you are."

Anthony stared at Michael, speechless, his face turning whiter even than his spotless linen shirt. He sat down abruptly in the nearest chair. "My God! But why—why would he do such a thing?"

"He said that you paid him to put arsenic in Mrs. Birkshaw's food, that he was to do it while you were gone. But he could not bring himself to finish her off, so you returned, he said, and did the deed yourself."

Anthony's mouth dropped open. "Sweet heaven! How could he do this? Why?" He looked pleadingly at Michael, then Rachel. "I did not do it, I swear. You must believe me. I would never have harmed Doreen. Sometimes she was silly, and she was not a woman of great grace or intellect, but there was no wickedness in her, and I never felt anything more than irritation now and then. We did not quarrel. We had a pleasant life. I would not—I could not—"

He turned away, shoving his fingers distractedly through his carefully arranged locks. "Will people believe this, do you think? Will—will the authorities?"

Michael shrugged. "It is a difficult accusation to overlook, Mr. Birkshaw."

"But it is untrue! It's unfair! I have no opportunity to defend myself against him."

"Yes," Michael agreed without any sign of sympathy. "I would say your only hope is to help us find out what really happened. I don't think that you have been honest with us, have you, Mr. Birkshaw? There is more here than what you have told us."

Anthony turned to him, startled. "What do you mean?"

Rachel read the guilt that flitted across Anthony's face. She jumped to her feet, anger surging through her. "Michael is right! You have been lying to us! Anthony, how could you!"

"No! I mean, I did not hurt Doreen. I swear that to you on all that is holy that I did not harm my wife.'' He stopped, then sighed. ''But…yes…I was not…entirely truthful with you.''

''You lied to us? Why?'' Rachel asked. ''I don't understand.''

''I don't understand it, either!'' Anthony shot back. ''What I told you was all true. I didn't lie. Everything happened as I told you. Doreen died, and we all believed that she had caught some illness or other. Then, after I came to London, I got those letters that I told you about. The bit of the arsenic label, and then the other one saying that I owed someone a favor in return. I—it scared me. I realized that someone must have killed Doreen and that now they expected me to help them. I—I assumed that they were threatening to make the authorities think that I had done it if I didn't help them. Well, you see how it has turned out—they have made it look as if I killed her. And I did what he asked!''

''What? Who? Who asked you?'' Michael barked.

''I don't know! That is what is so ghastly about it! Oh, God! It is all ghastly!'' Anthony pulled at his hair, leaving it sticking out in clumps. His face was stamped with confusion and desperation, and Rachel thought that he might burst into tears at any moment.

''All right, Anthony, calm down,'' she said firmly but quietly, taking his arm and leading him over to a chair, then pushing him gently down into it. She sat down directly in front of him and looked straight into his eyes. ''Now, just tell me exactly what happened. Michael has to know everything if he is to help you.''

Birkshaw nodded, seeming somewhat less distraught. "All right. What I did not tell you before was that after I got the second note, I received a third. It said—it said that I was to become reacquainted with you."

"What?" Michael and Rachel said at the same time. Michael strode over to where Birkshaw sat.

"What do you mean, 'reacquainted?'" he asked, looking thunderous.

Birkshaw gazed up at him blankly. "I don't know. That is all it said. I think it read, 'Pick up your friendship with Lady Westhampton again.' Or something like that. I assumed that he meant I should call on her. I have no idea why. It made no sense to me."

"No doubt because it is senseless," Michael commented tartly.

"Was it the footman?" Anthony asked. "Hargreaves? Is he the one behind this?"

"No," Michael responded tersely. "If he had sent you those notes, he would have asked you for money to keep from implicating you. Most people would have."

"It seems absurd," Anthony went on. "I can see that anyone would disbelieve me if I told them. But it is the truth."

"Where is the note about Rachel?" Michael asked. "I want to see it."

Birkshaw looked sheepish. "I—it made me angry, and I wadded it up and tossed it in the fire. I don't have it. I see now that I should have kept it. It would be proof of some sort, but...well, I didn't think."

"Is that why you came to me and asked for Michael's help?" Rachel probed. "Did the note tell you to do that?"

"Oh, no. You see, at first, I thought, 'I won't do it.' I wasn't going to let him scare me, whoever he was. But then it seemed like such a little thing to do, especially compared to people suspecting me of killing Doreen. And it made me wonder, you know, if someone really had killed her and why. Just so I would pay you a call or two? That's insane."

"It would certainly seem so," Michael agreed.

"Then I remembered what Lord Arbuthnot said about you, Westhampton—about your having solved things when the Bow Street Runners could not. And it seemed to me that that was the way out of my predicament!" His face brightened a little as he remembered his cleverness. "I decided that I would call on you, Rachel, and whoever it was would know, I suppose, that I had done so. And he would not do anything to me. But while I was there, I would ask you to get your husband's help on the matter. And perhaps that would get me out of this thing altogether."

He paused, looking from one to the other in a hangdog way. "I'm sorry. I should have told you all about it right from the beginning. I realize that now. You are suspicious of me because I did not. It was just—I felt like such a coward for giving in to the fellow and calling on you. And it all seemed so ridiculous—I was sure you would think me a fool. I am sorry," he finished lamely.

"Is there anything else you have not told us?" Michael asked, looking stern. "Any more instructions from this man?"

Anthony shook his head. "No. He has sent me nothing. I cannot understand why anyone would do this to me. I did what he asked. Do you think he knows that I asked you for help?"

"It's possible."

"I don't understand. Why would anyone do this to me? Who hates me that much?"

"I'm not sure that it is you at whom all this is aimed," Michael replied, looking grim.

18

Michael turned to Rachel. "I think it is time we took our leave. If I were you, Mr. Birkshaw, I would be very careful over the course of the next few days. I will try to find out what is going on as quickly as I can. But I cannot rule out the possibility that you are in danger."

Anthony stared back at him, his eyes so wide that they looked as if they might pop out of his head at any moment.

Michael and Rachel left him there contemplating his future and started walking toward home. For a moment they strode along in silence, then Michael burst out, "What poppycock! That is the biggest bag of nonsense I have ever heard."

"You don't believe him?" Rachel asked, looking at her husband.

"No, but it is so idiotic that I cannot believe anyone would make up a story so feeble!" Michael exclaimed. "If he had really killed his wife, surely he could have come up with a more intelligent story than that.''

Rachel nodded. ''Yes. Well, I think we know one thing for certain. Anthony could not be the mastermind behind this...this web of crime. He is far too stupid.''

Michael let out a short bark of laughter and turned to look at her. Rachel's blunt statement let him know, more than any honeyed words of love and desire could have, that he had no need to feel jealousy where Anthony Birkshaw was concerned.

''Well?'' Rachel said somewhat defiantly. ''It is the truth.''

''Yes. It is. I think someone far more clever than our friend Birkshaw is behind this.''

''And when you said that to Anthony back there, that perhaps it was not aimed at him, what you meant was that by using Anthony he was aiming it at *you*.''

Michael nodded. ''I was foolish not to pay more heed to the highwayman's warning. I was so far from discovering anything that I felt sure no villain would have seriously thought he was in danger from me. I wrote the warning off as the highwayman's wanting money. I came to London only because as long as there was even a possibility, however remote, that someone might harm me, I feared that he might try to do it through you.''

''And he did work through me, didn't he?'' Rachel said. ''Why else would he have sent Anthony to visit me? He must have hoped that it would reawaken your dislike and mistrust of the man.''

"Yes, and I fell right into the trap."

They walked along for a few more moments in silence before Rachel said in a troubled voice, "Michael...if some person *is* planning all this, and if he *is* trying to make you believe that Anthony killed his wife, then he is using him as a sort of decoy, isn't he? To distract you and get you working on this murder instead of tracking him down?"

"It would seem so," Michael agreed.

"What a monstrous thing to do!" Rachel exclaimed. "That would mean he has taken an innocent man and made it appear that he is guilty of murder. Anthony could be put to trial, even hanged. And it would mean that this criminal killed the footman, as well, because that is the primary piece of proof against Anthony. And he would also have killed Anthony's poor wife, or he would not have been able to set up the whole thing."

Michael nodded. "I suppose that Mrs. Birkshaw could have simply died from natural causes, as everyone believed at the time, and that our villain simply saw the opportunity to turn my suspicions against Birkshaw. But certainly he would have had to kill the footman in order to leave the suicide note implicating Anthony. And, in all probability, he engineered the whole thing. I would suspect he hired the footman to kill Mrs. Birkshaw, then killed *him* to throw suspicion on Birkshaw."

"What a heartless, cold-blooded man he must be!" Rachel cried in a low voice. "To destroy people like that—not even out of hate or anger but merely to throw you off the scent! It is abominable."

"Yes, I agree. The man is inhumanly cold and calculating."

They continued to their house, thinking their own thoughts.

But later that night, as they were sitting in the music room after supper, as Rachel was idling over the keys of the piano, lazily picking out a tune while Michael read, she turned to him and said, "I am sorry, Michael."

"What?" He looked up blankly from his book. "Sorry? About what?"

"That he has used me to hurt you," she said. "Whoever is doing these things. That he used Anthony to divert you."

Michael shrugged. "It is scarcely your fault that his mind works that way."

"No, but it is my fault that you had reason to be jealous of Anthony. It is because of me that you dislike him." She paused, then asked tentatively, "Are you indeed that jealous of him?"

Michael brows shot up. "Jealous? Of course I am jealous of him." His voice roughened, and he stood up abruptly. "It scores my soul to know that he is the love of your life." Though he knew that Rachel did no longer love Anthony, he could not forget that Anthony, not he, was the only man to hold her heart.

"But I do not love him!" Rachel exclaimed, aghast. "I have not loved him for—oh, years and years. I don't even remember when I got over feeling the hurt. Frankly, I am not entirely sure that I ever loved him. I didn't really know him, you know. We were always surrounded by parents and friends and—well, it was never a natural situation. I had no way of knowing what sort of man he really was. All I knew was that my heart fluttered whenever I saw him. It was probably as my mother said, merely an infatuation.''

''There is no way of knowing, I suppose, since you were not allowed to follow your heart.'' Michael was turned away, not looking at her.

''There is no feeling in me for him any longer,'' Rachel told him. ''When he came here to ask for your help, I wondered what I would feel when I saw him, but the truth was, I felt nothing. Whatever I felt for him, love or infatuation, it died long ago. And, believe me, nothing I have seen of him since that day has awakened any renewal of it.''

''Rachel!'' Michael strode across the room to her and wrapped his arms around her, lifting her off her feet and kissing her fiercely.

Then he pulled away and swept her up into his arms and carried her up the stairs to her bedroom, not caring if any of the servants saw them. All he could think of was Rachel and his need to be inside her, to kiss and caress her until both of them were teetering on the edge of the dark vortex of passion.

They made love hungrily, passionately, like people too long denied the pleasures of their bodies, coming together at last in a wild cataclysm. Afterward they slept, curled together.

Michael awoke some time later, stirred to consciousness by the chill in the air. He got up and pulled the covers up over both of them. Rachel murmured in her sleep and snuggled up against him. He curled his arm around her and kissed the top of her head, feeling a happiness and peace he had never known before.

He lay there in the dark for a long time, thinking about love and jealousy and times past, of enemies and friends, and when at last he fell asleep, he knew what he would do.

"I think I may know how to solve this investigation," Michael said the next morning over breakfast.

Rachel stared at him, his words chasing away the last cobwebs of sleep. "What? How?"

"We may be able to smoke out the criminal."

"How?"

"I will tell you in a little while," Michael said, a smile touching his lips at her impatient expression. "But I need to talk to Perry about it, so it will be easier if I wait and tell you both at the same time."

"Perry? Perry Overhill?" Rachel asked, confused. She could not imagine their portly, genial friend being able to help them solve a mystery. "But why? What can Perry do?"

"Patience. I will explain it all to you."

Rachel was anything but patient as they strolled over to Perry's house. She peppered Michael with questions, which he deflected with a smile.

Overhill's butler showed them into the drawing

room, which was decorated with Perry's usual impeccable taste. A moment later Perry himself bustled in, beaming. He made an elegant bow and placed a kiss on Rachel's hand, though both gestures were rendered faintly absurd by his pear-shaped figure. "Rachel, my dear, you are lovely, as always. And Michael—such a pleasant surprise to see you back in town. When did you return?"

Michael smiled, shaking his friend's hand and saying, "It's all right, Perry, Rachel knows all about it."

Perry put on a confused air. "All about what?"

"Everything," Rachel said, chuckling. "Michael's sister Lilith, his disguises, his work. I know the whole story that you have tried so valiantly to hide from me—and, by the way, I have a bone to pick with you over deceiving me for years—so you can cast off that vague air."

"It was not my preference, I assure you," Overhill told her earnestly. "Gracious me, Michael, what has come over you?" He looked searchingly at his friend, and his eyebrows rose. "Ah…" he said almost to himself, nodding sagely. "I see."

"See what?" Rachel asked.

"Why, that our Michael is a changed man." His eyes danced as he turned back to Michael, saying a trifle archly, "One can only wonder what happened to the fellow."

"No need to wonder. You know as well as I do that the change is due to Rachel." Michael took his wife's hand and lifted it to his lips, smiling at her tenderly.

"Sit down. Sit down." Perry gestured them toward the arrangement of sofa and chairs that centered the elegant blue drawing room. "Let me ring for some refreshment. Then you can tell me what has brought you here, for I cannot feel that you are in need of company right now."

"I have a favor to ask of you," Michael said, getting immediately to the point as his friend tugged at the bellpull. He walked with Rachel over to the couch, but remained standing, his hand clasped behind his back.

Perry glanced at him and frowned as he saw the serious expression on Michael's face. "Westhampton...what is it? You look as grave as a parson."

"I am a trifle worried," Michael admitted. "It is this investigation I am working on. The thing is, I— I would like for you to escort Rachel to the opera tonight. I have things to attend to, and I want to be certain that she is safe. If I know that she is in your care—"

"Michael!" Both Rachel and Perry exclaimed, staring at him.

"What are you talking about?" Rachel went on, rising to face her husband. "Why would I not be safe? Where are you going to be? What are you going to be doing?"

"Yes," Perry agreed. "I must say, old chap, you are sending chills up my spine. What is the danger?"

"I think, perhaps, that I have been betrayed by...someone I am close to."

"Michael!" Rachel paled, her stomach suddenly

icy. "What are you talking about? Who? Why didn't you tell me?"

"I wanted to explain it only once," he said. "It is a difficult thing for me to say."

"I should think so!" Perry exclaimed, looking shaken, and he sank down in a chair. "Pray explain yourself."

"I have been working on a case. Several cases, actually, that have certain things in common. There is no need to go into all the details, but yesterday I began to suspect that I have been led deliberately astray, that I have been pointed in a false direction."

"Toward Anthony, you mean?" Rachel asked.

"Who?" Perry asked, blinking. "Anthony who? Oh!" His face cleared. "You mean the chap you were asking me about? You are investigating him? Why? Because of his wife? You think he killed his wife?" Overhill gaped at Michael.

"I have been suspicious of him," Michael replied. "You see, there were obvious clues pointing toward the man."

"Good Gad. That is incredible!" Overhill gasped. "I don't know the man well, but...well, I mean, not the sort of thing one would expect." He shook his. "Are they going to arrest him?"

"No. I haven't gone to Bow Street with this yet. No one knows but me...well, me and the real murderer."

"The real murd—" Perry gazed at him blankly. "You mean—it isn't Birkshaw?"

"I think not. It simply did not fit together well."

"What do you mean?"

"There were inconsistencies, things that might lead one to think it was not Birkshaw who killed his wife. But I had overlooked them, you see, because of my jealousy."

Perry stared. "Jealousy! What do you mean?" He glanced over cautiously at Rachel. "Had the fellow made...uh, unwelcome advances?"

"No," Rachel put it. "But once, a long time ago, before I married Michael, Anthony and I fancied ourselves in love with each. We hadn't seen each other in years, but..."

"But when his name came up, I reacted more like a jealous husband than an impartial investigator. Once I realized that, I saw that someone had used that knowledge against me. He had tricked me into suspecting Birkshaw, knowing my feelings about him would make me believe almost anything bad about the man."

"But why would anyone want to do that?" Perry leaned forward, enthralled with the story.

"To throw me off the scent. You see, I was working on another investigation, and I believe that the criminal thought I had learned too much, was getting too close to figuring it out. I don't know why, really, as I was hopelessly muddled. I think he threw this thing with Birkshaw in to distract me, send me haring off after him because I was personally involved in it, you see."

"But that's not all," Rachel put in. "I think he intends to harm Michael."

"What?" Perry gaped at her. "You aren't serious."

Michael, too, turned to look at her, startled.

She grimaced at Michael. "Did you honestly think I had not noticed?" She turned back to Perry, explaining, "There have already been two attempts on Michael's life."

"Good Gad!"

"Someone shot at him," Rachel explained. "And the other night, as he was coming home, three men set upon him."

"It is my belief," Michael put in, "that this criminal wants to do away with me and make it look as if Birkshaw is to blame for it."

Overhill stared at him, speechless.

"It will solve all his problems. I will no longer be pursuing him. And Anthony will be the obvious culprit, so there will be no investigation into anyone else."

"Of course!" Rachel breathed. "That makes sense. That is another reason he involved Anthony. Bow Street would doubtless leap to that conclusion."

"But that—that's diabolical!" Perry exclaimed, aghast.

"I think we are dealing with a diabolical mind here. However, I have a plan to catch him."

"You do?" Rachel asked, turning to look at Michael.

He nodded. "That is why I need Perry here to look after you tonight, to make sure you are far from danger. I intend to set a trap for the fellow."

"But how?"

"Well, you see, I think I know who it is."

"What?" Rachel's voice rose. "You know who it is, and you didn't tell me?"

"I am telling you now, dear," he said, smiling at her. "But first, let me explain to Perry about the crimes." He described to him the various unsolved cases that he and Bow Street had worked on the past few years and the bizarre way in which they were connected.

"So you see," he said, finishing, "I think the crimes have all been carried out by one man, someone very clever, who gets other people to do the various crimes, people he has paid or people who are completely disconnected from the case in question. Then he uses the people who have benefited from that crime to help him with some other crime that will benefit someone else. Only *he* ties all the people together, and he is always behind the scenes, manipulating everything."

"But how do you know who he is?" Perry asked. "I thought you said that you had not been able to solve the crimes?"

"I didn't know until this thing with Anthony. You see, I realized that whoever threw that in my path would have had to know about my jealousy of Birkshaw. The thing was, I haven't spoken about it to anyone."

"Nor have I," Rachel added.

"And the only ones who knew besides Rachel, Anthony Birkshaw and me were Rachel's parents, and I am sure they would not have let the story loose.''

''I have never heard a word about it,'' agreed Perry, frowning in a puzzled way. ''So how—''

''I mispoke when I said no one knew. I had told one person—my sister Lilith.''

A stunned silence hung in the air. The other two occupants of the room stared at Michael.

''Lilith!'' Rachel exclaimed at last. ''Michael, you cannot be serious! Lilith loves you, she admires you. She would never do anything to harm you!''

He smiled at her. ''I agree. I do not think that Lilith is behind the crimes. However, she has a lover, and she might have told him.''

''Sir Robert?'' Rachel gasped. ''You think that Sir Robert is the mastermind behind these crimes?''

''Sir Robert Blount!'' Perry echoed, looking as stunned as Rachel. ''Michael, really, I think you— well, that's absurd. You and he have been friends for years and years. How can you think that he would try to kill you? That he would do such things?''

''I know.'' Michael looked weary. ''Believe me, I did not want to believe it. I still don't. But I could not overlook the facts. First of all, he is one of the few people who could have known about Anthony Birkshaw. Secondly, he has a mind capable of deviousness. He used it for good, mind you, when he and I were fighting Bonaparte's spy ring. But if he turned his mind to crime, he would be able to think of something of this complexity and inventiveness.''

"But that doesn't mean he has done so," Rachel protested. "He is your friend. He loves your sister."

"I know. I have to believe that in the beginning he had no intention of harming me. That he thought his scheme so clever it would escape detection. And it would have, if he had not overestimated my abilities. But I think when I was working on two cases that related to him, he began to get worried that I would figure it out. Then, when I started looking into Mrs. Birkshaw's death, he decided he could not risk that I would put all the pieces together. I would like to think that the first time he shot at me, it was a warning shot, designed to make me give up the investigation. He is an excellent marksman, yet he hit only my shoulder. But then, the other night when I was attacked…I had just left Robert, and I had told him about the progress we had made on the case. I think he realized that he could not afford to let me live any longer."

"Still…" Perry said, shaking his head.

"There's more. There is the factor of money. His father left him nothing but a title and a house, which he had to sell to settle the estate's debts. He worked for the government because he had to earn a wage in order to live. All through the time we worked together, he was always strapped for money. But now he has enough money that he is able to live quite nicely without working. He even purchased Lilith's gaming establishment for her. He told me that he received a small inheritance from an aunt, which he subsequently built up through wise investing."

"But such things do happen," Perry pointed out. "That happened to me—not the wise investing, of course, but the inheritance. My grandfather left me money when he died."

"Yes, it happens. But we don't know that he really did inherit. It could have been a lie to explain away his sudden increase in funds. All we really know for certain is that he did not have money in the past and now he has a good deal. Also, because he is a member of the *Ton,* he knows all the gossip—who badly needs money and would receive it if an inconvenient relative dies, who has valuable objects to be stolen, what wife or husband would be glad to pay to get rid of a spouse. He has necessary knowledge that most members of the criminal class do not. And, unlike most aristocrats, he also has access to a large number of criminals through his years of working with the spy ring and then with Bow Street. He would know burglars, pickpockets, men who would murder for pay."

Rachel frowned. "Yes, I can see how it would be possible for him to be the mastermind, but that doesn't mean that he *is.* I mean, a number of those things apply to you, as well."

Her response startled a laugh from Overhill. "A direct hit, Rachel!"

Michael smiled. "I know—although I think we can absolve me from having hired someone to kill me. The most damning thing is the knowledge the man obviously has about Anthony."

"But even that is only a possibility. You don't

know that Lilith told him. You have no proof,'' Rachel insisted.

"Quite right," Perry agreed. "You can scarcely go about accusing the fellow."

"I know. That is why I have decided to set a trap for him."

"A trap!" Rachel narrowed her eyes. "What kind of trap? Is that why you want Perry to take me somewhere, to get me out of the way so that you can do something dangerous?"

"I will feel much better knowing that you are somewhere safe, yes," Michael told her. "There is nothing wrong in that."

"Only the fact that it means that where you are will *not* be safe," Rachel retorted. "Michael, what are you planning?"

"It is simple, really. I shall tell Sir Robert that I plan to meet Anthony tonight at a certain place and time. If he is the man behind all this, I believe that he will get there before then and try to kill me so that he may lay the blame on Anthony."

"Michael!" Rachel exclaimed, horrified. "Have you run mad? You are going to provide him with yourself as a target just so that you can prove that he is the man behind these crimes?"

"You might have a little faith in me, my dear," Michael returned mildly. "I will get there earlier than Sir Robert does, and then when he arrives and hides, preparing to shoot me, I will have the proof I need."

"You *are* mad," Rachel said.

"She's right," Overhill agreed. "You cannot go there alone."

"He won't be, because I am going with him," Rachel put in.

Both men swung on her, protesting.

"No! Rachel..." Perry looked horrified. "That would just put both of you in danger."

"Absolutely not." Michael crossed his arms and looked forbidding.

"Well, I cannot go to the opera while you are out trying to get yourself killed!"

"Then stay at home. You and Perry could have an evening of cards, say."

"You need someone with you. Someone to help you watch for Sir Robert. To guard your back. You cannot see everywhere at once. He could sneak up on you."

"I can take care of it. I promise you, I will be fine."

"You need a witness!" Rachel cried, pleased at having come up with another argument. "Someone to corroborate that Sir Robert came there to ambush you."

Michael raised an eyebrow. "You think that my word would not be good enough?"

"Don't try to throw me off course. You know I'm right. Of course you are trustworthy—everyone knows that. But Sir Robert is also a man of breeding and apparent honor. He was a hero alongside you in the war. You have a difficult case to prove. It would help greatly if you had another witness to his perfidy,'' Rachel argued reasonably. ''Besides, if there are two people there, he will be less likely to shoot you. He cannot go about leaving dead bodies strewn all over the place.''

''If he is cornered, I'm not sure what he is capable of doing. I cannot risk it, Rachel. Not you.''

''You are risking yourself!''

''That is different. I have had some experience in these matters. I will have my pistols with me, and Sir Robert is well aware of my accuracy with them. You, on the other hand, would not only be vulnerable, you would make me vulnerable. I would have to worry about you. I could not simply concentrate on the matter at hand. Your presence would distract me, and that could prove fatal. Besides, he would know he had only to threaten you and I would be rendered harmless. If I had a pistol on him, he would know that even if he shot me, he would die, too, whereas if you were there, he would need only to point his gun at you and I would have to give up. You would endanger me, not help me.''

Rachel scowled. She would have liked to argue, but she knew that he was right.

''I will go with you,'' Perry announced. ''Don't look at me like that. I'm not completely useless, you know. I may not be the marksman you are, but I have clipped a few wafers at Manton's. I can guard your back. And Rachel is right—two people's testimony would carry more weight.''

''Yes, take Perry with you,'' Rachel agreed. She did not really think that Perry Overhill would be adequate protection—she wished desperately that Richard or Devin were there—but having him with Michael would be better than Michael's facing an enemy alone.

"No. I need Perry to stay with you," Michael said. "I have to be sure that you are safe."

"I will be at home, with servants all around," Rachel pointed out. "And the man you suspect will be with you. What could happen to me? I will be perfectly safe. You need Perry with you much more than I need him."

"She is right," Perry added. "Be sensible. I am sure—if Blount is your man—that he does not want to hurt you. He simply wants you out of the way. All harming Rachel would do is wound you and make you even more determined to capture him. It would be foolish in the extreme of him."

Michael hesitated, obviously swayed by the arguments. Finally he sighed and said, "All right. But only—" he fixed Rachel with a serious look "—if you stay at home, locked in and with the servants around."

Rachel rolled her eyes. "I promise. But I do wish that you would hold off on this, Michael. We could write to Dev and Richard, and they would come to help immediately. I know they would."

"No. I need to do this now. And I do not need an army. Perry will do fine."

So it was that several hours later Rachel settled down to spend an evening at home. Michael, thrusting a brace of pistols into the pockets of his jacket and looking grim, gave her a goodbye kiss and turned to go pick up Perry at his home.

"Michael, wait," Rachel said, catching hold of his sleeve. "I don't think this is a good idea. I cannot imagine why I thought Perry would be any protection. Please, wait. I will write to Richard this very evening."

Her stomach had been in knots ever since their conversation that afternoon, and now, with the moment actually upon them, she did not think she could bear for Michael to leave. What if he was taken from her now, when she had finally realized that she loved him?

"No. I cannot wait. Besides, until I catch our villain, I will still be in danger of his killing me."

"This is just so awful. I don't know what I would do if anything happened to you."

Michael kissed Rachel on the cheek, saying, "I am glad that you are concerned for me. You have no idea how much." He smiled down into her eyes. "But there is no need for you to worry. I promise you. This will soon be over, and I will be back here."

Rachel managed a smile for him and kept it in place until Michael was out the door. Then she dropped down into a chair and put her head in her hands. She did not know how she would get through the next few hours. There was nothing she could think of that would take her mind off Michael and what was about to happen. Reading was out of the question, and she was certain that if she started work on any of the delicate clothes for Miranda's coming baby, she would just have to rip out all the stitches the next day.

"My lady." Rachel looked up in surprise to see one of the footmen standing at the door. "A Mrs. Neeley is here to see you."

"Lilith?" Rachel stared at him. Her anxiety flared up into full-blown fear. It was not like Lilith to come calling on her; she was always concerned about not presuming in any way on her relationship with Michael. Rachel feared that only some sort of bad news would have brought her here.

"Show her in," Rachel said, rising to her feet. She crossed the room, meeting Lilith as she entered the doorway. "Lilith! Is something wrong?"

Lilith looked somewhat taken aback. "No. I mean…should there be?"

Hastily Lilith handed her cloak to the footman, and both women waited until he had left the room.

"I—I was just surprised to see you," Rachel said. She could not tell Lilith what Michael was doing this evening. If Michael was right in his suspicions, Lilith would find out about her lover soon enough. And if Michael was wrong, the fact that he had been suspicious might put a strain on the siblings' relationship.

"I knew I should not have come," Lilith said. "I told Robert it was not appropriate, but he was so insistent."

"Oh, no! Don't think that," Rachel said hastily. "You are always welcome in this house. You are Michael's sister. I was merely surprised to see you.

My, uh, nerves are a trifle unsettled this evening. Please, come in. Sit down.''

Rachel rang for a servant and requested tea, then turned back to Lilith. She smiled as she sat down beside the other woman on the couch and said, ''Sir Robert wanted you to come here?''

''Yes. I cannot imagine why, really,'' Lilith said, looking a little worried. ''I asked him, and he would say only that he thought you were feeling rather lonely and would welcome a bit of company.''

''That was very kind of him,'' Rachel replied, her heart sinking. She could not think of any good reason why Sir Robert would suddenly decide to send Lilith over here. It must be that he wanted Lilith out of the house this evening—perhaps so she would not see him leave and ask where he was going? Or it might be that for some reason he wanted to make sure Rachel was occupied. Whatever the reason, it seemed suspicious that Sir Robert would choose this very evening to push Lilith into paying a call on Rachel.

The tea was brought, and Rachel poured, trying to keep up a polite conversation when all the while inside she was racked with worry. It was difficult, and she could see Lilith frowning, wondering what was wrong.

''I am sorry,'' Rachel said. ''I am afraid that I am a trifle distracted.''

''Then I must ask you what you first said to me— what is wrong? Is there any way that I can help?''

''How kind of you to ask, but, no, I do not think that you—or anyone—can help.''

Lilith looked alarmed, and Rachel realized how dramatic her statement sounded. She began to flounder about, searching for an acceptable excuse for her distraction, when the same footman appeared at the door.

"Mr. Birkshaw to see you, my lady."

19

"What?" Rachel stared at the footman. Who else was going to pop in on her? Tonight, of all nights! "Umm. Well, show Mr. Birkshaw in, Debney."

She turned toward Lilith, shrugging apologetically. "I am so sorry. I had no idea that he was coming."

Anthony strode into the room, looking distraught. "Rachel! Where is Lord Westhampton? I must see him. I have had another missive from—" He glanced around and saw Lilith for the first time and gave a little start of surprise. "Oh—I beg pardon. I did not realize that you had guests. I am most sorry."

"It's all right. Mr. Birkshaw, I do not know if you are acquainted with Mrs. Neeley."

"No—yes, I mean, that is, I believe we have met on one or two occasions. How do you do, Mrs. Neeley?" Anthony looked thoroughly ill at ease. No doubt he was startled, Rachel thought with a burst of amusement, to find the owner of a gambling establishment in Rachel's drawing room.

"I am fine, thank you, Mr. Birkshaw." The twinkle in Lilith's eyes told Rachel that she was well aware of the comic undertones of the scene.

"I—I must speak to Lord Westhampton," Anthony said, starting over again.

"Yes, you said you received a message from—I assume from the man who has sent you the other messages?"

"Just so." Anthony looked relieved that Rachel understood and sent a cautious glance Lilith's way.

"You may speak in front of Mrs. Neeley," Rachel said. She sincerely hoped that whatever he had to say would not be about Sir Robert. "What sort of message did you receive?"

"An odd one. Well, they always are, aren't they?" He shrugged. "It said that I was to go to a certain address at nine o'clock. It—I believe it is somewhere near the docks."

"What?" Rachel sat up straighter. The warehouse where Michael and Perry were going was near the docks. "What is the address exactly?"

"Water Street at Conover," he said, frowning. "Something of a seedy area at this time of night, I'd say."

Rachel was glad she was sitting down. That was the address of the warehouse where Michael had told Sir Robert that he was to meet Anthony, but the time was an hour later than what Michael had said. It seemed clear proof that Sir Robert was the man who had been sending the messages to Anthony, which would mean, by what Rachel and Michael had surised, that he really was the mastermind behind the whole criminal scheme.

"I don't know what to do—whether I should go r not. What does he want of me? What does it nean?"

"I am not sure what it means, exactly," Rachel eplied. "But I think you probably should not go. It night interfere with a trap that Michael has laid or...someone."

"A trap!" Anthony goggled at her. "You mean he has set a trap for...for this man?"

"Yes." Rachel stopped. How could she explain the scheme without implicating Sir Robert? She glanced over at Lilith, who was frowning.

"I don't understand," Lilith said. "I thought Robert said that Michael was meeting Mr. Birkshaw tonight. That that was why you would be here alone and might welcome company."

"What?" Anthony looked even more confused. "But I had no plans to meet Lord Westhampton. Was I supposed to?"

"No. No. That was merely part of, um, this trap." Rachel shifted uncomfortably in her seat.

"But why would he say—" Lilith began, then stopped abruptly. Rachel looked over at her. Lilith was staring at her, shaking her head. "No," Lilith said in a way that made the word almost more a prayer than a statement. "No. You can't be saying that Michael set a trap for Robert."

Rachel cast about frantically for something to say, but her silence was answer enough for Lilith.

"That *is* it, isn't it?" she cried. "You are sayin[
that Michael lied to Robert. That he is trying to tra[
him! Why?"

"I'm so sorry," Rachel said. "Please, Lilith, be[
lieve me, Michael doesn't want to believe it."

"Believe what?" Lilith said, her voice rising emo[
tionally. "What is he trying to trap him into? Wha[
does he think Robert has done?"

"He doesn't know for sure," Rachel said quickly[
"He doesn't want to believe Sir Robert has done anything wrong, but there was the possibility.... He had
to find out."

"Find out what?"

"He thinks that Sir Robert might be—well, behind
some crimes Michael has been investigating."

"What he has been working on the past weeks?"

Rachel nodded. "And, if it is Sir Robert, then he
may also want to get Michael out of the way."

"Out of the— You mean kill him?" Lilith jumped
to her feet, eyes flashing and her cheeks flushed.
"That is absurd! Rob would never hurt Michael. He
is like a brother to him. You might as well say that
I would hurt him or the duke or your own brother!"

"Lilith, please." Rachel went to her, taking Lilith's hands. "Michael is by no means certain. That
is why he—"

"Set a trap for him?" Lilith burst out. "As if he
were an animal. A common criminal. Robert should
not have to pass a test for Michael! He has proven
his loyalty and friendship time and time again."

"I know. Michael does not want to believe it. Nei-

er do I. I was sure that tonight would prove that
Michael was wrong, and we would be happy about
that. But now, this letter to Anthony…''

Lilith whirled to face Anthony. ''This letter—do
you have it?''

Anthony brightened. ''Yes, I saved this one. I was
sure Michael would want to see it.''

''Show it to me,'' Lilith demanded, going toward
him. ''I can tell you whether the handwriting is Sir
Robert's.''

Anthony glanced uncertainly at Rachel. She nodded.

''Yes. Go ahead, Anthony. Let her see.''

He reached inside his coat and drew out a folded
sheet of paper, which he extended to Lilith. She
snatched it from his fingers and began to read.

''It is not his handwriting!'' Lilith looked up, tri-
umph glowing on her face. ''This was not written by
Robert.''

''Are you sure? He could have tried to change his
hand, make it unrecognizable.'' Rachel crossed the
room and took the letter from Lilith's fingers. She
looked down at it, ready to point out an attempt to
disguise his handwriting in block letters or a messy
script.

She froze, staring at the page in front of her, all
the blood draining out of her face. ''My God!'' she
said, her voice barely above a whisper. ''I know this
hand.''

The warehouse was dark and deserted, as Michael
had known it would be. It was owned by an importer

for whom Michael had found a thief who was raidin
his goods. The man had been happy to lend Michae
the use of the place for the evening and had give
him a key to the smaller side door, which led int
the warehouse through the offices.

Michael unlocked the door and led Perry past th
office and into the vast cavern of the warehouse. I
was dark inside, the only windows high up in th
walls and admitting very little of the moonlight outside. The light of Michael's lantern, shielded on one
side, lit up only a small semicircle of the room,
enough to reveal vague humps of the merchandise
stored there—crates, sacks and stacks of bales—an
eerie sight in the dim light.

"I say, Michael, couldn't you have found a more
propitious place for a meeting?" Perry whispered behind him.

"It's good for my purposes," Michael replied.
"Places to hide and only one obvious entrance."

He turned first right, then left, and made his way
around a mound of huge sacks, smelling redolently
of coffee. He peered around the stack, and Perry
could see that he had a direct view of the door
through which any visitor would enter.

"Well," Perry said, his voice still hushed and nervous, "I guess all we have to do now is wait for
Blount to arrive."

"Yes." Michael's voice was tinged with sadness.
"I can only hope that he will not come. It is a hard
thing, to find that a long-trusted friend is really a thief

nd a murderer. It would be far better if this whole
hing turned out to be a fruitless endeavor.''

"Oh, I don't think it will be," Perry said, no
onger whispering.

Michael turned around to look at his friend. Perry
stood facing him, a pistol in his hand, pointed directly
at Michael.

"We must go!" Rachel cried, turning to Anthony.
"Michael is in grave danger. We have to go!"

"Go where? I don't understand."

"To this address. This warehouse."

She ran out of the room, leaving Anthony gawking
after her. Lilith, quicker of mind, was right on her
heels.

"Wait!" Anthony started after them. "Rachel!
What is going on?"

"Michael is in terrible danger," Rachel explained,
though she did not pause in her headlong rush out
the front door. "We need a hansom."

"But—"

As he spluttered, Lilith was already waving her
arm frantically at a hansom cab down the street. The
three of them piled in, Anthony still asking questions.

"Whose handwriting is this? Why is Michael in
danger?"

"It belongs to Perry Overhill."

"Overhill! Are you sure? It can't be him. I know
the chap. Well, I haven't seen much of him for years,
but I—he—" He looked faintly embarrassed. "He

was a friend to me when...during that rough tim
after you became engaged to Lord Westhampton.''

Rachel looked at him sharply. "Perry? Perry is
friend of yours?''

"He was. He was in love with you, too, you know
We commiserated with each other over our broker
hearts. He knew he didn't stand a chance with you,
of course. He was aware that you loved me.''

Lilith, sitting beside Rachel, stared at him, astonished. She turned to Rachel, her face full of questions.

"Yes," Rachel said quickly, "I once fancied myself in love with Mr. Birkshaw. It was many years
ago, before I married Michael.''

"It was Overhill who encouraged me to not give
up on you," Anthony went on.''

"What do you mean, not give up on me?" Rachel
asked, suspicion tinging her voice. "Are you saying
that Perry encouraged your coming up to Westhampton and asking me to run—''

Anthony nodded, looking a little shamefaced. "He
told me that he was sure you still loved me, that you
would want to escape your forced marriage.... I guess
neither he nor I thought about the consequences.''

"I have a feeling Perry thought about them," Rachel said dryly.

"Who is this Perry?" Lilith asked.

"He is a friend of ours—or so Michael and I
thought. But that was his handwriting on that note. I
have seen it many times on cards he sent with flowers
or a gift. Oh, God, I've been such a fool! I never

realized that it was true! I always thought he was exaggerating his feelings for me, putting on a show of being a romantic. I didn't take him seriously. No one did.''

"But where are we going?" Lilith asked. "Why is Michael in danger?"

"Because when he set up the trap for Sir Robert, he took Perry with him!"

Michael looked from the pistol leveled at his chest up to his friend's face. "So," he said slowly, "it is you who was behind the crimes."

A smile quirked up one corner of Overhill's mouth. "Yes," he replied, his voice changed from its usual tone, harder and more sarcastic now, sure of himself. "It was I—poor foolish, bumbling Perry. Rather a good disguise, don't you think? No one would ever suspect such a fool to be the mastermind of such a scheme."

"Actually, I had assumed you were too honest and good a man," Michael replied. "Obviously I have been sadly mistaken about you all this time."

"Rather." Perry smirked. His demeanor had changed. He stood straighter, holding the gun easily, naturally, as if it were something he was accustomed to doing. "You were almost as easy to play as that idiot Birkshaw. Most people are, I find—a few threats, a bribe here and there. And the rest is pretense. My scheme has been amazingly easy to run."

"But why? Why did you start this?"

"Money, of course. I did not inherit a vast estate

as you did," Perry sneered. "My father was not a wealthy man, and even with what my grandfather left me, I was fast running out of money. I have rather expensive tastes, you see. And women like Leona cost a pretty penny to keep happy."

"Leona Vesey! You were one of her lovers?"

"You find that difficult to believe? I realize I hardly look the part of a ladies' man. God knows, Rachel never saw me as such. But women like Leona are easier to convince—I find that diamonds usually do the trick." Perry's eyes were cold and remote. Michael realized looking at him, that he had never known the real man at all. Perry had worn a disguise, a mask of personality, the entire time.

"Of course. Leona. So you no doubt put her up to telling Rachel that Lilith was my mistress," Michael ventured.

Overhill chuckled. "Yes. It wasn't difficult to persuade her to do Rachel and you a bad turn."

"But why?" Michael asked, his tone that of mild puzzlement. "If you were planning to kill me anyway, why did it matter that Rachel thought me a philanderer?"

"Well, dear fellow, it is preferable if a widow isn't overly grieving her husband's death," Perry explained. "Much easier to give her comfort."

The look on his face made Michael want to shove the man's teeth down his throat, but he forced himself to remain calm, and said merely, "And it bothered you not at all that you were causing pain to the woman you profess to love?"

Perry shrugged. "Pain passes."

"Hardly actions motivated by what I would call love," Michael shot back. "More obsession than any real feeling."

"Call it what you like, dear fellow," Perry retorted, looking smug. "Your scorn doesn't bother me. You are still the fool who has been caught in his own trap."

"Not precisely." A male voice spoke out of the darkness to the side of them.

Startled, Perry glanced over to the right as a dark figure stepped out of the shadows and walked to the edge of their lantern light. It was Sir Robert Blount, and he held a gun leveled at Overhill.

"Leaving it a bit late, aren't you, Rob?" Michael asked lightly.

"We were interested in hearing the story," Sir Robert replied.

"Aye. That we were." Cooper stepped out of the shadows a few feet down from Blount. The Bow Street Runner also carried a pistol—indeed, one in each hand. "I warrant the magistrate will be even more interested in hearing it."

Realization swept over Perry that it was he who had been tricked, and with a cry of rage, he fired.

Rachel and the others stepped down from the hansom. As Anthony paid the driver, Rachel and Lilith hurried toward the door of the warehouse. Just before they reached it, a shot rang out, followed by two more. With a scream of anguish, Rachel ran into the building, Lilith and Anthony following her.

She ran past the offices toward the glow of the lantern inside the cavernous warehouse. When she reached the scene, she stopped short. Sir Robert Blount and Mr. Cooper, pistols in hand, were hurrying over to where two bodies lay on the floor. One was Perry. The other was Michael.

Pain shot through Rachel, rooting her to the floor. She could not breathe. All she could think was that her life was over. Just when she had at last found happiness, everything had fallen apart.

Then Michael sat up, one hand going to his head. "Bloody hell! I hit my head on that crate as I went down."

Rachel went limp with relief. Her heart began to beat again.

Blount reached down and hooked a hand around Michael's arm and helped him to his feet.

"Michael!" At last Rachel's feet came unstuck, and she ran across the room to throw her arms around him.

"Rachel!" Startled, Michael folded his arms around her automatically. "What are you doing here?"

"Are you all right? Were you hurt?" she asked, not answering his question. She stepped back to look him over for wounds. Tears swam in her eyes, and she was breathing in hasty jerks.

Michael smiled. "No. He missed me. I'm fine. I think it is Perry who got shot." He turned toward where Perry Overhill lay, Cooper squatting down beside him. "How is he?"

"Blount hit him. I think I went wide of the mark," Cooper said, ripping off Overhill's cravat and pressing it against the man's shoulder. "He's still alive, though. I'll get him to a doctor."

"Good." Michael turned his attention back to Rachel. "Now, why are you here? If you had come any sooner, you might have been shot!"

His gaze went beyond Rachel to where Anthony and Lilith stood. "You, too?" he asked in astonishment.

Sir Robert turned, too, and saw Lilith. "What the devil!" He went over to her, curling his arm around his shoulder. "What are you doing here!"

"We came to rescue you," Rachel said. "We realized that the real mastermind behind the crimes was Perry, and I thought you were alone here with him. I was afraid we would be too late." She stepped back, crossing her arms, and frowned at Michael. "Obviously we were not needed."

"Yes," Lilith put in tartly. "Which we would have known if anyone had bothered to tell us the truth."

Michael and Sir Robert cast a glance at each other.

"I told you," Michael murmured.

"I think I shall go find a hansom for Cooper to take Overhill in," Sir Robert announced quickly.

"Coward," Lilith told him as he walked past, but the smile on her lips took any sting out of her words.

The men helped carry the wounded Perry out to

the cab, and Anthony, incensed by the way Perry had used him over the years, said to Cooper, "I will go with you, just to make sure he doesn't give you any more problems." He cast a grim look at Perry, adding, "You have played me for the fool for years. I'll be glad to see the jail doors lock on you."

Perry, conscious now, one hand clutching the bloody bandage on his shoulder, did not look as if he would be capable of putting up much resistance.

The others took another cab home to Michael and Rachel's house, where they had a late supper and went over what had occurred that evening.

Rachel and Lilith related Anthony's visit to Michael and Sir Robert and described how they had realized that Perry was the real criminal and had gone running to the warehouse to save Michael from Overhill.

"And then to find out that you had it taken care of—that you had planned it all!" Rachel exclaimed, with mock irritation. "How did you know it was Perry? You were so convincing when you explained why it must be Sir Robert."

"He has always been good at casting blame on me," Blount commented.

"Well, it was true that I realized that for the criminal to have employed Anthony as he did, he must be someone who knew about me and my past history with Anthony. But I never thought that it was Rob," Michael admitted. "He and I had been through too much together. I knew him too well. So I turned to the others who might know. I never told Perry. I didn't think he knew about that night that Anthony convinced you to elope with him—until just now, when you told me that it was he who encouraged Anthony to do so. But I knew that Perry had always been around during that period when we were engaged and that he was one of the many men who had been courting you, too. I thought it was possible that he could have guessed that Anthony loved you or that you had a preference for him as a suitor.''

"But there were many other people about at the time who could have guessed, as well,'' Rachel pointed out.

"Yes. But I also knew that in the past Perry had had money difficulties, though it occurred to me that in the last few years I had not heard anything about it. However, the most telling thing was the fact that whoever was behind all this had forced Anthony into the situation. It was the piece of the puzzle that made no sense. Why involve Birkshaw? At first I thought it was to throw me off the real criminal's trail, and no doubt it was, partially. But when I realized that the intent must be to kill me and blame it on Birkshaw, I knew that it was not just practical but personal, as well. Whoever was doing this wanted both me and Birkshaw out of the way. The connection between us, obviously, was Rachel. I knew then that the man behind this must be obsessed with Rachel. Why else try to get rid of Rachel's husband and the man she had once loved, all in one neat stroke? I was sure he was afraid that if he killed me, leaving Rachel free, she might turn to her old love, Anthony, instead of to him. So Anthony had to be gotten rid of, as well. Therefore, it had to be a man who had loved Rachel since she made her debut. Perry was the obvious choice.''

''I never thought he was serious!'' Rachel exclaimed. ''I mean, he made all those extravagant compliments, but I thought he was mostly joking. That it was just an easier course than actually courting and marrying another woman. He always seemed so…ineffectual.''

''Yes, he seems to have fooled a number of people into thinking he was a bumbling, good-hearted chap,'' Sir Robert added. ''He was the sort of man that any man assumed was safe to escort his wife or sister.''

''But how did he know the criminal element, the people he used to commit the crimes?'' Lilith asked.

''I don't know. But obviously, none of us knew the real Perry. He has always been something of a gamester. I remember he used to frequent some gambling hells that I would not have gone into,'' Michael commented. ''Perhaps he first made his criminal contacts there.''

Rachel shook her head. ''It is so hard to believe. I *liked* him.''

''We all did,'' Michael agreed sadly. ''The sorrow I felt was genuine. It was just the person I felt it for was not Rob.''

It was quite late by this time, and a short while later, Lilith and Sir Robert left. Rachel and Michael went upstairs, hand in hand.

"There is no need to wake your maid," Michael said, smiling. "I shall act as your lady's maid."

He reached up and pulled the hairpins from Rachel's hair, and it fell in a tumbling mass of curls to her shoulders. She picked up a brush and began to brush her hair out.

After a moment, she said in a quiet voice. "It is all my fault, isn't it?"

"What? Perry's going bad?" Michael asked, surprised. "No. Of course not. You had no control over that."

"But he tried to kill you because of me."

"No. He tried to kill me because he was wicked. You cannot help that you are a lovely, desirable woman." He grinned, taking her hands in his. "No doubt there are dozens of men out there pining away for you. But only Perry saw killing a few of us as a way to win your heart."

"But I made such a mess of things back then...when I first met you and Perry. Even now, you still don't trust me."

"What?" Michael took her chin in his hand and tilted it up so that she had to look up into his face. "What are you talking about? Of course I trust you."

"You did not tell me the truth about Perry. You told me the same story about Sir Robert that you told Perry."

"Not because I did not trust you!" Michael exclaimed. "Dear girl, you must not think that. I did not tell you because you are too honest, too trustworthy. I was afraid that you would not be able to dissemble in front of Perry, that if I told you what I suspected him of, it would show in your face. And I could not make him suspicious. I knew that if I told both of you the same story, your concern for my safety would make the story all the more believable, and that then his devious mind would see it as a way to get me alone, kill me and blame it on someone else. He would know that Sir Robert was not the criminal, so he would not guess that Blount would really be there. I thought he would work it so that it looked as if Anthony was to blame, but I didn't much worry about that, since Sir Robert, Cooper and I would already have caught Perry trying to kill me. It never occurred to me that if he sent Birkshaw to the scene, Birkshaw would come running to you with the note.''

He raised her hand to his lips and laid a gentle kiss in the center of her palm. ''But it was not because I did not trust you. I trust you with all my heart.''

''How can you?'' Rachel cried. ''After what I did to you back then?'' She pulled away from him in her distress, tears glittering in her eyes. ''I betrayed your trust. You had to marry me to protect your name, but I know it killed your love for me. You cut me out of your life. You told me nothing about your real life—your sister, your work. And now—now I love you so. I want to have your children, to live a normal, happy life. But I am afraid that I will never be able to get back the love you had for me!''

''Rachel! No. No.'' Michael reached out and grasped her shoulders. ''You think I married you for

the sake of my name? This is why I married you.''
He pulled her to him and kissed her.

When finally he raised his head, he said, ''That is
why I married you. Because I loved you too much
not to. I could have lived with the scandal. But I
couldn't have lived without you. I wanted you, and
I was willing to do whatever it took. I knew that I
was doing you a disservice, forcing you into a marriage you did not want. But I could not let you go. I
could not bear the thought of living without you. I
did not tell you about my work because I was afraid
that you would not like it, that you would think it
silly or dreadfully common of me. I—I was afraid to
look foolish in your eyes. I love you. I always have.''

''Really?'' Rachel looked up at him, smiling almost shyly.

''Yes, really.'' He kissed her again, then raised his
head and looked deeply into her eyes. ''I love you. I
just didn't know that you loved me. Of course I love
you. I would never have asked you into my bed if I
did not love you. And I want exactly what you
want—children, a happy life....''

Rachel went up on tiptoe and kissed him lightly.
''And perhaps a little mystery now and then?''

He chuckled. ''Yes, perhaps a little mystery now
and then—as long as you are there to help me
solve it.''

''I will be,'' Rachel promised. ''I will always be
there.''

''Good,'' he said, cupping her face with his hands.

"Now, about those children…what do you say we get to work on them right away?"

"I think that is the best idea you've had all evening," Rachel responded.

Michael bent, swept her up in his arms and carried her to the bed.